Marguerite

by

Carol Edgerley

Marguerite

by Carol Edgerley

Published by Brightwater Publications

Author Services by Pedernales Publishing, LLC.
www.pedernalespublishing.com

ISBN 978-0-9853660-2-5

First Edition September, 2012

Printed in the United Kingdom

FOREWORD

The story of Marguerite de Merencourt is inspired by the life of my adventurous French great-grandmother. It all began when I was thirteen years old, and back from boarding school for the summer holidays. My report for Mathematics was poor as always, but this time my mother decided to arrange Maths coaching for me. Two hours—three times a week. I was appalled!

Recently returned from India, my unfortunate great-aunt, a Maths teacher, was given the unenviable task of teaching me. Subsequent to the first two-hour session, the thought of weeks ahead of the same filled me with horror. In an effort to distract her from the business in hand, I asked her about her childhood in India with my grandmother and her other siblings. What were her parents like? Did she know her grandparents? Where was she brought up?

Well! The poor old lady was off and running. Over the following weeks, not very much in the way of Maths was achieved. Instead, I heard a story that amazed and fascinated me, and which I carried in my head for years meaning to write it down for my own children. Subsequently, I have been encouraged to share the story of the indomitable Marguerite with a wider readership.

Acknowledgements

I am indebted to my late great-aunt—Christina in the story—who provided me with a wonderful tale of adventure and destiny.

My thanks to Madeline de Suyrot, who tirelessly read each version of the manuscript and gave me her opinion—not just what I wanted to hear! And to my husband, Ian, who sorted out computer hiccups, and to Guy, Ashley and Michaela, my children, whose enthusiasm motivated me to write the story at the outset.

My deepest gratitude to my mentor, Barbara Rainess, without whose guidance and supreme confidence in my ability to write, the story of "Marguerite" might never have seen the light of day.

CHAPTER ONE

1875
SOUTHERN PERIGORD
FRANCE

"Take it away! I said take it away!" screeched the woman on the bed, shrinking away from the infant lying beside her. "Oh, I cannot bear it! How can something so ... so *hideous* be mine? Oh, someone just take the horrid thing away!"

Francine, Marquise de Merencourt, had just been delivered of a daughter. The baby was large. A mop of dark hair capped her head, lying in damp tendrils about the wrinkled little face.

A sharp smack having been administered to the small rump, the infant was bawling in red-faced outrage. Shocked by the Marquise's outburst, one of the attending midwives hurried to take the squalling baby.

The Duchesse de Saint Aubrey stood to one side, attempting to conceal acute consternation over her daughter-in-law's reaction to the new infant. She had just entered the room, intending to congratulate her.

"*Chèrie*, whatever can be the matter?" The Duchesse moved forward to lay a comforting hand on the young woman's shoulder. "Why, you have the most beautiful little girl. Charles will be so pleased, as I know he has always wanted a daughter. Do you have a name for her yet?"

"*Beautiful?*" shrilled the new mother, half-sitting up in the bed. "I assume you mean to joke, Madame? In the event my baby turned out to be a girl, I was considering Eugènie or maybe Carinne. But just look at it! How can I call that by a pretty name like Carinne? For God's sake, the horrid thing could be taken for a changeling." Francine turned her face into the pillow, sobbing wildly.

"Dearest, I believe you cannot be quite recovered from the birth," the Duchesse soothed. "Try and rest awhile, and I am sure you will see everything in a different light tomorrow."

"Never!" Although muffled, the Marquise's voice was strident enough for her mother-in-law to frown and step back. "The thing disgusts me. It's squat, sallow and positively hirsute … so unlike my lovely boys with their rosy cheeks and fair curls."

"I'm sorry, Francine, but I cannot begin to understand you." The Duchesse looked upset. "It's not the baby's fault she has a full head of dark hair … rather like her father's. As for being "squat"— such an unpleasant term—she's just a sturdy little mite. Healthy too, and we should give thanks for that, at least. In any event, the baby must have a name, so what do you wish her to be called?"

"Call it whatever you like," came back the ill-tempered response. "It is of no interest to me."

The Duchesse indicated to the midwives that the baby should be taken out from the Marquise's bedroom. It was obvious Francine was not herself. For the moment, it might be better to keep the infant out of her daughter-in-law's sight, until such time as she had recovered her spirits. Glancing at the bed, the old lady observed the new mother's back was now presented to her. Shaking her head, the Duchesse followed the midwives from the room.

As soon as the door closed behind her mother-in-law, Francine rolled over on her back and stared at the ceiling. All the disgusting business of childbirth–the dreadful, dreadful agony–only to be landed with that grotesque creature! God, it even had beetling brows like its father. Easy tears filled the young woman's eyes.

Was it not enough that she was rotting her life away in this dismal backwater? She, who once had Parisian Society at her feet? That is, until her father married her off to the oafish son of the Duc de Saint Aubrey.

Marquis he might be, but in her opinion Charles's comportment was little better than that of a coarse peasant. A sex-obsessed hog who assaulted her reluctant body night after night. Sated at last, he would snore off his depravity whilst she lay sleepless and sore … and as far away as she could from his revolting hairy body.

Oh, how different her life could have been. Soirées! Balls! Stimulating company! She could have had her pick of any one of the eligible young men crowding about her at social gatherings. Verses celebrating her ethereal silvery fairness had even been written by besotted admirers. How she had *loved* that exciting, if long-ago lifestyle.

Instead, she was saddled with a dull-as-ditchwater husband. Who not only stank of horses, but also had little conversation other than related to the stupid animals.

And now she must put up with his equally unappetizing daughter, who even at this early stage of infancy looked exactly like him. *Ugh!* Francine shuddered.

The disgruntled woman's glance fell on a heavy cut-glass bottle of perfume on her bedside table. A card was attached around its neck by a silken cord.

"From Charles, with my love."

Tcha! What did he know of love? Francine's mouth twisted in scorn. Seizing the bottle, she drew back her arm and hurled it at a nearby cheval mirror, watching the glass shatter into a cascade of glittering shards.

Broken! Fractured! Just like her life.

Throwing herself back against the pillows, Francine indulged in a storm of self-pitying tears …

Ten months later

One summer day, a black-clad woman was on her way to the Haras, puffing with the effort of trundling a rather antiquated pram, in which a baby girl lay fast asleep. Although late in the afternoon, the air was still and warm, the sweat trickling inside the nurse's serge garments causing them to become prickly and uncomfortable.

Halting in the shade of a clump of tall trees, Jeanne caught her breath, and tried to ignore her aching joints. Looking down at the sleeping little face under its riot of dark curls, the nurse sighed. Minette was such a lovely baby girl … if only her own mother could see it.

As it was, the Marquise only had eyes—and time—for her two sons, Jérome and Christophe. Why, she had left the choice of the child's very name to the Duchesse, who had chosen a perfect one for her granddaughter.

Marguerite—the name of an elegant flower.

Disagreeable as always, the Marquise had complained the name was too pretty for such an unattractive creature. How could she be so hard? In an effort to diffuse a tense situation, she, Jeanne, had begun calling the baby, Minette, an affectionate diminutive of Marguerite.

Everyone at the château adopted the pet name, including the baby's father and her grandparents. And her mother? Alas, no. Despite the Marquise having nothing to do with the baby girl, she demanded the child be called by her given name. It was clear to Jeanne that Madame didn't care to see affection bestowed on the poor child … even through a pet name.

Mon Dieu, but there was no pleasing some people.

Marshalling her strength, the old nurse plodded on her way. Little Minette loved to watch her brothers having a riding lesson. Should she be awake, the baby girl would be allowed to sit on a pony for a minute or two. Jeanne did not want to miss that by being too late.

Arriving at the Haras at last, the old nurse made her way behind the stabling to a fenced-in sand arena. Inside, both Merencourt boys were mounted on fat little Shetland ponies ambling around the perimeter. Their father stood in the centre, instructing his sons.

Flushed with excitement, Jérome drummed his heels against the pony's sides in the hope of encouraging his mount into a reluctant trot. The younger boy sat hunched over the saddle, his expression tense, clutching handfuls of thick black mane with both hands. His pony was almost asleep on its feet.

Choosing a shady spot close to the arena fence, the nurse positioned the pram next to a few bales of straw lying nearby. Hitching up her skirts, Jeanne sat down on a bale with a huge sigh of relief to be taking the weight off her feet.

A few minutes later, lulled by the warmth and somnolence of the afternoon and the chirruping of cicadas, the nurse's eyes closed and her chin came to rest on the bib of her white apron. In the pram beside her, the baby girl slept on.

The sound of carriage wheels startled the old nurse into wakefulness. *Holà* ... was that not the Marquise's carriage approaching? Knowing of her mistress's intense dislike of horses, Jeanne assumed she was coming to watch her sons ride for a few minutes. Hurriedly edging down from her perch, the nurse moved the pram away to allow the carriage driver to halt his vehicle in the shade of overhanging trees. Finding herself under the Marquise's cold gaze, Jeanne lowered her eyes and dipped a respectful curtsey.

"*Maman!*" Jérome had seen his mother. "Look, *Maman*—look how fast I can trot."

"Excellent, my darling," the Marquise called out with a smile. "I'm so proud of what a good rider you are becoming."

"I'm much better than Christophe, *Maman*. He's too scared to even try and trot."

"That's enough, Jérome!" his father barked. "Attend to the pony you are riding, and keep your remarks to yourself if you please."

"But he is! He's a silly little coward ... anyone can see that," Jérome sulked. "I'm brave, aren't I, *Maman?*" The boy appealed to the Marquise. "I want to gallop now, but I need a stick to beat this lazy pony to go faster."

"*Jérome!*" Charles strode over to his elder son, and brought the pony to a halt. "First, you will never beat an animal in my presence. If I ever find out you have done so, you won't be able to sit down for a month. Secondly, I warned you about taunting your brother, and I will not allow you ignore me."

Grasping the boy's pony by the bridle, the Marquis led it over to the arena gate and summoned his groom. "Your ride is at an end for today."

"*Papa!*" Jérome burst into tears of chagrin.

"Perhaps you will obey me in future, young man. Now, off you go."

The Marquis' personal groom arrived and took over the pony and the blubbering boy. Watching them disappear into the stabling, Charles was satisfied his groom would ensure Jérome dried off his small mount and prepared its feed.

Turning to his younger son who had been watching the scene with anxious eyes, Charles smiled reassuringly. "Christophe, you are doing very well. Now, sit up straight and use your heels to make that lazy fellow move forward."

The Marquise's face had darkened with annoyance to hear her favourite son being disciplined by his father. After all, Jérome was only pointing out the obvious. In fact, the entire business was becoming too, *too* ridiculous. Depriving one boy of the riding he loved ... to then bully the other petrified child into continuing? It was nonsensical! She would make a point of having words with Charles over the issue.

At the end of the riding lesson a few minutes later, Charles watched his younger son stumble towards the stables leading his pony. The boy's expression was almost comical, so relieved was he to be once more on *terra firma*. Charles shook his head. Never mind. With the right handling, Christophe should overcome his fear in time. Meanwhile, it was good for the boy to face a minor challenge on occasion.

Walking over to the arena gate, Charles noticed the nurse standing some distance away, rocking the pram. He made his way over to where his baby daughter was lying fast asleep. With a smile, he bent to examine the peaceful little face under its cloud of curls—as dark as his own. Almost as if sensing his presence, the baby opened vivid blue eyes. Breaking into an engaging smile, she displayed her latest acquisition of four tiny teeth.

On impulse, Charles lifted the child out of her pram and cradled the sturdy little body in his arms. With a gurgle of delight, she grasped the cravat at her father's neck and with surprising strength, tried to ram the lacy ends into her mouth. Laughing, Charles bent to kiss the baby girl's chubby cheek.

Seated in her carriage, the Marquise watched the interlude between Charles and his small daughter with thinning lips. She burned with resentment, comparing her husband's absent-minded ruffling of his sons' hair, with a sickening display of affection for that fat lump of a child.

Determined to break up the scene, the Marquise descended from her carriage, and swept over to her husband who was still entranced with his little daughter. Noticing dribble on the excited baby's chin, Francine's mouth turned down in disgust.

"Jeanne, take that child back to the nursery and give it a good wash, if you please. Can't you at least make sure it's clean before it goes out?"

"But Madame, Minette had a bath just before … "

"Don't argue with me, you insolent old woman! Anyone can see it's filthy. Charles, give the child to the nurse, if you please!"

"Aside from the fact that Minette is far from dirty—must you refer to your own daughter as *it?*" Charles looked at his wife. "I find it particularly offensive, and so does my mother."

"I'll thank you not contradict me in front of a servant, Charles," the Marquise snapped. "And *do* stop using the nurse's stupid diminutive for that child."

"Tell me, Francine, why are you the only person not to call our daughter Minette?" Charles was annoyed. "Even my mother thinks it is sweet, and suits her well."

"Ah yes. Your mother. Of course, she would think it is just the thing. Thanks to you and your doting parents, that child is becoming disgustingly spoiled. I am asking you once again to hand it over to the nurse, Charles!" The Marquise's shrill voice rose, attracting the attention of passing stable-hands.

With a sigh of resignation Charles handed the baby back to her nurse. It wasn't worth entering into futile arguments with Francine, or to endure an unpleasant scene. Finding herself abruptly deprived of her father's arms, Minette set up a piercing howl.

"Jeanne, just take that damned child and *go*, will you!" The Marquise was at the end of her patience. "And make sure it's clean the next time I see it.

Ensconced once again in her carriage, Francine glanced at her husband who made no move to join her. "I take it you mean to remain here for the time being?"

"I shall be back with the boys in about half an hour, when they have finished their duties. They are required to take care of the ponies they were riding just now."

"Duties?" echoed the Marquise, her eyebrows lifting in disdain. "Why do you make those poor children work when there are stable boys to see to all that?"

"Madame, I have explained it to you a thousand times, so I do not intend to waste my breath yet again." Irritated, the Marquis bowed to his wife, and then strode towards the stables without a backward glance.

Francine's inexplicable hostility towards their baby girl was of immense concern to Charles. He could only hope his wife would warm to the poor little thing in time.

It was not to be.

Minette grew into a charismatic child, if decidedly wilful and headstrong at times. Bewildered by her mother's chilliness that compared badly with the loving attitude shown to her brothers, the resentful child began to go out of her way to annoy. Any attention being better than none, after all.

Invective and threats were followed by punishment, but the girl ignored the Marquise's fury with cool indifference. As time passed, animosity between mother and daughter escalated, the girl seeking further ways to irritate in order to avoid being ignored. It became a vicious circle, for which there seemed no easy solution.

Fearless from an early age, Minette managed her Connemara mare with ease, weathering the horse's occasional energetic bucking with apparent enjoyment. To her mother's chagrin, however, she refused to conform to riding side-saddle like other girls of her age. Minette steadfastly insisted on riding astride like a boy.

Francine was beside herself with mortification. Without exception, the daughters of her friends wore elegant habits when out riding. But not her husband's hoyden daughter. Oh no! Grubby britches and a shirt was the damned girl's preferred attire.

Proud though he was of Minette's undoubted horsemanship, Charles bowed to his wife's demand that she be forbidden to ride astride in public. It would be shameful, Francine acidly declared—if the girl was seen to career about the place like some Amazonian savage. An indifferent Minette shrugged, and went her own way, continuing to ignore her mother's infuriated dictates.

By the time Minette was ten years old, the frustrated Marquise decided a governess should be employed. The girl's immoderate behaviour and impertinence required stamping down hard. Especially since neither Charles nor his parents seemed to notice Marguerite's flagrant dismissal of social etiquette. It enraged Francine to hear them lauding the beastly creature as a "free spirit."

Disobedient baggage was more to the point—she thought sourly.

Well, Marguerite could be a thorn in somebody else's flesh for a change. Yes, a strict governess who could do something about the girl's lack of propriety. Enquiries to find such a person should be set up at once, and neither Charles nor his doting parents would be allowed a say in her final choice.

Francine smiled grimly. Without doubt, there would be fireworks when the reins were pulled tight. However, it might be wise to warn Marguerite of her intention, thus avoiding a scene when the governess arrived which might put the woman off.

Seated on a garden bench one morning, the Marquise sent a footman in search of her daughter. Whilst waiting for the girl, she rehearsed her intended approach to the change in the girl's education.

"So, what do you want me for, Maman?" Minette demanded from behind the bench, causing the Marquise to start in fright.

"Don't *do* that, Marguerite! Don't you know how impolite it is to creep up on people like that?"

"Well, I'm here now so what do you want? I was having an exciting game with Papa's hounds until Pierre came to get me. Such a nuisance."

Irritated, the Marquise surveyed the girl standing in front of her. It never failed to amaze how Marguerite seemed unable to keep a civil tongue in her head. And God, just look at her! Green knees from crawling in the grass with those smelly dogs, a pocket in her smock almost ripped off. Even the girl's plait had loosened, releasing tendrils of dark hair clinging to her damp face.

Resentful under her mother's glacial stare, Minette flung herself down on the bench beside her, knees apart. Stiffening over the unwanted proximity, the Marquise inched away, watching in awful fascination as the child produced a grubby sweet from the remaining pocket of her smock. Popping it into her mouth, she waited to hear what her mother had to say.

"I shall be employing a governess to teach you in future, Marguerite," began the Marquise. "So when she arrives, you will no longer be sharing your brothers' lessons. Oh, for heavens' sake, will you kindly take that disgusting sweet out of your mouth when I am talking to you!"

Spitting the sweet into her hand, Minette held it out for a nearby dog to savour before shoving it back in her pocket for future consumption. "Who is this person coming to teach me, then?" she demanded. "I should have a say in that, don't you think?"

"I am more than capable of selecting a governess for you, Marguerite," The Marquise struggled to maintain an already tenuous hold on her temper. "There will be no more loafing about with those abominable dogs, looking like a ragamuffin. As a matter of fact, it is high time you learned to appreciate feminine interests, such as painting, embroidery, and pretty clothes. You may go now, and please see to it that you are washed and changed before coming to the lunch table."

Jérome soon learned of the intended change in his sister's education. Secretly delighted to be ridding himself of the regular challenge to his own intelligence, the older boy lost no time in poking fun at Minette whilst sitting at the supper table.

"I hear you are soon to have a ferocious old dragon to teach you, Minette," Jérome chortled. "Hairy warts and greasy grey locks scraped back in a bun! What, with all those new interests such as sewing, deportment lessons and poetry readings, your riding is sure to take a back seat."

"I can't see why it should. In any event, I ride far better than you do," Minette mumbled through a mouthful of bread. "Face it, Jérome, you could do with lots more lessons from Papa in the sand school."

"Maybe you haven't heard yet, but Papa is giving me his old stallion, Orpheus," Jérome chose to ignore his sister's taunt. "As for you, sister mine, I can see you are destined to keep riding your fat mare forever. Serves you right for not riding side-saddle like a proper young lady … God, you're *such* a disgrace! Everyone says so."

"So what? I bet you couldn't stay on even one of my horse's bucks!"

"I'm not interested in riding your bad-mannered animal, thanks!" Jérome returned in a lofty tone. "Especially since I will soon have Orpheus to ride."

"Oh, do stop bragging, Jérome! I couldn't care less that Papa is allowing you to ride his worn-out old horse. Besides, Orpheus is such an easy-peasy ride that even Christophe could manage him."

"Ooo … Mademoiselle Jalousie! Do I see you turning green with envy?" Jérome sniggered, delighted by his own wit. "Yes, I can just picture you in years to come. Snaggle-toothed old trout, fat legs sticking out each side, squatting on her sway-backed cart-horse … what a hoot!"

"Well, I feel sorry for poor Orpheus having a porker like you bouncing about on his kidneys all day," retorted Minette, not to be outdone.

"Minette, don't say silly things," exclaimed the old nurse, who was supervising the children's supper. "Look child, you haven't even started your soup. It must be almost cold by now."

"I like cold soup," muttered Minette, nevertheless picking up her spoon. Hoping she had managed to get under her brother's skin, she cast him a surreptitious glance from under her eyelashes. To her disappointment, Jérome was flapping his elbows and blowing out his cheeks in grotesque mimicry of a fat woman riding a horse.

"Stop it! Stop it Jérome, or I'll … "

"You'll what, dear baby sister?" Jérome crossed his eyes and hung his top teeth over his bottom lip in a hideous grin, a parody of the snaggle-toothed old woman.

With a scream of rage, Minette launched herself at her brother, fingers hooked to claw at his sneering face. Flushed scarlet, she was dragged off by her nurse and stormed from the dining room, followed by gales of jeering laughter.

"Minette, can't you just ignore what that boy says to you?" the old nurse tutted crossly. "You must know by now he wants you to attack him … so he can report to your mother."

"I really hate Jérome!" Minette was still fuming. "And how come he has been given Orpheus to ride, when everyone knows I am a much better rider than he is."

"Perhaps because he is the eldest, *ma chèrie*" suggested the old nurse, hoping to defuse the situation. "I feel sure it has nothing to do with ability, *n'est-ce pas?*"

"Nou-nou Jeanne, does everyone think I'm a disgrace?" Minette asked as she was getting into bed, her brother's earlier comment having reached its mark. "At least I'm not snooty with the servants like that beast, Jérome."

"Darling, we all love you, I promise!" soothed the nurse. "Now go to sleep, and all will be well tomorrow, you'll see."

CHAPTER TWO

Minette lay sleepless in her bed, feeling very hungry indeed. Her earlier fury against Jérome had all but dissipated, and she now regretted not having eaten her supper. Unable to settle, she threw back the covers and wandered over to the window, settling herself on the wide sill. Gazing out across the moonlit gardens, her expression was glum, her brother's taunts still ringing in her ears.

It was all the more galling, since Minette knew them to be accurate. Not only had she defied every dictate to ride side-saddle, but she had aired her views in no uncertain terms. What? Bundled up in a tight habit, nasty, scratchy veil over one's face? No fear.

It was also true that until she complied, she would never be offered another horse, although her mare was getting on in years. To think that idiot Jérome was inheriting a lovely old boy like Orpheus— it was so unfair.

With a determined effort, Minette relegated the humiliating scene at supper to the back of her mind. Her stomach felt uncomfortably empty. No good hoping it would pass—she would have to go downstairs and find something to eat. Barefoot, she made her way across the landing and down the servants' stairs to the kitchens. With any luck, the cook might have left a cake in the larder, or maybe a pie of some sort. And there was always fresh milk in the big, wooden urn.

To her relief, Minette found a bunch of black grapes in a basket. Taking them over to the window seat, she demolished them with relish. She dragged a chair over to a kitchen cupboard containing glasses. Climbing on to the chair, she reached up to retrieve a glass from a shelf, and filled it to the brim with creamy milk from the urn in the pantry. Feeling better for her alfresco meal, Minette resumed a resentful contemplation of Jérome's good fortune.

It was disgusting how that rotter gloated over her. And he hadn't even been on the stallion's back yet. Struck by an idea, a slow smile spread across Minette's face. Perhaps she could trump her brother after all … if she could claim to have ridden Orpheus before he had? What a wonderful joke to play against Jérome! Leaning back against the wall, Minette imagined her brother's unbearable chagrin with immense pleasure. But how might she go about achieving such a thing—and when?

She didn't stand a chance during daylight hours. The stable hands were far too vigilant. Well, what about now? The moonlight was so bright it could almost be day. Why, there was the kitchen tabby cat, striding across the yard towards the shed where Minette knew five kittens waited to be fed. Yes, it must be now—or never.

Half way to the kitchen door, Minette stopped, remembering she was clad in her nightgown … with nothing underneath. God! She really couldn't ride a horse with her bare bottom on view. Running back upstairs, Minette groped on her chair for the pantalettes she had taken off before going to bed. She found the garment under a pile of clothes, and dragging it on under her nightgown, she returned to the kitchens.

All was still quiet within the household.

Grinning to herself, Minette unlocked the kitchen door and sidled through. She closed it behind her, but made sure the key was left on the outside—just in case. She padded across the courtyard and out through the stone archway to the front of the château. Grasping handfuls of her nightgown, Minette broke into a run over flower beds, across sweeping lawns and down towards the Haras stables. Damp grass under bare feet, a gentle night breeze ruffling her hair, the girl laughed out loud, revelling in an unaccustomed sense of freedom.

The shortest route was through two large white-fenced paddocks. Large dark shapes moved slowly about, recognisable as grazing mares. They lifted their heads in alarm at the unexpected intruder, and then relaxed as the child whispered softly to them. Reassured, the horses resumed their peaceful occupation.

Minette stumbled on, wading through long grasses heavy with dew, hampered by the sodden nightgown clinging to her bare legs. At last, in the distance, she could make out a silvery outline of the darkened stables against a starry night sky. The silence was profound, only broken by the chirruping of crickets, and the occasional snuffle and stamp of horses from within the stabling.

The Haras was an attractive building consisting of three wings around a quadrangle. The right one contained young stock and a few breeding mares. Minette's own mare and her brothers' horses were housed in the centre. The Marquis' personal string of horses, including Orpheus, lived in loose boxes on the left wing.

Standing outside the heavy doors to where her father's old stallion was stabled, an unexpected *frisson* of unease seized the child. Suppose she was caught by one of the stable lads? Might ... might there be a bandit hiding in the shadows, getting ready to leap out? Straightening her shoulders—and her resolve—Minette grasped the heavy bolt on the doors with both hands and pulled it back.

As she stepped inside the building, several heads turned towards her, their nostrils fluttering in recognition of the small figure in the doorway. Appreciatively breathing in the warm pungent horse scent, she entered the tack room in search of a bridle. No time for a saddle, but riding bare-back was preferable, in any event.

A sudden noise!

Minette froze, her heart pounding with fright, her breathing ragged.

Half-hidden in the gloom by rows of saddles, a dark shape lurched up from the floor with a menacing growl! The shape quickly resolved itself into a large black dog, and the child almost wept with relief.

Bruno ... it was only Bruno!

Belonging to the Head Lad, the dog was on excellent terms with Minette. She had quite forgotten he was left to guard the stables at night. Squatting on her heels, the child wrapped her arms about him in an affectionate hug. The animal responded at once by an enthusiastic licking of his young friend's face. Cautioning him to lie down again, Minette seized a bridle from a wooden peg and hurried from the tack room. Time was running on.

It was dark as pitch in the stable building, the high windows being small and festooned with ancient cobwebs. Feeling her way along the wall, Minette was thankful she knew Orpheus's loose box was fourth from the far end. As the door to his box creaked open, the horse looked round in surprise. It was not his routine to go out at night! A piece of carrot was then offered, which was accepted with alacrity. Lowering his neck, Orpheus allowed Minette to slip the bridle over his head.

The child led the big horse out through the stable doors, wincing as steel-shod hooves struck the cobbles with a resounding ring. She decided on using the old sand school behind the stable building where she and her brothers had learned to ride. Perfect for a midnight ride.

Closing the arena gate behind her, Minette tucked her now decidedly muddy nightgown into the waistband of her pantalettes, rolling up the legs to well above her knees. She clambered up the white-painted fencing around the arena, and taking a handful of silky mane, eased herself astride the stallion's glossy back. Looking down, the child marvelled at how far from the ground she now was.

At the touch of Minette's heels, Orpheus set off round the arena with his beautiful rolling stride. Laughing in exultation, the girl clicked her tongue and closed her legs around the stallion's body. He obliged by breaking into a canter, his gait balanced and controlled. Sheer enchantment to his young rider.

Several circuits later, a reluctant Minette brought the horse to a halt with a squeeze of the reins. The temptation to continue riding was strong, but common sense told her it would be very foolish indeed. Several horses inside the stables had begun to neigh, and the noise might well bring someone from their bed to investigate! Slipping to the ground, Minette kissed Orpheus's soft nose, and then led him through the arena gate.

With a sudden scream of terror, the stallion reared violently, his front hooves thrashing close to the child's head. Clinging to the reins, Minette gasped to see dark figures looming eerily from the shadows. One carried a lamp, its flickering flame lending a sinister cast to the phantom's face.

Almost witless with fear herself, the child fought to control the plunging terrified animal. Reins, slippery with sweat, slid through numbed fingers desperately clinging to them. A large stone suddenly landed close by, causing the horse to rear once again. And another! The third stone hit Minette on the ankle.

A familiar mocking laugh rang out … Jérome!

Although relieved the two "ghosts" had turned out to be her brothers, Minette's relief was transformed into fury. The implications over what might have happened had the stallion broken loose were nothing less than a nightmare.

"You blithering idiot, Jérome!" the girl raged. "Aside from making my ankle bleed, how dare you fling stones at poor Orpheus?"

Grinning with malice, her elder brother emerged from the bushes. Christophe followed close behind, holding up a lamp, his mouth falling open in disapproval at his sister's grubby appearance.

"It's perhaps more to the point to ask how *you* dare to take Apollo out at midnight?" Jérome's voice was silky. "Papa's new stallion. Damned nerve, if you ask me. I dread to think what he's going to say about that."

"Just look at the state of you, Minette," Christophe interrupted. "Don't you realise your nightgown is still tucked up, and your legs are all bare for anyone to gawp at?"

"I don't care a fig about that, Christophe!" Minette's mind was focused on Jérome's last statement.

Apollo?

No … no, it couldn't be. "This is Orpheus, you dummy!" Minette blustered. "And we've just had the most brilliant canter round the school. He's absolutely fabulous, and I got to ride him before you."

"*You're* the dummy, Minette!" The older boy smirked. "Of course, it's Apollo. Orpheus has a white sock on one hind leg, but Apollo has socks on both. Otherwise, I suppose they look much the same in the dark."

Blanching, Minette stood back to peer at the stallion's hind legs. To have ridden her father's personal horse did not bear thinking about. But yes. Two white socks gleamed mockingly in the moonlight.

"But … but Orpheus has been in the same loose box for years. I can't for the life of me understand … "

"Use your brain, Minette. Since Papa retired Orpheus a couple of days ago, he ordered him moved to the central wing for me to ride next week," Jérome bent double in a mocking bow. "The stable manager must have installed Apollo in Orpheus' old loose box."

"So, are you going to tattle on me, Jérome?" Minette's tone was truculent as she yanked down the crumpled nightgown in an effort to cover her legs. "If you don't, I'll clean your tack after riding each day for ... for a month." She knew how much her brother resented this particular chore. As a matter of discipline, their father insisted upon his children cleaning their own tack, and grooms were forbidden to assist.

"Hmm!" Jérome pretended to consider. "All right, but it's for two months."

In no position to argue, Minette nodded. Quickly rubbing down the sweating horse, she returned him to his box with some hay. The three children then walked back to the darkened château, their absence having gone unnoticed by anyone within.

Back in the safety of her bedroom, Minette scrubbed at her stained nightgown with a towel soaked in cold water from her jug. Giving it up as a bad job, she pulled off the offending garment and stuffed it behind the armoire. She would get rid of the beastly thing the next day. Pulling out a fresh nightgown from her drawer, Minette slipped it on, and then wiped her feet clean with rather more success. She hopped into bed, and was soon sound asleep.

The following morning, Minette woke early. Hands clasped behind her head, she remained in bed for a few minutes to re-live the adventure of the previous night. Aside from the near disaster of the stallion breaking loose—that idiot Jérome's fault for flinging stones—what an unforgettable experience her ride had been! After riding such a gorgeous horse, her mare might seem a bit on the dull side ... .

Sitting at the breakfast table, Minette could not help but notice a crafty smile playing about Jérome's mouth. Her heart sank. From previous experience, that smirk did not bode well.

"Why are you grinning like an ape, might I ask?" Minette favoured her brother with a ferocious scowl. Crunching up his toast, Jérome did not deign to reply.

"You utter, *utter* beast, you've already blabbed on me, haven't you?" his sister hissed, clenching her fists.

"Why must you always think the worst of me?" Jérome opened his eyes wide in simulated injury. "I promised not to tell Papa … and I won't."

"And what are you are not going to tell Papa?" demanded the old nurse who had just entered the dining room. "Minette?"

"Er … nothing much! It's … um … a silly joke between Jérome and myself." Minette prevaricated.

"Really? Since when have you two ever shared a joke?" retorted the nurse, but said no more as she refilled Minette's glass with milk.

With an infuriating grin, the older boy continued to eat his breakfast. Sipping her milk, Minette regarded him across the table, her expression thoughtful. Perhaps Jérome was just out to torment her. She wolfed down a pain au chocolat and drained her glass of milk. Excusing herself from the table, Minette ran upstairs to her bedroom to retrieve the nightgown from behind the armoire before her nurse detected it!

To her astonishment—and intense dismay—the nightgown had vanished.

Sinking down on the edge of her bed, Minette's mind remained an obstinate blank. She supposed Jérome must have purloined it to ensure her co-operation over cleaning his tack. God, what a weasel that boy was!

A tap at the door interrupted Minette's disgruntled reflections. Jérome coming to gloat, she thought furiously. Yanking open the door, she was astounded to see Christophe standing in the doorway, casting furtive glances over his shoulder.

"Don't just stand there, Christophe, come in. What's the matter? And where is Jérome?" Minette stuck her head out to look up and down the corridor.

"*Shh*, Minette!" The boy grimaced. "I've come to warn you about what Jérome is up to. It's so mean to go behind … ."

"Get on with it, Christophe!" Minette snapped impatiently. "What has Jérome done now? I know he's pinched my nightgown to make sure I clean his beastly tack, so you can tell him from me—"

"I'm trying to tell you something rather more important," interrupted the boy in an injured tone. "Jérome happens to be with Maman right now, telling her about your ride on Papa's horse last night. He's showing her your muddy nightgown as proof."

Christophe shifted uncomfortably. "I thought it was only fair to warn you, as it was nasty to split on you behind your back. Anyway, I'd better go before Jérome finds out I've spoiled his nasty surprise."

"Yes, of course ... and thanks, Christophe." Although stunned by what she had just been told, Minette was aware of the risk her brother had taken on her behalf. Should Jérome discover such perfidy, painful retribution would be inflicted.

Leaning against the closed door, Minette's mind was in a whirl. Her mother's reaction was a foregone conclusion. She could deal with that. But what about Papa ... when he was told of it? Minette's knees turned to water and she flopped back on her bed, staring into space.

"Minette? Whatever are you doing in here, *chèrie?*" The old nurse looked into the bedroom. "Leave tidying up for now. Your mother wants to see you straight away."

"Do ... do you know why?" the girl's mouth felt dry.

"No, but she didn't look best pleased. What on earth have you done now, *chèrie?*"

White-faced, Minette got to her feet, unable to answer her nurse. Taking a deep breath, she lifted her chin and left the room. With troubled eyes, the old woman gazed after her. It was unlike the child to look ... well, frightened! *Eh bien!* Jeanne supposed she would know about it in due course.

On reluctant feet, Minette made her way to the Marquise's private apartments. Tapping on the door to the salon, she slipped inside. Her mother was standing by the window, her back to Minette. The Marquise allowed a full two minutes to pass, in the knowledge that it would further unnerve the girl fidgeting behind her. At last she turned to face her daughter, her pale eyes glacial.

"This time, my girl, you have gone too far!" The Marquise's disdainful glance swept over the quaking child. "God in heaven, this latest escapade of yours beggars belief. To think of all those tongues wagging about the Marquis' ten year old daughter ... last seen cavorting about the countryside in the dead of night. *Alone.* Not to mention wearing next to nothing, her legs and feet bare for all to see. Have you *no* sense of propriety, you stupid girl?"

"God, how I hate Jérome—the beastly tattle-tale-tit! Yesterday at supper, it was sickening the way he was bragging about being given Papa's old stallion to ride! I only wanted to serve him right by riding Orpheus first … "

"Your brother has shown an excellent sense of responsibility in coming to me," the Marquise continued, ignoring the child as if she had not spoken. "He was feeling concerned for your personal reputation, not to mention safety."

"I don't believe that nasty little sneak feels anything but pure joy to be getting me into as much trouble as he can manage," Minette regretted her impulsive words upon seeing her mother's face ominously darken.

"What a *very* unpleasant girl you are, Marguerite," The Marquise's lips twisted in annoyance. "Always ready to think the worst of poor Jérome."

Minette remained silent. What else was there to say? From the beginning, Maman had seen her elder brother as the next best thing to a saint! Awkward under the Marquise's gaze as it travelled over her person, the girl wished she had taken more care of her appearance. Her shoes were scuffed. Chocolate had dribbled down her clean pinafore, and her hair ribbon was hanging undone on the end of her plait.

"It is nothing short of scandalous the way you dismiss standards expected from a girl of your station," the Marquise shrilled. "You are nothing but a constant liability to your family, and I will not tolerate it, do you hear?"

Long minutes ticked by, increasing the child's apprehension.

"As from this moment, you are confined to the house for an entire week. Use that time to reflect on your wild behaviour." The Marquise paused to ensure her next words had maximum impact. "You are also forbidden to ride until I give you my permission. And that, of course, depends on you."

"Not ride?" Minette flushed bright red. "You can't stop me riding—again! Last time you forgot, and a whole month went by!"

"Oh, indeed I can stop your riding, you impertinent girl," the Marquise's smile was grim. "Remember your father has yet to learn of this shameful business. I very much doubt you will be able to wheedle your way out of trouble this time. Now, just get *out* of my sight!"

Horrified by her mother's words, and not least by the manner in which they were delivered, Minette fled from the room. She stood outside the door on unsteady legs, aware there had been a departure from the customary chilly attitude she had come to expect from the Marquise. Was...was that dislike she had seen in her mother's eyes?

Taking a shaky breath, the child ran down the stairs, desperate to be away from the perfumed stuffiness of her mother's salon. Ignoring the Marquise's order, Minette left the house and tore towards the woods beyond. All she wanted at this moment was to hide from the world. Gasping for breath, she scrambled up a favourite oak tree, her thin body racked by suppressed sobs over the injustice of the punishment. High up amongst the branches, she howled like a wounded animal.

With an effort, Minette regained control of herself. The deed was done, and she must accept the consequences. Utter misery would be what the Marquise wished to see in her above all things, so she must make sure her mother did not have that satisfaction. But what of her father's anger? That needed more thinking about …

Rustling in the bushes below her perch attracted Minette's attention. God! Had her father sent someone for her already? The child tensed. If she remained still, whoever it was might just pass on by. She needed a lot more time to work out how to explain her nocturnal excursion to Papa.

"Minette!" A familiar voice was calling her name. "*Chèrie*, where are you?" The child relaxed with a sigh of relief. It was only her nurse. The relief, however, turned out to be short-lived.

"Your mother saw you running off—and she's furious," huffed the old nurse, her forehead beaded with sweat as she gazed wildly about. "Minette, answer me!"

Agile as a cat, the child slid down from the tree, landing on her feet only a short distance away from the agitated woman. "Here I am, Nou-nou. Maman saw me leaving the house?"

"Yes, she did. She was shrieking the place down about rank disobedience, and that she intended to see you lived to regret it."

"But Nou-nou, she told me I am not to ride until she says so," Minette exclaimed, fresh tears threatening. "Knowing her … it could be months and months."

"Well, you haven't improved matters by tearing off through the woods like someone demented, you silly girl. Come, we must go back to the house, or Madame might send Jérome to find you. Think how you would hate that."

"Yes, but do I have to see Maman again?"

"Of course you do, Minette. It was the Marquise who sent me to find you."

Twenty minutes later, Minette stood in front of her mother. The Marquise was reclining on a pink velvet chaise-longue in her salon, her face set like a stone. On her lap, a fashion magazine lay open. Avoiding her mother's disparaging gaze, the child was conscious of an even scruffier appearance than before. There had been no time to do anything about that. Awkward under such close scrutiny, she stood on one leg, staring at the floor, grimy hands hidden behind her back.

"Don't you ever learn, Marguerite?" the Marquise spoke at last. "Disobedient to the bitter end, you appalling creature."

"It was just that—"

"Silence! Your confinement to the house is hereby increased to two weeks. Now, get out of my apartments. Go!"

CHAPTER THREE

Fourteen year old Minette leaned her forehead against a window pane in the school-room. Disconsolate, she stared out at the grey afternoon, watching her breath misting and then fading on the glass. Raindrops dripped from overhanging tiles on the roof, and the surrounding countryside was cloaked in constant drizzle.

It crossed the girl's mind to risk sneaking outside into the fresh air—despite the rain. No. It would be just her luck to be caught in flagrant disobedience. Over a week ago, she had been gated because she had refused to wear the new riding habit her mother had insisted upon.

After much resistance, she had agreed to wear the beastly thing when riding in the public gaze. But to insist she wore it whilst working at the Haras with her father's young horses? *Absolutely not!* It was ridiculous. Even Gran'père thought so!

Meanwhile, she had been trapped in the abominable stuffy atmosphere the Marquise preferred for eight whole days. And there were still two more to endure. The entrance of her governess into the schoolroom interrupted Minette's dismal ruminations. With a rustle of black bombazine, Mademoiselle Bonnaire swept over to Minette's desk to seize the blank sheet of paper lying on the top.

"*So!* Is this an example of how hard you are working on your devoir, Marguerite?"

"Sorry, Mam'zelle, I was trying to think of what to write." Minette hurriedly returned to her desk and picked up her pen.

"Too late by half, my girl—you've had your chance!" barked the governess, her spectacles glittering. "Of course, I am obliged to report your laziness to the Marquise, whom I know will be far from pleased to hear what I have to say."

Minette had long been aware that the governess disliked her intensely. Perhaps unsurprising, if one considered the practical jokes played on the unsuspecting woman subsequent to her arrival at the château four years ago. Tying her shoe-laces together whilst she dozed at her desk had not endeared her to the governess. Neither had a dead mouse in her bed, nor a live frog in her reticule. The outraged woman had never forgiven the girl.

"Mam'zelle, I've said I'm sorry. I'll make a start on my work right away. Please don't say anything to Maman," Minette pleaded, averting her eyes from the satisfied expression on the governess's face.

"Ah, but you are going to be sorrier still when I recommend your riding should be curtailed for a further month. It will also put an end to the unsuitable familiarity you enjoy so much with those vulgar stable-hands at the Haras. Hardly the behaviour one expects from a girl of noble birth."

"You cannot be serious!" The girl's jaw dropped in horror. "Stop my riding for even longer? I've done nothing to deserve that, for heaven's sake. And what do you mean by that last remark?" Minette flushed red. "What a nasty mind you must have, Mam'zelle, to mistake ordinary courtesy for something dirty."

"In my opinion, you deserve every misfortune which comes your way!" hissed the governess, white spittle appearing at the corners of her mouth. "You are an impossible girl, spoiled rotten by your father and besotted grandparents. The Marquise and I are the only ones to see through the sugary veneer you assume for their benefit."

Minette watched in horrified fascination as the gloating woman licked thin lips in anticipation of her pupil's fate. "Oh yes, you are sorely in need of a lasting lesson ... and I intend to see that you receive it."

Listening to the ranting woman, it became clear to Minette the governess had abandoned any pretence towards the niceties of a professional relationship with her pupil. She was also aware the Marquise would be only too delighted to take up the recommendation for further punishment. Driven beyond endurance, Minette leaped to her feet and faced her tormentor.

"You spiteful old witch," the girl shouted. "If you tell Maman wicked lies about me, you deserve to go straight to hell!" Sweeping her arm across the desk—pen, a full ink pot and paper flew towards the governess's person. Minette stared—horrified—as globules of blue ink trickled down the woman's skirt to pool on floor.

Desperate to get away from the governess's apoplectic glare, the girl pulled open the door and dashed from the schoolroom. Disregarding the fact she was supposed to be gated, Minette ran out into the gardens. Blinded by tears, she stumbled straight into her grandfather who happened to be on his way back from the Haras. The amazed Duc put his arms about the sobbing girl to steady her, clucking softly as if to a fractious horse.

After a few minutes, Minette managed to catch her breath sufficiently to relate the sorry tale to her grandfather. Innate honesty directed her not to try and minimise her own impassioned outburst against the governess. Twisting her hands together, the girl gazed at him with agonised eyes.

"Gran'père, what shall I do now?" she whispered. "How can I give up riding for another whole month? As things are, I haven't left the house for eight days. Before that, it was two months without riding! Now that ghastly woman means to tell Maman horrid lies about me being over-familiar with stable-boys."

"What?" The Duc's white eyebrows drew together. "Your governess said that? What nonsense!" The old man thought for a moment. "*Chèrie*, I can promise you nothing, but I imagine you already know that. Leave this business with me for the time being, and I will see what I can do."

The Duc looked up at the sky, in which patches of blue were appearing through the lowering greyness. "Why don't you take advantage of a pause in the rain, and have a look at your father's latest arrivals from Ireland? There is a very nice bay filly by the name of *Ariadne*. You will find her in the same wing as the other new youngsters. If anyone asks, you may tell them you have my permission to leave the house."

With a tremulous smile of gratitude, Minette set off down the driveway to the Haras stables. Watching his granddaughter walk away, her body drooping dejectedly, the Duc's face was grim. He returned to the house, and summoning a footman, he directed him to ask the governess to attend him in his study at once.

Seated at his desk, the Duc mused about how best to handle this unfortunate state of affairs. It was to be hoped the woman had not already blabbed to Francine. That would make the whole business rather more difficult to resolve.

Personally, he had never liked the Bonnaire creature. There had been something sly, almost rat-like about her that he found unpleasant. He had no difficulty in believing she was capable of the spite ascribed to her by Minette.

It must also be remembered that his granddaughter's own behaviour had been far from exemplary—by her own admission. In his view, however, the girl had been provoked to breaking point, and did not deserve further deprivation from her horses.

The Duc leaned back in his chair, his lined face pensive. Francine's inexplicable and ever-increasing hostility towards Minette was in direct contrast to the affection his daughter-in-law lavished on her sons— Jérome, in particular. Both he and the Duchesse felt sure Minette must be bewildered by a continuing inability to please her mother. A worrying situation, he thought, and it did not bode well for the future.

A scratching at the door broke through the Duc's sombre thoughts. He responded at once, and the governess sidled into the study. With a pleasant smile, he indicated she should sit, explaining there was a matter he wished to discuss. From the look on her face, it was obvious the woman was already intimidated by the unusual summons. The Duc de Saint Aubrey was not known to concern himself with domestic matters. Excellent! It suited his purpose very well.

"Mademoiselle Bonnaire, I must apologise for my granddaughter's behaviour in the school-room a short while ago. Minette told me about it herself. You will be receiving a sincere apology from her in due course."

Mesmerised, the governess stared at the Duc. The last thing she had expected was an apology. Sensing there must be more to come, she managed a tight smile.

"However, I do not believe that anything constructive would be achieved by informing the Marquise of such an insignificant matter," the Duc continued smoothly. "Neither do I recommend you pursue your intention to further curtail Minette's riding. She has already been confined to the house for a considerable time. I am sure you will agree it is better for a young girl to be exercising outside in the fresh air. Should the need arise to punish her, perhaps a different method might be chosen?"

The governess sat bolt upright in her chair, bereft of speech. Despite the Duc's reasonable approach, she was aware of an underlying threat in the tone of his voice. Seized by an acute desire to flee from his unwavering gaze, she was nevertheless anxious to retain her well-paid post. But in order to do so, she realised she would be obliged to eat humble pie on this occasion.

"Of course, Monsieur," she managed through stiff lips. "Perhaps I did react too strongly over Marguerite's lack of application to her work. I … er … seem to recall I had a bad headache at the time."

"That would explain great deal, Mademoiselle. I trust you are feeling better now?" The Duc's tone was solicitous. "Rest assured, I shall be making it clear to my granddaughter that discourtesy is never acceptable under any circumstances," he glanced at the governess over the top of his spectacles. "Regardless of what the provocation might be."

The Duc rose to his feet, indicating the interview was at an end. "Thank you for coming to see me, Mademoiselle Bonnaire. I am pleased we understand one another so well."

The governess scurried from the Duc's presence, secretly raging over having been out-manoeuvred in such a clever manner. That nosey old man! But she would bide her time. Sooner or later, an opportunity to inform the Marquise of that girl's cunning machinations was bound to present itself, she felt sure. And she, Bonnaire, would rejoice to see the Duc's little angel getting her come-uppance at last.

Subsequent to a stern lecture from her grandfather, Minette sought out her governess to humbly apologise for her earlier rudeness. Raising her eyes, the girl was taken aback to encounter a burning glare of hatred from the woman.

"Don't imagine that by bleating to your grandfather, you have heard the last of this, you nasty piece of work!" spat the governess, her eyes bulging with impotent rage. "One of these days, you will come to regret it … oh, I promise you that."

Minette recoiled, bewildered. Gran'père had assured her an apology would suffice on this occasion. It was obviously not the case. The horrible woman was still out to make trouble, so tremendous care must be taken to avoid further confrontation. It was vital that Bonnaire had nothing to report to her mother.

TWO YEARS LATER

At the fashionable seaside resort of Saint Jean de Luz in the South of France, it was high summer. Fine, silvery sand on the beach shimmered in the heat of the blazing sun high in a cloudless azure sky. Seagulls circled lazily, their keen eyes able to detect morsels of food far below.

Promptly at eleven o'clock each morning, elegant ladies and gentlemen and their families emerged from luxurious holiday residences. It was almost de rigueur to take a leisurely stroll at this time along the esplanade stretching the entire length of the sea wall. Aside from the social aspect of morning exercise, it sharpened one's appetite for an extended *déjeuner* at noon, Afterwards, everybody would return home for a few hours of *sièste* during the hottest time of day.

Countless restaurants competed with one another for lunchtime *clientèle*. A wide variety of fish and shellfish in delicious sauces were chalked on blackboards for the edification of passers-by. Waiters were busy laying tables within restaurants, as well as those outside, shaded from the sun by striped awnings. Sunshine filtered through gaps, dappling the array of silver cutlery and sparkling wine glasses upon snowy tablecloths.

The *sièste* at an end at five o'clock in the afternoon, the town would come alive once more to make the most of transient but wealthy holidaymakers. An enjoyable, if frenetic holiday atmosphere prevailed throughout the popular resort.

Luxurious villas were set back from the esplanade, many of

them situated within the security of walled gardens. One such property belonged to the Duc and Duchesse de Saint Aubrey, and they and members of their family came each year to spend the two hottest summer months at Saint Jean. The Saint Aubreys, together with their son, Charles and his family were recently arrived from the Périgord a few days ago.

One sweltering afternoon the town was deserted, everyone having retired home for a few hours *sièste* after their *déjeuner*. Down on the beach, the lone figure of a girl was sitting in the shadow of an upturned boat, her mouth trembling with emotion. Absently trickling warm sand through her fingers, she was relieved to have managed an escape from her family, subsequent to a humiliating scene over lunch.

Seated next to her grandmother in the restaurant, Minette had been uncomfortably aware of her mother's pale eyes resting on her in apparent distaste. Confused, she had tried to pinpoint the reason for such disagreeable scrutiny. Was she talking too much? Laughing too loudly? Had she spilled gravy down the front of her gown? Maybe all three—had been the girl's glum conclusion.

It was Minette's sixteenth birthday at the end of the following week. No plans, as yet, had been suggested by the Marquise to celebrate the event. In direct contrast, dear Jérome's birthday celebrations of three months ago had been organised weeks in advance.

Her brother had received many expensive gifts, one of which was a young stallion imported from Ireland, solely for his benefit. Minette had been green with envy over his good fortune— undeserved, in her opinion.

Despite the fact she had finally acquiesced to the Marquise's demands, and now rode side-saddle whilst in the public eye, Minette still had no horse of her own. Her mare, now too old to be ridden, spent her days out to pasture in the company of a few brood mares. Minette tried not to mind. After all, she rode regularly, and often helped with the schooling of her father's young horses at the Haras. Still, how wonderful it would be to have ...

"Marguerite!" Her mother's shrill voice had grated through the girl's thoughts. "Do take that bored expression off your face. It is not very flattering to see how we are of little interest to you. And kindly keep your knees together in a ladylike manner … you are not astride a horse now."

"Oh, but I am always fascinated by everything you have to say, Maman," Minette had retorted with spirit. "And my knees are positively glued together, I promise. "

"Don't answer back, you impertinent young madam," snapped the Marquise. "Your manners are abominable. Doubtless due to the unseemly horseplay with common stable-boys that you enjoy so much—and to a shocking degree, I am reliably informed."

"*What?*" Minette had gaped, flushing scarlet to the roots of her hair. "I have done nothing of the sort. If that old witch, Bonnaire, has said I have—she's a beastly liar!"

"How dare you speak to me in that rude tone?" Red patches of temper appeared on the Marquise's pale cheeks. "Mademoiselle Bonnaire has no reason to invent such a story. It is obviously true."

"Bonnaire has got a nasty mind, Maman," Minette had retorted. "She has been accusing me of over-familiarity with stable-boys since I was twelve."

"And not without reason, my girl! Mademoiselle Bonnaire told me that the day before we left to go on holiday, you were missing from the schoolroom. She was obliged to go in search of you at the Haras, where she was appalled to discover you cavorting, half-clothed, with some oaf in a hay barn. She was so distraught over such vulgar behaviour on your part, that she sought my advice. So Marguerite, are you still daring to contradict the word of a responsible adult?"

Her eyes burning with unshed tears, Minette glanced round the table. It was surely inconceivable that anyone in her family would believe such a monstrous accusation?

"This poor child might not dare to contradict the dratted woman, Francine—but I most certainly do," rapped out the Duc de Saint Aubrey. Everyone at the table turned to look at him in astonishment. "The inference that Minette is capable of this sort of behaviour is nothing short of iniquitous."

"Oh, you must always protect your darling granddaughter, mustn't you?" The Marquise sneered. "I prefer to believe … "

"It is not a question of who—or what—to believe, my dear

Francine," the Duc interrupted. "I happen to know it is sheer nonsense, fabricated to cause trouble by that blasted governess. I demand that she goes ... and without delay."

"Well, in my opinion," blustered the Marquise, unwilling to be foiled in humiliating her daughter, "the truth of the matter is still open to ... "

"This sorry business first came to my notice two years ago or so," continued the Duc, ignoring his daughter-in-law. "The governess was accusing Minette of something similar at the time. Not for a moment did I believe the child had been over-familiar with stable-hands. However, I made my own enquiries in case one of the lads had made inappropriate overtures, that had been misconstrued by the governess."

The Duc paused to stare coldly at the Marquise. "You will be relieved to know, Francine, that nothing of the sort had ever taken place. Nor has it since. Minette is on good terms with our stable staff ... and that is all."

Minette gazed at her grandfather, her heart filled with gratitude. Someone had, at last, stood up to her mother on her behalf! Even Jérome was looking stunned—if disappointed a potential drama was on the way to fizzling out.

"Minette, *chèrie*," the Marquis' voice broke into her thoughts. "Gran'père and I were going to wait until your birthday, but in light of this nonsense, I feel you should have something to look forward to. That bay filly you admire so much—Ariadne—she is to be your birthday gift."

"M-mine?" Minette was ecstatic. "Oh, thank you both so much."

There came the rattle of cutlery as the Marquise flung down her fork. "This is too, *too* much! Now this disgraceful girl is to be rewarded after ... "

"For God's sake, what are you talking about now, Francine?" impatiently barked the Marquis. "It is not a question of "reward" since the horse happens to be our daughter's birthday present. I imagine you must have momentarily forgotten the fact that it is her birthday next week?"

Her lips pursing, the Marquise picked up her fork. Conversation around the table resumed. But Minette's appetite had vanished, and the remainder of the meal seemed interminable. Upon leaving the restaurant at last, the family set off down the esplanade to the villa for a sièste. Deliberately lagging behind the rest of the family, Minette had slipped away, unnoticed.

Making her way along the sea front, she located a set of stone steps leading down to the beach. Kicking off her shoes, she rolled down her stockings, and ran barefoot down the steps to the warm sand and onward to the sea.

Handfuls of gown grasped in each hand, Minette paddled in the shallows for a few minutes. Then, rubbing her feet dry on the edges of her gown, she flopped down in the shade of an upturned boat to reflect on the awful scene in the restaurant ...

The sound of voices startled Minette. Heavens, she must have dozed off! Two fishermen were dragging nets towards the very boat beside which she was sitting. Amazed by the unusual sight of an unaccompanied young girl, they halted whilst Minette scrambled to her feet. The sun was now lower in the sky, indicating that considerable time must have passed since she arrived at the beach.

Frantically brushing sand from her gown, Minette decided against trying to slip back into her shoes—easier to run home. To avoid awkward questions as to where she had been all afternoon, she must enter the house unseen. Picking up her skirts, she raced back across the sand and up the steps of the promenade. Ignoring astonished glances from odd passers-by, Minette slipped on her shoes and hurried back to the villa.

Removing her shoes once more, she tip-toed through the front door and closed it with care. Before she could escape up the stairs, her elder brother emerged from the sitting room, a few magazines under his arm.

"Good God, where have you been?" Jérome demanded, casting a disparaging eye over his sister's untidy appearance. "What a sight! And why are you carrying your shoes and stockings ... oh, you weren't running around outside with bare feet were you? And what's that on the hem of your gown?" Jérome stood back to peer at the damp edges of Minette's skirts.

"*Sand!* You've been loafing on the beach, haven't you?" the young man smirked maliciously. "And all by yourself, I take it. My, oh my, Maman is going to love this."

Shouldering past her grinning brother, Minette entered her bedroom where the old nurse was busy ironing at a table by the window. Jeanne's eyebrows flew upward at the girl's precipitate entrance, not to mention her windblown appearance.

"I was wondering where you were, *ma chère?*" Jeanne attempted a diplomatic question. "Everyone came home from lunch for their sièste—except you."

"Oh, I just went for a short walk along the esplanade, Nou-nou," Minette replied evasively. "Er … nobody noticed my absence, did they?"

"No. Luckily for you, they went straight upstairs to rest. Minette, I trust you weren't alone out there?"

With a vague smile in her nurse's direction, Minette walked over to the long mirror in her bedroom. A somewhat untidy girl gazed back at her, pink-cheeked, her skin lightly tanned from outdoor activity in all weathers. Beads of sweat pearled on her upper lip and tendrils of dark hair clung to her damp face.

"*Chère*, do have a wash and brush up," Jeanne advised her charge. "Better to avoid trouble, *n'est-ce pas?*"

Splashing her hot face with water, Minette dragged a brush through her hair, replaced her stockings and shoes, and then left the room. Skipping down the staircase, she almost collided with her mother, about to leave the house with her younger son, Christophe.

"For God's sake, watch where you are going, you clumsy girl!" snapped the Marquise, her gaze sweeping over Minette's person. "I hope you don't mean to come with us in that filthy gown? It seems you have not bothered with a corset yet again, judging by your baggy appearance. And look at all that frizzy hair. Go back upstairs and do something about yourself. You are far too old to run around looking like a scruffy street-urchin."

Taking her son's arm, the Marquise pushed past Minette. "We are to meet your father down near the post-office. Make sure you are not in the same condition by the time we return, if you please."

Minette went back upstairs. Her nurse was hovering at the top of the staircase, and had overheard the Marquise's caustic remarks.

Poor child! Never mind, Jeanne knew exactly what to do to help her young charge redeem herself in her mother's eyes.

Opening the armoire, the nurse selected a sea-green organza gown. Ignoring Minette's immediate complaint that it was too "frou-frou," she laid it on the bed, assuring her it was ideal for this time of day. She also laid out the dreaded corset, which Minette generally refused to wear on principle.

Lacing a grumbling Minette into the corset, Jeanne slipped the gown over her head, and then brushed out the tangled hair until it shone. She seized handfuls of dark curls, twisting them away from Minette's face to the crown of her head. A few ringlets were allowed to escape and fall over a slender shoulder. Looking about her, Jeanne purloined a sprig of tiny white flowers from a vase, pinning it into the knot of curls on the girl's head. The nurse then stood back, satisfied with her efforts.

Glancing into the mirror, Minette gasped to see the radical change in her reflection. The dishevelled girl of half an hour ago was no more. Instead, an attractive young woman possessing the most enviable cheekbones was gazing back at her!

"See how you can look with just a little effort, *ma chèrie?*" Smiled the old nurse. "Quickly now, I think I hear your parents returning. Go and surprise them."

Beaming, Minette hugged her nurse in gratitude. At long last, she was going to see approval reflected in her mother's eyes. With as much dignity as she could muster—assisted by the rigidity of a corset—the young girl descended the staircase.

Charles was ushering his wife through the front door, when he glanced up to see his daughter coming down the stairs towards him. Gone was the *gamine* he was used to seeing, replaced by a vision. With a pleased smile, he moved forward to hold out a hand to Minette.

"Marguerite, why on earth have you dragged your hair up in that ridiculous way?" the Marquise shrilled from behind her husband. "God in heaven, it makes you look like a cheap third-rate actress—at best!"

"Francine, I beg you not to—"

"Go back upstairs and brush out your hair at once," the Marquise interrupted her husband's attempt to stop the flow of invective. "And in future, refrain from wearing flowers in your hair—only gypsies and harlots do that sort of thing."

Scarlet with humiliation, the girl's eyes brimmed with tears. Turning to flee, she caught a glimpse of the angry look her father directed at his wife.

Once again in the sanctuary of her bedroom, Minette flung herself on the bed in a storm of weeping. A worried Jeanne sat down beside the girl, mystified by the girl's abrupt return and her distress. The violent sobbing abating, Minette gave the old nurse a halting account of what had transpired below.

"But Papa thought I looked nice," the bewildered girl sniffled. "And I've seen lots of ladies with silk flowers pinned in their hats, and they weren't harlots!"

Fetching a bowl of water from the wash-stand, the nurse sponged Minette's tear-stained face. Her mind was whirling. What can have possessed the girl's mother to attack her so viciously? She, Jeanne, had brought up Francine from babyhood, and accompanied her upon marriage to her new home. Although her charge had been spoiled and given to tantrums, the nurse did not recall quite this level of nastiness.

Jeanne shook her head in bewilderment. Was it possible that Francine was jealous of her own daughter? Of her youthful freshness? For heavens' sake, she was still a beautiful woman, and had no need to feel sour towards Minette.

The old nurse was thoughtful as she brushed out the girl's hair. If she went to see Francine, might she be able to make her see sense over her treatment of this poor girl? After all, she had been the only one able to control her erstwhile charge's screaming tempers! Yes, it was worth a try, so she would choose a quiet moment ...

At dinner that evening, Minette was unusually withdrawn. Concerned, her grandmother attempted to engage in conversation, but elicited largely monosyllabic answers. Then, just as coffee was being served, Jérome leaned forward to drop his bombshell.

"By the way, Minette, I don't think it's a good idea to go off on your own, as you did this afternoon. Besides being unsafe, it is not at all *comme il faut* for girls of good family to wander about unaccompanied. Bound to encourage unpleasant gossip."

In the sudden silence at the table, Minette felt herself shrinking under her mother's triumphant stare. It was certain the Marquise had prior knowledge of Jérome's intention to humiliate her at some point during the evening meal. Before the beleaguered girl could think of a reply, the Duchesse placed a hand over Minette's clenched fist in an overt gesture of affection. The old lady hoped to prevent her impulsive granddaughter from exploding over her brother's duplicity.

"*Ma pauvre chérie*," murmured the Duchesse. "I'm sure the matter of étiquette did not occur to you at the time. It must be difficult for a modern girl to understand there are still things one should, or should not do."

The Duchesse turned a glacial eye on her elder grandson. She was well aware that, far from a sense of responsibility, Jérome's sole intention had been to cause trouble for his sister. Truly, there seemed little to admire in that boy's character.

"No harm done, in any event," the old lady continued smoothly. "I am sure Minette will remember in future."

The Marquise looked on in frustrated annoyance, still smarting over a recent row with her husband over the stupid girl's hairstyle. She had hoped Jérome's remarks would prompt outrage from the family against the sly creature. It simply hadn't crossed her mind that her mother-in-law might step in and neatly defuse the situation.

After the meal had ended, the younger members of family took themselves off to their individual pursuits. Charles and Francine remained at the table to enjoy a *digestif* with the Duc and Duchesse before retiring to bed.

Casting a surreptitious glance at her glowering daughter-in-law, the Duchesse wondered if Francine would be foolish enough to accuse her of interfering. After a few moments of awkward silence, the old lady took the initiative.

"Francine, *chérie*, why you are always so ... so angry with your little daughter? Not only is she a sweet child, but so very attractive! With those vivid eyes and dark hair, she makes most other young girls of her age look quite insipid."

Tears of suppressed fury sprang into the Marquise's eyes. "Madame, you must realise by now I cannot abide that girl. She is cunning, underhand, and deceitful. As for her colouring, it is as commonplace as that of an itinerant gypsy. *Ugh!* Positively brown-skinned. Furthermore, Charles makes me sick the way he is besotted with her. One might think the sun rises and sets with his darling Marguerite."

The Duchesse gazed at her daughter-in-law in shock, this being far from occasional friction between mother and daughter. Francine was displaying open antagonism towards a vulnerable young girl, which was quite another thing altogether.

"I don't think Minette merits rank hostility from her own mother, Francine," the old lady looked the Marquise directly in the eye. "Neither is the child's colouring up for criticism, thank you. It happens to be typical of my husband's side of the family. And is it not natural for Charles to be fond of his daughter?"

"No!" the Marquise's response was strident. "Not to the degree where he is actually drooling over the awful creature—to the detriment of my two sweet boys. How I long for the time when I am rid of that girl—permanently."

Upset, the Duchesse rose to her feet. The conversation was leaving an unpleasant taste in her mouth. Gathering her possessions, she turned to face her daughter-in-law.

"I do not care for your turn of phrase, Francine," she told the Marquise, her voice cold. "Neither will I enter into a debate over the ridiculous remark that Charles neglects his sons. I bid you good night."

Charles stood and watched his mother leave the room, accompanied by the Duc. Although deep in conversation with his father, he had nevertheless overheard most of the exchange between his wife and mother. White with anger, he addressed Francine who was flouncing towards the door.

"Madame, I wish to have a word with you—now, if you please."

Disturbed by the unusual chill in her easy-going husband's voice, the Marquise threw herself down in a chair with a long-suffering sigh.

"Understand once and for all, that I will not tolerate your unwarranted denigration of our daughter. It is a singularly unattractive trait in you, Francine."

The Marquise's mouth had fallen open in amazed fury. That Charles should address her in that icy manner? Criticise her?

It was that damned girl's fault—as always.

"Charles!" Francine made her voice plaintive. How can you speak to me so..."

"In future, I shall be keeping an eye on Minette's welfare," Charles interrupted, his tone still cold. "You would do well to bear it in mind, Madame." Without glancing again at his wife, he strode from the room.

Snatching up her reticule, the Marquise stormed through the door and pushed past a hovering footman. At the foot of the staircase, she screeched for her maid to attend to her without delay. If the lazy besom was sleeping, she would not only find herself dismissed, but she would be minus a reference.

Instead of her maid, however, the Marquise found her old nurse waiting in her boudoir. Jeanne bobbed a respectful curtsey as her mistress stalked in.

"What are you doing in here, Jeanne?" Francine's tone was truculent as she flung down her reticule on the dressing table. "And where the hell is that stupid maid who is supposed to attend me at all times?"

"Madame, I told her to retire as I wished for the pleasure of attending to you myself. I also hope to discuss a small matter with you, should you not be too tired," the nurse explained, suddenly nervous over her own temerity. "It is to do with Mademoiselle Marguerite ... "

"What about her?" snapped the Marquise, displeased to hear her hated daughter's name mentioned again so soon. "What could you possibly have to tell me about that blasted girl? Speak up, woman!"

"Madame, it was I who arranged Mademoiselle Marguerite's hair this afternoon," whispered the nurse. "She wanted so much to please you, and I remembered how I had done the same for you at much the same age ... "

Jeanne's prepared speech faltered upon seeing the Marquise's lips draw back in a snarl of rage. Patches of colour stained the woman's cheeks as she advanced on the quaking nurse.

"How dare you compare me with that creature, you

presumptuous hag!" Francine screamed. Her hand flashed out to deliver a resounding slap to the wrinkled face staring up at her in frozen horror.

Blood oozed from where one of the Marquise's sharp nails had ripped the thinned skin, but the nurse valiantly tried once more. "I beg of you Madame, please listen to me. Your daughter is much in need of you—"

"Silence! Have you forgotten yourself sufficiently to make overtures to me on that vile girl's behalf? Well? Have you?"

Fearing another blow, the nurse retreated a few steps. "No, Madame, I only—"

The Marquise sucked in her breath. "Unbelievable! You seem to imagine that because you have enjoyed the benefit of being in my family's employ for years, it entitles you—a stupid ignorant peasant—the right to criticise me?"

The woman's hand whipped out once more, but this time the nurse managed to duck the intended slap across the face.

"You have either lost your grip on reality, or you are becoming senile," spat the Marquise, her pale eyes dilating with incandescent rage. "In any event, you have outstayed your usefulness. Pack your bags and get out of my house—*now*! And send that lazy good-for-nothing maid to me before you leave."

Her eyes blinded by tears, a gnarled hand to her bleeding cheek, the old woman fled from the room. How could this woman whom she had mothered from birth be capable of such abuse? The child she had protected with her life? Slowly, the bleak realisation dawned that a lifetime of unswerving loyalty meant nothing to Francine— the woman who had just so brutally broken her heart.

And what of poor, insecure little Minette? How would her sudden absence be explained to her? Jeanne only hoped the child would eventually realise this abandonment of her was not through choice.

Maybe then, she would come to forgive her old nurse.

CHAPTER FOUR

The following year was uneventful, if not a particularly happy one for Minette. Her beloved nurse had vanished in the dead of night, plunging her into an abyss of insecurity and loneliness. The girl suspected her mother was somehow responsible for Jeanne's disappearance, but she professed complete ignorance of the matter.

"For God's sake, do stop whining about the old hag," the Marquise drawled with an ill-concealed yawn. "One can never expect loyalty or gratitude from these people whom one takes into one's home. I don't wish to hear another word."

"I don't believe Nou-nou would just disappear without saying a thing to me, Maman," Minette persisted. "Something must have happened, and … "

"Enough!" snapped the Marquise. "Really, you are boring me to tears. In any event, you are far too old to need a nurse-maid."

Clamping her lips together, the girl bobbed a curtsey and left the room. That the Marquise had a hand in her nurse's sudden departure, the suspicion had just intensified to certainty. And she would never, never forgive her mother for it.

Upon the family's return from Saint Jean de Luz, Minette rushed down to the Haras stables to claim her birthday present—her very own horse.

Ariadne.

Riding the horse became the highlight of Minette's subsequent days. It wasn't long before the once-fractious filly became the most docile of mounts for her young mistress. Even better was the fact that Ariadne was not broken to side-saddle—the perfect excuse for Minette to ride her astride.

Every morning at day-break, field hands yawning on their way to work would hear the distant thunder of hoofs. From out of the morning mist came a young Amazon, bareback on a galloping horse, dark hair streaming out behind her. The workers smiled and nodded to one another. It was only that nice child again—the Marquis' daughter.

Minette's education was placed once again in the hands of her brothers' tutor. Thankful to see the back of the hated governess, she began to enjoy her lessons, despite being plagued by the jealousies of her older brother. Little by little, Minette's spirits began to lift, and her many activities helped fill the void her nurse's abrupt disappearance had left in her life.

Twelve months later, a Ball was being arranged at the home of Minette's maternal grandparents, the Comte and Comtesse de Beaurepaire. The event was to mark the twentieth birthday of Minette's favourite cousin, Camille, the daughter of her mother's eldest brother, Maximilian.

Minette arrived at the Château de Beaurepaire well in advance of the event, to spend a few enjoyable days with Camille before other relatives arrived for the Ball. The girls were delighted to see one another, and went for daily rides through the woods, a disgruntled groom in attendance. Sharing a bedroom, Camille and Minette stayed awake long into the night, exchanging giggling confidences and plans for the future.

Two days before the Ball, family members living in other regions of France began arriving at the château. Max and his wife, Amélie, went out of their way to organise games and different kinds of races for the younger generation. Delicious fruit punch, wine, and champagne flowed from midday through to late evening, and the château atmosphere was festive indeed!

On the evening of the Ball, Minette and Camille stood side by side in front of the cheval mirror in Camille's bedroom. It was the first time Minette had been allowed to attend such a function, and the anticipation of the evening ahead was thrilling for the seventeen-year-old girl. Gazing at her reflection, Minette's eyes became fixed on the depth of her neckline. God! The thing seemed far too low.

The young girl wore a simple, midnight blue crêpe gown, its graceful skirt falling from an elegant Empire line bodice, reminiscent of the Romantic Period. The décolletage was low, but in impeccable taste, displaying her lightly tanned skin to perfection. A diamond necklace—on loan from her grandmother—was threaded through the shining chignon Camille's maid had created from Minette's mass of dark hair. Two heavy curls escaped to fall over a bare shoulder, and diamond studs sparkled in her ears.

Standing beside her, Camille resembled a pretty Tea Rose in pink taffeta. Her honey-coloured hair hung in ringlets about her face, and a single string of pearls glowed about her neck. Camille, however, was not looking at her own reflection. She was staring—open-mouthed—at her cousin, whom she was used to seeing as a tousle-haired *gamine*. In a few hours, Minette had been transformed into an unrecognisable beauty, generating an impression of sophisticated *jeunesse*.

With a smile, Camille restrained Minette's hand from straying towards her neckline, knowing her cousin intended to try and hitch it further up.

"*Chérie*, do leave your dress alone! The neckline isn't too low. As a matter of fact, you are looking quite beautiful tonight, Minette."

"Me? Beautiful?" Minette was incredulous. "Maman is always telling me how plain I am—verging on the ugly. Oh God, Camille, suppose she starts passing embarrassing remarks? I'll die!"

"*Tsk!* That sort of rubbish is best ignored, Minette. As for making nasty remarks this evening, I imagine Aunt Francine will be far too preoccupied with her own *entourage* to bother."

The two girls linked arms, and made their way to the top of the staircase. Looking down at the throng of guests milling below in the Great Hall, Minette was seized by an unexpected attack of nerves. Suppose she tripped over the hem of her gown whilst descending these stairs? Would people stare in disapproval at her definitely over-exposed bosom? At her too-plain ball-gown? And … and where was the Marquise?

Sensing her cousin was about to flee back to the bedroom,

Camille took Minette's elbow and engineered her further down the staircase. Once the younger girl began to mingle with the crowd, Camille hoped she would feel more secure from her mother's gimlet eyes.

Minette hesitated for a moment, awed by the elaborate finery of the ladies present, and the sophisticated elegance of the gentlemen. Silks, taffetas, brocades and satins of every imaginable shade and nuance whispered past her. Precious stones adorning necks, wrists, and coiffed hair blazed in the flickering light of chandeliers. Feathered fans cooled too-warm faces.

Gentlemen of varying age, handsome in frilled shirts under dark evening attire, stood in groups discussing topics of interest. Waiters threaded their way through the crowded guests, trays of canapés held aloft, or were pouring bubbling champagne into shallow glasses. The buzz of animated conversation rose and fell.

Rooted to the spot, Minette's eyes were still searching for the Marquise, her anxiety almost tangible. Camille gently prodded her cousin, and the two of them continued down the staircase.

A sudden prickling of her skin caused Minette to stiffen, her gaze inexorably drawn to where her mother was reclining on a velvet chaise longue. Vivacious and laughing, the Marquise held court to a group of youthful acolytes. Jérome stood close by, a possessive hand resting on his mother's shoulder.

Galvanised, Minette lost herself in a convenient crowd of younger people standing close by. Seconds later, she was swept up by a tide of young men, jostling to stake a claim on the Dance-card dangling from the new beauty's wrist!

No time left for dismal introspection!

A familiar voice caused Minette to whirl with a glad smile. Her father had come up behind her, approval reflected in his eyes. "How enchanting you look this evening, *ma petite!*" Smiled the Marquis. "Can this really be the same girl who gallops about the countryside when it is barely light?"

"Papa!" Minette was radiant. "Grand'mère helped me choose this gown, and she lent me her diamonds for the evening."

"A perfect choice, *chérie*. I am very proud of you. Off you go now, and enjoy yourself on the dance floor."

After a magnificent dinner, the music struck up and dancing resumed. Half an hour later, Minette took the opportunity of a pause to wander outside to a terrace. She wanted cool off a little in the night air, before being sought out by her next partner.

Standing alone beside the balustrade, the young woman was unconscious of the attractive picture she made against the velvet darkness of the evening sky. Flames from garden *flambeaux* lent mysterious shadows to the angles of her face, and the diamonds woven through her hair glittered their own cold brilliance.

Leaning against the stone surface of the balustrade, Minette breathed in the fresh air with appreciation. A sudden unexpected sound made her look round, startled.

On the far side of the darkened terrace … a movement!

Minette took a nervous step towards the doors to the ballroom. Then the glow of a cigar pierced the gloom, followed by a reassuring male voice.

"Do not be afraid, Mademoiselle. I had need of some cooler air, perhaps like yourself."

"Oh!" Minette was still faintly alarmed. "As a matter of fact, I was about to go inside, Monsieur."

"Please don't leave on my account, Mademoiselle Marguerite," the gentleman emerged from the shadows. "I would very much appreciate it, if you could keep me company a moment longer. May I introduce myself? Jacques Briand at your service. I happen to be an old friend of your mother's family."

Minette relaxed with a sigh of relief. As the gentleman moved into the light of the *flambeaux*, it became clear he was somebody's father, or perhaps an uncle. A pair of warm brown eyes gazed back at her.

The man was of medium height, dark-haired, but greying at the temples. His immaculate evening suit strained a trifle at the seams, indicating Monsieur Briand must really enjoy his food—thought the girl with an inward giggle.

"How did you know my name?" Minette asked with interest.

"Your mother pointed you out to me," replied the gentleman. "We watched you coming down the staircase with Camille."

"My…my mother?" Minette thought to have escaped the Marquise's notice.

"Frankly, I am amazed the fair Francine's daughter should turn out to be a dark-haired young Diana ... Goddess of the Hunt." the gentleman continued with a smile. "A divine creature with stars in her hair, and skin like melted honey."

Minette smiled uncertainly. A man of his advanced years shouldn't be saying such things to a girl of her age, for heaven's sake! Somehow, it seemed inappropriate.

Maybe it was time to leave.

"Goodness, there is my partner for the next dance. Please do excuse me, Monsieur Briand, I had better go inside and join him."

"Of course, my dear girl," the man moved aside. "I have enjoyed our chat, and hope we may continue it another time."

Jacques Briand's gaze was speculative as he gazed after Minette's retreating back. Yes, indeed! The girl was fresh, delightful, and very attractive into the bargain—he thought with satisfaction. He would confirm to Francine that he wished to pursue a suit for Marguerite, as soon as possible.

Of course, she was still on the young side, so a betrothal would be acceptable for the time being. Marguerite was worth waiting for, and he was a patient man. A wedding the following year would do very well.

Hastening back to the ballroom, Minette felt unaccountably disturbed. She meant to ask Camille who the man was ... and how best to avoid him in future. It was also odd how the Marquise had been happy to claim her as a daughter. As a general rule, it was something her mother wished to avoid at all costs.

Shrugging off her disquiet, Minette was caught up once more with the excitement of the Ball. She forgot about the odd man on the terrace, and did not see him again during the rest of the evening.

A month later, it was Minette's own birthday—her seventeenth. The Marquis had arranged a Drag Hunt on horseback for his daughter and her friends, followed by an alfresco *déjeuner* set out in the château gardens.

The Hunt was a wild success, involving much whooping and shouting from the youthful huntsmen, and those who followed on foot. At noon, the tired participants, now washed and changed, made their way outside to trestle tables set up in the shade of giant chestnut trees. On a wide buffet table, baskets of still-warm crusty bread were interspersed with platters of charcuterie and cold chicken. A variety of salads were also on offer, followed by apple tart and cream.

At the end of the meal, Minette leaned inelegant elbows on the table with a sigh of satisfaction. It had been a wonderful day, and so much nicer than those soppy *soirées* her girlfriends seemed so fond of! All that hysteria over what to wear, and having one's hair teased to death with curling irons—no thank you!

"Excuse me, Mademoiselle Minette." A footman appeared at her elbow. "Monsieur Charles requests you attend him in his study when you have finished your *déjeuner.*"

"Thank you, Pierre, I shall go straight away."

On the way to her father's study, Minette wondered about the summons she had received. Might it be another gift? Or maybe he wanted to arrange some other activity for her friends? She would soon know, in any event.

Tapping on the study door, she slipped inside. The Marquis was sitting at his desk, preoccupied by a heavy ledger in front of him. He glanced up at his daughter, smiled, and indicated one of the shabby armchairs on the other side of the desk. After a moment, the Marquis rose to drag over the other armchair and sat opposite Minette.

"So, *ma chèrie!* Are you enjoying your birthday? The Hunt went well, I am told. Excellent! And I have seen the astonishing array of presents you have received."

"Oh, Papa, the whole day has been wonderful, and I shall never forget it. Thank you so much for everything."

"Minette, there is an important matter I must discuss with you. Nothing to be alarmed about!" the Marquis smiled reassuringly, and patted his daughter's hand.

"Following your undoubted success at Camille's Ball, it is clear you are well and truly out of the schoolroom, *n'est-ce pas?* In fact, not far off a marriageable age."

"Marriage?" Minette pulled a face. "Papa, I'm only just seventeen! I don't want to even think about such a thing for ages yet."

"Minette, as your father, my duty is to arrange the best possible alliance for you. Of course, it would be to a man of impeccable lineage, and wealthy enough to take good care of my darling child."

"But Papa, I don't want to marry anyone!" Minette exclaimed in alarm. "I want to stay here, at home with my family!"

"Yes, yes, I understand, Minette. But you must also realise that one day, you will have to leave here to live at your husband's home. Possibly, you are still a little young, but next year I daresay you will think differently about everything."

"I don't want to think about it at all!" Minette retorted with heat. "Besides, there isn't a single boy I know who would want to marry me."

"A foolish boy is not at all what your mother and I have in mind for you, Minette. As it happens, a gentleman has approached me with regard to making you his wife in the fullness of time. It is an offer of the highest order, and one which I believe would be perfect for you."

Minette frowned. This was becoming a great deal too serious for her liking.

"Papa, can we talk about this another time? I don't want to spoil my birthday."

"Very well. But I am asking you to consider what we have been discussing with care. It is all about safe-guarding your future, Minette—of vital importance to me. But a betrothal at this point will suffice."

A betrothal? Stunned, Minette rose to her feet and turned to go. She hesitated a moment, then looked back at her father. "Papa, this man who is so anxious to marry me … when am I to meet him?" she asked.

"You have already met him at Camille's Ball, a month ago. It seems the two of you spent a pleasant moment taking the air outside on a terrace."

The girl's mouth fell open. Not … surely not that old fellow with the cigar? Why, he was as old as her father—maybe even older!

"Is this a joke, Papa? The man I spoke to at that Ball was old, sweaty, and bursting out of his clothes. He also made personal remarks … so embarrassing. As a matter of fact, I thought him rather peculiar."

"I am not joking, Minette. Far from being peculiar, Jacques Briand would be an ideal husband for you. Being an older man he would give you stability, happiness, and it would be his pleasure to spoil you." Charles glanced at his daughter's glowering face and sighed. It was clear Minette was not going to be easily convinced.

"As Jacques' wife, you would have the choice of several homes throughout France, the principal residence being a lovely old château in Provence," Charles persevered. "He is very wealthy, so you could have all the dogs and horses you desire. On the death of his father, Jacques will become the Duc de Mont-Ravelles, and of course, you would … "

"*No!*" Minette burst out. "Papa, I can never marry that man! I don't care how much money he has, or how many houses he owns. It's disgusting that a man of his age should be chasing after a girl of seventeen, don't you think?"

"Watch your tongue, Marguerite!" the Marquis was taken aback. It had not crossed his mind that his daughter might argue with him. Neither had she ever spoken to him in this explosive and disrespectful manner. He was unimpressed.

"I will not allow you to describe Monsieur Briand in such derogatory terms. He is a very pleasant man, and your mother's family have known him since he was a lad."

"In that case, they must have known him for an absolute age," muttered the girl under her breath. "Seeing as how ancient he is!"

"That's enough, Marguerite!" barked the Marquis. "Your attitude is disrespectful, and does not reflect well on your upbringing. It is my wish that you become betrothed to Jacques Briand, so there is no more to be said. As you are still young, the wedding will not take place until after your eighteenth birthday. You may go now."

The Marquis returned his attention to his ledger, not looking at his daughter who slunk from the room, her expression thunderous. He was astounded over what he perceived as impertinence in Minette, that she should dare to make unjustified and crass remarks relating to Jacques Briand's person and character. Could it be that Francine was right all along about the girl being out of hand? A disturbing thought.

Charles shook his head. No. It was too soon to think along

those lines. Minette must be brought to understand—and accept—that a father invariably arranged his daughter's alliance. It was only to be expected of a girl of her rank. Jacques Briand's offer was excellent, and Charles would not allow girlish tantrums to jeopardise a matter of such importance.

Minette fled from her father's study, and rushed up to her bedroom. Throwing herself on the bed, she gave way to a storm of weeping, banging her fists against the pillows in frustrated rage.

Her wonderful birthday was turning into a hideous nightmare!

Bartered to that old fellow like … like a blasted sow at the market! It was too much to bear. Who could she ask for advice, since her beloved nurse on whom she had always depended had gone? Nobody. Fresh tears trickled down the girl's cheeks, as she saw her once-bright future yawn dismally before her.

A light tapping at her bedroom door, and Camille peeped in. Her face registered concern to see her cousin huddled on the bed, her eyes reddened and swollen.

"Dearest Minette, whatever is the matter? "Camille sat down beside the distraught girl. "Is it something to do with your Papa? I wondered why you had to run off to see him straight after lunch."

"Camille, I want to die!" Minette whispered. "They mean to marry me off to some fat *vieillard* my dear mother has netted. Papa is furious because I won't agree. God, I can't bear the idea of that man ever touching me."

"What man?" Camille stroked Minette's hair back from her damp face. "He can't be as bad as all that, if your father likes him."

"It's Briand … Jacques Briand," Minette sniffled. "And I hate him."

"Come on, Minette! How can you say you hate him, when you don't really know the poor chap," Camille smiled in amusement. "I have met Monsieur Briand, and he strikes me as being a nice man. He's fearfully rich, you know, and his family live in a gorgeous Provençale château. The old Duc de Mont-Ravelles is said to be terminally ill, so when Jacques inherits the title, you … "

"I don't care how rich he is, Camille," Minette interrupted. "And I've heard all about becoming his Duchesse. Can you imagine it—me, a snooty Duchesse? *Pah!*"

"Minette, do take a moment to think the whole thing through," Camille replied, perturbed by her cousin's vehemence. "If your father has agreed to this alliance with Jacques Briand, it cannot be easily set aside. To be frank, Minette, I don't believe Uncle Charles would arrange something as important as this, if he was not certain it was right for you."

"Never! I will not tamely allow myself to be married to that pink porker!" Minette exploded. "Oh, I know who is behind this plot ... it's my dearest Maman! Ever since I was a small child, she's been longing to see the back of me."

"Minette, you must calm down!" Camille advised her volatile cousin. "It will not do to let everyone see a defiant attitude, because I'm convinced you would be the loser in the end!"

"Papa loves me, and won't want to make me miserable," Minette declared with conviction. "I shall tell him how Maman pointed me out to the Briand man at your Ball. He can then see for himself the cunning plan she's concocting to be rid of me."

Camille shook her head. "Don't, Minette! For heaven's sake don't confront your mother. To be honest, I would not care to find myself at odds with Aunt Francine! It's a frightening thought!"

"We'll see, won't we?" Minette's was mutinous. "I'm damned if I'm going to allow my mother to ride rough-shod over me this time. Not when the ruination of my whole life is at stake."

CHAPTER FIVE

The Duchesse de Saint Aubrey was sitting on a bench in her rose garden, her face pensive. Earlier that morning, her son had approached her with a request she was unwilling to undertake. It was with regard to the betrothal he had accepted on behalf of his daughter to a gentleman, Monsieur Jacques Briand. His father not being long for this world, Jacques would then inherit the title, Duc de Mont-Ravelles. It was an ideal match, but Minette was resisting the suitor with surprising energy.

The Duchesse had already come across Jacques Briand, and recalled a pleasant enough man with charming manners, if a trifle on the chubby side. Being one of the wealthiest men in France, he was in an excellent position to care for a wife, indeed, to indulge her every whim. On the face of things, the suit was a superb marital prospect.

However, the Duchesse was unable to imagine her exuberant, often impetuous young granddaughter becoming a dutiful wife. In addition, she would probably be obliged to assume the heavy mantle of Duchesse at the age of eighteen. *Ah non* – the old lady's mind boggled at the thought. Minette was still far too much of a *gamine*, and not ready for anything of the sort.

There was another worrying aspect for the Duchesse. It was the disparity of age between Minette and the intended bridegroom. It would not have posed a problem with a more malleable girl. But Minette? The old lady knew her granddaughter would never willingly marry a man old enough to be her father, for heaven's sake.

The Duchesse was at a loss to understand why Charles had consented to this ill-matched alliance in the first place. Francine must be at the bottom of it—she thought, determined as always to rid herself of the poor girl.

Nevertheless, she had agreed to speak to Minette, in the vain hope she might induce her granddaughter to see reason. It went against her better judgement, but Charles was insistent. His view was that marriage to an older man would spell stability for his volatile and headstrong young daughter. Jacques was known to be a kind man. He was also very taken with Minette, so she would be able to indulge her love of horses and dogs to her heart's content. In short, she was certain to enjoy an enviable lifestyle.

As if on cue, her granddaughter arrived in the company of Charles' hounds. Dressed in her habitual checked shirt, riding britches and boots, Minette threw herself down in the grass by her grandmother's feet. The two hounds followed suit and rolled over on their backs, hoping for a tickle. Laughing, Minette scratched each warm stomach in turn, the dogs' jaws falling open as they panted in ecstasy. The Duchesse couldn't help smiling to see the young girl happy and relaxed.

"I imagine you have been down to the Haras to school that naughty Minèrva," the old lady asked. "How is she coming along?"

"She's so much better balanced now, Grand'mère. She isn't bucking like she used to, and neither does she shy at everything. I can even ride her out in the woods without much drama these days."

"I'm sure your Papa is delighted with the change. He was very concerned about that filly managing to get rid of every single lad who tried schooling her."

Minette laughed, running a hand through her mass of dark curls. "It's taken a little time, but we're getting there."

The Duchesse looked at her granddaughter, thinking she had never seen the girl look more beautiful. There was something about the exposed, honey-tinted throat, rosy lips, and a hint of colour in her cheeks that spoke of health and vitality. Precisely what had attracted the attention of the unwanted suitor in the first place—was the old lady's wry reflection.

"Just what do you think you are doing, Marguerite?" the Marquise's shrill voice grated on the girl's nerves. "Good God, look at the state of you! Why, pray, are you garbed like a stable-hand?"

Scrambling to her feet, Minette faced her mother who had just arrived on the scene. "I was playing with Papa's hounds just now. And I'm still in my riding clothes because I was schooling a youngster down at the Haras earlier this morning."

"I won't have it, do you hear?" the Marquise ordered. "You have been told time and again to dress in a proper manner at all times, Marguerite. As the future wife of Monsieur Briand, it is unacceptable that you romp about the place, filthy dirty, and wearing your brothers' old clothes."

"I am not anyone's future wife yet, thank you Maman."

"Don't answer back! Imagine if your fiancé happened to call, and clapped eyes on you looking like you do? How shameful."

"That man is not my fiancé. Nor is he ever likely to be." Minette glowered. "Why are you trying to push me off on the fellow like this?"

"How dare you address me in that impertinent manner?" Tell-tale patches of red stained the Marquise's cheeks. "You forget yourself, my girl!"

"Minette, *chérie*, why don't you get yourself washed and changed since it is almost lunch-time?" the Duchesse interceded, in an effort to avoid further confrontation. "I will come down to the stables later this afternoon. Perhaps you can show me the progress your beautiful Ariadne has achieved in her dressage? I understand you mean to compete with her later in the year? She should do well, by all accounts."

Her eyes veiled against her mother, Minette dropped a curtsey to both older women. Calling to the hounds, she walked quickly towards the house.

"Francine, why not allow Minette her freedom for the time being?" The Duchesse asked, ignoring her daughter-in-law's infuriated exclamation. She is hardly in the public eye when working down at the Haras. To tell the truth, I'm pleased to see a smile back on the child's face, something which has been conspicuous by its absence for quite some time."

"Madame, I ask you not to encourage that girl so," the Marquise held her temper in check with an effort. "It is expected that she conforms to her future role as Monsieur Briand's fiancée, and shortly thereafter, his wife. That does not include rough-housing with those smelly dogs, dressed like some hobble-de-hoy.'"

"*Chérie*, have you and Charles considered the probability that there will be other very good offers for Minette a little later on? On reflection, if this particular match comes to nothing, it might well be a blessing in disguise … "

"What?" the Marquise flushed scarlet. "The alliance with Jacques Briand must go forward without delay! That damned girl has blighted my life long enough. One should be deeply grateful for this genuine offer for Marguerite. For God's sake, Madame, any other suitor would take to his heels in the belief that Marguerite must be of peasant origin with that bush of hair and swarthy skin."

The Duchesse looked at her daughter-in-law's beautiful face, mottled red and contorted with vitriol. Heavens, she really was obsessed with getting rid of the girl. True, Minette had never been a docile child, but she was brave and loving, and in possession of many attributes which Francine preferred to ignore.

Such a tragedy.

"I have promised Charles that I will speak to Minette about this betrothal," the Duchesse said at last. "It is, however, unfortunate that she has taken so violently against Monsieur Briand. I wonder why? Is it possible he has made an unsuitable approach which has given offence?"

"Of course not, Madame," the Marquise retorted. "Jacques is a gentleman to his finger-tips. The stupid girl is probably put out over Jérome teasing his little sister about having a suitor. Nothing untoward, I'm sure."

"Yes, I can well imagine what was said," said the Duchesse grimly, ignoring Francine's offended expression. "Knowing my elder grandson, it would not surprise me if the poor girl is appalled by the prospect of marriage … to anyone."

Later that afternoon, the Duchesse drove down to the Haras in her own trap drawn by a stocky pony. She drew up beside the sand school, where Minette was riding her own mare, Ariadne. Watching the sheer grace of the horse's paces as she danced past, the old lady smiled with pride. It was amazing what her granddaughter had achieved with the flighty little filly Ariadne had been only a year ago!

Bringing the horse to a halt, Minette slid off her back and kissed Ariadne's soft nose. She led her over to the arena gate where her grandmother was waiting, a bulging string bag over her arm.

"Grand'mère, I'm so pleased you have come!" Minette's brilliant smile flashed out. "Ariadne has been a darling, and hasn't put a foot wrong this afternoon."

"She looked wonderful to me, *ma chèrie*. So effortless!" declared the Duchesse in genuine admiration. "If you are finished, perhaps we can take advantage of the sun's last rays to drink a glass of lemonade and share a biscuit or two."

Five minutes later, Minette and her grandmother made their way down to a bubbling stream behind the stabling. It was home to a quantity of wild ducks that registered the intrusion into their world by a cacophony of loud quacking. Taking the string bag from Minette, the old lady extricated a tartan rug that had seen better days, and a flask of lemonade.

"There, spread this out for yourself, but I shall use my old camping stool. I would join you on the rug, but I rather fear I wouldn't be able to get up again."

"This is gorgeous lemonade, Grand'mère! I was so thirsty just now, it was tempting to take a swig from the horse trough" Minette grinned, wiping her mouth with the back of a none-too-clean hand.

"Darling, I want to have a private chat with you," the Duchesse began. "I regret it is to do with a matter I know you detest," the old lady was sorry to see the joy die from her granddaughter's face.

"Oh! That. I suppose you mean dear Maman's efforts to fob me off on the old codger she dug up from somewhere?"

"He's not that old, Minette," the Duchesse hid an involuntary smile over the disrespectful terminology. "I happen to know Jacques Briand, and found him to be a very nice man with quite a sense of humour. "

"He cannot be that nice, since Jérome told me Monsieur Briand was itching to—"

"*Chèrie*, you know better than to believe everything that young rascal tells you," hurriedly interrupted the Duchesse. "At least think about it, my darling. You would look forward to a wonderful future as Jacques' wife. Provence is not so very far away, and we could often visit—"

"No! I will never agree to marry that man. He's old, fat, and he sweats a lot. Why the hurry to get me married off?" Minette truculently demanded. "I'm only seventeen, Grand'mère! Of course, I know my dear mother has always wanted to be rid of me."

Minette's hands were gripped together so the knuckles shone white. "What I cannot understand, is how Papa seems happy to go along with her plotting."

Unable to answer that particular question, the old lady remained silent. "Very well, Minette," she said at last, sad to have ruined what had been a companionable and relaxed atmosphere between them. "But on your own head be it, my poor child. It is not an easy road you are choosing to take. Come *chérie*, let us pack up our things and go. The sun has gone down, and I'm beginning to feel a trifle chilly."

Three weeks later, Minette was sitting in the salon with her grandfather, reading aloud to him in English. The Duc de Saint Aubrey, himself fluent in the English language, had ensured his granddaughter spoke the language both colloquially and well from the time she was small. He wanted Minette to discover the vast range of fascinating literature available to her, consisting of both English and American authors. Over the past year, the old man's eyesight was gradually failing, so the reading sessions were becoming more frequent.

A knock at the door announced a footman. "Excuse me, Monsieur, but I have a message for Mademoiselle Marguerite. Please would she attend Monsieur Charles in his study as soon as it is convenient."

"Thank you, I shall go immediately." Minette dismissed the footman. "Gran'père, what do you suppose this is about? I couldn't bear it if Papa starts talking about that beastly betrothal business all over again."

"Minette *chérie*, it would not be advisable to allow your father to see such defiance in you," was the Duc's quiet admonishment. "Try to use a little diplomacy, instead of rushing at things like a wounded bull."

"But Gran'père, I have to put a stop to Maman's horrid plans to get rid of me! I told Papa how she raked up this old fellow at Camille's Ball, but he became angry, and wouldn't listen."

"Minette, you must understand that you are obliged to fall in with your father's wishes as regards your future," exclaimed the Duc, his tone unusually sharp. "It is the requirement of every young girl of our station. You are no exception to the rule, so my advice would be to accept this betrothal—an excellent offer—with grace."

"But Gran'père, I really ... "

"Minette! Are you not listening to me? There are no "buts" in this case. Jacques Briand is a good man, and I am confident he will treasure you. Go now to your Papa, and try to be an acquiescent daughter for a change. Or I may begin to wonder if we have not brought you up very well."

Minette stared at her grandfather, incredulous that he, too, seemed happy to fob her off on the Briand fellow. Her expression stony, she rose without a word, bobbed a curtsey to her grandfather, and left the room.

The Duc gazed at the closed door, and shook his head. His wife had told him of her own attempt to make Minette see reason, which had been to no avail. He had deliberately spoken sharply to his granddaughter, in the hope that Minette might be jolted into being sensible. But seeing the mutinous expression on her face, the Duc had serious doubts about the outcome of this interview with Charles ...

The Marquis looked up with a smile, as Minette tapped at the door and came into his study. "Thank you for coming so quickly, chèrie ... sit down over there, and I'll be with you in a moment."

Minette settled herself in a chair, apprehensive of what further horror might be coming her way. The betrothal business was bound to come up.

Pushing his papers to one side, Charles gave his full attention to his daughter. "I wanted to let you know your mother has sent out invitations for a formal soirée next week, marking your engagement to Monsieur Briand. I thought you might like to have a new gown made up for the event?"

Minette sat frozen to the chair. This was a terrifyingly swift escalation of the matter of her betrothal. How to handle matters in the diplomatic manner her grandfather was advising? But this was her darling Papa, who had always wanted to see her happy. Maybe an appeal to the side of him that she knew so well?

"I ... I truly don't want to be betrothed, Papa," Minette entreated, gazing up at her father with ingenuous eyes "I'm not ready for that sort of thing yet. Please let me stay at home for a few more years. I'm sure I shall have other offers ... "

The Marquis' dark brows flew together. "I trust you are not about to give me a repetition of the juvenile charade you enacted the other day, Marguerite!" he enquired, his tone icy. "You will accept Monsieur Briand's proposal with a show of good manners, if you please. This wilful attitude of yours is unacceptable, so perhaps marriage to an older man will keep your feet firmly on the ground."

"No!" Minette threw caution to the winds. "The so-wonderful man selected for me is not only old and fat, but he's lecherous into the bargain. *Ugh!* Just the idea of such a person touching me makes me want to be sick."

The Marquis stood up, his expression thunderous. "Marguerite, I fear you forget yourself. How dare you speak of Monsieur Briand with such disrespect, and nothing to back up your vulgar assertion? I have never heard a lady speak thus, and do not wish to again. The matter of your betrothal is settled. You may go."

Aghast, Minette rose to her feet and left the room without a word. This was the first time in her life that her father had shown real anger towards her. It did not sit well. The net was inexorably closing about her, and there was nothing she could do to avoid it. Or was there?

What if she appeared to accept the engagement to the Briand fellow, but asked that the actual marriage be delayed for an extra year? That might buy valuable time to think up an escape plan. Such tractability on her part would also reinstate her into her father's good graces. Yes, a demure approach could well work out to her advantage.

It was the evening of the soirée to celebrate the betrothal of Marguerite de Merencourt to Jacques Briand. The flower-filled Salon was already buzzing with guests and relatives from both families, many of them having travelled considerable distances to be present.

The Marquise, resplendent in ice blue silk, stood by the Salon doors to welcome new arrivals, her elder son, Jérome, by her side. Champagne fizzed, and liveried footmen offered silver salvers heaped with delicious canapés to guests.

Upstairs, Minette stood in front of the cheval mirror in her bedroom, gazing at her reflection with a critical eye. She had chosen to wear a dusty pink gown in fine lawn, which she knew suited her well. No jewellery, except for a single string of pearls about her neck. At the last moment, she had pinned a pink rose into her mane of dark hair. In doing so, she felt a small, if illogical satisfaction to be flying in the face of the Marquise's dictates about the wearing of flowers.

Despite assurances to herself that the plan she had rehearsed in her bedroom was sound, her stomach was nevertheless churning over what lay ahead. It was a matter of retaining cool self-control. Pray God she remembered that when face to face with the prospective bridegroom.

Taking a steadying breath, Minette lifted her chin and left the sanctuary of her bedroom to descend the staircase. A footman darted forward to open the Salon door for her, and she entered the room, an artificial smile on her lips. The Marquise who was standing close to the door, treated her to a brief examination, then nodded, seemingly satisfied. Amazing to have won my mother's approval, just so she can sell me on—the girl thought, her lips twisting with the irony.

"Mademoiselle Marguerite." Jacques Briand was at Minette's elbow. "How very beautiful you are looking this evening, my dear," he bent to kiss her hand.

"Thank you, Monsieur," Minette cast down her eyes, "You are very kind."

"Dearest girl, with your father' permission of course, will you take a short turn in the garden with me? Although formal details of our betrothal have obviously been completed, a personal element should be an integral part, do you not agree?"

"Er … yes, indeed, Monsieur Briand. But surely the speeches are soon to begin?"

"Not for a while yet, *ma chèrie*," the Marquis broke in from behind

Minette, his smile approving of his daughter's demure demeanour. "A short promenade with Monsieur Briand will not interfere with the evening's arrangements."

Placing her hand on the man's proffered arm, Minette realised she had no choice but to allow him to lead her out into the Duchesse's rose garden. The evening was pleasantly warm, but Minette found herself struggling to control shivers running through her body. What was he going to say? Might he try and kiss her? God forbid.

After a moment, Jacques Briand turned to face the agitated girl. "Please don't be nervous of me, Marguerite," he said gently. "I count myself a fortunate man to have won your father's consent to make you my wife in due course. Please believe me when I say I shall cherish you to the end of my days, dearest girl."

"Mon…Monsieur Briand, I am truly flattered you hold me in such high regard," Minette stammered, hoping her confusion would be put down to maidenly shyness. "But I should point out that I am sadly lacking in the necessary skills I shall require upon marriage to you. There will be much entertaining to oversee, and households to run. I admit to being nervous of dealing with such responsibilities as would be mine."

"Dearest girl, my mother will be there to help, and one of my sisters—"

"What I am asking of you, Monsieur, is that our marriage be delayed for a further year … until after my nineteenth birthday," Minette continued determinedly. "Given this time for instruction in various issues by my mother and grandmother, I shall feel much more confident by the time I stand beside you as your bride."

Without amusement, Minette noted the expression of dismay clouding her suitor's features. No doubt it was dawning on him that he might not lay hands on his youthful intended for a long time to come—the girl thought dryly.

"My dearest Marguerite." Jacques struggled to conceal his disappointment. "If allowing a year or two to go by will make such a difference to you, I must agree."

"Thank you so much, Monsieur Briand." Minette's smile of gratitude was genuine, "I shall make good use of the time, I promise you."

Groping in a pocket, Jacques produced a small, gilt-embossed leather box, snapped it open and offered it to the girl. "I trust you will wear this ring for me as a symbol of our attachment, dearest Marguerite? It has been created especially for you."

Resting on its tiny velvet cushion, a ring of large and priceless diamonds blazed their fire in the last rays of the evening sun. In spite of herself, Minette's jaw dropped in awe. Extracting the ring from its nest, the man slipped it over the girl's finger. A perfect fit.

"I ... oh, it's beautiful!" Minette breathed, forgetting for a moment what the jewel represented. "I have never seen anything quite like it before."

Overcome with pleasure, Jacques leaned towards Minette, meaning to place a light kiss on her lips. Sensing his intention, the girl turned her head at the last moment, and the kiss landed on her cheek. Apologising for his forwardness, Jacques hastily stepped back. Scarlet with embarrassment, Minette suggested they return to the Salon to show off her ring to the assembled company.

With a grim inward smile, Minette wondered how the Marquise was going to deal with having to put up with her daughter yet awhile? She did not have long to wait. Learning of the postponement of the wedding by a full year, the ever-ominous red flags of temper flared in the Marquise's cheeks. Grasping Minette by the arm, she hustled the girl from the room.

"Just what do you imagine you are achieving by this ploy, Marguerite?" she hissed, lips drawn back over her teeth. "A further year's delay on your marriage? Impossible! I will not tolerate such nonsense, do you hear me?"

Wrenching her arm from her mother's painful grip, Minette smiled. "But Jacques has already agreed to it, Maman dear. He sees my point of view perfectly."

"Insolent girl! Just wait until your father hears of this," spat the Marquise. "He will soon put you right, my young madam!"

"I take it you are referring to the delay on the marriage, Francine?" the Marquis's voice intervened, having joined his wife and daughter, unobserved. "Jacques has already told me of it, and I am inclined to agree on principle. I can see that Minette could feel herself unprepared for the role of Jacques' wife. One should also bear in mind the heavy mantle of Duchesse she would bear in the event of his father's death. Nobody is better qualified than you and my mother to instruct our daughter in the skills she is likely to require."

"But the whole thing is a yet another cunning ruse by this girl, Charles … can't you see that?" argued the Marquise, anxious to reverse her husband's unexpected consent to the postponement of the marriage.

"Nonsense, Francine," Charles frowned in irritation. "Jacques is agreeable to waiting a further year, so the matter is settled."

Incandescent with impotent rage, the Marquise flounced away without a further glance at her triumphant daughter. All her carefully laid plans overturned on that blasted creature's whim … and Charles' foolish connivance! It made her sick to her stomach. Jérome must be told at once, and perhaps he would have a suggestion to recoup the situation. Dearest Jérome, he always understood her …

Although privately reeling over the condition imposed by his bride-to-be, Jacques Briand was nevertheless determined to see as much of her as possible. Seeing Minette return to the salon in the company of her father, Jacques hurried over to speak to the Marquis.

"Monsieur, I seek your permission to take Mademoiselle Marguerite on a visit to my parents in Provence—naturally chaperoned by her maid? My parents and one of my sisters who still lives at home are anxious to meet my fiancée. Marguerite would also see something of the surrounding area, and the château which is to be her home."

"By all means, I'm sure Minette would be delighted to meet your family. Is that not so, *chérie?*" the Marquis glanced over at his daughter.

"Indeed, Papa," Minette answered in a faint voice, privately horrified.

"With your approval, I shall plan on leaving in approximately ten days time." Jacques glanced fondly at his intended. "That should give Mademoiselle Marguerite time to make her own preparations for the journey."

The remainder of the evening seemed interminable to the girl.

There were endless speeches to be endured, congratulations to be accepted with grace, and exclamations of admiration for the ring sparkling on her hand. By the time the last guest had departed, Minette felt she was suffocating to the point of screaming.

Back in her bedroom at last, the girl relaxed her self-control and dissolved into tears. How in God's name was she to avoid the catastrophic abyss into which she was being plunged? Forced to visit that man's ancient parents. To be looked over by his spinster sister. How could she have been so stupidly naïve? So delighted had she been to achieve a hefty delay on her marriage, she had failed to take into account that in the interim, she was expected to participate in old Briand's day-to-day life.

And her father was happy for her to do so.

Minette dragged off her gown with leaden arms, but noticed something was catching on the material. It was the ring still adorning her hand, the diamonds seeming to sparkle mockingly. With an oath to make a seaman proud, Minette wrenched off the ring and flung it into a drawer in her dressing table. There! She would refuse to be bullied into advertising her "bondage" to the world by wearing the beastly thing!

Hours later, Minette was lying awake in her bed, her mind an obstinate blank. Try as she might, she could see no real solution to her problems. How delighted the Marquise must be to learn of recent developments in her daughter's life! Minette ground her teeth in frustration. Just as she thought to have triumphed over the vile woman's scheming!

Henceforth, it had been made clear she was to be chained to Monsieur Briand's side. Which, to all intents and purposes, would be almost as bad as being married to the fellow. Her active life at the Haras would be replaced by dull sorties in the company of that man and his circle of ancient friends. But how to extricate herself from the maelstrom of events she had unwittingly brought down on her own head? God alone knew—was the girl's dismal thought, before drifting into an uneasy sleep.

CHAPTER SIX

Early next morning, the rising sun cast its first rays through Minette's bedroom window, touching the girl's sleeping face with golden fingers. Traces of tears were evident on the pale cheeks, as that of an unhappy child. Conscious of the increasing warmth on her face, Minette stirred, and then opened her eyes. Her mind refused to function normally, but she was aware of a vague sense of foreboding.

Throwing back the bedclothes, Minette got out of bed and went to splash her face with water from the jug on her washstand. The water was very cold, and as she gasped from the shock, events of the previous evening came flooding back. Her spirits low, Minette blindly groped for a towel. But with the dawning of a new day, no fresh answers came to mind.

Seized by a feeling of suffocation, the girl was filled by a desperate desire to be gone from the château and its present associations. The only thing to do at this point was to take her mare for a ride through the woods. Exercise had always helped to blow cobwebs away and clear her mind. God knows she needed to think of a way of dealing with the situation … and fast!

Clad in her usual riding attire of britches and an old cotton shirt, riding boots under an arm, Minette crept down the back stairs. She slipped out through the kitchen door, put on her boots, and ran down the drive towards the Haras.

Ten minutes later, girl and horse were thundering through the early morning mist, across pastureland and up through woodland. Halting the mare beside a stream, Minette slid from her back to the ground. Immediately, Ariadne stepped forward into the shallows to drink, then settled down to graze on lush grass growing on the bank.

Sitting cross-legged beside the horse, Minette tried to focus her mind on her impossible situation, but with no success. Hearing Minette sigh, Ariadne sensed all was not well with her beloved mistress. Lifting her head, she pushed an enquiring nose into Minette's face, the tickling of her whiskers making the girl giggle. Satisfied she had improved matters, the mare resumed her pleasant occupation.

An hour later, Minette vaulted on to Ariadne's back, mentally refreshed, if still without a solution. They slowly ambled back to the Haras, which only a short time ago had been deserted, but was now a hive of industry.

Horses were being led out to grass, whilst stable hands busied themselves mucking out loose boxes. Raised voices berated youthful apprentices for sloth or inefficiency. A farrier hammered on his anvil, the horse he was shoeing held by a stable boy. It was a familiar scene that had always sustained Minette, and that she adored. A far cry from the life planned for her as Madame Briand … or the Duchesse de "What-not," thought the girl. The idea of giving it all up was intolerable.

Handing Ariadne to her groom to be showered off, Minette hurried back to the château. It was important she was washed and changed before anybody was up and about, if only to boost her flagging morale. The kitchen door was wide open, and maids scurried about their duties. The boot-boy sat outside in the sun, polishing rows of tall leather boots to a high shine.

Minette walked through the kitchens towards the backstairs, largely unnoticed, the servants accustomed to seeing the young girl come home from an early morning ride. Finding herself prevented from continuing on her way by a booted foot, Minette swung round to see Jérome, propped against a wall, grinning.

Hands on her hips, she surveyed her brother with scorn. God, how he had grown into a male version of their mother! Complete with perpetual dissatisfaction over his lot in life, and with the same vast capacity for venom. What could he want now, for heaven's sake?

"Well, well! What have we here, sister mine?" drawled the young man. "Out for a ride dressed like a ramshackle hoyden as usual, I see. Since you are almost a married woman, Minette, one really expects to see you dress appropriately—not like some loutish stable hand."

"Let me through, damn you, Jérome! And I can do without your pathetic comments so early in the day." Minette tried unsuccessfully to barge past her brother.

"*Oh, là, là!* Temper has always been your undoing, dear baby sister! Actually, I bear a message from Maman. She wants to see you in her boudoir at ten o'clock this morning, to discuss your forthcoming stay with old Briand's parents."

Jérome's teeth flashed in a malicious grin. "Such an exciting event for you to look forward to! I'm told that all three Ugly Sisters will also be there, desirous of clapping eyes on their future sister-in-law. At least one of them is permanently in residence with the parents, so there will always be someone there to keep you in hand."

"Shut up, Jérome! I won't ... "

"By the way, you can forget about putting off your marriage for two years," Jérome continued in a conversational tone. "Old Briand has changed his mind after a quiet chat with Maman. She pointed out that since his father is tottering on the brink, he should think about starting a family as soon as possible to provide an heir for himself. The old boy saw the sense of it at once, so a delay is right off the cards."

The young man laughed at the horror-struck expression on his sister's face. "Frankly, I shall be surprised if you do not find yourself wedded by the end of the year, dear girl. I can just imagine it. Our sweet Minette, perpetually *enceinte*, a gaggle of snotty brats whining round her feet. No time for riding then—horses, I mean!"

"Christ, Jérome ... you are so bloody crude sometimes!" Minette burst out angrily. "For your information I have no intention of becoming anyone's bride for years and years. So there is no question of being pregnant, thanks very much."

Opening his eyes wide, Jérome stared with interest at his sister's flushed face. Since the furore over Minette's energetic refusal to be betrothed to the old coot, life had been rather on the dull side. This latest tid-bit of information was maybe just the thing to liven it up! From what he had just heard, he guessed his dimwit sister might have staged the entire charade of becoming engaged … to keep the parents quiet for the time being. Stupid girl hadn't thought beyond that, it was clear.

"Whatever can you mean, sister mine? You are formally affianced to the old boy, aren't you? And the marriage is to be sooner, rather than later. Old Briand must be positively slavering at the thought of soon having the right to lay hands on the nubile body of his lovely bride."

"*Bah!* He'll have a long, grey beard before he touches me!" blazed Minette, outraged. "And it would be over my dead body, believe me!"

"Never a truer word spoken in jest … so the saying goes," remarked Jérome with pointed significance. "Personally, I should hate to be in your shoes when Papa finds out the truth of the matter, sister mine!"

Too late, Minette froze in her tracks. Once again, her impulsive nature had taken control and common sense had flown. To have lost her temper was bad enough … but to Jérome? Of all people? Minette could have kicked herself. If she had thought her situation to be bad, it would be ten times worse once Jérome had delivered his report to the Marquise—well embellished, no doubt! Minette vainly tried to remember exactly what she had said to him in her fury.

"Go on then—tattle away! I know there is little point in asking you not to say anything," Minette finally snapped. "Seeing as how your favourite pastime has always been to land me in as much trouble as possible."

"Trouble? In capital letters, dear girl—*in capital letters!*" chortled Jérome as his sister pushed past and disappeared up the stairs.

Filled with trepidation, Minette wriggled out of her riding clothes, washed, and put on a morning gown in a blue and white pin stripe. She brushed out her hair, securing it with a white bandeau. At least her mother should not have the opportunity to find fault with how she was dressed. But how she was to escape the proposed visit to those ancient parents in Provence, she had no idea. But go there— she would not.

Minette was sitting alone in the dining room, breakfasting on a slice of warm bread and apricot jam, when a tap at the door announced a footman.

"Mademoiselle Marguerite, I bear a message from Monsieur Charles to inform you the appointment with your mother is cancelled. Instead, he asks that you attend him in his study instead, and without delay."

Minette quailed. It was obvious bloody Jérome had wasted no time in tale bearing.

"Thank you, Pierre, I shall go at once."

Standing outside her father's study, Minette took a ragged breath and raised her chin. After all, what could they do to her? Force her up the aisle to marry old Briand? Of course not. She was too old to confine to the house, or to be punished like a child and have her riding stopped. A ghastly storm was looming ahead … but that was all. No need to be afraid—the girl shakily tried to reassure herself.

Before Minette was able to knock at the door, it was pulled open by Jérome. With a flourish, he stood back to allow his sister to enter. Standing in the doorway, Minette could see her grandparents seated in armchairs to the side, visibly upset. The Marquise occupied another chair, centre stage, whilst her father stood, staring out of the window. Straightening her shoulders, Minette walked into the study.

The ensuing silence greeting her entrance was deafening in its intensity. The girl's face paled with apprehension. At last, the Marquis turned to face his daughter, his expression cold.

"Marguerite, I understand you have no intention of fulfilling your promise to marry Monsieur Briand—at any point in time. Your fiancé is an honourable man, and undeserving of any such cruel charade on your part. May I remind you that you were happy to accept his betrothal ring … with exclamations of joy, as I recall?"

"The ring? Yes, it was beautiful, but … "

"What a shallow, nasty piece of work you are turning out to be," the Marquise's strident voice cut in. "Of course, I have always known you to be sly, but the gross deceit you have displayed on this occasion is breath-taking."

The beleaguered girl turned her head to look at her mother, whose lips were twitching with a scarcely concealed smile of satisfaction—despite her grave words.

It was too much to bear.

"Yes, I can see how thrilled you are to see me brought down

like this," Minette shouted at the author of her misery. "But why should I be surprised? Haven't you always been an unnatural mother to me? Never missing an opportunity to humiliate or cause me huge embarrassment? How I *hate* you!"

"Marguerite! How dare you speak to your mother like that— apologise at once!" barked the Marquis, appalled.

"Apologise for what?" the girl was beyond control. "Apologise for being born perhaps? After all, that has to be my greatest sin against Madame, la Marquise."

"Silence!" thundered the Marquis. "Look at how you have upset your mother."

Minette looked. Her expression tragic, the Marquise was delicately dabbing an apparent tear from her eye with a tiny lace-trimmed handkerchief. A faint sob could be heard, followed by another.

"Humph!" Minette grunted scornfully. "Such theatrics merit applause, Maman dear. Should I clap now … or later?"

"I told you to be silent!" the Marquis roared, his face stiff with anger. "Are you so puffed up in conceit that you imagine yourself exempt from respecting your elders and betters? As things stand, Marguerite, you are not fit to be anybody's wife."

Her father's next words were to stun Minette beyond her worst imaginings.

"In light of this last monstrous outburst, I intend to take the advice of your mother to send you away to the Sacred Heart Convent in Ireland. It comes well recommended by your Beaurepaire grandmother, who has personal contacts in Dublin. You will spend the next two years there, learning how a young lady of standing should conduct herself in a proper manner."

"Please, Papa! I'm so sorry, but I couldn't bear it any longer."

Charles ignored Minette's desperate appeal. "Neither will I allow you to cast a shadow of dishonour on our family name by jilting your unfortunate fiancé. At the end of your time at the Convent, you will return home and take your place as the bride of Monsieur Briand without fail."

The Marquis paused to glance at his daughter, who stood as if transfixed, her eyes wide with horror. "You have brought this on yourself, Marguerite," he added in a gentler tone. "Your absence will be explained as the sudden onset of illness, and it was decided to send you to recuperate in a climate conducive to your health."

The room appeared to rock under Minette's feet, and she staggered slightly. Two years under the thumb of nuns in flapping, black habits? Soured hags with pursed mouths and a penchant for inflicting unpleasant penances? Did she truly deserve such a terrible fate?

Minette's eyes were drawn to the triumphant smile playing about the Marquise's mouth. Sick at heart, the girl wondered anew about the woman who could engineer her own daughter's banishment from home … to then openly gloat?

"When must I go?" she asked through stiff lips. "And please may I come home for the holidays?"

"You will leave as soon as it can be arranged," replied the Marquis. "And no, you are not to return for holidays. Your mother thinks it will be too disruptive: not merely for you, but for everybody else besides."

Minette's final weeks at home proved both difficult and depressing. There had been the agony of saying goodbye to her mare, Ariadne. The girl's self-control was stretched to breaking point as she walked away from the Haras for the last time, halting briefly to glance back at her beloved horse.

Just the thought of leaving her beloved grandparents was also more than Minette could bear. They had represented the only emotional security in her life since the old nurse had vanished. And worst of all, she was betrayed by the one person she had idolised throughout her life—her father. Scalding tears burned in her eyes, but pride forbade them to fall. Minette clutched her dignity about her like a protective garment.

Each night, the girl lay awake for hours, wondering what lay ahead. Time and again, she re-lived the traumatic scene in her father's study. Her grandmother had hurried from the room in tears, unable to bear further unpleasantness. Gran'père rounded on Jérome for "disturbing a hornet's nest" through deliberate mischief making. Affairs would have resolved themselves satisfactorily—declared the Duc—without resorting to such draconian measures as sending the girl away from her home.

But Charles was too angry to listen.

And so Minette's banishment stood. Arrangements with the Convent in Dublin were formalised by the Comtesse de Beaurepaire with astonishing swiftness. She enlisted the assistance of her younger son, Emile, with regard to arranging a reliable escort to Ireland for her granddaughter.

Fond of his lively young niece, Emile had been astounded to learn the reason for Minette's expulsion from home. Apparently an obstinate refusal to accept the superb alliance arranged for her. *Alliance?* Emile frowned. Apparently Minette was betrothed to Duc de Mont-Ravelles' son, who—unless he was mistaken—was almost in his fifties!

His niece, on the other hand, he recalled as still being something of an untidy, horse-mad *gamine*. Emile had difficulty in envisaging her coupled with anybody, never mind a mature suitor. With reluctance, he complied with his mother's demand.

Over the years, Emile had become a personal friend of John O'Hara, the owner of a respected Racing Yard near Dublin. On Charles de Merencourt's behalf, Emile regularly visited the O'Hara Yard, with a view to purchasing breeding mares and promising young stock for export to France. Emile discovered that John's brother, Robert, happened to be on holiday in France with his wife and daughter. It was subsequently arranged that Robert and his family would escort Minette to Ireland, and see her safely to the Convent.

The day of Minette's early morning departure finally dawned. Neither of the girl's parents joined her at the breakfast table. The Duc and Duchesse de Saint Aubrey were there, however—ignoring the Marquise's directive that no fuss was to be made of Minette prior to her departure. The girl was in deep disgrace—Francine had forcefully declared the evening before.

All too soon, it was time to leave. Dry-eyed and stony-faced, Minette hugged her grandparents for the last time. Climbing into the coach, she was followed by her maid, Lucie, who was to accompany Minette on her journey to Tours. It was there the O'Haras would be waiting to take charge of her. Her hands clenching with the effort of self-control, the stricken girl stared straight in front of her. She did not dare to glance at her grandmother again, fearful of bursting into noisy tears, and immediately compromising the dignified departure she was determined upon.

Picking up the heavy reins, the coachman clucked to his six horses, and the coach rolled forward down the drive. Unable to prevent herself, Minette twisted round to see if, after all, her father had come to say goodbye to her.

But there was no sign of the Marquis.

Her mouth trembling with hurt, the girl gazed back at the château receding into the distance. Unexpectedly, she was seized by the disturbing notion that she might never see her childhood home again. Chilled by the thought, Minette dismissed it as being fanciful. It was only two years that she would be away ... .

CHAPTER SEVEN

The journey to Tours was both wearying and tedious. With considerable envy, Minette regarded the maid slumped opposite, snoring away the hours of uncomfortable travelling. Several changes of horses were necessary, and Minette took advantage of each halt to jump down from the coach and stretch her stiffened limbs. The basket of bread, cheese and cold meat that the maid had brought with her, provided an occasional alfresco meal for them both.

Towards the end of the journey through an ever-changing landscape, twilight was falling when the coachman gruffly announced their destination. He pulled up his horses outside an imposing *aubèrge*, the exterior of which was illuminated by lanterns strung over the sign. Relieved to finally be free of the constant lurching and rolling of the coach, Minette stepped down from it for the last time.

Having heard the coach arrive, the innkeeper emerged from within to welcome the tired traveller, bowing courteously. "*Bonsoir,* Mademoiselle de Merencourt, we have been expecting you for the last hour, and are much relieved you are arrived without incident. Bad people sometimes roam the roads, in particular after nightfall. Monsieur and Madame O'Hara await you in the private salon, and ask that you join them directly."

Turning to her maid who was standing a respectful distance away, Minette gave the amazed woman a quick hug, thanking her for all she had done. Pink-cheeked with pleasure, the maid bobbed a curtsey and disappeared into the nether regions of the *aubèrge*. Aware of the unpleasant issues affecting her young mistress—as were all the château servants—Lucie was touched by the impulsive gesture. Mademoiselle Minette was a nice girl, and she was sorry to be losing her.

Minette followed the innkeeper into a small salon, in which a log fire was blazing in a granite fireplace. An elegantly dressed lady was seated beside it, and she rose with a smile to greet the young girl standing hesitantly in the doorway. A tall gentleman leaned on the mantelpiece, and he too greeted Minette pleasantly.

"Marguerite, my dear, how lovely to meet you at last!" exclaimed Jennifer O'Hara. "Your uncle Emile has told us so much about you. You must be exhausted after such a long journey, so I hope speaking English to us will not tire you even further. Emile did mention you spoke the language fluently?"

"It is very kind of you to allow me to accompany you to Ireland, Madame, and no, I do not find speaking English in the least way tiring."

"This is my husband, Robert, and you will shortly meet our daughter, who is only a little older than you," Jennifer told Minette. "Belinda went upstairs to fetch something for me, but she should be here directly."

Minette was weak with relief that she was to be in the care of this kindly couple. She had expected to find herself in the clutches of disapproving strangers, who would be watching her every move in order to report back to the Marquise.

The door to the salon burst open, and a girl with startling red hair rushed in, a sheaf of magazines under an arm which she handed to her mother.

"You must be Marguerite!" the girl's freckled face split into a wide grin. "Gosh, I couldn't believe my luck when Mama told me you were to join us. Holidaying with one's parents is all very well—but!" Belinda O'Hara grinned mischievously at her parents.

Amazed, Minette noted that both Robert and Jennifer were smiling indulgently at their daughter's saucy remark. The atmosphere was relaxed—quite unlike that to which she was accustomed. A tentative smile tugged at her mouth.

"And you are Belinda, Madame O'Hara's daughter? I am also very happy to have your company on the way to Ireland."

"Well, that's the formalities dealt with," Belinda laughed.

"Marguerite, you must be hungry after all that travelling. Come, I'll show you your room, and we can both have a wash and brush up before joining Papa and Mama for a scrumptious dinner. You must try the crème caramel here, it's out of this world."

Linking her arm through Minette's, Belinda swept her from the salon. Watching the two girls go off, Robert and Jennifer smiled at each other with relief. All their earlier forebodings over taking charge of a defiant young virago now appeared quite unnecessary. They had seen no sign of undesirable behaviour—in fact, to the contrary, the child seemed a trifle timid.

And what was that business Emile had mentioned to John? Something about the girl rejecting an arranged marriage to an older man? Surely not! Why, the poor girl was barely out of the schoolroom!

As predicted by Belinda, the meal was excellent, and Minette discovered herself to be very hungry indeed. Soon after, Robert and Jennifer went up to bed, leaving the girls chatting over cups of hot chocolate in front of a dying fire.

It was not long before Belinda wanted to know why her new French friend was being dispatched to a convent in Dublin. Haltingly at first, Minette recounted the chain of events leading up to her expulsion from home. Then the floodgates opened, and out poured a devastating tale of hostility and even hatred from Minette's own mother.

It culminated in the Marquise's efforts to arrange her daughter's marriage to a man old enough to be her father. The girl told of her sense of betrayal when her father supported her mother's plans, and the final blow when he did not even come to say goodbye.

Scalding tears—long suppressed—filled Minette's eyes and trickled down her cheeks. She cried from the sheer relief of being able to talk about the whole sorry affair to a sympathetic listener.

Listening to the French girl's account, Belinda placed a gentle hand over Minette's. It was beyond belief that this poor girl—barely seventeen—should be forced into marriage with a man more than twice her age. Belinda tried to imagine her own parents attempting to engineer her into something similar—and failed.

"Marguerite, sweetie, the first thing to accept is that it is not your fault. Anyone knowing of these events would understand the devastation you are feeling," she said quietly. "It sounds a bit trite, but time will heal a lot of this stuff, and you will begin to feel less mortally wounded. It's only then that you will be able to think clearly about your future."

"That seems rather distant at the moment, Belinda. But I can't help feeling a bit apprehensive over what is awaiting me at that convent. I have never been away from home before, and the nuns I have come across seemed rather … stern."

"Oh, don't you worry your head about the nuns. Most of them are quite sweet. I used to attend the Sacred Heart until the end of last year, and it's not so bad."

"Oh, I didn't know that. But Belinda, imagine what they must have been told about me, as Grand'mère Beaurepaire does not mince her words, believe me."

"Once they know you, Marguerite, they will see for themselves you are no hooligan. Stop worrying sweetie, and now it's time for bed."

"Thank you for listening, and please call me Minette—everyone does. Except for my mother, that is."

Arm in arm, the girls trudged sleepily upstairs. Depositing a light kiss on the French girl's cheek, Belinda disappeared into her bedroom.

Climbing into bed, Minette was caught unawares by a surge of homesickness. What of her beautiful Ariadne … was the mare missing her? Had she broken her grandmother's heart by her intransigence over that betrothal? And her father? Did he hate her so much that he could not bring himself to see her off? Gritting her teeth to maintain a semblance of self-control, the girl eventually slipped into an exhausted sleep.

A light tapping at the door awakened Minette, and she looked about her in vague alarm at the unfamiliar room. Memory then came flooding back, and she leaped out of bed. Grabbing a robe, she opened the door to Belinda who was standing there, fully dressed, a laden tray in her hands.

"Oh God, am I late?" Minette exclaimed in a panic. "I must have over-slept! Is everyone waiting to leave?"

"Calm down, sweetie!" Belinda grinned. "You aren't in the slightest way late. Mama told me to leave you to sleep after that ghastly journey. Anyway, here's some breakfast–only hot chocolate and a couple of croissants, I'm afraid."

"Thank you so much, Belinda." Minette was relieved not to have already blotted her copybook. "What time are we leaving?"

"Not until nine o'clock, so you still have loads of time. See you downstairs in half an hour or so?"

Barely half an hour later, a refreshed and neatly dressed Minette joined the O'Haras in the little salon. Accepting a cup of coffee from Jennifer, Minette laughed to see Belinda grimace.

"*Ugh!* Why is the coffee always so strong in France? Could it be a cunning ruse to dissuade foreigners from staying too long?"

"The coffee here is a bit strong, even for France," Minette admitted with a grin. "I had better make the most of it, since I don't suppose the nuns serve coffee for breakfast."

Forty minutes later, Robert O'Hara arrived with the information that the coach was waiting outside. It was important to make a start if they were to reach Rennes before dark. The luggage was soon loaded, and the passengers installed as comfortably as possible. The coachman clucked to his horses, and the vehicle rolled out of the *auberge's* courtyard to join the road to the north.

The journey was uneventful, both girls sleeping a good deal of the way. Good weather allowed meals to be taken picnic-style on grassy patches, well away from the main highway. The coach arrived at a hotel in Rennes late in the afternoon, having required only two changes of horses. Minette reflected on how less tired she was, than after the helter-skelter journey from the Périgord.

Anxious to stretch their legs, the two girls went for a walk along the banks of a stream behind the hotel. A disgruntled chambermaid was delegated by the hotel management to accompany them.

"From what you have told me, Minette, it does rather seem that your parents are not going to change their mind about marrying you off to the old gent," Belinda remarked. "Do you think you could ever accept such a marriage?"

"I haven't much idea about anything, except that I shall never marry a fellow chosen by my mother," Minette's brave words rang hollow even to her own ears.

"Well, you have two years to think of something," comforted the Irish girl. "Just imagine if they had tried to marry you off right away? In some circles, girls can be considered ripe for marriage by sixteen, you know."

"God forbid! Seventeen is more usual in France, but in my case, they seem to think eighteen is an ideal age to fob me off."

"What about your brothers?" Belinda asked with interest. "Have suitable brides been selected for them?"

"*Huh!*" snorted the French girl. "Jérome is chained to his mother's side, and she would never welcome a rival for his affections. As for Christophe, he will soon be off to pursue a religious life in a Normandy monastery."

"You never know, sweetie, your old codger might become fed up with waiting for you, and go off with someone else?" Belinda suggested. "And then you would be free to choose your own husband."

"Not in a month of Sundays ... as I believe the English expression goes," replied Minette gloomily. "My mother would make certain of that."

The girls walked on in companionable silence, broken by heavy sighs from the chambermaid stumbling along behind them.

"Perhaps we should be turning back." Belinda patted her stomach. "It's been ages since lunch, and I'm starving!"

Early next morning, the O'Haras and Minette set off on the last stage of their journey. Robert was anxious to ensure their arrival at Le Havre would be in plenty of time to catch the boat for Ireland. After what seemed an eternity, the coach arrived at the docks where three steam-ships were tied up at the quayside. Armies of porters bearing piles of luggage swarmed over decks, trying to dodge seamen handling heavy ropes in preparation for their ship's departure.

Dusty and chilled, the air temperature having dropped significantly as the coach proceeded northward, the travellers descended stiffly from the vehicle. Robert hurried to the Company Office, to complete necessary paperwork for the journey to Ireland, and to identify their ship. Jennifer and the girls waited on the quayside, Minette striving to control her shivering, partially due to the unaccustomed cold, but also in apprehension of what might be in store.

Collecting his extended family, Robert ushered them up the gangway and through swing doors into the ship's saloon. Grateful for the warmth of the interior, the four travellers collapsed into comfortable wicker chairs chained to the Saloon's wooden flooring. Minette idly wondered why such a thing was necessary? Belinda assured her she would, in all probability, soon discover the answer to that.

Two hours later, the sturdy vessel edged away from the quay, to then make its way towards the open sea. Standing in the stern, the two girls watched the coastline diminishing, until France became a grey smudge on the horizon. Noticing the French girl's hands gripping the rail, her knuckles gleaming white, Belinda realised Minette was probably emotionally devastated to be leaving her homeland ... and in such unhappy circumstances.

"Come, sweetie," she said, putting an arm about the French girl's shoulders. "I think we should go in now, and warm ourselves up with a hot drink."

Whilst the two girls were still outside, Jennifer O'Hara voiced thoughts to her husband about the possibility of Minette spending occasional weekends with them.

"It seems too cruel," she declared, "to deprive the poor child of everything she loves. We are in a position to allow her contact with horses, and also to ride. Have you not noticed how she and Belinda have taken to each other? Yes, I shall ask Mother Superior for permission to take Minette out."

"Dearest, just make certain you don't inadvertently make things difficult for her with the nuns," Robert cautioned. "God alone knows what the Convent has been told about Minette—remember the exaggerations we heard about the poor girl."

A few hours later, the weather deteriorated, the ship rolling and bucking as it ploughed its way through mountainous seas. Succumbing to seasickness, both Jennifer and Belinda retired to their cabins to suffer in private. To her surprise, Minette remained unaffected by the heavy weather. She remained in the saloon with

Robert, passing the time by leafing through newspapers from a nearby stand. It was also now clear to her why the furniture was chained to the floor.

Two hours later, the worst of the storm abated, except for sheets of driving rain from leaden skies. Robert decided to check on his wife and daughter, so Minette was temporarily left to her own devices. Desperate to escape from the stuffy atmosphere in the saloon, she staggered towards the doors leading to the deck outside. Pushing past a pasty-faced steward uttering dire warnings about falling overboard, Minette burst out into the fresh air.

A blinding blast of spray stung the girl's face, making her gasp for breath and cling to the railing. Her hair, sodden in moments, broke loose from the restraining bandeau to whip painfully across her face. But Minette was uncaring of the cold, or of her drenched clothing.

Looking down at the foaming greyness of the sea rushing past, she was forcibly reminded of being distanced from everyone and everything she held dear. And with every mile that went by, she was drawing ever closer to the dismal future awaiting her at the Convent of the Sacred Heart.

Difficult tears trickled down Minette cheeks to mingle with the rain. Knowing she was quite alone, Minette gave way to her misery, throwing back her head and howling like an agonised animal. Eventually, there seemed no tears left to cry.

Once more in control of herself, Minette returned to the warmth of the saloon, where Belinda was anxiously waiting with her father. Without commenting on the French girl's sodden outer garments and hair, Belinda hurried away to look out a spare cloak from her valise.

It was with immense relief that newly arrived passengers to Dublin discharged themselves on to dry land. Several, still clearly queasy, tottered down the gangway to the cobbled quayside below. Jennifer and the two girls stood to one side of the gangway, watching the crew's deft unloading of luggage from the ship's hold. Robert had already gone to enquire if the carriage from the O'Hara Yard had arrived to collect them. Despite being well wrapped up in the warm cloak Belinda had lent her, Minette was shivering from the chill of the Irish air.

Now she had arrived in Dublin, the prospect of the convent loomed large to the French girl. Her spirits sank, thinking of the two years she was to be incarcerated. No horses, no dogs, no friends ... only nuns. Jennifer O'Hara noticed the girl's sudden depression, and quickly came to the rescue.

"Minette, this may be a trifle premature, but I would like you to know I intend asking Mother Superior if we might take you home with us for the odd weekend."

"Take me out?" Minette repeated, unable to believe her ears. "Oh, I should love that! Thank you so much, Madame."

"I don't anticipate any difficulty in gaining permission," Jennifer continued with a smile, "since we have been acting in *loco parentis* since you arrived in Tours. We have enjoyed having you with us, Minette, and it is obvious you and Belinda are already firm friends. It would be lovely for you both to continue seeing something of each other from time to time."

The O'Hara carriage had arrived on time, and the travellers were soon on the way to their first stop—the Sacred Heart Convent, situated only a few miles from the docks. Gazing out of the carriage window, Minette was mesmerised by the vibrant green of the countryside, almost emerald in colour.

Cattle and sheep grazed in lush pastureland stretching for mile upon mile. Herders whistled up their sheep dogs to dart after strays, some animals scattering in fright upon hearing the rumble of carriage wheels on the highway.

Anxiety must nevertheless have been evident in the French girl's face, for Belinda leaned forward to take her hand comfortingly.

"Try not to worry about things, sweetie, I'm sure everything will work out well in the end. Mother Superior will let you out of jail from time to time ... she's not a bad old stick at heart, you'll see."

"Belinda!" Jennifer pretended to be shocked. "A little more respect, if you please. And do try and behave in a proper manner when we see Mother Superior. Remember we intend asking a huge favour of her."

All too soon, the carriage halted outside heavy wrought iron gates and a Lodge, from where an ancient porter emerged to ascertain the identity of the carriage. Satisfied, he opened the gates wide to allow the vehicle to drive through and along a winding driveway, lined by tall, blue-green conifers.

The carriage rolled on for half a mile, before pulling up outside an attractive building, its warm red brick walls partially covered by evergreen creeper. Despite being a Convent, the house lacked the air of an institution, but possessed that of a private residence.

Climbing down from his perch, the carriage driver located Minette's trunk and valise, which he placed by the front steps. Jennifer, meanwhile, rang the bell by a heavily carved door, its chimes sounding distantly within. Behind her stood the two girls, their hands clasped demurely, eyes lowered. Glancing behind her in astonishment, Jennifer's lips twitched to see her vivacious daughter attempting to be decorous for a change.

The door opened to reveal a young nun, who led the O'Haras and Minette into a wood panelled sitting room smelling pleasantly of beeswax and lavender. Inviting the visitors to sit down, the nun told them she would inform Mother Superior of their arrival.

Minette looked about her in surprise. The convents she had been accustomed to seeing in France were grey austere buildings, often encircled by high walls. This house did not remotely resemble those forbidding places ... goodness, there was even a fire crackling in the grate!

A few minutes later, the nun reappeared with the announcement that Mother Superior was ready to receive her visitors. The O'Haras and Minette were ushered into a study, where a diminutive figure garbed in the black robes of a nun came forward to welcome them. Within the white coif framing her face, the nun's expression was sweet, her clear blue eyes and unwrinkled skin belying a lady of considerable age.

"Good-day to you, Mr and Mrs O'Hara ... and to you, Belinda dear. How nice to see you again after so long!" the elderly nun turned to the French girl, her kind eyes noting violet shadows beneath the sapphire eyes in her rather pallid face.

"And you must be Marguerite? Welcome to our Convent, my child. I imagine you must be tired after your long journey."

"Not very much, Mother," Minette answered, bobbing a nervous curtsey. "I managed to sleep a little on the boat."

"Good. Sister Genevieve should soon be here to take you to meet other girls of about your age. They are also here to finish their education.

The nun paused, glancing down at the letter lying open on the desk in front of her. Minette had no difficulty in recognising the copperplate handwriting of her Grand'mère Beaurepaire. Her heart sank like a stone, knowing the contents were likely to be damning.

"I understand you speak English fluently, Marguerite, which will be of great help to your tutors. I hope you enjoy gardening, because we grow all our own fruit and vegetables here, assisted by the young ladies in our care."

"Er ... yes."

Minette was saved from dredging up a suitable reply by a tap at the door. A portly nun entered, greeting the visitors with an amiable smile. Knowing Belinda O'Hara from her school days, she turned to Minette.

"Marguerite, I assume? I am Sister Genevieve. Mother, I shall take Marguerite with me now, and introduce her to some of the other girls. They can then show her the ropes, and perhaps take her to meet Sister Benedict."

Ropes? Minette was bewildered. What ropes? And what might they be used for?

"Thank you, Sister," said the old nun. "But please make sure Marguerite is in the front entrance in fifteen minutes. I feel sure she will want to say goodbye to her friends, who have been looking after her during the journey from France."

With an apprehensive glance at the O'Haras, Minette silently followed the waddling nun out of the room. The door closed, and Mother Superior returned her attention to the letter on her desk, her eyebrows lifting in evident concern.

"Mother, I am certain I know what is written about the French child in that letter." Jennifer sought to prevent any prejudgment of Minette. "We, too, received dire warnings from the Comtesse to expect all manner of undesirable behaviours. To the contrary, my husband and I have been agreeably surprised. The girl is charming, and it has been a singular pleasure to have her in our care."

"Is that so?" the nun adjusted her spectacles. "I am very happy to hear it, Mrs O'Hara, since I was led to believe we should expect a rebellious young virago."

"Utter nonsense! Minette is verging on the timid, and she is, in fact, quite a calming influence on my extrovert Belinda."

"*Minette?*"

"A diminutive from her childhood, I believe." Jennifer hesitated, before plunging on. "As I understand it, Mother, this so-called rebelliousness stems from the girl's refusal to accept an arranged marriage to a man twice her age. It appears that disobedience of this kind is poorly tolerated within elite French circles. I feel you should know this, because it simply would not do for the poor girl to begin life at the Convent with an unmerited stain on her character."

The elderly nun smiled. "Mrs O'Hara, I hope Marguerite is deserving of the excellent reference you are giving her."

"I'm sure she will. As a matter of fact, I would like to request that Minette is allowed to spend the occasional weekend with our family. She and Belinda have taken to one another, and Robert and I are much in favour of the friendship continuing." Jennifer held her breath as she waited for the old nun's decision.

"Do you believe the girl's parents would approve of such an arrangement?" the nun asked, gazing at Jennifer over the top of her spectacles. "I should really have their written permission. However, you have already taken responsibility for Marguerite during the journey from France, so I cannot see any harm in allowing it. Naturally, it goes without saying that Marguerite's own behaviour must merit the concession."

"Thank you, Mother." Jennifer stood. "Minette is an intelligent girl. And I am sure you will find her an exemplary student. Now we must be on our way, since there are still a few miles to go before reaching home."

Minette was waiting in the hallway, alone and subdued. Walking out with the O'Haras to the waiting carriage, she leaned close to Belinda, anxious not to be overheard. "Did you know they call a bedroom a cell here? Like in prison! There is nothing in it, only a bed and a chair. No mirror, so how are you supposed to do your hair in the morning?"

"Don't worry about that, old bean," Belinda laughed. "Nobody cares much how you look, provided you are clean and tidy. Listen, the best news is that Mama has persuaded Mother Superior to allow you to come home with us now and then. It's on the proviso that you behave impeccably, of course. After that beastly letter from your grandmother, you'll have to go out of your way to be virtuous."

"Belinda, do come along!" Jennifer called from the carriage. "And Minette, we will expect to take you home with us a month from today."

The carriage rolled off down the drive, Belinda waving frantically to Minette until it disappeared round a bend. Disconsolate to be losing her only friends, the French girl turned back towards the Convent. Now she must face what was to be her life for a considerable period of time.

CHAPTER EIGHT

The first days of life at the Sacred heart Convent proved somewhat trying for the French girl. There were all manner of rules to adhere to—in fact, a list of them to remember in order to avoid committing an offence.

> No crossing of one's legs—ankles only.
> No fidgeting during Mass.
> No laughing out loud.
> No running in the house, nor outside unless taking
>   part in sport.
> No visits to bedrooms during the day.
> No looking staff members in the eye.

The list was endless. And there was Sister Benedict.

Tall and scrawny, the nun's black robes hung loose on her spare frame. Cold black eyes surveyed Minette from head to foot on that first day. The almost lipless slash of a mouth thinned even further in disapproval.

"Well, Marguerite de Merencourt—such an odd name—you would do well to understand certain things from the outset. This is a House of God, where there is no place for vanity, gluttony, or self-indulgence." The nun paused to examine the French girl's face for any sign of the predicted rebelliousness.

"Amongst other things, you are here to learn humility, and appreciate the glorious history of the Catholic Faith."

"Yes, Sister," murmured Minette, as humbly as she could manage. "I understand, and will try my best to comply with what is required of me."

Benedict looked sharply at the girl before her, suspecting dumb insolence. But Minette's eyes were cast down, her face without expression.

"Good! Now, let us attend to the matter of your clothes. Most of them are quite unsuitable for a girl of your age, if you ask me. You will hand all of them over to me, with the exception of your under-things, and I shall provide you with a uniform. If all of you girls are wearing the same thing, it leaves no room for jealousy or sinful envy!"

"Now, hand me your cloak," the nun held out a bony hand. "That ridiculous fur around the hood must be removed at once. Our Lady had no benefit of fur—neither shall you. In future, you do not wear outside garments like this inside the house." Minette relinquished the cloak with reluctance, since it was the only thing keeping her warm against the chilliness of the Convent.

Bundling up the offending cloak, the nun departed, having instructed the girl to attend her office to collect her uniform after Chapel. Confused and cold, Minette closed her bedroom door. How, she wondered, might a scrap of fur offend the Virgin Mary's sensibilities? Seconds later the door re-opened, and a fair-haired girl looked in.

"I say, don't close your door for heaven's sake!" whispered the girl. "It's forbidden to shut it—even at night—Sister Benedict's rule."

"What?" Minette was horrified by such a loss of personal privacy. "But, how does one get to sleep at night?"

"You'll get used to it. I'm Alice Bingham-Jones, lately from Hertfordshire in England. Someone mentioned we have a French girl in our midst … is that you?"

"Yes, my name is Marguerite de Merencourt—Minette to my friends. Now, about this door, why on earth … "

"Actually, they have only just put the doors back on their hinges," Alice cut short the question. "Ten days ago there weren't any, until someone fell ill with a nasty bug. Mother Superior ordered the doors to be put back, supposedly to keep the disease from spreading."

"But that's ridiculous—"

"Ours is not to reason why, dear girl! The nuns are a law unto themselves. But now, we had better get a move on. If we are even a minute late for Benediction, we'll go without supper!"

Fortunately for the girls, they were in plenty of time, and joined the queue outside the dining hall. A bell rang, and Alice led the way to a table where several older girls were already standing behind their chairs. Following her mentor's meek example, Minette bent her head to hear Benediction. A nun presided at each table, and with a rush of relief, she saw it was not Sister Benedict at the head of theirs.

By any standards within her experience, Minette considered supper to be almost inedible. The watery soup doled out by the nun at their table was nothing less than disgusting. Lumps of unidentifiable vegetable floated on its greasy surface, and Minette could only manage a few spoonfuls, washed down with gulps of water.

A thick slice of surprisingly fresh and tasty bread lay beside her plate, but it was not enough to satisfy the girl's healthy appetite. An apple completed the meal. The girl wondered gloomily how she was to manage until breakfast the following morning.

In the senior girls' Common Room, Alice introduced Minette to other girls sitting about in somewhat seedy armchairs. For an hour, they were free to chat, read magazines or books approved by the Convent. Another bell rang, and everyone proceeded to the Chapel to hear Mass before bedtime.

After the short service, Alice directed Minette to Sister Benedict's office, saying she would wait for her in the Common Room. Before going to bed, the girls were provided with a mug of hot milk and a biscuit. Minette felt almost cheerful that she was not destined to cope with an almost empty stomach until morning.

"Come!" rasped the nun's voice in answer to Minette's timid knock. Entering the office, the girl saw Sister Benedict poring over papers at her desk. Seemingly absorbed by her occupation, she ignored the girl standing in front of her for several minutes. At last, the nun glanced up.

"You are to have five white blouses and two navy skirts," Benedict announced, indicating shelves stacked with neat piles of clothing. You are also to take a pair of those black lace-up shoes. Make sure you have the correct size. Give me those you have on your feet, if you please." The nun held out a hand for Minette's shoes, which the stunned girl slipped off and handed over.

"You will be responsible for washing your own clothes in the laundry room next to the kitchen. Anything ruined will be added to your end of term bill. Mondays are allocated to senior girls for laundry and shoe cleaning."

The nun's cold black eyes flicked over Minette's person. "Something must be done about that frightful hair of yours. Either I cut it to a sensible level, say just below your ears, or you will wear a hair net. Please yourself."

Minette hardly trusted herself to speak. First, she was obliged to exchange her soft leather shoes for clumping, black atrocities— and it was now her bloody hair. The old witch wanted to hack it off! Summoning up a fast-evaporating self-control, Minette turned to the nun, a pile of clothes in her arms.

"I shall see to it that my hair is neat and out of the way, Sister Benedict. But not cut off. May I go now, please?"

"I suppose so," replied the nun, her tone grudging. "But you may be sure that I shall inspect your efforts tomorrow morning. Then we'll see." Pursing thin lips, Benedict returned to her papers.

Assuming she was dismissed, Minette bobbed a brief curtsey, the customary mark of respect for adults in France. She was horrified to see the nun leap to her feet in apparent outrage, her long face mottling a dull red.

"Why … why you impertinent young hussy!" Benedict advanced on the shocked girl. "How dare you exercise impious sarcasm on your elders and betters?"

"But Sister, I-I don't know wh-what I have done wrong?" On the verge of tears, Minette's voice began to wobble. "Was it the curtsey? Yes? In France it is a s-sign of respect for one's elders, Sister B-Benedict."

"I see." The hectic colour in the nun's face began to subside. "In future, kindly devote your curtseying to Our Lady. We won't tolerate your peculiar Frenchified ways here. I'm afraid."

"Yes, Sister. May I go now, please?"

"You may, but you would do well to remember I shall be submitting a weekly report on your behaviour to Mother Superior."

The door closed quietly behind Minette. Benedict sat down at her desk, satisfied she had triumphed over that bold French girl with her foreign habits. With a rush of pleasure, she recalled seeing the glint of incipient tears in the hussy's eyes. Well, she had been warned to expect possible trouble, so it was her duty to stamp down hard on the slightest sign from the outset.

Fighting for self-control, Minette made her way to the Common Room, only to find it empty. Well, she had been rather a long time with Benedict, and it was now past bedtime. In the flickering light of a small lamp, Minette saw a flask on the table—presumably the hot milk Alice had mentioned. Beside it was a plate, empty of biscuits. At least she would have a warm drink to help stem the chills running through her body. Minette tipped the flask over a clean mug, and small amount of tepid milk trickled out—evidence she was too late for that as well. Minette drank what little there was, and then turned down the lamp. Groping her way in relative darkness, she went in search of her tiny bedroom.

Huddled on the narrow cot, Minette shivered with cold as she reflected on this first day at the Irish Convent. Inedible food! That dreadful scene with Benedict! It really couldn't have been worse, except for being taken under Alice's wing. The girl's mind flew to her home in faraway France. If only she was still there! Minette pressed both hands over her mouth, desperate to avoid bursting into tears. The humiliation of being overheard through the open door would be unbearable.

Teeth chattering, Minette got out of bed and padded barefoot over to her chair. She groped about in the pile of clothing she had thrown there, and grabbed the heaviest and most voluminous garments. Returning to bed, she heaped them over her shaking body. She shut her eyes tight in the hope that sleep would overtake her, allowing her to forget the stark loneliness of her soul for a few hours.

To the French girl's relief, the following three weeks passed without event or momentous drama. In accordance with Sister Benedict's directive, Minette had dragged her hair back from her face into with a length of plaited wool. Each night, taking care to avoid direct contact with the nun—and the chilly floor—Minette leaped into bed. Only then could she release her hair, vigorously rubbing her scalp to ease tingling at the roots.

Minette discovered she thoroughly enjoyed her studies. She was introduced to subjects unknown to her, and lessons were both interesting and absorbing. Noticing the French girl's dedication to her work, she basked in the warmth of the nun-tutors' approval.

Alice remained her friend, and Minette also befriended a Scottish girl, Jane Ogilvy. The three girls became inseparable, eyed by Sister Benedict with thinly veiled suspicion. "Divide and Conquer," was her favourite motto, but thus far, she had been unable to disrupt the girls' friendship.

Every Sunday, the girls trooped in "crocodile" to hear Mass at a little church a mile away from the Convent. The Service was conducted in Latin, the psalms and chants resonating in the incense-scented dim interior poignantly familiar to the French girl. Once, she had seen the O'Hara family sitting at the back of the church, but had been denied contact with them. As soon as Mass came to an end, the girls were always quickly herded from the church by accompanying nuns, to then assemble their "crocodile" for the return to the Convent.

Minette enjoyed the walk to church, her youthful body revelling in the exercise. Having been accustomed to riding her horse every day, she was finding the once-a-week period of gymnastics a poor substitute. "Grace and Bearing" sessions, however, held little attraction for the French girl. Strutting about, a sprig of holly fastened under her chin and books wobbling about on her head—seemed irrelevant and a singular waste of time.

Doing her laundry presented Minette with a new set of problems. White blouses turned grey after her efforts, and undergarments assumed unrecognisable shapes. Hot, frustrated and annoyed, she was obliged to ask the nun in charge of the laundry room how she might resurrect her clothes back to their original state.

Minette's preferred chore was working in the gardens. She found herself looking forward to the seasons when she would see, or taste the result of her labours. The physical effort of digging and raking helped keep her muscles supple, a welcome improvement on her restrictive lifestyle.

It was on such a day that Minette was hoeing out a lettuce patch in the kitchen gardens, when Sister Genevieve came puffing round the corner.

"Marguerite, Mother Superior asks that you present yourself in her study in half an hour. Do make sure you are clean and tidy, dear."

Minette was conscious of a *frisson* of apprehension. Had she somehow blotted her copybook? Heaven knew she had tried not to. She had always been anxious to do nothing to preclude her from the longed-for visit to the O'Hara home.

Twenty minutes later, Minette was standing outside Mother Superior's study. Tucking a wayward curl inside its restraining band, she knocked at the door. There came a murmured reply, and the girl slipped into the study. The elderly nun looked up with a smile, and indicated a nearby chair.

"Marguerite, my dear—how well you are looking. Convent life seems to agree with you," the nun's smile grew wider, and Minette could have sworn there was a mischievous twinkle in the faded blue eyes.

"I have received very good reports about you, both from the aspect of your studies, and your general demeanour. It is obvious that you are making every effort to settle in, Marguerite."

"Thank you, Mother … I'm happy you are pleased with me."

"I have received a letter from Mrs O'Hara, requesting that you be allowed to spend the following weekend with her family. In light of your good conduct, I have no hesitation in granting my permission. Please see to it that you are back in time for Chapel on Sunday evening."

"Yes, Mother!" Minette's face shone with joy, and she unthinkingly dropped a curtsey to the nun. She stiffened in horror, belatedly recalling the ugly scene with Sister Benedict over that simple gesture of respect. To her infinite relief, the old nun smiled with apparent pleasure.

"It is such a shame that these days, the curtsey seems to have largely vanished from the comportment of modern youth. Personally, I find it quite charming. You may go now, Marguerite."

The rest of the week passed with lightning speed for Minette.

Casting a shadow over the prospect of her visit to the O'Haras, was that she had received no letters from home. She had written to her father, and to her Saint Aubrey grandparents several times, but had received nothing in return.

A brief missive from her Beaurepaire grandmother arrived, exhorting her to reflect on her personal situation. It was desirable— wrote the Comtesse—that her granddaughter redeemed herself by viewing her betrothal in a more sensible light. The tone of the letter did nothing to cheer Minette.

At last Friday came, and Minette stuffed a few garments into her small travel bag. She let herself out by a side door at four o'clock, the appointed hour for the O'Haras to collect her. Greatly daring, she dragged off the restraining wool band, and shook out her curly hair over her shoulders.

A distant rumble of wheels heralded the approach of a carriage. Within minutes it had drawn up, the door was flung open, and an exuberant Belinda jumped out.

"Minette!" Belinda hugged her French friend. "How wonderful to see you again, and looking so well. Must be all that lovely grub they serve up here."

Linking arms, the girls hurried to where Jennifer was waiting. Impulsively, Minette flung her arms about the delighted lady.

Standing at the tall, sash window of her study, Mother Superior watched the excited interchange of the two girls. It was pleasing to see the improvement in Marguerite's general health and uplifted spirits in only one month. She had been concerned over the girl's nervousness and strained pallor upon her arrival.

It was also true she had received excellent reports from all members of staff concerned with the French child. With the exception of Sister Benedict. Uneasily, she recalled the peculiar exchange she had with the nun, when Benedict had come striding into the study a few days ago.

"Good morning, Mother. I have come to give you my report on the French girl," Benedict began with an important air. "I'm sorry to say that Marguerite is a devious young madam, with a marked leaning towards dumb insolence!"

"I ... see. Can you give me some examples of such instances, Sister?"

"Well, there have been so many, and it is difficult to record everything, as I am sure you will appreciate, Mother."

"Sister Benedict, I must point out that you are the only member of staff to make a complaint against Marguerite," said the older nun, with a penetrating gaze at the woman opposite. "Without exception, I have been told how pleasant the girl is, how helpful, and how interested she is in all she does, academic and otherwise. You will appreciate, therefore, my difficulty in associating the girl they describe in glowing terms with your own unhappy assessment."

"Oh, I can see how easily people have been taken in by this girl," Benedict declared earnestly. "Marguerite is a sly, nasty piece of work, believe me! But there is another worrying development that I must, with reluctance, bring to your notice, Mother. That girl has inveigled two others into an unhealthy relationship—far, far too close to be natural."

The nun sat back in her chair, certain this unwholesome titbit of information would scupper the French besom's chances of a weekend away. She smiled, displaying a set of yellowing teeth in anticipated pleasure.

Mother Superior rose to her feet. Sister Benedict's unmitigated denigration of Marguerite gave rise to a definite whiff of vilification towards the girl. Deplorable. Not for the first time, the elderly nun wondered if Benedict was the best person to handle these older girls? In the meanwhile, she saw no reason whatsoever to deprive Marguerite of the exeat she had earned.

"Sister Benedict, you do realise this is a very serious allegation you are making against these girls—Marguerite, in particular. To pursue such a distasteful avenue would result in unpleasant repercussions, not least for the Convent. In my view, these girls are probably drawn to each other in pure friendship, finding themselves in similar situations through being away from their families."

"But Mother, surely ... "

"Meanwhile, I see no reason to prevent Marguerite from spending the weekend with her friends. Now, if you will excuse me, Sister, I have a great deal to do."

To have her plan so neatly foiled, Benedict's frustration was almost palpable as she flounced from the study. That *dratted* foreigner had somehow managed to fool everyone! But she would trip herself up one day, and she, Benedict, would be there to catch the hussy in the act. The nun seemed oblivious that her own stance was fast degenerating from that of a guiding adult. The embittered woman persuaded herself that the French girl's natural charm in addition to the unconscious grace of her class, was nothing but rank arrogance.

Later that Friday afternoon, the object of Sister Benedict's acrimony was sitting in the O'Hara's sitting room. Minette was enjoying her second slice of Victoria sponge with jam and cream, having already devoured several sandwiches and two scones.

"Minette, how do you get away with scoffing all those sandwiches and lots of cake ... but still staying lovely and slim?" asked Belinda enviously. "I only have to look at a slice of bread to put on an extra pound."

"I don't eat much as a rule," Minette mumbled through a mouthful of cake. "But all this is sheer heaven after the pigs' swill they serve up at the Convent!"

"Tell me, my dear, what news from home?' Robert O'Hara enquired. "Mail seems to take an age these days, but I imagine you must have heard by now?"

"No, I haven't," Minette replied, mortified by her family's apparent lack of interest in her welfare. "I did receive a letter from my Beaurepaire grandmother, lecturing me on my shortcomings, but nothing from my father or my other grandparents."

"Oh, I am sure there will be a very good reason why you haven't heard from them!' Jennifer exclaimed at once. "As Robert says, the post can be terribly unreliable ... "

"Minette, if you have finished scoffing, there are a few things on your bed to try on," Belinda swiftly changed the subject. "You can't be expected to wear that ghastly uniform all weekend."

Thankful for the distraction, Minette excused herself and followed Belinda upstairs. In less than half an hour, she had been kitted out with an assortment of garments, including some innovative riding attire. Divided skirts—so that a lady might ride astride with perfect dignity!

Later that evening, Belinda and Minette sat together in the sitting room after an excellent dinner. Robert and Jennifer had retired to bed, leaving the girls to chat.

"It's just as well Oliver likes voluptuous girls, or I would never dare introduce you to him," Belinda remarked, taking a swig of her hot chocolate.

"Oliver?"

"He's a front-runner for my hand in marriage. A real sweetie," Belinda answered with unconscious pride. "He's coming for lunch on Sunday, so you will meet him then. The only problem is that he's a junior partner in a firm of snooty solicitors in London—much too far away, for my liking."

"Is Oliver ... did your parents?"

"No, sweetie." Belinda replied gently. "Oliver is entirely my own choice, but both Mama and Papa like him lots, thank goodness."

"Lucky you, Belinda. If you like him so much, he must be very special."

Belinda looked curiously at her friend. Minette somehow always managed to look elegant—even when garbed in those frightful Convent rags. Those vivid blue eyes of hers were so striking in contrast to that dark hair! It seemed inconceivable that her parents found it necessary to palm her off on an old fogey ... almost as if they were frightened of being saddled with an old maid.

"Shall we go up to bed now?' Belinda stood up with a yawn. "It's not late, but we do need to make an early start if we are to beg a ride for you from Uncle John. The Yard is only just a short way down the lane, but I want to make sure of having enough time for a decent breakfast."

The next day dawned fine and clear. Clad in Belinda's riding costume, Minette was intrigued with the divided skirts she was wearing. She wondered how it was that women in France had not yet discovered such a thing? So much better than putting up with an uncomfortable habit, perched sideways on a horse. A short, black jacket matched the divided skirts, under which Minette wore a white shirt. A pair of Belinda's black riding boots completed the ensemble.

God, I look almost Spanish—thought a fascinated Minette, gazing at her reflection in a long mirror. Coming up behind, Belinda peered over her shoulder.

"Heavens, I'm sure I never looked like you do when I could still squeeze into that outfit," she commented without rancour. "You look gorgeous, Minette!"

The two girls set off down the lane to the Yard, Minette riding George, Jennifer's gelding, whilst Belinda walked alongside. "I really need the exercise," she declared, "to offset the four slices of buttered toast I had for breakfast."

Hearing the clatter of hoofs on cobbles as the girls entered the yard, a grizzled old man emerged from a stable block. Respectfully touching his balding pate, he treated the girls to a toothless grin.

"Top o' the mornin' to yer, Miz Belinda! Blaze is all ready for yer friend. She c'n ride proper, oi tek it?"

"Thanks, Eric, and don't worry, my friend is more than capable of managing Blaze. She has her own horse in France. Can you take George and give him a handful of hay in one of the boxes? We won't be long, but I want to take my friend to meet Uncle John up at the house."

Eric bobbed his head, and taking over George's reins, disappeared inside the stables. Belinda grinned after his retreating back.

"Eric is Uncle John's personal groom," she explained, "and he's very protective of the horses he looks after. I've known him all my life."

Ringing the front doorbell, Belinda told Minette her uncle was a darling. Her Aunt Serena, however, could be … difficult. Privately, Belinda was hoping today was not going to be one of those occasions.

An ancient manservant appeared at the door, his lined face wreathed in smiles to see Belinda, and he nodded politely to Minette.

"Michael, me ol' fruit," Belinda grinned at the old man. "An' how are we on this foine sunny mornin'? Is me onckle out from his bed, then?"

"Och, but ye're an impudent wee article, so y'are Miss Belinda!" replied the delighted old retainer. "Ye know foine the Maister is up at fust loight! Oi reckon ye'll foind 'im in t'study wi' young Sean."

"Thanks Michael." Belinda marched across the hallway and knocked on a door. Hearing her uncle's voice, she swung it wide and walked in, Minette following close behind.

John O'Hara was seated at a large desk. Perched on a corner was a youth, his hair the same fiery red as Belinda's. Leaping to his feet, the lad's freckled face split into an infectious grin. "Belinda! I was hoping you would call round. Is this your French friend who is to ride Blaze?"

Before introductions could be initiated, the door opened to admit a lady, tightly corseted, her silver hair swept back into a bun. Must be the aunt, Minette supposed. With lifted eyebrows, the lady turned to her niece.

"Well? Where are your manners, Belinda? Are you not going to introduce your friend to us?"

"I was about to do so, Aunt Serena. May I present Marguerite de Merencourt? She is spending the weekend with us, to … er … polish up her English," Belinda improvised hurriedly. She knew Minette would not want the real reason for her presence in Ireland to be common knowledge.

"Good morning, Madame." Minette bobbed a curtsey, somewhat disconcerted by the lady's appraising stare. "It is very kind of you to lend me one of your horses. Of course, I shall take great care of him."

Serena O'Hara acknowledged the courteous gesture, by a brief nod in the French girl's direction. The little foreigner had a few manners, at least! None the less, the French girl had to be classified as one of those vulgar outsiders that were currently infiltrating Ireland in droves.

"You are most welcome, my dear," John broke the awkward silence. "You will enjoy Blaze. He used to race for us, but now has a lazier time of it. He occasionally comes out on the gallops to provide a young horse with a steadying influence."

"By the way, I'm Sean—the better-looking of my parents' two sons," broke in the red headed youth. "I've never met a French girl before … most exotic."

"Stop talking ridiculous nonsense, Sean!" his mother snapped. "Anybody overhearing such drivel might be forgiven for assuming you to be a country dolt."

Poor chap! Glancing away from Sean's acute embarrassment, Minette hoped Belinda would take her aunt's unpleasantness as a cue to leave.

"Sean, as it is Sunday we will be at Mass tomorrow morning,

why don't you come out for a ride with Minette and me later in the afternoon?" Belinda asked her cousin.

"Wonderful idea!" Sean's face lit up. "What time are you planning on ... "

"I imagine Sean will be far too busy in the Yard," broke in Serena. "Don't bother to wait around for him, in any event."

"It won't be a bother, Aunt. See you tomorrow at around three, Sean. Come on, Minette, we'd better be on our way."

"Minette?" Serena frowned. "I thought the girl's name was Marguerite?"

"I am known to my family and friends as Minette, Madame," the French girl explained quietly. "I believe it was my old nurse who first called me that during my babyhood. I would very much like it, if you would also call me Minette."

"Minette, Minette! Good Lord, I should feel as if I were calling in the cat from a farmyard! No, I shall call you by your given name, if you don't mind."

"*Mama!* Must you be so beastly rude?" Sean glared at his mother. "For heaven's sake, you have only just met the poor girl!"

"I agree, that was quite unnecessary, Serena," John also looked upset.

"Oh, I answer to both names!" Minette tried to offset the tense atmosphere. "Belinda, come and show me this lovely horse I am to ride."

Walking back to the stables, Belinda's usually sunny face was clouded by annoyance. "God, Minette, I'm sorry. My aunt is such a harridan at times."

"Don't worry about it, I'm used to far worse, believe me."

"Poor Sean, having to put up with a Mama like her!" Belinda said with feeling. "No wonder Patrick took to his heels, and ran off to London."

"Patrick?"

"Sean's older brother, around twenty five or so. He was Aunt's favourite son—until he decided to become a doctor. Aunt was furious, and Pat was immediately classed as the "black sheep" of her family. She expected him to take over the Yard from John when he retired, and live at home with Mama, naturally!" Belinda grimaced.

"Sean has since been lined up for the take-over, but Aunt still gives the poor thing a mostly undeserved tongue-lashing whenever she feels like it. God knows why he puts up with it."

"I'd have thought your aunt would be pleased her son is doing something intelligent, such as studying medicine," Minette commented. "I don't imagine he bothers to come home much, if he gets the cold shoulder from his Mama?"

"Actually, he does. I think it's mainly to see Uncle John, but he comes back to Ireland every few weeks as his studies allow."

The old groom led Blaze out of the stable for Minette, a big bay gelding with a streak of white down his face. As Blaze snuffled at her pockets for a titbit, Minette was poignantly reminded of Ariadne, her own mare. Leading the horse to the mounting block, Minette stepped up and then slid into the saddle.

On their return to the Yard, both girls were tingling from the exercise of a good canter along the lanes. A healthy pink had invaded Minette's cheeks, banishing the pallid cast induced by the rigidity of her life at the Convent. Her dark hair was a riot of curls about her face, and she and Belinda were both laughing from the sheer pleasure of their ride.

Sitting confidently astride the big horse, Minette presented a striking image to the two young men standing, unseen, by the stable block. She brought Blaze to a halt and slid to the ground, then leaned forward to give the horse an appreciative kiss on his nose. Taking a few slices of carrot from her pocket, Minette offered them to Blaze, who crunched them up with evident pleasure.

"Pat!" A sudden exclamation from Belinda made the French girl look round. "I didn't know you were home. How long are you staying this time? Come and meet my French friend who is staying with us."

Sean came forward, accompanied by an older version of the young man with the same burnished head of hair. Evidently the medical student brother, Minette guessed.

"Minette, this is my cousin, Patrick—surgeon in the making," Belinda drew her friend forward. "Pat, don't you speak French after all those school holidays you used to spend in Brittany?"

"*Enchanté, Mademoiselle,*" Patrick O'Hara touched his lips to Minette's gloved hand. "*Que je suis content de faire votre connaissance!*"

"I am also very happy to meet you!" Minette was almost speechless to hear her mother tongue spoken with a commendable accent.

Patrick regarded the French girl with interest. His brother had said something about a friend of Belinda's staying with her for a few days, and he had idly imagined it to be some convent chit. This girl, however, whose colour was deepening under his open scrutiny, was no awkward schoolgirl.

"Sorry chaps, but Minette and I must be getting back to change before lunch," broke in Belinda. "Why don't we all ride together tomorrow afternoon?"

"An excellent idea!" Sean was ecstatic. "We had also be making tracks, or Mama will be on the war-path—again!"

It was Belinda's turn to ride George back to the house. Walking alongside, Minette glanced up to see Belinda grinning meaningfully at her.

"Well, you seem to have bowled over *both* my cousins, my fine French friend. Sean was positively drooling, and even Pat was having a good stare."

"Rubbish!" Minette giggled. "Sean is just a boy, and I could see that Patrick thought me gauche."

"We'll see what happens tomorrow when we go riding with them, won't we? I wouldn't mind betting there will be an escort glued to each side of Blaze."

Laughing, the two girls made their way back to the house.

CHAPTER NINE

Back once again at the Convent, Minette and her two friends were seated on the stairs, waiting for the supper bell to ring. Alice and Jane were riveted to Minette's account of her exciting weekend away with the O'Hara family. Of particular interest, were details of Belinda's two good-looking cousins. Minette's face was animated as she talked, her bubble of happiness not yet pricked by a return to the humdrum regimentation of convent life.

"Own up, Minette," Jane demanded. "Which of those two chaps did you fancy the most?"

"Difficult to say, since they were both very nice to me," Minette prevaricated. "I suppose Sean is nearer my own age, as Patrick is in his mid-twenties, I believe."

"Aha, a budding romance in the making, perhaps?" Alice grinned. "What fun!"

"Tell us about the older brother—a medical student, you said?" Jane asked. "How long is he staying in Ireland?"

"I think he has already gone back to London," Minette replied. "As for what he is like—a bit on the stuffy side, I thought."

"Practising his bedside manner, I imagine," Jane laughed. "In any event, all doctors need to be pompous, don't they? I know my uncle is."

The supper bell rang and the three girls hurried into the Dining Hall. Minette had long since lost her acute distaste for convent meals, and now ate what was available as hungrily as the rest of the girls in the Hall.

Later that night, Minette lay awake, her head pillowed on her arms. She wanted to re-live that fateful Sunday, when her life had unexpectedly shifted in a different direction. A young man had made her heart beat faster for the first time in her life, but it had not been sweet Sean O'Hara! No, it was his elder brother, whom she had earlier described as being "stuffy." Minette smiled to herself, remembering ...

The O'Haras and Minette had attended morning Mass in the ancient church frequented by the Convent, and familiar to her. On that Sunday, however, there had been periodic bursts of rain, so no girls or nuns were present in the congregation. A few minutes before the service was due to begin, John and Serena O'Hara arrived at the churchyard, in the company of their two sons.

Turning to speak to Belinda, Minette had been amazed to notice a beatific expression on the Irish girl's face that spoke volumes. Intrigued, Minette followed her gaze to see a young man hurrying towards them. Of course, this must be Oliver—the "front runner" in Belinda's love life. Minette felt a brief twinge of envy, that her own family were determined to deprive her from a similar joyful liaison.

During the service, Minette stole a surreptitious glance at the older O'Hara son. Although red headed like his brother, Patrick had been spared the freckles adorning Sean's face. Taller than his brother, the young medical student's lithe body possessed a natural grace. Without warning, Patrick O'Hara turned his head to look at Minette, an eye closing in a deliberate wink. Mortified to be caught staring, Minette looked hastily away, her cheeks on fire.

Mass having ended, the congregation emerged into weak sunshine. Jennifer rounded up her family, and took her leave of John and Serena. Following his parents to their carriage, Sean mouthed a reminder to the girls that they were to ride together after lunch. Minette glanced over at Patrick, who nodded pleasantly, but gave no indication of his earlier humorous gesture during the service. Maybe it was her imagination after all ...

Later that afternoon, the five young people met up in the Yard, and set off on a ride across the countryside. Twisting in the saddle, Minette saw Belinda and Oliver were engrossed in one another, seemingly happy to bring up the rear. Sean, following her gaze, raised his eyes heavenward, and suggested a canter along a track. Minette needed no second invitation, taking the lead on Blaze who extended his stride upon hearing hoof-beats close behind. In seconds, the canter had developed into a full gallop!

Breathless and exhilarated, Minette eased Blaze to a walk, turning to watch Sean and Patrick catch up only moments later. Belinda and her young man were nowhere to be seen. It was clear the horses had enjoyed the exercise, necks damp with sweat, bright-eyed and relaxed, nostrils flaring. Halting Blaze by a grassy patch, Minette kicked her feet free of the stirrups and slid to the ground.

"I thought to give Blaze five minutes or so to regain his wind, if you don't mind," she told the young men, half-apologetically. "It's something I always used to do with my own mare."

A little surprised at her thoughtfulness for the horse, Patrick and Sean also dismounted to join Minette. Loosening the girth, the girl tossed the reins over Blaze's head, and the horse settled to graze. Sean sprawled in the grass with a contented sigh, Minette next to him. Patrick placed himself slightly apart, his expression a touch whimsical.

"That was such fun," Sean declared, squinting up at the sun through the trees. "You're a hard one to beat, Minette. You were riding Blaze like a jockey, and the old boy knew it. He loved stretching his legs ... just like old times!"

"Blaze is a dream, and it's a privilege to be riding him," Minette replied with genuine pleasure. "It's wonderful enough for me to have these weekends away from the Convent, never mind riding this lovely horse."

"You really are rather special, Minette!" Sean grinned and closed his eyes. "A girl who is not only gorgeous but loves horses as much as we do ourselves."

"I can't imagine how anyone would think your grasp of the English language required sending you overseas for improvement," Patrick suddenly intervened. "Can't help thinking it to be an unnecessary move, since your English is excellent."

"*Christ!*" Minette was saved from answering by Sean's anguished exclamation. He had failed to retain a hold on the reins, and his horse had strayed further away than was wise. "Billy, come here you damned rogue!" Sean lunged for the trailing reins. With rolling eye, Billy shied, whirled, and took off at a gallop back down the track towards home.

Laughing helplessly, Minette and Patrick watched the hapless youth stumbling in the wake of his horse, audible profanities wafting back on the still air.

"This is not the first time Sean has done this sort of thing," Patrick remarked. "Last time, he had the embarrassment of collecting his horse from grazing on a neighbour's manicured lawn. Upon the discovery that his precious lawn resembled a ploughed field, old man Jones could be heard a mile away!"

Minette dissolved once more into giggles, imagining poor Sean attempting to extricate his horse from the enraged neighbour. Glancing at Patrick, she coloured under his frank gaze and began scrambling to her feet, but the young man put out a hand to restrain her.

"No need to tear off right away, Mademoiselle Marguerite. You have as yet to tell me why a French girl has been locked away in an Irish convent."

"But you already know why," Minette mumbled, feeling cornered. "My English needed … "

"Rubbish!" Patrick's retort was succinct. "As I said before, whoever taught you to speak English did an excellent job. Now, tell me the *real* reason!"

Minette stared at this overly perceptive young man. Another lie would not do—he would know it at once. Perhaps it would be better to make a clean breast of things, even if it meant he began viewing her in an adverse light.

"My parents want me to marry a man old enough to be my father," Minette stated baldly. "I refused, my father was furious, so it was decided that I should be sent away to learn the error of my ways. There! Are you satisfied now?"

The silence following the girl's humiliating confession was profound. It was clear the man was shocked. Unable to bear it, she got to her feet, and began brushing down her skirts with unnecessary concentration.

"Minette, forgive me for being an insensitive beast." Patrick was standing beside her, a placatory hand on her arm. "I should never have pressed you to tell me something so private and painful."

"It's just that people assume I must be some kind of hooligan to be sent away from my home," Minette muttered. "The nuns did at the outset. In fact, there is still one who watches me like a hawk, convinced I'm a nasty piece of work."

Close to tears, the girl requested a leg-up on her horse. Patrick complied, and she placed a foot in his clasped hands. "Do not despair, little Minette," the young man whispered against her hair. "A good deal can happen to change things. For instance, the old chap in France might not care to wait around much longer?"

"Unlikely. He seemed determined to marry me, come what may," Minette replied gloomily, as she slid into the saddle. "My mother would see to it, in any event."

Touching her heels to Blaze's sides, Minette departed at a brisk canter, unwilling to prolong the conversation further. Back at the Yard, she found Belinda and Oliver waiting, and discovered that Sean had managed to retrieve his horse.

"Cheer up, young lady,' Patrick told Minette, unnecessarily helping her to dismount. "You never know, you might even find yourself pursued by another, more acceptable suitor for your hand in marriage," he ended enigmatically.

Lying awake in her little bed, Minette sighed, wondering what Patrick could have meant. He must realise she was hardly likely to meet another man whilst locked away at the Sacred Heart! Might it be that he was interested in her? No. Minette dismissed the idea. He was taken up with his medical studies: and besides, it was unlikely a chap of twenty-five or so would seriously consider a Convent girl. Turning over in bed, Minette dragged the covers over herself and drifted off to sleep, a smile on her face.

The next few months flashed by. With a mighty effort, Minette managed to avoid confrontation with Sister Benedict, who nevertheless continued to eye her with disfavour. Her visits to the O'Hara home continued at regular intervals, and Minette regained her natural insouciance in the relaxed atmosphere.

It wasn't long before it became noticeable to the French girl that Patrick O'Hara somehow managed to be in Ireland for a good many of her visits. She wondered how he managed to manipulate his studies to fit in with her exeats—but he did! The five young people spent many a happy afternoon that summer, exploring the beautiful Kildare countryside, on horseback or on foot.

For Minette, it was a magical time, even if it poured with rain. Just to be with Patrick, who was giving her the affection and attention she craved—the deeper and more ecstatically she fell in love with him.

For his part, Patrick was fascinated by the French girl's soft, faintly accented voice, her sense of adventure, and fearlessness on horseback. So refreshing after the restrained, nervous females of his acquaintance. Their first kiss had been a revelation! Far from pretended fright at such forward behaviour, Minette had returned his ardent kisses with open enthusiasm. Of course, there was always the shadow of that arranged marriage to an old coot looming over her. Pity, and such a waste of a lovely girl.

By that September, Patrick O'Hara had come to a decision. The idea of Minette returning to France to marry another man had become anathema to the medical student. He realised that he wanted her for himself, and he was certain Minette felt the same about him. If it meant travelling down to the Perigord to ask the Marquis for his daughter's hand in marriage—he would do so. She was only betrothed to the French fellow, after all.

Patrick chose a weekend when he knew Minette was due to stay at his uncle and aunt's home. During a ride down the lanes, Patrick and Minette enjoyed a fast canter, whilst Oliver and Belinda lagged behind, as was their habit. Exhilarated and laughing, Minette halted Blaze, meaning to allow him his usual graze.

Sliding to the ground, she found herself enveloped in Patrick's arms. Smiling, she looked up, and was surprised to see a serious expression on the young man's face. Tracing her lips with a finger, Patrick looked deep into the vivid, sapphire eyes.

"Marguerite de Merencourt, would you do me the singular honour of becoming my wife?" Patrick smiled to see the astounded expression on the girl's face. "I have come to love you passionately, and I flatter myself you have feelings for me."

"Oh, I do!" Minette's eyes shone with undisguised joy. "I love you so very much, Patrick. But … but what about my frightful situation?" her face fell. "They will never allow me to break free from that betrothal to old Briand."

"Look darling, suppose I go to see your father and explain the situation? You have often told me how close the two of you were for the greater part of your life. That being so, he is hardly likely to thrust that aside when your happiness is at stake."

"We can assume *nothing*, Patrick," Minette was emphatic. "These days, my father seems to fall in with whatever my mother wants, and she is unlikely to abandon her plans for me. I can just imagine the frightful scene … "

"It must be worth a try, though?" Patrick persisted. "If we do nothing, we both know you will be dragged back to France at the end of your time at the Sacred Heart."

Minette hesitated. "You are right, of course," she admitted dubiously. "But you don't know what my dear mother is capable of! Until we decide what is to happen, let's keep everything secret for the moment—except for Belinda, of course."

Later that same evening, Jennifer came into the sitting room where the girls were playing cards, to tell Minette there was a surprise for her. The French girl looked up to see a tall man entering the room behind Jennifer.

Emile!

Uncle Emile was here, in Ireland. With an exclamation of joy, Minette cast herself into her uncle's open arms. A member of her family had come to see her at last.

"How well you are looking, *ma chère* Minette!" It was clear Emile was delighted to see his young niece. "It seems life with the nuns is suiting you well. So much so that you have quite forgotten to write to your family."

Minette looked blank. "Of course I have written to my father, and also to my Saint Aubrey grandparents. But nobody answers my letters. The only letters I have received are from Grand'mère Beaurepaire."

"Yes, my mother mentioned she often hears from you, Minette. Extraordinary!" Emile frowned, recalling a distasteful visit to his sister and brother-in-law's home not so long ago.

From the outset, it had been clear that Charles badly missed the young daughter who shared his passion for horses.

"Emile, I am of a mind to bring Minette home sooner than arranged," Charles told him over lunch. "Sending her away was a mistake. Her place is here with her family, and we should have dealt with the matter of her betrothal at home."

"*What?*" Francine banged her cutlery down on the table. "I can scarcely believe my ears! You want that disloyal, selfish creature to come back into our home, only to cause further trouble? Remember this is the girl who cannot be bothered to write to anybody here, not even to the grandparents she professes to love. We might as well not exist where she is concerned."

"Forgive me, Francine." Emile addressed his sister with a puzzled frown. "But Maman says she regularly hears from Minette, who often mentions in her letters that she receives no news from home. "How do you explain that, might I ask?"

"Oh, I cannot bear this!" screeched Francine, scarlet flags of fury staining her cheeks. "That poisonous creature has even managed to inveigle my own brother into championing her cause. Is there no end to her lies and deceit?"

"I did not know the Comtesse has been receiving letters from Minette," Charles interjected with a cold glance at his wife. "I shall be looking into the matter. But for now, let us enjoy what was intended to be a pleasant lunch together."

Disturbed by his sister's venom towards her own daughter, Emile allowed the matter to drop. He only hoped Charles was strong enough to fly in the face of Francine's wrath to discover what kind of skulduggery had been going on.

Jerking his mind back to the present, Emile managed to smile at his niece, whose lips were twisting in obvious scorn. It was clear that Minette understood exactly why her letters had never reached their destination. "Tell me about your life at the Convent, *chèrie*," Emile sought to change the subject. "Are they making a little nun out of you?"

Minette shook her head. "No chance of that. Had it not been for these weekends with the family, I think I would have gone mad with all their rules and regulations, most of which are quite potty."

"*Potty?*" Emile looked askance.

"A new English word Belinda taught me, which means silly," grinned his niece. "Will you be adding that to your vocabulary, Uncle Emile?"

"Maybe not … as it might not go down well with my *clientèle*! John tells me you and Belinda regularly go for wild rides with his sons in all weathers, leaping hedges and ditches in the countryside. Sounds most ladylike, *chèrie!*"

At the mention of Patrick, Minette felt her cheeks colouring, and hoped it would be put down to Emile's gentle teasing. It would not do that her uncle suspected anything.

During dinner, however, it occurred to Minette that Emile could prove to be the perfect ambassador to approach her father. He possessed the necessary diplomatic skills to broach an escape from her engagement to Monsieur Briand. Since he had known the O'Hara family for years, her uncle might even persuade her father to consider Patrick as her future husband. Minette brightened. A tiny light seemed to be appearing at the end of the dark tunnel of her life, after all.

Even so, she knew she must tread carefully with her uncle. Emile might be an approachable member of her family, but he was still party to what was *comme il faut* in French society—and what was not! Minette was certain there would be a sticking point over honouring her given word to Jacques Briand.

At the end of the meal, Robert and Emile remained at the dining table to enjoy a glass of port and a cigar. Jennifer and the two girls removed to the sitting room, where coffee and a silver dish of chocolate mints awaited them on a side table. Catching Minette's eye, Belinda mouthed that Jennifer should be told of her relationship with Patrick. Her eyebrows lifting, Jennifer looked up from pouring the coffee.

"Girls, I have a feeling that I am about to be told something momentous! Belinda, I hope you are not about to tell me you intend running off with Oliver in the dead of night, or some such thing?"

"I don't need to, Mama," grinned her daughter. "Poor Oliver is still trying to screw up his courage to ask my ogre of a father for my hand in marriage. No, it's Minette who has interesting news for you," Belinda looked encouragingly at Minette, who seemed unaccountably tongue-tied. Shaking her head at her friend's arrant cowardice, Belinda continued with enthusiasm.

"Our Patrick seems to have fallen head over heels for Minette's considerable charms, and is even talking marriage, Mama. Isn't that wonderful? She will then truly be a member of our family."

"Just a moment, Belinda," Jennifer interrupted, a tiny frown creasing her forehead. "How does Minette feel about this development? She hasn't had much happiness in the romance department, as I recall."

Rising to her feet, Minette went to kneel beside Jennifer. "Madame, please feel reassured that I love Patrick with all my heart! I never dreamed I could feel such a wonderful sense of belonging to another person."

"Minette, my dear, have you thought of the serious problems you will be facing from your own family? I am certain they will be far from delighted over the proposed abandonment of your existing betrothal."

"I know." Minette was despondent. "Added to which, it seems my mother has been intercepting every single letter I have written to my father and grandparents, as well as those written to me. Destroyed, I imagine. She could then point out to everyone how little I care about my family."

Jennifer was silent. The situation was indeed dire, and she frankly did not know what advice to offer. The problem of the suitor in France cast a long shadow over any possibility of a future together for these two young people. That was certain.

"Let me talk to Robert about it, "Jennifer said finally. "Perhaps he can better advise you over resolving this unhappy situation. Aside from that aspect, Minette, I want you to know how delighted we would be if one day, we could welcome you into our family."

"Of course, Uncle John and Aunt Serena are not yet in the picture," Belinda supplied. "I do hope I'm there when Aunt is told— she's bound to turn up her toes, being such a possessive old trout!" she added with relish.

"So disrespectful about your aunt, Belinda!" Suppressing a smile, Jennifer finished her coffee. "I'm off to bed now, girls, but why don't you ask Patrick and Sean for lunch tomorrow? Emile will also be coming," she added with significant emphasis.

Lunch the following day proved an enjoyable affair. Emile was at his most entertaining, relating amusing anecdotes from his visits to breeding centres all over Europe. He chatted to Sean about the horses he intended to purchase, and complimented Jennifer on her *cuisine*.

"I imagine your parents must be proud of your choice of career, young man," Emile turned to Patrick. "I'm told you intend to specialise in Medical Research?"

"Yes sir. Rather more interesting than spending one's life dealing with gout or pneumonia. I'm obliged to qualify first in General Medicine, after which I shall do a stint in surgery. It's only then that I shall be free to embark on my chosen career."

"Excellent! Your Finals are imminent, I believe? The best of luck, my boy."

Sensing an appropriate moment to initiate the delicate subject of his nephew's relationship with Minette, Robert O'Hara refilled Emile's glass. Taking a deep breath, he embarked on a hastily rehearsed speech.

"Emile, my friend, there is a family matter about which I would seek your advice. It concerns Patrick and your niece, and I seem to have been elected spokesman on their behalf."

Startled, the Frenchman glanced at Minette, whose colour was draining away, leaving her pale as milk. *Nom de Dieu*—what was this? Emile's heart sank, guessing what was coming. Returning his gaze to his host, Emile was reluctant to hear more.

"I want to make it clear that I am aware of the circumstances leading to Minette's relegation to the Sacred Heart," Robert continued. "As I understand it, your niece was resisting being affianced to a man not only much older than herself, but not of her choosing."

"A regrettable situation, but that is correct." Emile nodded. "Minette was sent away to rethink her attitude, and wait out the period before her marriage takes place."

"I do not wish to involve myself in the rights or the wrongs of this affair, merely to tell you that Patrick and Minette are very much in love. They wish to marry in due course, after Patrick has completed his Finals."

A long silence followed Robert's speech. Emile's expression was grim, knowing the advice he was obliged to give was not what his niece was hoping for. Granted, the dismissal of the poor girl to an Irish convent was excessively severe. But it did not alter the fact that in families such as theirs, marital alliances were invariably arranged.

Added to which, Emile was certain Charles de Merencourt would not entertain the dismissal of Jacques Briand's suit for his daughter. It would be considered a direct slur, in particular since the girl had accepted the engagement herself. The Frenchman sighed, and shook his head.

Minette's eyes were burning with unshed tears. Was she destined to lose Patrick now, after all the years of rejection and loneliness? A man who was offering her unconditional love—despite her difficult circumstances?

"*Cherie*, you must know what your parents will say to this," Emile's voice was gentle. "What of the unfortunate man waiting patiently for the return of his fiancée? Have you considered how your father might explain away your broken promise? Think of the stain on the family's honour? How am I to advise you, Minette?"

"If I travel down to the Périgord to personally ask the Marquis' permission to marry Minette," Patrick interjected. "Might that change his mind? I would be able to present my prospects to him, and reassure him that his daughter would be safe and happy as my wife."

Emile shrugged. "I doubt that very much, Patrick. But if you wish to make such an attempt, I would be happy for you to accompany me back to France. Of course, you are more than welcome to stay with me at my home on the Beaurepaire estate."

"Thank you, sir. I still have a few days leave outstanding, so I accept your kind invitation with pleasure."

CHAPTER TEN

"Come along, Marguerite, it is not like you to be so inattentive!" Sister Emmanuelle's sharp voice jerked Minette from her reverie. "Whatever is the matter with you, child?"

"Sorry, Sister … I was listening,' the girl fibbed, hoping the nun would not question her further. The last thing she wanted was to draw attention to herself. She had been lost in thought over her uncle's parting words, spoken in rapid French. They were words that continued to reverberate through her brain.

"Minette, *ma chèrie*, I am not about to insult your intelligence by telling you all will be well. You must know I have grave concerns regarding Patrick O'Hara's mission in France. It is unlikely to be successful. However, let us hope that in this instance, I am proved wrong."

At the end of the period, the good Sister decided to question Minette once more, concerned that something might be worrying the girl.

"No, no, Sister Emmanuelle! I didn't sleep very well last night, so I am a little tired, that's all," the girl earnestly assured the nun.

"Hmm … I see. There goes the bell for Mass, so off you go." Sister Emmanuelle sent a relieved Minette on her way. The nun was thoughtful watching her hurry away. This "tiredness" was uncharacteristic of the usually vivacious French girl. She had never given the staff any trouble, despite unfortunate character references preceding her arrival. Perhaps she should mention it to Sister Benedict, who was after all, in charge of the older girls' pastoral care.

Thankful to have escaped so lightly, Minette rejoined her two friends in the Convent chapel. The familiar, musty atmosphere redolent of incense within the ancient walls helped calm the girl's ragged nerves. Despite that, the thought of losing Patrick forever brought tears to her eyes, to be fiercely blinked back.

Minette's distress was not lost on Alice and Jane. Since her return from the O'Hara home a week ago, she had been unusually reticent. It was clear to her friends that something momentous had happened, causing Minette to lose her usual irrepressible sense of humour. Seeing her trying not to cry during the short Chapel service, decided the girls to find out the reason—with *no* further prevarication.

Alice and Jane seized their opportunity the following day. The three of them were sitting on a low wall during a gardening break, gulping down much-needed water from enamelled tin mugs.

Taking the initiative, Jane fixed the French girl with a hard stare. "Now then, my girl, what is bothering you to the point that you can barely think straight? No, don't deny it, for that would be most annoying."

"I-I don't really —"

"Don't be a chump. Minette," Alice interjected. "Jane and I know you far too well to allow you to wriggle out of sharing the burden, so to speak."

With a weak grin, Minette capitulated. Patrick had asked her to marry him—she told the dumbfounded girls. The problem was the suitor in France, waiting for his bride to return. Her uncle had been visiting the O'Haras, and Patrick had gone back to France with him. His intention was to ask her father to dissolve the existing betrothal, and accept his own offer for Minette. Her uncle had been far from optimistic regarding Patrick's mission, and neither was she hopeful. In the meanwhile, there had been no news, either way.

"Minette, this may seems heartless, but the more you mope about the place, the more unbearable things will seem," Jane told her friend. "It will also alert the nuns, who have noses like bloodhounds for trouble of any sort."

"I know you are right, Jane, but I—"

"No 'buts' Minette!" Alice said firmly. "Are we agreed? Wait until you have some real news, instead of imagining the worst."

"Well! Well! Having a lovely Mothers' Meeting, are we?" exclaimed the nun in charge of garden duties, striding over to the girls. "Jane, go and help Sister Marcella please, and Alice, you will come with me. Marguerite, that bed over there needs weeding."

Late that same evening, Minette was preparing for bed when she became aware of a looming presence behind her. Whirling, she was dismayed to see Sister Benedict standing in the doorway, her lipless mouth twisting in a familiar sneer.

"So, Marguerite from France, what is this I am being told about you being tired? How is it that you—the athletic leader of your peers—can be "tired?"

Stroking her chin with a bony hand, the nun pretended to consider. "Now, what kind of high-jinks could it be that has made you tired after a weekend away with that family? Frankly, I am of the opinion that you should give your friends a miss for the time being," the spiteful voice continued. "It's clear these jaunts are exhausting to such a degree that you are incapable of concentrating in lessons."

Listening to the goading voice, Minette gritted her teeth, determined not to give the ghastly woman reason to report her. "Thank you, Sister Benedict, but I am feeling perfectly well," she said, her tone neutral. "The most strenuous exercise I undertake on my visits to the O'Hara home is a short ride on horseback every morning. All very relaxing. Thank you for your concern, in any event."

Frustrated, the woman glared at Minette, certain the foreign hussy was laughing behind her back. Insolence again. Pursing her mouth, the nun departed, irritably pulling her robes about her spare frame.

About this time, the object of Minette's affection was on his way back to resume his studies in London. Still stunned by recent events, Patrick O'Hara was glad of the hours of travelling to reflect on his interview with the Marquis de Merencourt. He had to arrange his scattered wits into some semblance of order, and then decide how to go forward.

His time in France had not begun well. During an excellent dinner with Emile's parents, the Comte and Comtesse de Beaurepaire, his hostess had turned to him with a charming smile.

"Emile tells me you are studying to be a doctor, Monsieur O'Hara? In London, I believe?"

"Yes, Madame. I was fortunate to be offered a place at a well-known teaching hospital. I have only a few weeks to go before taking my Finals, after which I shall spend a few months in surgery."

"Ah! You mean to be a surgeon?"

"Not as a career, Madame. My interest lies in Medical Research."

"How interesting! An unusual choice, but essential for discovering cures for disease, I imagine. But what brings you to this part of the world? It cannot form part of your medical agenda, surely?"

"I am seeking an interview with the Marquis de Merencourt, as soon as it is convenient to him," Patrick shifted uncomfortably under the Comtesse's pale blue gaze.

"To do with horses on your father's behalf, I assume?" the Comtesse appeared perplexed. "Emile, don't you usually deal with that sort of thing?"

"Patrick is here for himself, Maman," replied Emile. "It concerns Minette … "

"Minette? What on earth can she have to do with anything? The girl is locked up inside a convent, for heaven's sake!"

"Madame, I wish to seek the Marquis' permission to marry his daughter," Patrick decided not to beat about the bush. "Over the past year, we have come to love each other very much indeed."

"Emile? What is the meaning of this?" demanded the Comtesse, her eyebrows arching incredulously. "Marguerite is already betrothed to another gentleman. Has Monsieur O'Hara not been informed of this?"

"Madame, I am aware of the existing engagement," Patrick hastened to explain. "I hope to persuade the Marquis to absolve his daughter from the arrangement, it not being of her choosing from the outset."

The Comtesse rose to her feet, obliging the gentlemen present to follow suit. Fixing Patrick with an icy stare, she became a distant and intimidating personage—unlike her pleasant demeanour earlier in the evening.

"There is nothing to be discussed, Monsieur O'Hara. My granddaughter has been affianced for a considerable time to a gentleman of influence and social stature. For your information, we do not break our word for no good reason in families such as ours. I suggest you view your association with Marguerite as youthful infatuation on her part—nothing more. I would also advise you to reconsider your desire to present yourself to her father. It would be ill advised. I bid you good evening, Monsieur."

The Comtesse swept out from the dining room without a backward glance, leaving an uncomfortable silence behind her. Her husband, the Comte, was the first to recover. He sat down again, and indicated with a wave of his hand that the other two men should follow his example.

"I shall call for a good cognac, gentlemen," he declared, an amused twinkle lurking in his eyes. "An excellent tonic for frayed nerves, I find."

To Patrick's profound relief, his hostess remained absent, and the rest of the evening passed without further incident. As soon as it was polite to do so, Emile rose to his feet and took his leave from his father. Thanking the Comte for his hospitality, Patrick bowed, and followed Emile outside to a waiting carriage.

During the short drive back to Emile's residence, the Dower House, an awkward silence existed between the two men. There seemed little to say. Determined not be deterred from his purpose, Patrick politely excused himself and retired to bed.

The following morning, Emile rose early and rode off alone to visit his sister and brother-in-law. The sooner an interview with Minette's father could be arranged for his young guest, the better. The whole damned business was doomed, Emile was certain of that. But Patrick must be allowed to see for himself the reality of circumstance governing Minette's future. Only then would he understand the impossibility of a radical change—and accept defeat.

Charles welcomed Emile with genuine warmth, and immediately issued an invitation to stay for lunch. Francine wafted in later in the morning, offering a hand to her brother to avoid the customary kiss on each cheek. Nothing must risk ruining her perfect *maquillage*. Emile hid a grin. Some things never changed! However, there came a radical change in the atmosphere when his sister was told the purpose of his visit.

"*What?*' Francine exploded. "Who is this impertinent person attempting to wheedle his way into our home?"

"Patrick O'Hara is not in the least an 'impertinent person,' Francine," Emile explained, his patience already wearing thin. "He is the son of our close associate, John O'Hara, with whom we have done business for years. He is a medical stud..."

"I don't care whose son he is, or what the fellow is studying," interrupted the Marquise. "He's got a nerve coming here on such a ridiculous pretext—egged on by that stupid girl, I have no doubt."

"You are quite wrong, Francine … jumping to conclusions, as usual!" Emile breathed deeply to keep his temper. "Minette had nothing to do with instigating Patrick's visit. It was his own decision to come to see Charles, in good faith, wishing to be above-board and *comme il faut* in his approach. You have to admit that much!"

"Emile, how is Minette?" Charles asked. "Is she well, and coping with her environment?"

Emile smiled. "She is looking quite ravishing, as a matter of fact. So grown-up, and she seemed happy despite her circumstances. Of course, it is mainly due to having been so well looked after by Robert and Jennifer O'Hara, who … "

"Oh yes, wonderfully well looked after," cut in his sister, her voice dripping sarcasm. "Turning a convenient blind eye to the goings-on between that girl and this O'Hara fellow. Doubtless in cahoots! Weaseling one of their number into a family such as ours is bound to raise their kudos amongst the Irish peasantry."

"That's enough, Francine!" Emile snapped, angered to hear his friends abused. "I would have thought you would be pleased to know that somebody has bothered to look after your daughter's interests—having arbitrarily sent the unfortunate girl away to a foreign country."

Francine's pale eyes bulged. "What the hell do you mean by that remark, might I ask? Have you forgotten what that dreadful girl put us all through? The heartache she caused me?"

"Heartache? *You?*" Emile's teeth flashed without humour. "Because the miserable seventeen-year-old was resisting being paired off with a man almost in his fifties? Could you not have allowed her to grow up properly, Francine? It wasn't as though she was languishing in grave danger of becoming an old maid."

"Oh! You have no idea what ... "

"But no!" Emile ignored his sister's outburst. "You, and that son of yours persisted in hounding the girl until she was cornered—with disastrous results."

"How ... how *dare* you speak to me like that, Emile?" Spluttering with fury, Francine sprang to her feet and glared at her husband. "Charles, do you see what that creature has done now? Setting my own brother against me?"

Turning his back on his enraged sister, Emile addressed his brother-in-law. "Charles, I must admit to being at a loss to know why you are anxious to have news of Minette. Have you still not heard from her? She tells me she regularly writes to you and to her grandparents. Sadly, she has never received a reply from anybody here since she left."

Emile glanced meaningfully at his sister. "And Maman has confirmed she still regularly has letters from Minette. Inexplicable, *n'est-ce pas?*

Charles looked at his wife in distaste. During Emile's previous visit, he had been shocked to realise that Francine had been purloining Minette's letters home—as well as those sent to her. He had never taken up the matter with his wife over it, hoping she would be too nervous to continue intercepting. In which event, at least one or two should have slipped through her net.

Nothing had ever arrived.

"I cannot pretend to know what you are talking about, Emile," Francine blustered after a moment. "That girl is lying through her teeth in an attempt to conceal her gross lack of family feeling, not to mention sense of duty. I cannot believe how ... "

Seeing both men look away in disgust, Francine closed her mouth with a snap, her face thunderous.

"I think it would be best if you bring the young Irishman here tomorrow," Charles told his brother-in-law. "He has travelled all this way expressly to see me, so it is a matter of courtesy. It is to be hoped that he understands the impossibility of extricating Minette from her betrothal to Jacques Briand. A question of honour. Incidentally, Jacques is now the Duc de Mont-Ravelles, his father having expired eight months ago."

"Oh, for God's sake!" Francine interjected, having recovered her equilibrium. "The man must be a complete dolt not to have understood all of this, before embarking on a ridiculous wild-goose chase. One must surmise the concept of honour does not exist in Irish bogs."

"Francine, I've had quite enough!" Emile exploded. "This spewing of venom towards people you haven't even met is absolutely inadmissible! Not to mention the constant denigration of your own daughter. It makes me sick to my stomach." Furious, he strode towards the door, intending to depart forthwith.

"Emile, old fellow, wait a moment." Charles laid a restraining hand on the other's sleeve. "Come to my study ... I need a word with you in private."

Without glancing at his sister, Emile followed Charles and collapsed into one of the worn armchairs. Without speaking, Charles poured out two generous measures of whisky into heavy cut-glass tumblers. Handing one to Emile, he sat down in the other armchair.

"I-I didn't really want to send Minette away, you know, "Charles leaned back with a sigh, his eyes closed. "I realise I should have dealt with matters here, at home. Instead, I stupidly allowed myself to be influenced by Francine and her mother. Minette's own intransigence lent credence to their claim she was out of control. I suppose I was angry enough to lose perspective of the affair as a whole."

Charles opened his eyes. "All of a sudden, it was too late—my sweet daughter had gone. It's been lonely over these past months without her bright presence."

Emile was silent. There was little he could say. Charles' weakness in the face of his vitriolic wife was his business, and his alone. It was now up to Patrick to sway the Marquis—unlikely, despite his brother-in-law's regret. Poor Minette! But she was young, and would survive the disappointment. And from all accounts, Jacques was a kindly man, and apparently enchanted by the young girl. It stood to reason he would leave no stone unturned to make Minette happy.

Putting his glass down on the table, Emile stood up. "I shall bring Patrick O'Hara here by eleven o'clock tomorrow. Charles, please ensure Francine behaves in a proper manner towards the young chap. I have always enjoyed an excellent relationship with the O'Hara family, and I don't wish that to be spoiled."

Riding back to his residence, Emile made a conscious decision not to elaborate on the unpleasant scene earlier that day. It would be better not to risk Patrick forming a prejudice against Minette's parents from the outset. *Voilà!* He had done what he could. The outcome was now in the lap of the gods.

Patrick was jubilant. The fact the Marquis had agreed to see him must indicate an intention to consider his suit for Minette. Armed with proof of his credentials, and with an excellent future in the medical world, Patrick felt he could be quietly confident of success.

The next day, the young Irishman rose early, and took immense care with his appearance. His burnished hair shone from vigorous brushing, and his cream shirt under a dark suit looked properly dignified. As a doctor should.

Straightening his shoulders, he joined Emile at the breakfast table for coffee and croissants, the older man avoiding discussion of Patrick's mission. After the brief meal, the two men walked out to the closed carriage waiting in the drive. Emile was anxious to ensure his young visitor did not arrive windblown and gritty after a ride on horseback. First impressions were important.

Entering through heavy wrought iron gates, the carriage continued up a winding drive, pulling up in front of the château with a swirl of gravel. Stepping down from the vehicle, Patrick was conscious of the scent of roses. A profusion of the blooms wound their way along iron railings on either side of wide, stone steps leading to the front doors.

A grizzled gardener, secateurs in hand, was busily dead-heading faded blooms in a nearby bed, and respectfully touched his cap to the visitors. Looking up at the ancient walls of the château towering above, Patrick noticed with interest how different it was to the Normandy châteaux familiar to him. This was more in keeping with a substantial manor house in red brick, an attractive creeper adorning the front façade. So this was where his Minette had grown up.

Jolted from his musing by the realisation that Emile had already mounted the steps and rung the bell, Patrick hurried to join him. The front door swung open to reveal a liveried footman who bowed, and stood back for the two men to enter.

"Monsieur and Madame await you in the grand salon," the footman murmured. "Come this way, if you please."

Patrick's first impression of the Marquis was that of a masculine version of his daughter. Identical vivid blue eyes surveyed him from beneath dark brows, the greying hair at the temples giving him a distinguished air. Smiling pleasantly, Charles de Merencourt came forward to greet his guests.

"*Bonjour*, Monsieur O'Hara. I trust your long journey to the Périgord has not been too wearying?"

"Good day sir," Patrick bowed politely. "I must admit it was a considerable distance. Luckily I had the good fortune of Emile's company, so the hours of travelling passed swiftly."

From the corner of his eye, Patrick noticed a blonde woman reclining in an armchair. At a word from the Marquis, she rose to her feet with a show of reluctance, and unsmiling, extended a hand for him to kiss.

Patrick pasted a smile on his face as he bent over the Marquise's hand. So this was the woman who had caused Minette untold grief throughout her young life! Silvery of hair and slender as a reed, she exuded a fragility belying the steel beneath. Pale eyes gazed at some point beyond Patrick's head.

The awkward moment was broken by the entrance of a footman, bearing a tray laden with crystal glasses and a carafe of a local fortified wine. Hard on his heels came a second servant carrying a silver salver of canapés.

The conversation flowed to and fro for over an hour, touching on all things inconsequential. Patrick privately wondered if he would find himself leaving the château … without having discussed the reason for his presence.

"So, Monsieur O'Hara, I understand from Emile that you are very nearly a fully-fledged doctor," the Marquis's voice broke through Patrick's thoughts. "It is in London that you are studying, is it not?"

"Yes, sir. After surgery, it is my ultimate ambition to engage in Medical Research—genetic to be precise. Medical science has always fascinated me," the young man replied, wondering how the subject of Minette might be introduced without appearing brash.

"I imagine that to be very interesting. Emile tells me your younger brother is to take over the business of horses upon your father's retirement?"

Before Patrick could answer, the door opened and a fair-haired young man sauntered into the salon. He had such a look of the Marquise about him, that Patrick instantly identified him as Jérome, Minette's hated brother.

"May I present my elder son," the Marquis turned to the newcomer. "Jérome is my right hand concerning the day-to-day running of the Haras. How fortunate that you speak such good French, Monsieur O'Hara, or Jérome would find himself at a loss to understand the conversation. Unlike his sister, he did not pay very much attention to his tutor."

Pausing, the Marquis now looked directly at Patrick. "Monsieur O'Hara, you must indeed hold my daughter in high esteem to interrupt your studies in order to visit me. However, as I am sure you are aware, Marguerite has been formally promised to another gentleman for over a year. It is unthinkable to put that aside, in particular, since Marguerite accepted the gentleman's proposal of her own free will. A question of family honour, you understand."

Patrick's spirits sank like a stone. It seemed the Marquis had already made up his mind, regardless. Be that as it may, he intended to persist in explaining himself.

It was now—or never.

"Sir, of course I realise the difficulties," Patrick tried to choose his words with care. "But you must also know the existing engagement has never been what your daughter desires for herself. She and I met entirely by chance, and fell in love over the past year. Sir, may I emphasise that our every meeting has been conducted with the highest propriety. With your permission, we are anxious to marry and share a future together."

The Marquis nodded. "I must admit to some confusion as to how you came to meet Marguerite in the first place. However, Emile has been at pains to explain the situation to me. I regret it does not change matters, Monsieur O'Hara. As things stand, I am unaware of anything which precludes my daughter from honouring her given word."

"Please do consider a moment, sir," Patrick shook his head, as if to clear his mind. Noticing this, the Marquise rose from her chair and drifted over to a window. Turning back to the beleaguered young man, her well-plucked eyebrows were raised in apparent astonishment.

"Monsieur O'Hara, you must appreciate my daughter is a capricious girl, and given to wild fantasies. She has always been a flighty young madam, requiring a firm hand and a steadying influence. That is precisely what she will have once she is married to her fiancé, the Duc de Mont-Ravelles."

"Madame, I assure you Minette is not in the slightest way as you describe," Patrick restrained himself from firing up in Minette's defence, having noticed a distinctly triumphant smile playing about the Marquise's mouth.

"Naturally. I cannot comment on how she was as a child, but I find her to be a delightful girl, vivacious, loyal, and completely without deceit or subterfuge. I am honoured to know Minette, and feel she is being sadly misjudged here."

"How dare you presume to correct me with regard to my own daughter?" the Marquise rounded on Patrick. "Understand once and for all, that families such as ours always arrange marriages with those of a similar social level. I'm afraid *you* do not qualify in this instance. Marguerite is destined to become the Duchesse de Mont-Ravelles, so kindly refrain from regaling us with tedious declarations of passion for another man's fiancée!"

The silence following the Marquise's outburst was profound, broken by a muffled laugh from Jérome, her son.

"Why, Maman,*"* he sniggered with a significant sideways glance at the Irishman. "You forget how my sweet sister always had a taste for common stable hands—or the odoriferous equivalent. Old habits die hard, it might appear."

Patrick's jaw dropped as the insulting words sank in. So he stank of the stable, did he? Common as muck was he? A slow flush suffused his face as he turned to stare at the Marquise's son.

"Would you care to repeat that, Monsieur?" Patrick's voice was deceptively quiet. "Outside perhaps?"

"Jérome, keep your disgraceful comments for your equally unpleasant circle of friends!" roared Emile. "Patrick is my guest, and I will not allow you to subject him to such appalling discourtesy."

"Oh, stop exaggerating Emile!" the Marquise defended her son.

"Marguerite is known to have questionable tastes in the opposite sex. It's been such a problem … "

"*Be quiet*, Francine!' her brother barked, his face a mask of fury. "In a matter of minutes, you and your son have managed to undermine the family background and upbringing through a disgusting display of bad manners."

"You've got a damned nerve, Emile, speaking to me like … "

"*Francine!* That's enough," the Marquis belatedly turned on his wife. "Jérome, you will apologise to Monsieur O'Hara at once."

"Apologise? I have nothing to be sorry about, Papa." Jérome yawned, his tone indifferent. "The truth always hurts, so they say." Shrugging, he wandered through the glass doors and out into the gardens.

"Come, my friend, I think your business here is terminated," a grim-faced Emile told Patrick, "before I lose my temper entirely."

"Thank you for your … kind hospitality, Monsieur." Patrick formally addressed the Marquis, his face pale with shock and suppressed anger. After a brief bow to the Marquise, he noticed the delicate features had become mottled with temper, her mouth a rouged slit. Ignoring Patrick's courteous gesture, the Marquise pointedly stared out of the window.

Both men returned to the Dower House in relative silence. There seemed little left to say, on either side. Emile was deeply ashamed of the scene at his sister's home—the unforgivable insults hurled at the son of a man who had shown him nothing but friendship and hospitality. How was one able to offer restitution for such offence? Emile did not know.

Patrick was unable to trust himself to speak. What a ghastly family! Never had anyone subjected him to such unvarnished disrespect and blatant discourtesy. It was now easy to see why Minette had been nervous about his visit to her home.

Patrick's mind turned to the Marquis. He had seemed cordial enough, despite a refusal to even consider Patrick's suit. Less easy to comprehend was his retreat into cowardly silence whilst his wife and son launched a scathing attack on him. Only after Emile had upbraided his sister, had the Marquis spoken up. How was one to respect that in Minette's father?

Abundantly clear was the stark fact that his mission to claim Minette was a dismal failure. The reality was that it was a lost cause, and Patrick knew he would be wise to accept it as such. Only one question remained: how in God's name was he to bring himself to swallow rejection by that family of arrant snobs? *Christ*, how he itched to wipe the sneer from that young fop's face with a fearsome punch on his aristocratic nose!

Patrick wrenched his mind from brooding over his treatment at the hands of the de Merencourts—to assessing what remained to be done. It was essential to let Jennifer and Robert know of his failure. They were the ones who would face the unenviable task of breaking the news to Minette. God help the poor girl when she was once again in the grip of that family.

CHAPTER ELEVEN

Over in Ireland, a reluctant John O'Hara faced his infuriated wife over the breakfast table. It was the third morning that she had brought up their eldest son's marital affairs for discussion, and he was sick to death of it. Serena simply could not accept the fact that her darling boy intended to marry that little French girl after he had qualified. Stupid woman.

A letter had arrived that first morning with the information that Patrick was on his way to France with Emile de Beaurepaire. It was his intention to request permission from the Marquis de Merencourt to marry his daughter. John thought his son's choice to be in excellent taste, but Serena had been spluttering with rage. Today was the third morning, and the silly woman was still fulminating.

"John!" Serena banged the now-crumpled letter down on the table, teacups rattling in their saucers. "Say something, for goodness sake. It's hard to credit my son would do something like this to me."

"My dear, as I have told you several times over, I don't think Patrick is doing anything to you at all," protested her husband mildly. "He is almost twenty-five years old, and has the right to marry anyone he chooses. Frankly, I don't in the slightest way understand your objection to the little French filly, Serena. Tell the truth, I find her rather sweet."

"If Patrick thinks he can foist that foreigner on me as a daughter-in-law, he's got another think coming!" Serena spat, subsequent to her husband's frivolous remark. "John, you must put a stop to this nonsense right away."

"I shall do no such thing, Madam," John rustled his newspaper in irritation. "If you want my advice, keep your opinions to yourself and allow Patrick to lead his own life."

Abruptly rising to his feet, John left the room, shutting the door with unusual force behind him. Damn the bigoted, self-righteous woman! He hoped she would not alienate their elder son. If so, they would see even less of him in future.

Further up the lane, Belinda O'Hara had just finished having breakfast with her parents. She was scanning a telegram, her freckled forehead wrinkling in distress.

"Oh, Mama! Patrick says he was unable to make the Marquis see reason. He wants us to tell Minette … oh, poor, *poor* girl."

Jennifer sighed. "It is not unexpected, though, is it? Of course, I feel sorry for the two of them, but there you are. Sad to say, nothing can be done about it."

"It's my guess that now the parents have been alerted to the situation, no time will be wasted before Minette is dragged back to France," Belinda declared, "to then be bullied into marrying that old codger."

"When is she due to come out?" Robert asked from behind his newspaper. "Best get the bad news over with right away, and then the two of you can go on a ride. Minette seems a sensible girl, and not given to fits of the vapours. I feel certain she will accept her father's decision with dignity."

"I hope you are right, Papa," Belinda said unhappily. "It's an awful thing for her to come to terms with, in light of her joy over Patrick's attachment."

Ten days later, Minette was summoned to Mother Superior's study. Searching her mind, she was unable to pinpoint any infringement of rules, nor had she drawn adverse attention to herself. Vaguely concerned, the French girl made her way to the nun's study, and knocked on the door.

Moments later, she was standing in front of Mother Superior's desk. With no little trepidation, she noticed the nun's eyes regarding her coldly.

"Marguerite, I have just received a letter from your mother, the Marquise de Merencourt. I regret to say the contents are disturbing, to say the least. Not only have you abused my trust, but

I am disappointed to note the O'Hara family have also violated that which I unhesitatingly placed in them."

"Mother, I don't ... "

"*No, Marguerite!*" the nun's voice was sharp as she glanced down at the open letter in front of her. "You do not have my permission to speak. Rest assured, you will have the opportunity to explain yourself in due course."

"It appears you have been consorting with a man on an intimate level during your visits to the O'Hara house. To make matters worse, this man is from the lower orders, well beneath the social standing of your own family. This unsuitable person had the temerity to accost your parents in their own home, bombarding them with embarrassing demands to marry you." Mother Superior's expression was amazed.

Whilst the nun was speaking, Minette's mouth had dropped open, her mind grappling with her mother's denigrating description of Patrick O'Hara. Added to which, the blame was being laid at the door of her kindly benefactors.

"Mother, please may I speak?" At a nod from the nun, Minette drew a deep breath. "I beg you not to attach any blame to the O'Hara family over this," the girl got out. "They knew nothing of my involvement with Patrick, because our eventual relationship was always above board, I promise you. We were never alone, nor was there even a whisper of impropriety."

"In that case, Marguerite, I am thankful you are not entirely ruined whilst in my care," the old nun's tone was dry. "But to lower your standards to a base degree through an unseemly association with this person—that I do find quite shocking!"

"Patrick is not from the lower orders as that letter indicates, Mother. He happens to be Belinda's cousin. He travelled to the Périgord to seek my father's permission to marry me, not wishing to be party to subterfuge of any kind. Patrick wanted to deal with matters in a proper manner."

Mother Superior appeared slightly mollified by the French girl's explanation. Far from being a common individual, the man involved with Marguerite came from an excellent upper middle class Irish family. How odd that the Marquise should be so ill informed as to the chap's origins? However, there was something else she was obliged to tell the girl.

"Your mother has forbidden you to have further communication with any member of the O'Hara family. She feels they are no longer to be trusted. It is also her wish that you do not leave the Convent on any pretext, with the exception of Mass on Sundays. Is that clear?"

"Y-yes, Mother. May I go now?"

"Before you go, I am obliged to tell you arrangements are already underway for your immediate return to France."

Minette gasped in horror. "*No!* I can't go back there now, Mother! They will force me to marry that old man my mother dug up. Why, I would rather take the veil than accept him as my husband," she finished dramatically.

"*Tsk!* That's silly talk!" the old nun hid a smile at the thought of this vibrant, impulsive young girl taking Holy Orders. "You are not cut out to be a nun, believe me. For your own sake, Marguerite, try to accept that your parents must know what is best for you in the long term."

Stumbling from the study, Minette went in search of her two friends who were waiting for her in the Common Room. From the dismal expression on the French girl's face, it was easy to guess the news was not good.

It did not take long for Minette to tell the girls what had transpired in Mother Superior's study. She was to be taken back to France as soon as possible. Neither was she to leave the Convent premises except for Mass, and any contact with the O'Haras was forbidden.

Alice and Jane gawped in horror. It did rather seem to be the end of the road for Minette and Patrick. A solution at this point seemed improbable.

"I realise I've lost the battle with my parents," Minette said with unsettling calm. "But what I cannot bear is that Patrick must hate me … cursing the very name of de Merencourt!"

"Why?" Jane looked puzzled. "Why should Patrick hate you, just because his offer was refused?"

"It isn't only that, Jane. My mother wrote some very unpleasant things about Patrick's origins in that letter to Mother Superior. It wouldn't surprise me if she said something along the same lines to him personally."

"What about Patrick's origins?' Alice asked in bewilderment. "He's Belinda O'Hara's cousin, and isn't your Papa a business associate of his father's?"

"Minette is worried her mother may have called Patrick dead common to his face," Jane explained baldly. "And that he might now be tainting her with the same poisonous viewpoint."

There was silence as the girls digested this latest revelation. "We don't know what Patrick's current opinions are," Alice said at last. "It's also unlikely that he would ascribe her family's horrid ideas to Minette, herself."

"Then we'll just have to find out, won't we?" Jane decided. "We must think of a plan, and quickly!"

Four days later, the girls still had no realistic idea of how to proceed. An already gloomy Minette became still more dismal upon being told to present herself for the second time to Mother Superior. The nun was seated at her desk, and looked at the girl over the top of her spectacles. From what Minette could ascertain, the ice in the old lady's gaze seemed to have thawed a trifle. Any feeling of relief, however, was instantly dispelled with the nun's next words.

"Marguerite, arrangements have now been completed for your journey back to France. Your older brother and a female companion will be arriving to escort you home in precisely ten days time. Please ensure your possessions are packed up. Anything left behind will be donated to the Little Sisters of the Poor. You may go."

Minette felt numb as she stumbled from the study. She hadn't expected things to move quite this quickly. Or that the detestable Jérome would be sent to escort his disgraced sister. She could just imagine him crowing with glee.

Alice and Jane were equally horrified by this turn of events. "Bloody disaster!" was Jane's succinct exclamation.

"Wait a second, Sunday is the day after tomorrow, and we will be going to Mass." Alice mused. "You never know, with luck and a following wind, Patrick might be there. If not, one or two of the O'Haras are bound to be in the church. Maybe there will be a message of some kind for you, Minette?"

The following day dragged by for the French girl, exhausted from trying to appear normal for the benefit of the ever-vigilant nuns. Lessons passed in a less than riveting haze, and even a gardening session did not inspire Minette with her usual enthusiasm.

Sunday dawned at last, and Minette sprang out of bed. Soaking a corner of her towel in cold water, she pressed it against closed eyelids. Should Patrick be in church, he would not see her languishing with reddened eyes over his rejection. No fear! It was a question of personal pride.

Sitting in front of a cooling cup of tea in his parents' house, Patrick O'Hara was in a quandary. There was a strong possibility of seeing Minette at Mass later in the morning. However, he was unsure whether he should try to speak to Minette... or just allow the moment to pass?

Belinda had already told him that Minette knew about the outcome of his interview with her father. In which event, she would have realised their relationship was doomed. There was no solution—short of kidnapping the girl.

Kidnap?

Patrick's mouth stretched in a humourless grin, for the Merencourts' insults still rankled. What a slap in the face for that vile family to find their victim gone! It would also wipe the sneer from the face of that slimy little toad, Jérome.

A tempting idea, indeed ... but unwise.

Later in the morning, Patrick followed his parents and brother into the church. The dim atmosphere was heavy with whorls of candle smoke mingling with the pungency of incense. His eyes ranged over the pews filled with people quietly settling themselves in preparation for the service—then abruptly halted.

There, in the midst of a clutch of black-robed nuns sat his sweet Marguerite. His lovely girl, snatched out of his reach by domineering parents. Her eyes meeting his, Patrick was struck by her expression of pure joy. Earlier concerns as to the wisdom of pursuing this girl fled the young man's mind. He smiled, and holding Minette's gaze, unobtrusively pressed his fingers to his lips. He would have her ... and be damned to her snobbish family.

A sharp tap on the shoulder, followed by an order to stop looking behind, broke through Minette's glow of happiness. That loving gesture from Patrick would be kept in her heart forever— even if she never saw him again.

Seated next to the French girl, Jane Ogilvy had been observing the exchange between the two. Rising to her feet, she mumbled an excuse to the accompanying nuns that she felt sick, and wished to go outside for a few minutes. Fainting girls during a religious service was not unknown, and the nuns hastily agreed. Easier to let the girl go out, than to find oneself cleaning up a nasty mess!

On the way to the door, Jane managed to catch Patrick's eye and indicated with a jerk of her head, that he should meet her outside. Intrigued, Patrick emerged from the church minutes later, to join Jane in a secluded area behind the church.

"I think you should know that Minette is to leave for France in eight days time," Jane told him without preamble. "Her brother will be accompanying her home."

Patrick was appalled. "My visit must have unleashed quite a storm for them to have moved this fast! And to be sending that unpleasant little fop to escort her. God, how insensitive can they be?"

"Minette believes you must hate her after the beastly treatment meted out to you by her family. Tarred by the same brush, so to speak," Jane supplied. "By the way, I'm Jane Ogilvy, a close friend."

"I don't hate her!" Patrick exclaimed in amazement. "I happen to love the girl, and I mean to marry her regardless of what her family does."

"Jane, please ask Minette to wait outside the Convent after Mass next Sunday at precisely one o'clock, when everyone is likely to be at lunch," Patrick slipped off his gold signet ring. "Give this to her as a token that I will come for her, and thank you for taking the risk of meeting me here."

"Something had to be done to help the poor thing," Jane muttered gruffly as she stuffed the ring up her sleeve. "I had better get back inside the church now, or the nuns will be racing round the church in a black tide to see what I am up to."

At the end of the service, the Convent girls were ignominiously hustled out of the church by a side door. The nuns had received instructions to ensure the French girl had no contact with the O'Hara family. There was no time for Minette to even say goodbye.

On the way back along the country bridleway to the Convent, the accompanying nuns evidently felt their duty of overseeing the French girl to be done. They relaxed their vigil, and began to converse amongst themselves. Taking advantage of the situation, Jane pressed something solid into Minette's hand. Surprised, the French girl glanced down, immediately recognising the signet ring Patrick always wore on his left hand. Closing her fingers over it, Minette looked at her friend, a question in her eyes.

"From Patrick as a token of his love for you," Jane whispered, after a surreptitious look round in case a nun was in the vicinity. "Next week, after Mass, you are to wait outside the Convent at one o'clock, whilst the rest of us are inside scoffing lunch. Sweetie, you are to be rescued by a knight in shining armour!"

Minette gasped, one question after another racing through her mind. Could such a rescue succeed? What if they were caught? Would Patrick be thrown into jail? How were they to marry without parental consent? In her joy, all such obstacles seemed mere trivia— Patrick hadn't abandoned her!

Minette turned to her friend, her eyes shining with happiness. "Jane, how can I ever thank you for risking being caught by one of them?" she whispered, indicating two portly nuns waddling by. "I shall never forget it."

"My reward is to let me have a blow by blow account of this riveting saga of yours," Jane grinned, "Remember Alice and I will have nothing of interest to talk about after you go."

Back at the Convent, Minette escaped to the cloakroom where she knew she could expect relative privacy in one of the lavatories. Undoing the gold chain holding the gold crucifix she wore around her neck, she threaded the chain through Patrick's signet ring. Slipping the chain round her neck once more, she made certain its extra pendant was hidden from sight under her blouse.

Before the supper bell rang that evening, Jane, Minette and Alice decided to work up an appetite by going for a walk round the gardens. The weather was breezy, and rather cooler than was usual for the time of year. Feeling chilled, Minette ran upstairs to fetch her cloak—devoid of its fur trim—from her bedroom. She would also take the opportunity of secreting Patrick's ring under her mattress, the hiding place for anything precious to her.

Entering the cell-like bedroom, the French girl was horrified to discover Sister Benedict on her knees beside the bed. The mattress and bedding lay askew on the bed frame, and in her hand the nun held a letter she had been reading. Baring yellow teeth, Benedict got to her feet and waved it under Minette's nose.

"Well, well! The haughty little madam has been caught out in *flagrante delicto!* That's Latin for "caught in the act," in case you didn't know," the nun was enjoying herself. At last she had confounded this foreign hussy who looked down her snooty French nose at her!.

"Nauseating these letters are ... sloppy and sickening. *Ugh!* Worse than a kitchen maid's reading material, if you ask me," Benedict continued her rant. "Disgraceful to be carrying on with some common lout when you are engaged to marry another man."

"Sister Benedict, you have no right to ... "

"I have every right!" snarled the nun. "It is you who has no right to receive rubbish like this. Especially when you have been forbidden to communicate with this man. Doubtless, with the connivance of that flibbertigibbet, Belinda O'Hara."

Minette stood silently, her eyes lowered against the nun's gloating stare. She did not trust herself to speak. The letters were not dated, so Benedict was assuming them to be recent. Thank God the vile woman knew nothing about Patrick's ring hanging safe and warm between her breasts.

"Now, let's see what else we have here ... what's this rubbish you are hoarding?" the nun flipped through the pages of a heavy book, from which a quantity of dried flowers fluttered to the floor. Treading on the delicate blooms, Benedict smirked into the French girl's face.

"Oh, you frightful, *frightful* woman!" Minette yelled, driven beyond control. "I was making a collection of those as a gift for my grandmother." The girl was almost in tears as she knelt to gather up her ruined blooms. "See what you have done to my beautiful flowers, crushed to bits under your beastly boots—and you did it on purpose. Call yourself a nun?" Minette spoke through gritted teeth. "More like a horrible excuse for a human being."

The nun's face turned a satisfying shade of purple. "How dare you speak to me like that, you insolent young besom! Woe betide you when Mother Superior ... "

"Get out!" Minette hissed. "Get out of my room where you have no business to be, and keep your hands to yourself as you leave."

"You will regret this, *Frenchie*," spat the nun. "Oh yes, especially after Mother Superior has seen these." Snatching up a handful of Minette's letters, Benedict cast a glare of pure hatred at the trembling girl, and stalked from the room.

Minette stood as though turned to stone. Her own, foolish impetuousness was landing her in trouble yet again. The woman had been insufferable, but Minette knew she should have kept her mouth shut. There was so much at stake over these next few days, and she might well have ruined everything. In a daze, she picked up her cloak and left the room.

"Ah, there you are, Minette! We've been waiting ages, and the bell is about to go ... whatever is the matter?" Alice noticed the girl's desperation as she came down the corridor towards them.

"It's that vile woman—Benedict!" Quickly, Minette described the earlier scene in her bedroom. "She was reading one of Patrick's letters, and accused me of immorality with the most hideous grin on her face. Not content with that, she threw my dried flower collection on the floor, and deliberately stamped all over them."

"Don't tell me you lost your rag, Minette?" Jane demanded. "Not now? Not when things are so ... finely-tuned?"

"I'm afraid I did," Minette whispered in desolation. "I told her exactly what I thought of her. Of course, she's off to see Mother Superior."

Jane gave an inelegant whistle between her teeth. "Well, there's no point crying over spilt milk, I suppose. We'll just have to hope and pray you are not confined to the San until your brother arrives."

Minette blanched. It was a known fact that the nuns were given to incarcerating an expelled girl in the Sanatorium until her family collected her. And she was in this mess because, as usual, she had given way to impulse with little thought of consequence.

For the remainder of the day, Minette was on tenterhooks. At any moment she expected the dreaded summons to Mother Superior's study. Nothing happened. The following day passed without incident, also the next and the one after that. Even Sister Benedict was conspicuous by her absence. Minette wondered if she dared hope to have escaped the retribution she feared?

"Marguerite de Merencourt?" A junior girl peered round the door to the older girls' Common Room. "Excuse me, but is Marguerite here, please?"

"That's me," Minette looked up from the book she was reading.

"Mother Superior asks that you attend her in her study. At once, she said." The junior girl closed the door and disappeared, her mission accomplished.

Minette's hand flew to her throat in an unconscious gesture of fright. So it had come after all—the summons she had been dreading. Well, it had to be faced, so she had better get on with it and know the worst. There was little she could say in her own defence.

Standing in front of Mother Superior's desk, Minette licked dry lips. Her hands were clenched behind her back, lips firm, bracing herself for the storm about to break over her head.

The elderly nun sighed, surveying the girl standing before her, tall, strong-willed, and resentful! In her private opinion, the matter of Marguerite's betrothal was being handled in a singularly ham-fisted manner.

The girl was far too headstrong to conform to her parents' grim determination that she be married to a much older man. Neither was it helpful to the situation that she had taken an acute dislike to him. Also unfortunate was that the girl had formed an attachment elsewhere. Mother Superior thoughtfully pursed her lips.

Continuing to browbeat the girl was unlikely to have a happy outcome for all concerned. Including the fiancé in France, waiting patiently for his reluctant bride to return. The elderly nun shook her head. A sorry state of affairs. Nonetheless, the matter would soon be out of her hands.

"Marguerite, I feel certain I do not need to reprove you for your verbal attack on Sister Benedict the other day. Your upbringing must indicate that a young lady of standing never allows herself to lose control—regardless of the provocation," Mother Superior paused, her mouth quirking at the astonishment on the girl's face.

"It saddens me that you should be leaving under disagreeable circumstances, but there we are. Your brother will be arriving on Monday afternoon to collect you. I may not see you again, so *bon voyage*, my dear."

Minette hesitated, stunned by the radical change in the old nun's demeanour towards her. Also astonishing was her obvious understanding of the unpleasant scenario involving Sister Benedict. Sinking into a full curtsey, Minette asked for the nun's blessing— gladly given—and then quietly left the room.

Alice and Jane were waiting in the cloisters, filled with anxiety as to what the outcome of their friend's summons might be. Upon seeing Minette, they hustled her into the relative privacy of the gardens.

"It was incredible, Mother seemed almost sympathetic." Minette was still in a state of amazement. "And she said very little about Benedict, rather as if she was aware of what a vile person she is."

"If that's the case, I fancy old Benedict might soon be for the proverbial boot," Jane commented dryly, "and a good job, too."

The rest of the week passed uneventfully. Of Sister Benedict, there was still no sign—to Minette's intense relief. Out of the blue, a sweet-faced nun by the name of Sister Agatha, arrived to take charge of the older girls' pastoral care. Firm but motherly, she was an ideal person for the task.

As Sunday drew closer, Minette tried not to worry that Patrick might have thought better of his plan to rescue her. Might the thought of possible retribution weigh too heavily on his mind? She supposed she should prepare herself for every eventuality. Even the unthinkable, should she find herself hustled back to the Périgord, and forced into marriage with Jacques Briand.

The three girls spent their last evening together with mixed feelings. The two English girls were sorry to see Minette go, but pleased that her future now seemed so bright. For her part Minette was ecstatic, and then sad to be parting from the two friends in her life—the only real ones she had ever had. Promises were exchanged to keep in touch. And then it was bedtime.

CHAPTER TWELVE

Sunday dawned, a glorious autumnal day. Leaves on the trees and hedgerows were beginning to crisp, turning from pale gold through to the deepest russet. Fluffy clouds drifted across an azure sky, the watery sun cloaking the countryside with an artificial sense of warmth.

The "crocodile" of Convent girls were on their way to Mass, accompanied by several vigilant nuns. Minette generally enjoyed the brisk walk to church each Sunday, her youthful body relishing the exercise. But today was all-important to the French girl. It was the day when Patrick had said he would come for her—if he hadn't changed his mind. Whatever the outcome, it was preferable to this awful uncertainty. Rejection she would accept with dignity.

Arriving at the church, the nuns herded their charges towards the doors, uttering the usual directives to hurry along and stop talking! Waiting her turn in the queue, Minette surreptitiously scanned the groups of people chatting in the churchyard. Robert and Jennifer were immediately identifiable, speaking to John O'Hara. Then Belinda's burnished head came into view, her freckled face beaming.

Of Patrick, there was no sign.

Shuffling behind Minette, Jane Ogilvy noticed Belinda indicating by a discreet gesture that Jane should meet her behind the church. Assuming a sick expression, Jane abandoned her place in the queue, fanning herself with her Missal for the benefit of two suspicious nuns. Emitting ominous sounds of impending nausea, Jane rushed to where Belinda was waiting.

"This is for Minette," the Irish girl handed over an envelope, and then leaned over to kiss Jane's cheek. "Thank you, Jane … you're such a brick! Without you, Minette would have been be dragged off to France—unbeknownst to any of us."

Squeezing past other girls in the pew to reach Minette's side, Jane gave her a barely perceptible nod to indicate she was in possession of a message.

For Minette, Mass seemed interminable that morning. In light of Patrick's non-appearance, she was certain the message Jane held was simply his way of saying goodbye. She would not look at it until she was back at the Convent. It would be too embarrassing to burst into tears before the entire congregation, not to mention the beady-eyed nuns.

On the walk back to the Convent, Alice and Jane thought Minette to be oddly quiet. Even when Jane managed to slide the envelope over to her, she merely smiled and placed it between the leaves of her Missal … unopened. The girls looked at one another, perplexed.

Then Jane grinned. "I think Minette thinks Patrick's note is his goodbye … yes, that's it!" she whispered, "Of course we can't be certain, but from what Belinda said, Patrick means business. In any event, our French friend will bolt for the lav as soon as we get back. She always goes there to read her letters for some reason."

Walking into the convent hallway, Minette escaped to the girls' cloakroom, unaware of the grins her two friends exchanged. Locking herself into one of the lavatories, she sat down on the wooden seat. Only then did Minette slip the envelope from her Missal and take out a folded sheet of notepaper. Taking a deep breath, she opened it with careful fingers to avoid the noise of rustling.

One o'clock sharp. Bring nothing. I love you. Patrick

One line. That was all it took to infuse the girl's pale cheeks with colour, and return the missing lustre to her sapphire eyes. Kissing the flimsy paper, she folded it into a tiny square to slip inside her blouse. Minette let herself out of the lavatory and went in search of her friends, who were not far away. Alice and Jane saw at a glance the news was good, for her face was alight with transparent joy.

Alice and Jane's happiness for their French friend was plain to see—tempered with regret over the inevitable parting of their ways.

Both girls were leaving the Convent at the end of the following term. Alice to become a missionary in Africa, and Jane intended to take up nursing. Promises were exchanged to write as soon as things were more settled.

The clanging of a bell resounded. "Oops, off we go to lunch," Jane turned to give Minette a quick hug. "Do think of us feasting on stringy meant and soggy cabbage whilst you run off with a gorgeous man, won't you?"

"Bye, sweetie," It was Alice's turn to put her arms about the French girl. "I beg you to bear in mind that Jane and I will be dying for the next instalment of the saga. It would be *too* cruel to forget."

Minette watched her friends go off to join the queue of girls waiting to enter the dining hall. She had never imagined such selfless friendship existed before knowing these two girls. She resolved to move heaven and earth to somehow maintain contact with them both.

Briefly visiting her bedroom, Minette snatched up her cloak and ran downstairs, then through a side door to the gardens. It had not been easy to close her mind to the few treasured possessions she was obliged to leave behind, sternly telling herself to focus her mind on what really mattered.

Terrified that she might come face to face with a nun at any moment, Minette stealthily made her way to the front of the building. Glancing round for a suitable hiding place, she decided to conceal herself beneath the lower branches of a large conifer beside the drive. Her mouth was dry as dust, and each breath she drew was ragged with apprehension that her absence might be discovered at any moment. Without thinking, her hand sought the tiny gold crucifix hanging around her neck ... and her talisman, Patrick's signet ring.

No sign of a carriage yet. The minutes ticked by—an age to the girl crouched uncomfortably under the tree. At the sound of galloping hooves coming up the driveway, she stiffened, nerves stretched to breaking point. God, it might be a visiting cleric or nun—please let her not be seen—not now! Moments later, a horseman came thundering round the corner of the drive, leading another horse recognisable to the girl as Blaze from the O'Hara Yard.

Patrick!

Emerging from her hiding place, an ecstatic Minette wrenched off the plaited wool band restraining her hair, allowing a profusion of curls to bounce free on her shoulders. With a triumphant grin, Patrick pulled up in a spray of gravel and whipped off his hat with a flourish. More like a wild buccaneer than sober-sided doctor—thought the delighted girl as she ran towards her saviour.

Without hesitation, Minette took over Blaze's reins and put her foot in the stirrup iron. Careless that her skirts were in disarray, or that she was displaying a good deal of bare leg, the girl swung lightly up into the saddle. Leaning over to kiss her full on the mouth, Patrick thought he had never seen Minette look more beautiful. Wheeling the horses, the two set off at a brisk canter down the driveway to the main thoroughfare—and freedom.

Standing by the sash window of her study, Mother Superior watched their spectacular departure. At the unexpected sound of hoof-beats, she had been drawn to the window to witness the ecstatic reunion between Marguerite and the O'Hara lad. The old nun turned away with a sigh, vaguely conscious of something within her psyche preventing her from raising the alarm. A long ago—but never forgotten—trauma during her girlhood had inexorably led to Religious Orders.

Her duty was clear, but she deliberately chose to ignore it. Let the little chit have her chance of happiness with the man she loved. It would not be the case should she be forced into the marriage chosen by her draconian parents. The runaways should have until late evening, she decided, putting on her spectacles to peruse papers on her desk requiring her attention.

At a secure distance from the Convent, Patrick and Minette brought their horses back to a walk. Turning off the main road, Patrick led the way through the countryside, taking short cuts across fields and woodland. An hour later, they arrived at the O'Hara Yard.

"Darling, we have to leave for the coast at once," Patrick told Minette, as he helped her dismount. "It's too risky to do otherwise, although I know Jennifer and Belinda would love to see you."

"Yes, I understand," Minette answered. "And I'm sure they will too."

CAROL EDGERLEY

"We can catch the boat to Bristol on this evening's tide," Patrick continued, handing the tired horses to a passing stable hand, "after which, it's rather a tedious journey to London by train."

"How exciting … I've never been on a train before," Minette remarked. "I shall look forward to that."

Patrick glanced at the girl in surprise. He had forgotten how protected she must have been, buried in southern France for most of her life.

"Um … does your mother know about this, Patrick?" the girl tentatively asked. "I can't imagine she would like it!"

"No. My mother is not to be trusted with sensitive information. We will let her know when things are more settled."

"Where are we to live in London?" Minette asked. "I don't suppose I would be allowed to stay with you at your Chummery?"

Patrick laughed. "No darling! Our porter would have a blue fit. I've arranged for you to stay with good friends of mine, George and Maud Jennings. They live in Wimbledon Village, a rather nice rural part of London."

"But Patrick, we won't be together then, will we?" Minette's forehead wrinkled in anxiety. "I don't know these people, and—"

"Darling, we will see each other almost every day," Patrick hastened to reassure her. "It's better like this, because your reputation must remain unblemished. It is important your father has nothing to reproach us with when we seek his consent to marry."

Minette stared at Patrick in astonishment. "My father will never countenance marriage between us after this escapade," she stated positively. "I thought we could just get married—maybe in a church where we are not known?"

"It's not that simple, Minette. You are still under the age of consent, you know," Patrick told her, amazed once again by the girl's naïvety. "No priest would ever agree to marry us in such circumstances. We are obliged to somehow *force* your father to give his permission."

Minette frowned, small seeds of doubt infiltrating her haze of happiness. This was not at all what she had been envisaging during those last days at the Convent. Expected to lodge with strangers for an indefinite period, to wait for her father's consent? A consent she knew would not be forthcoming? Were those lovely daydreams of a glorious future with the man she loved ... a silly schoolgirl illusion? Was it possible that she had just done something unutterably stupid?

No! The girl shook her head in heated denial. She must remember that Patrick was a responsible person, soon to become a doctor. As such, he would be taking all eventualities into consideration. He loved her, so she must put her trust in him to take care of her.

"Minette?" Patrick's voice brought her back to the present moment. "Darling, please don't worry your head over silly little details. "Things will fall into place, you'll see. Your father may well decide you have been irrevocably compromised, in which event his permission for our marriage will be certain."

The rattle of wheels announced the arrival of John O'Hara's personal carriage into the Yard. Without his wife's knowledge, John had arranged for it to take the couple to the docks, to catch the steamer for Bristol.

"Come on, darling." Patrick held out his hand to Minette. "The second stage of our adventure is about to begin,"

The journey to London seemed to go on forever to French girl. During the choppy sea trip to Bristol, Minette was thankful once again not to suffer from seasickness, and she was able to doze a little. After disembarking from the vessel, Patrick and Minette made their way to the recently constructed Railway Station. It was an impressive building, light and airy, tall glass windows set within graceful arches, quite unlike the usual style of public building.

Minette had never actually seen a train. Exhaustion forgotten for the moment, her eyes sparkled with excitement. Supported by Patrick's hand, she stepped up into the railway carriage and sat down on a velveteen banquette seat. Three other ladies were also sharing the carriage with Patrick and Minette, all of whom politely nodded a greeting.

A piercing blast from the Guard's whistle signalled the imminent departure of the train, followed by a hiss of steam and clanking of metal. Huffing and puffing, shuddering then jerking, the monstrous metallic beast hauling the carriages moved slowly along the tracks. Once clear of the station environment, it rapidly picked up speed. Minette sucked in a breath with excitement, having read somewhere that a train travelled at unheard of speeds between destinations.

She spent the first hours of the journey to London gazing out of the carriage window, watching towns and villages flashing past like lightning. Cows and sheep grazing in fields raised their heads in alarm, unaccustomed to hearing the rhythmic clatter as the train sped by. Even distant passers-by stopped to watch its swift progression through the countryside.

Hours went by and Minette began to feel stifled by the over-warm atmosphere within the carriage. Before Patrick could stop her, she leaned over and pulled down the window for a breath of fresh air. A gale blasted through the carriage causing the ladies to clutch at their hats, uttering cries of chagrin. Before the window could be slammed shut again, the girl leaned into the wind, determined to cool her over-heated face.

A blast of smuts from the engine hit Minette full in the face! Recoiling in shock, she heard genteel tittering from the ladies sitting opposite—and noticed a wide grin on Patrick's face. Minette guessed something must be amiss with her appearance.

Standing up in the swaying carriage, she peered into a small mirror set into the wooden panelling above the seat. An astonished sooty face stared back at her! Still laughing, Patrick offered the disconcerted girl a clean handkerchief. The ladies also proffered a flask of cold water from their basket. Soaking the handkerchief with water, Minette wiped her face clean and dusted off her clothes. She only hoped the Jennings couple would not look too closely at her person.

At long last, the train chugged into London's Euston Station, halting beside a platform with much squealing of brakes, clanking, and hissing of steam. Weary passengers descended from the carriages, to hastily make their way out of the station. Emerging into chilly afternoon sunshine, Minette waited whilst Patrick hailed a passing hansom cab. The cabbie was instructed to go to an address in Wimbledon Village, and Patrick turned to help the tired girl into the cab.

Unused to the noise and bustle of London, Minette was relieved when after a few miles the cab entered a relatively rural area. As they progressed further away from the heart of the city, the girl was fascinated to see shops shouldering each other on either side of the thoroughfare. Buildings were sometimes interspersed by patches of grassland in which cows or sheep were grazing. Even the smallest hamlet though which they passed boasted a bakery and grocer's shop.

The hansom cab finally turned into a tree-lined avenue, pulling up outside a pretty brick-built cottage. A white picket fence enclosed a miniscule front lawn. On either side of the front door, wooden window boxes overflowed with scarlet late flowering geraniums.

The cabbie was paid off, and Patrick ushered Minette up an immaculately kept path to the front door. Before he had the opportunity of ringing the bell, the door swung open to reveal a tiny rosy-cheeked woman, beaming in evident pleasure. Close behind was a portly little man, his face also wreathed in smiles.

"Patrick, my dear, how lovely to see you again!" Maud Jennings held wide the front door. "Come in, please do come in! Everything is ready for your young lady."

"George, Maud … may I present Miss Marguerite de Merencourt, my fiancée." Patrick drew Minette forward. She happens to be French, but speaks our language as well as we do ourselves." Murmuring a greeting, Minette held out a hand to Maud, who clasped it between both of her own chubby ones.

"Why, she's delightful, Patrick. Fancy you keeping her a secret for so long, you naughty lad. You will stay for dinner, I hope?"

"I'd be delighted to, Maud. Your cooking has always been a welcome change from bangers and mash in Bart's canteen." Patrick laughed, noticing Minette's frown of confusion. "Sausage and mashed potato to you, darling!" he translated with a mischievous grin.

"George dear, do go and organise the drinks' tray," Maud instructed. "We will have a sherry before dinner, but I must just check our maid hasn't done anything too dire to the meal!"

"Well, what do you think?" Patrick enquired as the little woman bustled away. "Can you be happy here, until we marry and have a home of our own?"

"Of course, they are very kind, Patrick," Minette answered. "But, do you think I could buy something else to wear? As you know, I had to leave everything behind at the convent."

"I'm so sorry, darling, but it slipped my mind. I'll make an arrangement with Lombards Bank for you have immediate access to funds. Maud will take you shopping, as she is bound to know where to go for everything you need."

After an excellent dinner, Patrick excused himself, saying he had an early start the following morning. There was an important lecture he could not afford to miss. Accompanying him to the front door, Minette felt unexpectedly forlorn. She no longer had her stalwart friends at the Convent to fall back on for comfort. And the last link with a security she had taken for granted was about to vanish through the front door. The girl tried to smile and pull herself together, accepting Patrick's light kiss before he disappeared into the night.

Turning away from the door, Minette became aware that both George and Maud had noticed her distress with some concern. Not wanting to explain further, she told them she was exhausted due to days of constant travelling.

Maud nodded understandingly, and showed Minette into a cosy bedroom, a heap of burning coals glowing in a tiny grate. A vase of pink and white roses stood on the dressing table. Pink and white cushions were scattered over a polished brass bed. Damask curtains matching the colour scheme framed a bow window that overlooked the front garden.

Tears of genuine exhaustion smarted in Minette's eyes, and she longed to just sleep and forget everything for a while. Maud disappeared for a moment, returning with a voluminous nightgown draped over an arm.

"Patrick told me about your missing valise—how *very* vexing I thought," she remarked, holding out the garment. "Here is a new nightgown I bought for when my daughter next visits us. She invariably forgets to bring one. Extra toiletries are in the bathroom— please help yourself. Good night, my dear, and sleep well."

The door closed behind Maud.

Huddled in front of the fire after a thorough wash, Minette put on the borrowed nightgown. Just as well Patrick had thought to invent the "lost valise" story—she thought, her teeth chattering with a combination of tiredness and cold. How else could one explain a complete lack of luggage? Grabbing her cloak, she wrapped herself in it and climbed between lavender scented sheets. Within minutes, Minette was fast asleep.

CHAPTER THIRTEEN

The following week flew by for Minette. True to his word, Patrick made a generous sum of money available to her for necessary purchases. Never having been shopping in her life, Minette was fascinated by the novel experience. The wide selection of goods was sometimes confusing, but Maud was there for advice, and helped with the various transactions.

One morning, Patrick arrived with a letter from his cousin, Belinda. Aside from a demand to be given a detailed account of Minette's rescue, she wrote that her parents had been graced by a visit from an angry Jérome de Merencourt.

Arrogant in attitude, he had demanded to know the whereabouts of his sister. Jennifer had informed the young man that as far as she knew, Marguerite was locked up in the Sacred Heart Convent, awaiting the arrival of her brother. This statement had not convinced Jérome, and Belinda had added to his chagrin by pretending not to understand his stilted English.

Red as a turkey-cock, the Frenchman had spluttered, "*You peepel 'ave not 'eard ze las' of zees mattaire!*" In high dudgeon, he had flounced away in his carriage. Nothing had been heard of him since.

Although Minette had laughed with Patrick over the description of her brother's visit, she was secretly cold with horror that matters had gone so far. She hadn't thought further than the pleasure of envisaging Jérome's fury upon discovering the bird had flown! She had presumed he would have gone back to France. Now Minette wondered what her family's next move might be.

A few days later, nothing further had transpired with regard to her escape from the convent. Minette tried to relax, and believe her family had washed their hands of her. In some ways that would be the best solution, for Patrick's resolve to request her father's blessing now seemed even more far-fetched than before. It worried her that the fact didn't seem to have dawned on Patrick.

She was still only eighteen years old, so it looked if they would just have to live together until she had gained the age of consent. After all, she could hardly continue living with the Jennings indefinitely. She would wait another day or two, and then maybe bring the subject up when they had a moment alone.

The following day, Minette was waiting for Patrick to collect her from the Jennings' home. Jonathan Adams, a senior—and wealthier—medical colleague, had invited them for luncheon at the exclusive Savoy Hotel in London.

Minette was wearing a gown of soft rose wool—one of her new purchases. The scooped neckline showed off her slender throat, around which she wore a narrow black velvet ribbon. A black velvet cloak fell from her shoulders to the floor, its hood generously trimmed with fur—another recent purchase.

Anxious to avoid being thought of as mere schoolgirl with hair about her face, Minette enlisted Maud's help in arranging her rebellious curls into a glossy chignon. Standing back to examine her reflection in the mirror, she was reassured that nobody could possibly mistake her for a schoolgirl.

On his arrival at the house, Patrick was delighted by the radical change in Minette's appearance. The over-excited tomboy had miraculously become an elegant and very attractive lady, and with obvious pride he assisted her into the waiting hansom cab.

Deposited in front of the Savoy Hotel's entrance, Minette and Patrick entered the foyer. Never having been in such a luxurious hotel before, the grandeur of gilt panelling, velvet curtaining, glittering crystal chandeliers, and acres of marbled floors were awe-inspiring to the French girl.

Elegant clientele stood in groups, either passing the time of day, or sitting at small tables sipping expensive beverages. Threading her way through the foyer to the dining room, Minette felt confident she could hold her own amongst these well-dressed sophisticates.

Lunch was predictably excellent from all points of view. An aloof Headwaiter showed them to a table where their host, Jonathan Adams, awaited them. Rising to his feet, he bowed over Minette's hand, murmuring his congratulations to Patrick for having netted such a beautiful girl.

Handed an elaborate Menu to peruse by the Headwaiter, Minette had difficulty in concealing her astonishment over the extensive list of dishes from which to choose. In front of her lay an intimidating array of glittering cutlery and glasses on a snowy tablecloth, such as Minette had never seen even at formal dinners given by her parents. Relaxing with an inward sigh of relief, she recalled her grandmother telling her that one worked from the outside inward. The glasses? Not wishing to display her ignorance, she would wait to be see what her companions did …

During lunch, Jonathan told his guests he had recently purchased a Commission with a Mounted Regiment as a doctor-surgeon. He was certain it would be more rewarding than his present rather dull job in General Practice.

"I'm soon to be sent to Africa," he explained, "and I'm researching as much as I can about the place, to have some knowledge of what I'm getting myself into."

"Africa!' Minette breathed, her eyes shining. "How wonderful to live and work in such an exotic country, Jonathan."

"It will make a change from dealing with influenza, gouty old men, whooping cough and measles," Jonathan admitted. "It's also very well paid by comparison. What are your own plans after qualifying, Patrick?"

"I hope to devote myself to medical research—genetic in particular. Might have to do a stint of General Practice to shore up the old finances, though."

Jonathan leaned back in his chair with a quizzical expression. "In your place, I should think about joining the army abroad, like myself. You would earn a good deal more than working endless years in some dingy hospital, hoping to make enough to buy into a decent Practice. A few years under your belt as a doctor-surgeon—with the Indian Cavalry for example—you will have accumulated sufficient funds to do whatever you wish. When are your Finals over?"

"Surgery in three days time!" Patrick grimaced. "Nose to the grindstone from tomorrow, I'm afraid. Your idea about India sounds tempting, but remember I will have a wife to consider. I cannot expect Minette to expose herself to all the inherent dangers and diseases prevalent in the Far East. No, I ... "

"Patrick, it would be a wonderful experience," Minette interrupted. "I'm no ninny given to the vapours, you know. Besides, I am capable of all sorts of things you know nothing about."

"There you are, then!' Jonathan looked at Minette with interest. "You may as well give it some thought ... if only for your fiancée's sake," he smiled across at the French girl.

"Changing the subject, did you know the new anaesthetic is now routinely used not only to dull pain, but to render the patient unconscious? A real boon for amputation or even tooth extraction." Carried away by his enthusiasm, Jonathan looked apologetic. "Forgive me, Minette, I realise this sort of thing is hardly for a lady's ears."

Minette grinned. "Please don't be concerned about me ... I often used to assist with the foaling of my father's mares. I would like to know more about this wonderful-sounding anaesthetic—an advantage for women in labour, surely?"

Both men stared at the French girl in surprise ... and a dawning respect. As a matter of etiquette, unpalatable subjects such as blood or disease were generally never discussed in the presence of ladies. Aside from being an unusually attractive girl –Jonathan reflected— this girl was also amazingly emancipated. Pity she was already snapped up.

"By George, what a treasure you have in your betrothed, Patrick!" Jonathan declared with an infectious grin. "Better marry the girl quickly before she is snatched from under your nose by the likes of myself."

"I would if I could. Unfortunately, we face the problem of Minette still being under-age, so her father's consent is required," Patrick looked down at his hands. "As matters stand his permission is far from certain, so we might have to lead separate lives for three more years until Minette is twenty-one."

Minette stared at Patrick, horrified. For God's sake, he had dismissed her earlier worries about the future as mere "details" which would ultimately be resolved in time. *Three years?* She had expected to live with the Jennings for a question of weeks.

Jonathan Adams leaned back in his chair, nursing a fine cognac in a balloon glass. It was clear his friend had allowed his heart to rule his head in this instance. No parental consent, eh? That was bad—very bad. And judging from the appalled expression on the girl's face, it might appear he hadn't been entirely truthful with her regarding the situation in general.

"In light of your predicament, have you considered the possibility of Gretna Green in Bonnie Scotland, old chap?" Jonathan suggested—albeit against his better judgement. "A marriage ceremony conducted by the blacksmith over the anvil at the local forge ... all perfectly legal, of course. Not ideal, but I'm reliably informed that uncomfortable questions are not asked—a decided advantage in your situation, I would think."

Patrick looked disbelieving, suspecting a joke. "A forge, you say? Married over an anvil? Pull the other one, Jon, it's got bells on!"

Jonathan sat up to replace his glass on the table. "No jokes. All you need do is spend the requisite period of time—a matter of twenty-one days—after which the marriage can go ahead."

"Good Lord!" Patrick shook his head. "I've heard of Gretna Green weddings, but assumed it to be fiction, a feature of novelettes for kitchen maids."

Jonathan grinned. "Well, we won't go into how you happen to be conversant with kitchen maids' preferred reading, Patrick. And now I must be on my way ... a tea-time appointment with my aunt who becomes crotchety if one is a minute late."

"Goodbye, young lady," Jonathan bent over Minette's hand. "And Patrick, don't dismiss the idea of joining a Cavalry Regiment ... I say Cavalry, because like myself, you have a background of horsemanship. The Indian Cavalry should suit both of you very well."

"What a really nice man," Minette exclaimed as they watched Jonathan leave the dining room. "As a matter of fact, we had better go as well—George and Maud are expecting us for tea."

Minette saw little of Patrick over the next few days. He was working at the hospital during the day, revising throughout the evening, and into the early hours of the morning in preparation for his final examination. After which—all things being equal—he would be a fully qualified doctor, and free to pursue his dream of genetic research.

At last, Patrick appeared on the Jennings' doorstep, haggard, but exuberant. Giving Minette a hug, he told her they were going out to celebrate in style!

"Of course, it's the end of your examinations," Minette leaned back in Patrick's arms to look at him. "Such a relief to know all that hard work is over."

"It is, but that's not the only reason for celebration. Hurry up and fetch your cloak, my sweet, I have wonderful news."

An hour later, Patrick and Minette were sitting opposite each other in a small, but exclusive restaurant. Lunch had been ordered, and a bottle of fine champagne steeped in ice was to hand. For the French girl, the suspense was unbearable!

"So, what is the other reason for our celebration, Patrick?" Minette held her breath. "Has my father sent word that he is agreeable to our marriage?"

Well no, we still have to wait for that, I'm afraid," Patrick impatiently shook his head. "My news is that I've already been offered two very good jobs."

"Why, that's wonderful, darling!" Minette tried to hide her disappointment.

"I can remain at Bart's if I wish—a live-in surgical post," Patrick continued, "but I've been offered the opportunity of a career in medical research, to begin as early as next month," the young doctor grinned with delight, "exactly what I have been hoping for!"

"The only drawback is that the hospital laboratories are in Dublin. But that need not pose a problem as I can travel back ... "

"Patrick, you cannot be contemplating leaving me alone in London?" Minette exclaimed in alarm. "If you accept the position at Bart's, at least we will see one another almost every day."

"I realise that, but I must do what is best for my career, don't you see that?" Patrick was persuasive. "A post like this one in Dublin doesn't come up that often, you know. You seem quite happy with

George and Maud, so until we can change your father's mind, you can continue—"

"No, Patrick! I am not prepared to live alone in London for three years until I am of age. My father's consent will never be given—I told you that before," the girl was on the verge of tears. "Don't you care about leaving me to rot indefinitely like this?"

"Darling, aren't you being a little dramatic?" Patrick attempted to swallow his annoyance that Minette was being so uncooperative. "It's hardly the end of the world if I—"

"*Dramatic?*" Minette leaped to her feet. "Dramatic, when I am told I have to live on my own for years, whilst you chase off to a beastly job in Ireland? When you don't actually have to?" Tears of betrayal trickled down her cheeks.

"Sit down, Minette!" Patrick was embarrassed. "You are making a spectacle of yourself, and people are noticing. Look, let's just enjoy our lunch for now, and we can talk about everything afterwards."

Minette sank down in her chair, her face mutinous. She was also horrified that she and Patrick had come close to quarrelling. Suppressing her anger—and fright—she treated Patrick to a brilliant smile. "Of course. Isn't this fish quite delicious?"

Two hours later, Minette was cramming her possessions into a recently acquired valise, her heart hammering in fright and apprehension.

Her father was in London!

It seemed the Marquis had managed to trace her, and in the company of his son, arrived unannounced on the Jennings' doorstep. Maud had told of her shock upon opening the door to them. The older gentleman had been courteous, if icy in demeanour, introducing himself as Charles de Merencourt. He then stated he had come to London in search of his missing daughter, Marguerite.

George arrived on the scene, and Maud invited the visitors into the house, and into the sitting room.

"I hope you do not intend to pretend ignorance of my daughter's whereabouts, for in such a case, I would have no hesitation in calling the police," the Marquis had informed the stupefied couple. "Marguerite is only eighteen years old, and I imagine you will know that the abduction of a minor is a serious offence under both French and English Law. I should have no hesitation in pursuing that avenue in the event of obstruction from any quarter."

"*My seester ees not wors ze reesk of preeson, n'est-ce pas?*" the younger man had tittered, before reverting to French. "*Nom de Dieu, Papa—* that Minette should be reduced to living in a dump such as this?" Jérome gazed disparagingly about him. "Our servants are better accommodated."

George was unable to believe his ears, that this arrogant little twerp had the nerve to pass snide remarks about their home! It was unfortunate for Jérome that George had a sound knowledge of the French language from his time as chief clerk for a French shipping company. Placing himself in front of his trembling wife, he addressed the Marquis directly.

"I'll thank you to stop intimidating my wife, sir!" George snapped. "And I would be obliged if you would ensure your son keeps a civil tongue in his head whilst under my roof. As regards your daughter, she has indeed been staying with us. There is no question of denying that. However, Minette has gone to spend a few days with friends ... she did not say where."

Astounded by the courage and temerity of the little man, the Marquis was rendered speechless, if briefly. Jérome opened his mouth to speak, but a barked order from his father in rapid French reduced him to sulky silence.

The interview with this old couple was clearly not about to produce the desired information, so the Marquis turned to leave the house. Pausing by the front door, he glanced back to deliver a *coup de grâce.*

"Please oblige me by informing Marguerite that I am in London to escort her home to France, where she belongs. As for the fellow who abducted my daughter from her Convent in Ireland, I would advise him not to stand in my way."

The Marquis smiled without humour at the shock on the old couple's faces. It was evident they had no idea of the actual facts of the matter.

"Should this man fail to return my daughter to me, I shall not hesitate in bringing a charge against him. Abduction of a minor is a very serious crime, and would put paid to his aspirations of a career in medicine. Not to mention the possibility of a jail sentence. *Au revoir, Monsieur, Madame."* The Marquis bowed to Maud, and left without a backward glance.

Watching the hansom cab disappear down the road, Maud's legs gave way and she sat down on the doorstep, her face pale as milk. She and George led tranquil pleasant lives, and were unused to unpleasant drama. Despite his earlier bravado, George knew it was only a question of time before the Marquis returned. Possibly with reinforcements. His lips tightened in anger.

By God, Patrick and that young lady had some explaining to do when they arrived back! Minette was a minor? Abducted from a Convent? Untruths had certainly been told—if only by omission. Added to which, George did not care to have his wife terrified out of her wits, nor his home invaded by an enraged father. Who, by all accounts, had every right to be furious.

It was to this scene that Patrick and Minette returned from their "celebratory" lunch—a disastrous event as far as the French girl was concerned. Resentments were forgotten, however, when faced by a visibly angry George. He lost no time in detailing the scene with the *Marquis*, and demanded an immediate explanation.

"Maud and I are deeply disappointed that you did not see fit to let us know Minette was three years under-age, Patrick," George continued, "and neither did you trust us to know the background of her presence in our home. It was an abuse of our trust—quite unforgivable."

Patrick was silent as he digested this latest turn of events. Minette's face had blanched, too shocked to utter a word.

"As for you, Patrick—are you quite mad? Have you never considered what a scandal like this would do to your medical career?" George's voice was cold.

"Maud, George, I ... I'm so sorry you have had such a horrid experience," the French girl finally got out after a swift glance at Patrick's set face. "I had no idea that my f-father would actually travel to England."

"Yes. Well, never mind about that now!" George brushed aside Minette's stammered apology. "Please pack up your possessions and leave the house as soon as possible. Your father and that appallingly rude brother of yours are bound to return, doubtless with a police escort. In the event the house is searched, nothing belonging to you must be found. Disgraceful this affair is—utterly disgraceful!"

Watching George stamp from the room, muttering under his breath, Patrick's mind was reeling. Abduction of a minor? Prosecution? It had never occurred to him that Minette's father would resort to pressing charges. My God, was it possible? Had he realised this, he would never have—

"Patrick?" Minette's voice broke through his jumbled thoughts. "Please would you help me with my valise?"

"What? Oh, of course," Patrick seemed distracted, "and I had better see about calling a cab, hadn't I?"

"I knew exactly who the Marquis was from the moment I laid eyes on him," Maud suddenly spoke up. "You are the image of your father, you know."

Carrying Minette's valise outside on to the pavement, Patrick focused on George's last words. Wasn't it something about Minette's vile brother? That effeminate dolt who had sneered at himself, and cast aspersions on his family's origins? The young man's mouth thinned in renewed fury. Never, by God, would he allow that little bastard to get the better of him, and there was still one card left to play.

Patrick returned to the house and took Maud's chubby hand. "Please accept my humble apologies for what you have been through," he murmured softly, his tone penitent. "I also ask that you convey my regrets to George, if you would. Suffice it to say, I have no intention of returning Minette to the unhappy circumstances from which I rescued her."

He turned to the French girl, who was weak with relief she was not about to be abandoned. "Darling, go and fetch your cloak and anything else you need—we are going to Scotland."

CHAPTER FOURTEEN

Three hours later, Patrick and Minette were boarding a train to Liverpool. From there, they would be obliged to travel onward to Scotland by stagecoach. It would be a journey of daunting length, and promised to be both tedious and tiring.

Emotionally exhausted by the recent turn of events, Minette sat silently in the railway carriage, preoccupied with her own thoughts. Aware she should be feeling euphoric at the prospect of marriage, Minette was also unable to forget Patrick's cavalier attitude over leaving her alone in London. And what of the famous job, for which he intended abandoning her whilst gallivanting off to Ireland? There had been no further mention of it since the disastrous lunch.

Other people entering the carriage interrupted Minette's sombre thoughts. A youngish woman came first, clutching the hand of a small boy who kept up an irritating whine for sweets. Next came an ascetic-looking cleric. Casting a glare in the direction of the boy, he found himself obliged to sit next to the mother and her child. Disgruntled, the expression on his face conveyed that of having to endure an offensive stench under his nose. With a heavy frown, he fished in his travel bag and pulled out a newspaper, opening it wide behind which to bury his head.

Moments later, the carriage door crashed open once more to admit a stocky individual, who heaved his bulk through the door. Clad in a tartan kilt and long woolly socks, he wore a floppy tam-o'shanter crammed on his head. With a toothy grin to the other occupants of the carriage, the newcomer flung himself down on the other side of the discomfited cleric.

Ten minutes later the train rumbled its way out of the station precincts, the massive engine hauling the carriages slowly gathering speed with noisy blasts of steam. Every so often, the train would halt at a station for water and coal to be taken on to replenish the engine's hungry furnace.

During a halt, Patrick jumped down on the platform to buy hot pies and apples from a barrow boy. Following Patrick's example, the cleric also bought himself a pie and proceeded to nibble it, rather like a genteel mouse—Minette thought with amusement, eating her own pie with enjoyment.

The mother produced a stack of thick-cut ham sandwiches from her basket. To her travelling companions' dismay, she proceeded to wake the now-sleeping boy to offer one to him. Batting the sandwich away, the child started up his wailing and grizzling once again. The cleric sighed gustily in disapproval, reflecting the opinion of everyone else in the carriage.

Inspired by the tantalising smell of hot pies, the kilted fellow delved into his string bag. Groping about, he triumphantly extracted a packet of grease-proof paper, and revealed a rather hairy pig's trotter. His fellow travellers watched in fascinated horror as he wrenched off chunks of gristle with his teeth. Chewing with relish, he belched pleasurably between mouthfuls.

Disgusted by this display of gluttony, the cleric produced a silver hip flask from an inside pocket. Swigging back the contents, he unconsciously displayed a certain familiarity with alcohol, only belatedly noticing his companions' interest. Put out, the cleric returned to his newspaper with an irritable rustle.

Aside from the entertaining aspects of her fellow passengers' behaviour, the journey seemed to be taking an eternity to Minette. Her limbs felt stiff from hours of inactivity, and she had read her magazine from cover to cover. Only managing to sleep intermittently, she was also bored to tears as the hours dragged by.

At long last, the train slowed and then stopped at Liverpool station. Descending from the railway carriage, Minette and Patrick joined the tide of passengers hurrying to leave the station. From the over-warm atmosphere of railway carriage, the sudden chill of the northern English climate came as a shock to the girl. Shivering uncontrollably, she and Patrick set about locating the Coach Station, in order to book the onward journey to Scotland.

The Coach Station was at last discovered, where a sleepy clerk lounged behind an untidy desk in his cubby-hole of an office. His reply to Patrick's question was an unintelligible outpouring that required imaginative guesswork. Patrick finally deduced the stagecoach to Scotland was due to leave the following morning. Pointing a grubby finger, the clerk indicated an inn across the road where travellers could spend the night.

The interior of the inn was at least warm, Minette thought with relief. Two rooms were reserved for the night. She noticed with faint surprise, the innkeeper did not appear to find it odd that she was in the company of a man who was not her husband! In this uncomplicated atmosphere, the exhausted girl tried to unwind, and persuade herself the threat of being apprehended by her father no longer existed.

After a simple but well-cooked meal, Minette excused herself and went to her room. Undressing quickly, she fell instantly asleep in a clean and comfortable bed.

Left on his own, Patrick sat by the fire in the inn's parlour, nursing a full glass of whisky. During the journey north, he had plenty of time to reflect on the impossible situation in which he found himself. The blinding rage that had seized him upon hearing Jérome's hated name had subsided—with grim reality taking its place. What if the Marquis failed to abandon the quest for his daughter? Even after a marriage ceremony? What then? Was he prepared to sacrifice his entire career and risk possible prosecution? Christ, that would be sheer folly!

Taking a hefty gulp of whisky, Patrick shook his head in confusion. Common sense dictated he should take immediate steps to return the girl to her father. She would go without argument, and neither would she beg. Fierce pride would prevent that, Patrick knew. But could he face the inevitable scorn in Minette's eyes that her hero had turned out a broken reed after all? A weakling who fell apart over her father's threats? Patrick could not make up his mind.

The following morning, Minette was up at first light. Unaware of Patrick's agonies of indecision, she was filled with renewed energy and happy anticipation. Having mulled matters over in her mind, she had dismissed her distress over Patrick's desire to abandon her in London. He was here, wasn't he? They were soon to be married, so it was nonsensical to worry about nothing. After all, once she was Patrick's wife, she would be free to accompany her husband when he took up his new position at the Dublin hospital.

Minette wondered if her friend, Jane, had returned to Scotland. She remembered Jane had said her family lived in Dumfriesshire, not far from the English border. Perhaps she could stay with Jane during Patrick's period of residence? It would be great fun, and there was so much to tell her! Minette decided to send a telegram to Jane as soon as possible.

The parlour was chilly despite the fire having been lit, but Minette was well wrapped up in her warm cloak. Becoming aware of a strange absence of street noise, Minette glanced out of the window. To her dismay, a thick curtain of snowflakes danced in a sharp wind against the lowering sky.

Without being told, Minette knew it would be impossible to journey by coach in such conditions. The roads would be slippery and dangerous, even impassable in places. They would just have to wait until the blizzard cleared.

The wild weather continued to rage for a further two days. Minette nevertheless managed to send Jane a telegram, having bribed the innkeeper's son to fight his way through a blinding snowstorm to the Post Office, which amazingly remained open for business.

She passed the time sitting quietly in the parlour, reading, writing in her Journal, or merely dozing in front of the fire. Patrick sat with her, oddly withdrawn and uncommunicative. Shrugging, Minette assumed his mood to be annoyance over the unforeseen delay in their departure.

Then as quickly as it had blown up, the blizzard dissipated, leaving a sparkling blanket of snow over roof tops and roads. Children rushed about, shouting and flinging snowballs, happy to be out after being cooped up. Dogs barked with excitement, and carriages began emerging to make their cautious way through still-perilous streets.

Six fresh horses were harnessed up to the stagecoach, the driver holding them in check with visible difficulty. Climbing aboard in the company of only one other passenger, Patrick and Minette set off once more on their journey to Scotland.

As the stagecoach travelled northward, the landscape gradually changed with the miles, becoming bleak and less inhabited. Frequent patches of ice on the road forced the driver to slow his horses to a walk, so progress was necessarily slow.

During halts at Posting Inns along the way to change horses, the passengers took advantage of them to enjoy a brief meal. Together with a glass of spiced wine, the welcome break did much to drive the chill from tired and cramped bodies.

It was with infinite relief that all three occupants of the stagecoach finally heard the driver call out, "Gretna … Gretna Green!" The stage pulled up in the centre of the village, and Patrick jumped down from the mud-splattered vehicle. Turning, he helped a stiff Minette negotiate the coach's rickety little steps to the ground.

"Minette!"

The French girl whirled, amazed to hear her name screamed aloud. Amid a flurry of mittens and woollen cloak, Jane came bounding up, her round face split in a delighted grin. Flinging her arms first about her friend, Jane then turned to give Patrick a hug.

"I can hardly believe you are really here—in Scotland!" Jane grinned from one to the other. "Of course, I shall want to know absolutely everything that has happened since you left the Convent!"

Ever efficient, Jane had already organised a room for Patrick at a small hotel on the outskirts of Gretna Green. Minette, of course, would be coming home with her! The three took afternoon tea together at the hotel, tucking into delicious buttered teacakes and fingers of shortbread. Jane and Minette left shortly afterward for the Scots girl's family home, Briar House.

Lord Stanford and Lady Ogilvy welcomed their daughter's guest with genuine pleasure. Of course, they had no knowledge of the real purpose of Minette's visit to Scotland, assuming the two girls were catching up with their news. Jane showed her friend to a large guest bedroom, complete with canopied bed dressed with a satin eiderdown. A fire was burning in a vast fireplace, stoked by servants throughout the day—essential for one's basic comfort, Jane assured her friend.

Later that night, Minette was cuddled up in bed, warm and cosy under the eiderdown. Sleepily, she wondered if her father had given up the search for her? In the event he hadn't, Gretna Green would hold no significance whatsoever to a Frenchman. Reassured, Minette fell fast asleep.

Having advised the appropriate authorities of his personal details, and those of his intended bride, the weeks of Patrick's obligatory residency in Scotland crawled by. He still wrestled with the conundrum of whether to continue with this possibly ill-fated union with Minette … or to call a halt before it went any further.

Although Gretna Green might mean nothing to the Marquis, Patrick was certain the marriage would merely exacerbate his fury to further incandescence. Of course, there was a slender chance that Minette's father might have given up the search in disgust. But Patrick suspected he was not a man to give up easily, in particular where his daughter was concerned.

Several glasses of whisky under his belt by the time he went to bed each night, Patrick had always come to a decision. He would call a halt to this foolish elopement. By returning Minette to her father, there was a good chance the Marquis would not take matters any further.

But when he awoke the following morning, the thought of telling Minette was too daunting. Could he bear to be the cause of bewildered hurt in her eyes … and the inevitable contempt in Jane's? No, he needed more time to think …

The morning of Minette's wedding dawned cold, but sunny. She and Jane were still in dressing gowns and sitting at the breakfast table, discussing Minette's intended wedding attire.

"To be honest, Minette, I haven't seen a single garment of yours which might be suitable," Jane stated baldly. "You really do want to look rather special on your wedding day, you know."

"I thought perhaps my rose wool," Minette tentatively suggested. "It suits me well enough, don't you think?"

"It's a very nice gown, but not quite right for a wedding," Jane declared with conviction. "Hang on a sec, I have a brilliant idea which might suit the occasion. Go back to your bedroom, and I'll meet you there." Jumping up from the table, the Scots girl left the room, Minette staring after her in mystification.

Pulling her dressing gown more tightly about her, she made her way quickly down long, chilly corridors whose walls were hung with paintings of long-dead Ogilvy ancestors. Regaining the welcome warmth of her bedroom, Minette flopped into a chair close to the fire.

During these last weeks with Jane's family, it had been a secret worry that Lord and Lady Ogilvy might discover the real reason for her presence in Scotland. And that she was three years under-age. In which event, they were likely to regard it as their duty to locate and inform her father.

On Jane's advice, she had made no mention of Patrick's existence to her hosts. Better to be safe than sorry—Jane said. Thank God this unsettled period in her life was coming to an end, Minette thought with feeling. A tap at the door and Jane reappeared, her arms full of creamy material that turned out to be a beautiful gown in fine, almost fluid wool.

Cut to the ever-popular Empire line, it flowed from a high waistline to the floor. Before the stupefied French girl could utter a word, Jane produced a circlet of matching cream flowers with a triumphant grin.

"Where on earth did you get this utterly gorgeous gown?" Minette gasped in awe. "You can't seriously be suggesting I wear it—why, Jane, it looks brand new!"

"Hardly new, sweetie, as Mama wore it as a debutante hundreds of years ago. She recently donated it to me in the vain hope I would agree to a London Season. Don't worry, she knows I'm lending it to you. I told her we had been invited to a rather grand dance, and you had nothing to wear."

"But did she believe that?" Minette looked askance. "Didn't it seems odd that all of a sudden a formal dance was taking place in the wilds of Scotland?"

Jane shook her head. "Mama is so full of laudanum and sherry these days, she barely knows what is going on around her much of the time."

Reassured, Minette slipped the gown over her head, thrilled by the softness of the folds as it settled about her body. It was a perfect fit. Jane steered a euphoric Minette over to the dressing table, and pressed her down on the stool. Brushing out the dark curls into a shining cloud, Jane placed the circlet of silk blossoms on Minette head, the delicate petals brushing her forehead.

"Now you look like a bride, my girl!" Jane exclaimed with satisfaction. "When Patrick sees you, his eyes will pop out."

Later that morning, Patrick O'Hara was at the blacksmith's forge, waiting for his bride to arrive. His nerves were on edge, and he cast involuntary glances at the door as if he half-expected the local constabulary to march in and arrest him. For the umpteenth time, the young doctor wondered how it was that he had been plunged into this maelstrom of dangerous intrigue. And now it was too late to extricate himself from the tangled mess. All he could hope for now was that the Marquis had washed his hands of his errant daughter, and cleared off to France.

Patrick's jumble of apprehensive thoughts was interrupted by the sound of carriage wheels arriving outside the forge. Minutes later, the door opened and Jane breezed in to join Patrick, giving him the benefit of a conspiratorial wink.

The door opened once more, and the young man was confronted by a vision in cream. A circlet of blossoms crowned her dark hair, cheeks tinted pink with excitement. Gasping in delighted amazement, Patrick gazed into his bride's vivid eyes. All earlier fears now fading, he took Minette by the hand and the couple turned to face the officiating personage over the anvil.

A dazzling smile broke out on Minette's face as the simple gold circle was slipped over her finger. For the last time, she signed the register with her own name, Marguerite Anne de Merencourt. Accepting the congratulations of the borrowed witnesses, bride and groom left the forge still holding hands. Jane had left a few minutes earlier to summon the Ogilvy carriage from around the corner.

"May I tell you how ravishing you look, Mrs O'Hara?" Patrick whispered against his bride's hair. "I'm so proud you are my wife at last."

Speechless with happiness, Minette gazed up at her new husband, any lingering vestige of anxiety over his commitment to her vanishing. Both seemed oblivious of everything except each other, even Jane who had returned with the carriage. Smiling with pleasure to see her friend so happy, Jane ushered them into the vehicle. She instructed the driver to go to a hotel in the centre of Gretna, where a private parlour and double bedroom had been reserved for the bridal pair. The three of them would celebrate over a glass of champagne, followed by a special luncheon provided by the landlord.

Clearly of a romantic turn of mind, the hotel owner's wife had decked out the parlour with garlands of holly and mistletoe. A small wedding cake stood on a lace-draped table, a bottle of champagne steeped in a bed of ice beside it. The luncheon was delicious, but Minette could only pick at the food. She presumed it to be a delayed reaction after all the weeks of anxiety. Jane had no such reticence, however, and helped herself to liberal portions of the excellent meal.

Although only late afternoon, daylight was beginning to fade so Jane took leave of her friends. Exhorting them to furnish her with an address as soon as they were settled in their new home, Jane departed home in her carriage. Patrick and Minette stood in the hotel entrance, watching until the vehicle disappeared into the encroaching gloom of early evening.

Alone at last, the young couple went upstairs to investigate their room. Opening the door, Minette saw every surface had been decorated with boughs of holly laden with scarlet berries. The double bed was made up with crisp white sheets and the hotel's newest blankets, sprinkled with confetti. A wood fire crackled in the grate so the room was pleasantly warm.

Suppressing an unexpected attack of nerves, Minette held chilled hands towards the fire. What was she supposed to do now, she wondered, since it seemed rather too early in the evening for bed? Perhaps there was an en suite bathroom, where she could change into another gown—in privacy?

Behind her, Patrick grinned in amusement. Good God, his volatile and usually self-possessed bride was actually … shy! Putting his arms about her, Patrick kissed her neck and shoulders until Minette turned towards him, her eyes searching his face. He kissed her mouth, lightly, then with mounting passion. Her nervousness evaporating, the girl's lips unconsciously parted as a delightful, if unfamiliar sensation suffused her body.

With gentle fingers, Patrick unlaced Minette's gown, letting it slide to the floor unnoticed. A cascade of dainty under-things followed until the girl stood before him, glorious and unself-conscious in her nakedness. Picking her up, Patrick carried Minette over to the bed, noting her passion was equalling his own—a vital response he had always suspected lay just beneath the surface …

Bright winter sunshine streamed through the latticed windowpanes, causing Minette to screw up her eyes and snuggle deeper into the bed, closer to the warmth of her husband's body. How very pleasant, and doubtless decadent it was to sleep without the inconvenience of a nightgown! Turning her head, she saw Patrick was still asleep, his tousled hair a bright copper in the early rays of the sun.

Raising herself on an elbow, she gazed down at the man she adored. Heavens, what a wicked Irish seducer her husband had proved himself to be! A secret smile curving her lips, she recalled the night of passion they had shared, her cheeks warming with the memory of her own wild abandonment! Taking his time, Patrick had brought his bride to heights of ecstasy she had not dreamed existed. Dawn was breaking when the two of them finally fell asleep in each other's arms.

Smiling, Minette held up her left hand, turning it this way and that, watching the gold ring encircling her finger glitter in the sunlight. Madame Marguerite O'Hara! Stifling a giggle, she supposed she would become accustomed to her new status in time. But now—at last—she could put the unhappy past to rest, and look forward to a new and exciting future, a loving husband at her side.

CHAPTER FIFTEEN

Despite the temptation to prolong the halcyon hours of their marriage, Patrick and Minette travelled back to London the following day. As arranged, Minette left the borrowed gown at the hotel for Jane to collect, a note of gratitude pinned to it.

Time was running short for Patrick with regard to the post in Dublin that he so desperately desired. Before leaving for Scotland, he had provisionally accepted the job, and was hoping to find confirmation of his employment awaiting him at Bart's Hospital. The other important factor was, of course, the result of his Finals.

Patrick decided it would be prudent not to draw attention to themselves until he had managed to ascertain what the situation was regarding the Marquis. With this in mind, he reserved a room at a small, but genteel hotel in the relative obscurity of the London suburbs.

There was only one way in which to find out if anything further had transpired, and that was by paying the Jennings a visit. It was also necessary to apologise for the unseemly intrusion into their tranquil lives, and for what the couple saw as an abuse of their trust. Of course there was always a risk of the Jennings home being under some kind of surveillance. Nevertheless, Patrick knew it was a risk he must take—sooner or later.

Leaving a bored Minette in the hotel bedroom, Patrick made his way to Bart's. It was important to collect his correspondence and other documentation from the hospital. All being well, he would be a fully qualified doctor at last! On his way across the foyer, he came across an old friend and associate with whom he had shared a chummery with two other students.

"I say, old chap … jolly well done on your results!" Simon Prendergast clapped Patrick on the back. "Mine have also made the grade, thank God."

"Thanks Simon! Happy to see you, but must go as I have an appointment in an hour or so." Patrick hoped his chum would take the hint and continue on his way.

"Pity … I was hoping we could have a cup of tea in the canteen and catch up on what's what," Simon was disappointed. "Another time perhaps. Oh, before I forget, there's a French fellow hanging about outside who seems fearfully keen to find you, Pat. Spoke vile English, and the silly ass wouldn't accept the fact I hadn't a clue as to where you were. Where were you, by the way? Piers and Harry wanted to invite you to a celebration party last week at White's."

"A Frenchman? How odd!" Patrick evaded his friend's question. "Do you recall what the fellow looked like?"

"Um … longish fair hair, pale eyes, effeminate in manner. Bit of a fop, if you ask me," Simon replied. "Arrogant little devil though. Couldn't quite put his attitude down to the language barrier, if you know what I mean."

Jérome—it had to be.

No mention of the Marquis, however. "Must be the fellow I came across during a visit to France not long ago," Patrick said with a composure he did not feel. "Nasty piece of work, and I have no wish to renew the acquaintance. Should he accost you again, don't mention you have seen me, will you? Must get on now, Simon, so goodbye and all the best!"

Patrick hurried to retrieve the documents regarding his qualifications from his postal box—and discovered a letter from the Dublin hospital. To his relief, it was indeed confirmation of his employment on medical research, so at least his future was on the right track.

Of course, he and his new bride would be obliged to live with his parents until suitable accommodation could be located. Minette would not be thrilled at the prospect, his difficult mother being the fly in the ointment—Patrick reflected with a rueful grimace. Perhaps now that he and Minette were legally married, she might bring herself to accept her French daughter-in-law.

Exiting the hospital, Patrick was unable to prevent himself from a furtive glance to right and then left—to his annoyance. Christ, but he was beginning to skulk about the place like some bloody criminal! The sooner he left London for Ireland, the better.

No sign of Jérome, thank God.

Relieved, Patrick returned to the hotel to give Minette the news regarding his successful qualifications. Also that he would be taking up a position in medical research with the Dublin hospital in two months time. Although another doctor had been employed, his wife was unable to settle for the dullness of life in the Kildare countryside. He and his family would be returning to England at the end of his notice. The hospital authorities were therefore delighted that the other doctor taking up the post would be a returning Irishman.

Although pleased for her husband, Minette was predictably not enchanted to learn she would be living with Serena O'Hara.

"It would only be at the outset, darling," Patrick hastened to assure his wife. "And remember Robert and Jennifer, maybe even Belinda will be close by."

"Patrick, your mother doesn't like me ... even a little bit," Minette objected. "I should hate it, and so would she, I have no doubt. Besides, what would I do all day long, just to keep out of her way?"

"Well Sean will be at home, and you can always ride as much as you want, my sweet."

"I suppose so," Minette grudgingly agreed, "provided you swear to begin looking for our own home from the start. I'm afraid you will be so wrapped up in your work that you will forget all about it. I will live with your mother for one month ... six weeks at the most. Is that agreed?"

"Absolutely!" Patrick agreed with a grin. "Never fear, I don't believe I could bear living under her roof for longer than that, myself."

The weeks flew by, and Patrick decided he could not put off visiting the Jennings. Hiring a cab, Patrick instructed the cabbie to go to the address in Wimbledon. To his relief, the couple seemed delighted to see him, despite the unfortunate circumstances of their last meeting. They were amazed to learn that he and

Minette were now legally married, but then George's expression grew sombre. He had disturbing news to impart, and this marriage was not about to improve matters!

True to his threat, the Marquis had returned to the Jennings' home in the company of two policemen—and a search warrant. Finding no evidence of the French girl, the elderly couple were interrogated as to the possible whereabouts of Marguerite. Emphasis had been placed on the girl's under-age status.

To their utmost relief, George and Maud had been able to say with perfect truth that they had no idea. The police had made it clear that unless the matter was speedily resolved, Patrick O'Hara would face a serious charge of child-abduction.

Having allowed the police to make their inquiries, Charles de Merencourt turned to address George, his voice cold.

"Monsieur Jennings, dealing with this unpleasant business has obliged me to stay away from my home for an extended period. I imagine you will understand how this absence has seriously inconvenienced me. It has since occurred to me that my foolish daughter may have been persuaded to participate in an illegal marriage of sorts. Should I discover this to be the case, immediate steps will be taken to ensure an annulment. I shall then instigate proceedings against that scoundrel, O'Hara for the *seduction* of my under-age daughter. The English authorities have already endorsed my intention, and they are aware of the circumstances concerning Marguerite's removal from the Convent in Ireland. *Au revoir*, Monsieur Jennings."

Grim-faced, the Marquis had bowed courteously to the stupefied couple, before departing in the company of his sulky son and the two policemen.

Patrick stared at George in horror. It was manifestly obvious the Marquis had no intention of abandoning the quest for his delinquent daughter. In addition, he appeared determined to prosecute him for the heinous crime of seduction—as though he was guilty of bedding a twelve year old, for Christ's sake! Nevertheless, he doubted the authorities would bother to engage in an argument over the finer points of Minette's current status.

How to avoid the looming catastrophe that would effectively

throw away years of medical training, not to mention his future career? For the sake of a romantic liaison, it seemed he was now facing a possible jail sentence.

Patrick forced himself to acknowledge the fact that his actions had also been motivated by a thirst for revenge on the Marquise and her vile son. Those people who inferred he stank of manure, and then had openly insulted his family. Of course, he adored his sweet girl, but there had to be a limit to what he was prepared to sacrifice.

But how to break it to Minette, that perforce, the marriage was over? Should he instruct George to furnish the Marquis with details of the hotel's location, and allow matters to take their course? He could then unobtrusively disappear …

Patrick pulled himself up. That would be the easiest way … and also the most cowardly! No, Minette deserved better. He would explain things to her, and hope to God he would be spared an over-emotional scene. She was intelligent, and should understand her father had created an untenable situation. In the existing circumstances, there was no other solution but to return to her family.

As things stood, it was not even certain the Marquis would be satisfied in regaining his daughter: she could, after all, be considered "spoiled" goods. Patrick swallowed convulsively. With Minette's agreement, he supposed he could claim the girl to be sexually untouched? It was a chance he felt obliged to take …

"Patrick?" Maud's voice broke through the confusion in his mind. "You must do the right thing, you know. Lovely girl though she undoubtedly is, you were very wrong to seize Minette from her family. If you give her back now, there is a chance the Marquis will drop these dreadful charges against you."

"She's right, Patrick," George broke in. "You don't want to jeopardise your entire future, do you? And you cannot hide forever. Sooner or later, the law will catch up with you … and what then? Prison?"

"No … no, of course not! I'm due to leave the country shortly for Dublin to take up a position in medical research. What I always wanted. I'll go back now and tell Minette what has happened, and she must accept it. Perhaps if I bring her back here, you can leave it a couple of days, and then inform the police she has been found? It will give me a chance to get myself out of the Marquis' way."

"Very well." George looked doubtful, clearly unwilling to be further embroiled in the distasteful intrigue. He supposed it would be the end of it, however.

On his way back to the hotel, Patrick was apprehensive over what he should say to Minette—despite his bold words. He would explain what had transpired at the Jennings' house, and the dire threats made against him by her father. It was important to be decisive, and leave no room for argument.

Patrick's spirits lifted with the thought that soon, very soon, he would win back his personal freedom from this nightmare of a situation. No more skulking round corners, and hasty glances over his shoulder in future!

Patrick had just fitted the key into the lock of the bedroom, when it swung open. Minette stood in the doorway, her eyes shining with happiness.

"Darling, I've been longing for you to come home! You've been ages," she gazed up at her husband. "I've exciting news ... we are expecting a baby!"

"*A baby?*" echoed Patrick stupidly. "If this is your idea of a joke, I—"

"Of course I'm not joking, Patrick!" Minette stood back, her face clouding in bewilderment at the chill in her husband's voice. "I've suspected for some time that a baby might be on the way. Our landlady recommended her personal doctor, and he confirmed it this morning."

"*Christ*, Minette, how could you allow such a thing to happen? It's going to ruin everything!" Agonized, Patrick envisaged his careful plans disappearing into thin air. Now there was *no* chance of pretending the French girl was as virginal as she had been upon leaving that blasted Convent.

"Don't you think we have enough problems on our plate without the complication of a squalling infant? What the *hell* were you thinking, you stupid girl?"

Minette had lost colour with the shock of Patrick's accusation. So this was all her fault was it? Anger began to burn and colour returned to her cheeks. Following her husband into the bathroom, she saw him pouring a hefty measure of whisky into a tooth glass. Throwing back a huge swallow, Patrick swung round to glare down at Minette.

"It seems your blasted father is still dogging my footsteps on your account! And now—damn it to hell—you have seen fit to land me with a bloody *baby!*"

"Allow me to remind you this baby is your responsibility as well as mine, Patrick O'Hara!" Minette's voice dripped ice, her eyes flashing blue fire. "Don't you dare to lay the blame entirely at my door!"

Having expected tears and entreaties, Patrick stepped back, startled, in the face of his wife's fury. "It's just that I don't want ... "

"*What?* What don't you want, Patrick?" Minette's eyebrows rose in chilly disdain. "If you don't want children, then you should take more care, don't you think? You are a damned doctor, after all!"

"You obviously haven't taken in what I was saying about your father, Minette," Patrick blustered, taking a swallow from his third glass of whisky. "The Jennings told me he intends to have me arrested for seducing you—an under-age child! This blasted pregnancy rather confirms that, don't you think? A jail sentence if I'm caught. Oh, how the hell did I get myself into this mess?"

"You went into this marriage with your eyes wide open, Patrick O'Hara!" snapped Minette tartly. "You were fully aware of the implications. Do allow me to reassure you this is not some Machiavellian plot I conceived to anchor you to my side," she added bitingly, unaware of how close to the truth she had come.

Patrick glowered into his glass of whisky. He was still reeling from the shock of Minette's announcement. Unsure of how to proceed, his earlier plans having blown up in his face, alcohol-fuelled frustration reached boiling point.

"Damn it to hell, can't you understand I have no desire whatsoever to reproduce myself—at any point in time?" snarled the man, his lips drawing back over his teeth. "And if I lose the job in Dublin because of this damnable farce, I shall never forgive you!"

"In that case, I take it you won't be sharing my bed in future!" Minette retaliated, her face pale as milk.

Shaken to the core by her husband's words, she grabbed her cloak from a nearby chair and stalked out of the bedroom, slamming the door behind her. Minette had no idea of where she was going. She was conscious only of an overwhelming desire to get away from the stale atmosphere of the bedroom, and her husband who had metamorphosed into an unpleasant stranger.

Seated on a bench in a nearby park, Minette was trembling with a combination of hurt and resentment. The injustice of Patrick's hurled accusations had shocked her beyond belief—not least coming from a man who professed to love her.

Accusing her of deliberately setting out to become pregnant— how dare he infer such a thing! God, she had entrusted this person with her very life, to the point of estrangement from the father she had always adored.

In danger of dissolving into futile tears, Minette pulled herself together with an effort. A baby was on the way, so a strategy to resolve matters had to be found.

And what about the position in Dublin upon which Patrick placed so much value? Minette's mind shied away from the inescapable fact that Patrick could no longer risk taking the job. Yes, she could understand how upset he must be feeling, and she supposed she was indirectly the reason. But to continue indulging in bouts of recrimination was futile, and served no purpose.

In order to escape her father's net, she and Patrick must somehow contrive to vanish from the scene. Leave the country perhaps? Minette sat up, recalling the luncheon at the Savoy with Patrick's doctor friend. Jonathan Adams had suggested Patrick should consider joining the Indian Cavalry, declaring it to be an excellent idea, and very well paid.

Filled with renewed hope, Minette jumped to her feet and hurried back to the hotel. Going to India was a perfect solution to the situation, besides being an exciting prospect! She only hoped Patrick would see the sense of it.

Patrick was not in the bedroom. The bottle of whisky stood empty on the dresser. Somewhat deflated, Minette sat down on the bed to wait, hoping her husband had gone out to buy food—and not another bottle of whisky.

Hours passed. Darkness was beginning to fall, but there was still no sign of Patrick. Minette couldn't make up her mind whether to be concerned—or furiously angry. Granted he was upset, but to effectively abandon her for an entire day was not in the least way acceptable. There was no food in the room, and neither did she have any money to buy something to eat—even had she known where to go.

Minette remembered the bowl of fruit provided by the hotel, but upon inspection, only two rather wizened pears remained. Hungry, she ate them both with relish and drank a glass of water. Minette hoped the small meal would be sufficient for an hour or two.

Three hours later, Patrick had still not returned, and Minette was now ravenous. Tantalised by delicious cooking smells wafting from the hotel dining room, her stomach protested its emptiness by an audible rumbling. Although aware that it might seem odd to the hotel proprietor, Minette decided she would ask if she might join the other guests for the evening meal ... alone.

Tidying her hair in front of the bathroom mirror in preparation of going downstairs, Minette heard a key scrape in the lock of the bedroom door. Moments later, she was confronted by an obviously inebriated Patrick, clutching a full bottle of whisky. It was the first time Minette had seen anyone in such a condition, and aside from being horrified she was also unsure how to handle the situation.

"So there y'are madam!" the man slurred, glaring at Minette from red-rimmed eyes. "Where th' helluv you been, eh? Pleased with y'self are you ... saddling me with an unwanted brat? Should'a given you back to your damned father long ago."

"*Patrick!*" Minette's face was pinched. "Don't ... don't you love me any more? Are you already regretting our marriage?"

Patrick hesitated, something deep within his intoxicated brain preventing him from confirming Minette's question. Had he done so, the fiercely proud French girl might go to the nearest police station and request her father be notified. It would be perceived that a very young girl had been driven to wander the streets of London— alone and penniless. Inevitably, the Marquis would discover the condition of his abandoned daughter. Despite his befuddled brain, Patrick knew the consequences of that did not bear thinking about.

Pulling himself together, he attempted a reassuring smile. "Don … don't be silly, darling, 'course I love you ver' much! Jus' had a lil' too much whisky on an empty st-stomach, th'ass all. C'mere for a kiss!" Patrick staggered as he leaned forward to embrace his wife.

"No thank you, Patrick!" Minette stepped back in disgust. "Certainly not whilst you are in this revolting state. Since I have spent my day cooped up in the room waiting for you, with only a little fruit to sustain me, I'm going downstairs to have some supper. I suggest you go to bed and sleep it off."

Minette left the room, willing herself not to cry. Patrick's words had cut her to the quick, and she wondered if there was a grain of truth in them—despite his denial. She would have her meal, and then think about what she should do.

The hotel proprietor readily agreed to Minette joining the other guests for the evening meal. Although sick at heart, Minette's young body demanded to be fed, and she enjoyed the simple but well-cooked dinner. Excusing herself from the other diners, she went back to the bedroom—apprehensive about what she was about to find. She only hoped Patrick had not started on the full bottle of whisky he had been holding in his hand.

To the girl's immense relief, Patrick had taken her advice. He was in bed, albeit still half-dressed, and snoring loudly. The atmosphere was disagreeably rank from exhaled alcoholic fumes, and wrinkling her nose, Minette held her breath until she reached the bathroom and closed the door. Undressing quickly, she wondered if she dared open a window to clear the air a little. Otherwise, it would be impossible to sleep in such a disgusting stench.

The window creaked open, and Minette froze, hoping her husband would remain asleep. Standing by the open window in her nightgown, uncaring of the evening chill, the girl filled her lungs with fresh air. Tip-toeing to the bed, she slid between the covers, lying as far away as possible from the snoring man. Staring bleakly into the darkness, Minette pressed a hand over her mouth to prevent herself from crying.

What had happened to the fearless champion who had so

gallantly rescued her from the terrible fate of an arranged marriage? *Bah!* Such a person simply did not exist. Placing her hands protectively over a still-flat stomach, Minette wondered at her own naivety. Hours later, the devastated girl drifted into a fitful sleep.

Early morning rays of the sun stroked Minette's tear-stained cheeks with golden fingers. Opening her eyes, she squinted against the unaccustomed brightness. The memory of the previous evening rushing back, she quickly turned her head to where her husband was sleeping. The bed was empty. Gripped by the possibility that Patrick had already abandoned her, she tried not to let panic overwhelm her. The hotel bill … she had no money to pay it! Patrick always paid for everything, deeming it unnecessary to give Minette any money for herself.

Think! How should she avoid handing herself in to a police station with a request to contact her father? Trying to explain the inexplicable to him? Cast out by her family when her condition became known? God, anything was better than enduring the shame of that! She would find work. She would …

The bathroom door opened, and Minette almost wept with relief to see Patrick, fully dressed and shaved, his expression sheepish.

"Good morning, darling," Patrick's tone was penitent. "I've a feeling I may have behaved rather badly yesterday—said some unpleasant things, maybe?"

"Yes, you did," Minette's tone was uncompromising. "Unforgivable, beastly accusations which I find hard to forgive, never mind forget."

"It will never happen again, sweetie, I swear," Patrick wheedled. "It was a shock to find out your father is hell-bent not only on destroying my career, but anxious to see me thrown me into jail."

"I understand how unpleasant it is for you, Patrick," Minette said coldly. "But tell me, is this supposed to explain your regret in not having handed me back to my father? I don't care to be treated as a leech, from which you can shake yourself loose at will."

"*A leech?* For God's sake, darling … you are my much-loved wife! How can I make things up to you?"

"Patrick, I cannot stand the person you become when you have had too much to drink." Chilled by the distress of the moment,

Minette dragged the blankets up the bed and huddled into them. "I would rather we went our separate ways, than be obliged to endure *that* again."

"Look, I've said how sorry I am – "

"And then there is prospect of the coming baby, an idea you seem to find intolerable, and for which you hold me to blame," Minette continued inexorably. "Hardly a happy start to a child's life, wouldn't you agree?"

"Darling, please forget I ever said that," Patrick entreated. "I was drunk. It's true to say a child has never featured in my scheme of things for the future. But a baby is now on the way, so I will try my best to be a good husband ... and father. Just promise me I won't have to play second fiddle to an infant, I beg you."

The tension in the atmosphere lightening, Minette relaxed with a watery smile. "Competing already with your unborn child? Shame on you, Patrick O'Hara!"

CHAPTER SIXTEEN

The following day, Patrick and Minette went for a walk along a pathway beside the embankment of the River Thames. The weather was mild for the season, but a brisk wind tossed fallen leaves into a dancing russet cloud about their ankles.

The conversation between the two was desultory, punctuated by an occasional awkward silence. Patrick's eyes were reddened, and he was suffering from a splitting headache, the result of alcoholic indulgence. Minette was anxious to put the disillusionment and misery of the past days behind her—no easy thing.

A factor uppermost in the girl's mind was the importance of suggesting the possibility of going to India to her husband. However, the queasy look on Patrick's face was less than encouraging. But time was of the essence, so Minette chose a moment when they stopped to watch a group of excited children flying a kite.

"Patrick, have you given any thought to Jonathan Adams's suggestion of joining the Indian Cavalry?" she began tentatively. "He seemed convinced it would suit you well, besides being well paid."

"No." Patrick's answer was short. "Having accepted the position in Dublin, nothing else required consideration ... so I thought."

"I think we both know that to be impossible now," Minette continued, trying to choose her words with care. "Dublin would be one of the first places the police would look for you. It would be safer to spend few years out of the way of their clutches. Once I am twenty-one, we can come back to England, and then you can do as you please."

Patrick turned to look at his wife, his expression bleak. "You seem to think jobs in medical research are two a penny! I was extremely fortunate to be selected for the Dublin post ... and now I am prevented from taking it up."

The words "because of you" hung in the air between them, but remained unsaid.

"I know, and I'm so sorry things have turned out the way they have." Minette ignored the profound silence. "Darling, don't let's go over old ground again, because it serves little purpose. We must think of what to do now, in order to avoid endless problems."

"It seems I have little choice in the matter!" Patrick retorted. "I suppose I may as well serve out a term in the jungles of India, instead of languishing in some filthy prison. I'll get on with it then."

Minette was silent. Patrick's capitulation was grudging, but she was relieved to have achieved it without further recrimination or argument. At least now there was a sense of direction. She would pray that Patrick would discover an element of satisfaction in the work he would be undertaking for the Indian Cavalry. Her burden of guilt might then become lighter...

Patrick had little difficulty in purchasing a commission with the British Army Medical Corps. He became a doctor-surgeon with The Queen's Own 16th Lancers, a Cavalry Regiment. Basic training was to take place at the Depôt in Aldershot, during which Patrick would be required to reside on site. Lodgings were located for Minette with a somewhat dull couple, the advantage being that their home was no great distance away.

The young doctor's battle training was necessarily brief due to the urgent requirement for doctors throughout British Regiments in India. It was nevertheless intensive over a period of four months, leaving Patrick little time to spend with his wife. To Minette, he appeared preoccupied, often distant, and she reacted fiercely to being thrust to one side—as she viewed it. She was also bored stiff.

Having received short shrift from Patrick to her pleas for attention, Minette began work at the local Cottage Hospital. Her boredom magically evaporating, she assisted with the delivery and after-care of newborn infants.

In due course, she was motivated to undertake a short course in midwifery and childish ailments. Possessing a working knowledge of medication, delivery and breast-feeding would stand her in good stead to assist her husband upon his eventual return to England. The French girl felt at peace with herself for the first time in many months.

Despite her new preoccupation, Minette was never quite free from the spectre of her whereabouts being discovered by her father or the police. Upon her return to her lodgings each evening, she would ask her landlady if any visitors had enquired after her. The answer was invariably negative, and Minette was awash with relief that she had lived through another day without detection. Nevertheless, she knew she would not feel safe until she and Patrick were on board ship, and on their way out to India.

In the fullness of time, Patrick completed his training and received Orders to join the Regiment in the garden city of Lucknow. He and his wife were to sail on an ocean-going liner from Southampton docks, the voyage to Bombay taking several weeks. After disembarkation, they would travel under military escort to the Regimental cantonment in up-country Lucknow.

Leaving the Cottage hospital proved to be something of a wrench for Minette. She had felt herself to be of value there, besides being in control of her life for the first time. The work had been engrossing, and time passed with little opportunity for introspection. She would also miss the nurses, some of whom had become good friends—only to lose them—Minette wryly reflected.

Preparations for departure were intense and complicated. An approved London tailor made up Patrick's uniforms of scarlet and black encrusted with gold braid, an assistant visiting the Depôt on several occasions for fittings. Two different types of headgear also had to be obtained. One was the *czapska*, a parade helmet adorned with white swan feathers. The other was the *solar topi*, a much lighter pith helmet and decidedly more comfortable to wear.

Horses also had to be acquired. Chargers for active duty, polo ponies, and a hunter or two for fox hunting.

An elegant, dark bay thoroughbred mare was purchased for a thrilled Minette, which went some way towards melting the ice that had formed around her heart. All the horses would be travelling with them, housed in specially constructed stalls in the ship's hold. Throughout the long sea voyage, Cavalry grooms would see to the horses' needs, as well as maintaining a vast collection of harnesses, saddles and miscellaneous other tackle in pristine condition.

On the day of departure, a perpetual drizzle was raining down from a leaden sky. On board ship, seamen scurried about the decks, unworried about being soaked to the skin, busy with final preparations for the long voyage ahead. Despite the dismal weather, all the arrangements of past weeks fell neatly into place. The horses were loaded into the ship's hold without incident, together with colossal quantities of feed and hay.

Patrick and Minette boarded the ship up a swaying gangway, followed by a trail of porters struggling with a not inconsiderable amount of luggage. Following the Purser's instructions, they located their cabin on an upper deck. Patrick oversaw the stowing of their personal valises, whilst Minette removed her hat and sank into a chair. Glancing round the cabin, she was surprised by its comfort and attractive décor. A far cry from the little steamer in which she had travelled from France!

An hour later, a loud-hailer message instructed those who were not travelling to leave the ship, followed by blasts from the vessel's siren indicating her imminent departure. In only minutes, with a rumbling of huge engines, the great ship inched away from the quayside to make her slow way to the open sea. She was escorted by a flotilla of little tug-boats, to ensure the ship negotiated her way out from the harbour in safety.

Preoccupied by their own private thoughts and emotions, Patrick and Minette stood apart by the stern rail. In silence they watched the misty land that was England gradually diminish, and then fade from sight.

The great liner sailed swiftly towards the east. Crossing the Bay of Biscay's notoriously rough seas, a large percentage of passengers took to their bunks, stricken with seasickness. Neither Patrick nor Minette suffered, but subsequent to mandatory confinement to the ship's interior during storms, they were glad to emerge once more into the fresh air on deck.

Progressing up the Suez Canal, Minette marvelled at the

Captain's expertise in manoeuvring the huge vessel along an almost impossibly narrow waterway. On either side, caravans of camels undulated along sandy banks, Bedouin riders perched on their humps. Clad in voluminous garments and seemingly oblivious of the intense heat, they easily rode the swaying gait of the animals.

Halfway along the canal, the ship slowed and then halted. From nowhere, scores of tiny "bum-boats" swarmed around the ship. Tradesmen manning them shouted out the desirability of their differing wares, interspersed by curses as they fought for position beside the liner.

Passengers began to appear at the ship's railings, intrigued to see members of the crew throwing down rope ladders to the boats. Jostling one another, the tradesmen clambered up the ladders to the deck, and set about arranging their goods with a speed indicative of much practice in the exercise.

One trader sported a monkey on his shoulder. Clad in a scarlet bolero and tasselled hat, the tiny creature held out a wizened hand, begging for *baksheesh* from his delighted audience. He would then drop the coins into a bowl held by his master. Another individual performed "magic" tricks with blown eggshells and half a dozen fluffy yellow chicks. Luxurious carpets in brilliant jewel colours were unrolled, and people exhorted to buy trinkets purporting to be antique.

All too soon, it was time for the ship to resume her journey. A shrill blast from the siren signalled the traders' immediate return to their vessels. With a speed equal to their arrival, they collected up their possessions, and vanished over the railings to their boats bobbing in the waters below. Wasting no time, they pulled away from the liner and made for the shore.

Anchor chains rumbled and clanked, engines surged, and the ship continued on her way along the canal. Eventually reaching open sea, the liner began her long traverse across the seemingly endless expanse of the Indian Ocean.

The climate changed radically with the miles, a blazing sun beating down on those daring to venture out on deck. Brought up in southern France, Minette had learned from an early age to be judicious about exposing herself to damaging rays. Nevertheless, she acquired a warm, if unfashionable tan to her skin bringing out the vividness of her blue eyes.

Gentlemen noticing the young Frenchwoman taking her habitual early morning walk round the decks, secretly admired her unusual colouring. Their ladies, however, huddled under canvas or covered decking, were openly horrified that Mrs O'Hara should allow herself to become so... well, *ugly!*

Minette saw little of her husband during these days at sea. Patrick spent much of his time with the ship's doctor in his cabin. A man in his sixties, who told Patrick he had only taken this last job as he was on the verge of retirement. Most of his earlier years had been spent in the Indian Army, and he had seen enough blood and gore to last him a lifetime.

In his personal view, most Indians did not care for the British presence. Resentment manifested itself on occasion in butchery of the white overlords who had taken over their country. Uprisings were quashed with equal violence—but a simmering hostility remained. Disturbed by the memory, the good doctor fetched two glasses and a bottle of whisky from his cupboard.

Patrick listened silently. This aspect of the British Army was not at all what he had learned during his training at Aldershot! If he had thought about what to expect as an army doctor in India, he supposed it had been a vague idea about general care for army personnel and their families. Dealing with horrific battle wounds simply had not occurred to him. It was a grim prospect.

Minette was pleased when a lady travelling on her own asked if she might accompany her on her morning walk. Sally Walters was on her way to rejoin her husband, a civil servant in Calcutta, the capital of India. She was a fount of information about life in India, and the young Frenchwoman absorbed a great deal about daily life for the expatriate.

During their conversations, Minette heard about the *caste* system prevalent in Indian society. Even more rigorous than the class system in Europe, it was why the employment of several servants in a household became obligatory. Individuals would only perform tasks specific to their caste. It was important never to challenge it, Sally warned.

Minette also learned simple Hindi words to enable her to communicate with her servants. The most important person was the *bearer*, whose principal duties were to care for a husband's clothes, and to wait at table. An *ayah* would look after the lady's wardrobe and care for the children. Another *ayah* of lesser importance would attend to the family's washing. Sheets and towels were sent out to a *dhobi* who would return them sparkling white. A *mali* looked after the garden.

The remainder of the voyage passed uneventfully, with no further violent storms to contend with. Approaching the Indian continent, the heat intensified and Minette noticed the crew's uniforms changed from navy to the cooler tropical whites.

With regret, she and Sally were forced to confine their morning walk to the covered deck areas, the heat from a blazing sun becoming intolerable. It wasn't long before they abandoned even that, being obliged to dodge perspiring nannies, prams, and fractious children!

Uncomfortable with her rapidly increasing girth, Minette took two showers a day in an effort to refresh her hot and sticky body. Water for showering was necessarily seawater, and she made the dismaying discovery that the simple act of soaping herself was next to impossible. It also resulted in her skin feeling chapped and sore, adding to the discomfort of her condition.

Liking the pleasant young French woman, Minette's steward took pity on her plight, secretly passing her a small pail of fresh water for a final rinse. In days, her roughened skin recovered its elasticity, and Minette was everlastingly grateful for the steward's kindness.

Resting on her bunk one hot afternoon, a fascinated Minette watched her stomach shift and change shape under its own volition. What began as feather-light nudging, over subsequent weeks the baby she carried became a great deal more active. In particular, it seemed to enjoy keeping its mother awake at night—she thought ruefully.

She would have liked to point out the baby's antics to her husband, but she rarely saw him during the day. Neither was Patrick there when she retired for the night, and he frequently did not return to the cabin at all. He offered no explanation, and she asked for none, fearing angry accusations of spying or unwarranted interrogation.

Suddenly, the door to the cabin opened, and Patrick entered, his gaze sweeping the girl lying on the bunk. Pushing herself awkwardly up on an elbow, Minette reached for the sheet to pull over her swollen body.

"Darling, such a surprise to see you at this time," the girl tried to smile. "I've just been watching my stomach move all by itself … would you like to see?"

"No thank you!" Patrick retorted. "And must you lie like that, Minette? You begin to look like a beached whale. I sometimes wonder what happened to the attractive slender girl I married?"

Minette blanched, dragging the sheet up to her chest. "Patrick, why must you be so unkind? In case you have forgotten, it happens to be your child I am carrying."

"As if I could forget. I don't care to see you in this condition, that's all."

"Well, it's not through choice, besides being damned uncomfortable!" the girl snapped, her patience exhausted. "So don't look."

Patrick walked over to the table beside his bunk, and picked up a book. "I only came to fetch this, as John Holmes, the ship's doctor, would like to read it. Seeing as you are so ill-tempered, I'll make myself scarce."

"What do you expect, Patrick O'Hara, when you make such *beastly* personal remarks … " Minette's voice trailed to a halt, for her husband had gone.

Agitated and tearful, the girl tried to reassure herself that Patrick's hostile attitude would change when he saw his own child for the first time. And she should be grateful there had been no sign of that dreadful whisky drinking, although she thought to have smelled it on his breath just now.

The weeks of her voyage almost at an end, the liner steamed into Bombay's wide harbour, dropping anchor some distance from the jetty. An announcement by loud-hailer was made to inform passengers they would be ferried to shore by small transport boats.

Standing by the rails to watch the ship's advance into the harbour, Minette's nostrils were assailed by a pungent, and very unpleasant stench. Gasping, she attempted to breathe through her mouth, wondering what on earth was the source of the awful smell. She would later learn it was particular to the waters in Bombay.

The harbour was alive with vessels of all shapes and sizes, manned by dark-skinned people going about their work. Some paused to watch passengers from the newly arrived liner stagger down a swaying gangway to a ferry bobbing unsteadily on the dark green waters below.

Hanging on for dear life to her husband's arm, Minette negotiated her way down to a waiting ferry, and thankfully sat down on one of the wooden benches. Pushing away from the ship, the small boat set off towards a flight of steps leading up to the jetty.

The ferry arrived at the foot of well-worn, rather slimy stone steps, and Minette took care climbing up to the quayside. Dry land—she thought joyfully—for the first time in weeks on end!

"Good morning, sir!" An officer in uniform marched up and saluted Patrick. "Doctor O'Hara, I believe? Lieutenant Crossley-Montague at your service."

"Thank you." Patrick nodded. "I wonder if you would mind helping my wife with her hand luggage? I must check on what is happening with the horses."

"No need, sir," the officer assured Patrick. "Two grooms have been sent down from Lucknow to help your fellows on board ship." He turned to Minette with a smile. "May I help you with your valises, Ma'am?"

"Thank you, Lieutenant, it's very kind … *oh!*" Minette staggered and almost fell, the ground appearing to heave beneath her feet. "God, it's happening again!"

The officer grinned. "Don't be concerned, Ma'am! You probably feel a trifle unsteady as the middle ear is out of kilter. It's on account of having been at sea for so long. Don't worry, it will right itself very quickly."

"I've arranged transport to the army bungalow," he now addressed Patrick. "You and Mrs O'Hara will be spending a couple of days there, to acclimatise and recover from your journey."

Patrick and Minette followed their guide threading his way through a forest of rickety food stands, some of which sported dried fish hanging in festoons. Shallow wicker baskets were heaped with exotic-looking fruit and vegetables. Vendors squatted in groups to watch the world go by, the air around them redolent with the aromatic smoke of *beedies*.

The transport turned out to be two covered carriages drawn by sturdy ponies that were patiently waiting in the inadequate shade of a nearby tree. Minette climbed into one, relieved to have the opportunity of sitting down again. Patrick stowed overnight valises into the baggage space, before joining his wife.

The lieutenant informed Patrick that he and the two Lucknow grooms would remain at the docks to supervise the unloading of the horses and tackle. They would also locate the bulk of the luggage for transport to the station *godown*, ready to be loaded on the train to Lucknow.

Closing the carriage door, the lieutenant leaned into the open window. "I'm sure you will be very comfortable at the army bungalow in Breach Candy," he assured the couple. "It's cool, and the servants are top notch!" With a smile, he stood back to watch the vehicle depart.

To Minette's heartfelt relief, the stench from the docks diminished noticeably as the carriage bowled down the road along the sea front. By the time they turned off to clatter along a cobbled tree-lined avenue, it had all but dissipated.

Moments later, the carriage turned in through wrought iron gates and headed up a short drive. It pulled up outside a low sprawling building encircled by a covered veranda, its wooden railings entwined with boughs of purple wisteria.

At once a dignified manservant emerged to greet the visitors. Smartly attired in spotless white livery, he wore a scarlet and gold brocade cummerbund about his waist. The traditional *pugri* of white muslin adorned his head, into which was tucked a flash of the same brocade.

Dredging up Sally Walters' informative lectures, Minette guessed this to be the *bearer* ... and what a magnificent personage he was!

"*Salaam, Sahib, Memsahib*," murmured the manservant with a courteous bow, his eyes lowered and the palms of his hands together in greeting. "Welcome to Bombay-side!" Turning, he led the way into the dim interior of the bungalow.

Patrick and Minette were ushered into a covered veranda

equipped with rattan armchairs and a low table. After the stifling heat in the carriage, the atmosphere in the veranda was pleasantly cool, protected from the sun's glare by white-painted bamboo blinds known as chicks.

With another dignified bow, the manservant disappeared silently on bare feet. Moments later, he returned carrying a jug of iced *nimbu pani*, the most delicious fresh lemonade Minette had ever tasted. After downing a tall glassful, Patrick went to identify the pieces of baggage they would require over the following two days.

Left on her own, Minette got up and wandered down the veranda's wide steps into an immaculate garden. The air was filled by an unknown exotic scent, which so intrigued the young woman that she wanted to discover the source. In a nearby flower bed, a skinny old man whose skin was burned black after years of working under a blazing sun, was deadheading scarlet cannas lilies.

Seeing Minette approach, the old gardener straightened to bestow a toothless grin. Placing his palms together, he greeted her politely. "*Namaste Memsahib!*"

"*Namaste* ... er ... *mali*," Minette replied, hoping her Hindi was correct. The old man qualified her response by delightedly wagging his head from side to side in acknowledgement. Walking over to a bush heavy with large white flowers, he snipped off one of the waxy blooms with a short knife and presented it to the young woman.

Accepting the offering with a smile, Minette bent her head to smell the flower in her hand. To her delight, it possessed the very scent she had hoped to identify.

"*Frangipani!*" said the old gardener with another toothless grin.

The next two days proved extremely trying for Minette. Hot and uncomfortable, her bulky body preventing sleeping the night through, further misery was in store when her skin exploded in tiny blisters. Minette recalled Sally Walters mentioning a condition known as prickly heat, which she supposed this was!

The constant irritation and itching nearly drove Minette to distraction, in particular when under claustrophobic folds of mosquito netting at night. In an effort to cool her burning skin, she stripped off traditional nightwear down to the bare minimum ... in disregard of her husband's clear disgust.

The *ayah*, a small Indian woman of indeterminate years, clucked in disapproval upon seeing the young woman's cracked and reddened skin. Producing a mixture of soured milk and herbs, she smeared generous quantities on the rash. The strange concoction alleviated much of the discomfort, to Minette's relief and gratitude. She wondered miserably if she would ever acclimatise to the ghastly Indian climate.

All too soon, it was time to resume their journey northwards to Lucknow. On the morning of their departure, Patrick and Minette rose at dawn to take advantage of the relative cool of early morning. Leaving Minette to finish her breakfast of papaya and lime, Patrick went to see to the baggage and check that none of their possessions had been left behind. The horses had already departed for the railway station, to be loaded into stalls on the train to Lucknow.

Before leaving the bungalow, Minette thanked the servants for their care, whilst Patrick handed the *bearer* a generous sum of money as a tip to be shared amongst the others. The dignified manservant smiled for the first time.

Taking a deep breath, Minette heaved herself into the carriage, unwilling to let Patrick see the effort it was costing her. Before she was able to sit down on the carriage seat, she was obliged to step over baskets piled high with fruit. On the seat opposite were boxes of various foodstuffs that would not spoil in the heat, and bottles of boiled water for the journey ahead.

Patrick joined Minette in the carriage, having first settled his account with the Army Quartermaster who had arrived at the bungalow with Lieutenant Crossley-Montague. The young lieutenant was anxious to complete his task of seeing the O'Haras safely on their way to Lucknow.

Bombay's Victoria Station was both vast and impressive. An immense array of windows, many of them stained glass, illuminated soaring arches that supported the roof area of the building. A thick pall of pungent *beedie* smoke hung in the atmosphere over the hordes of humanity scurrying in different directions.

Scrawny *coolies* bearing impossible loads on their heads, a valise under each arm, trailed after well-to-do passengers to earn a few coins. Stalls on all the platforms offered bowls of steaming curry and garishly coloured drinks to hungry passengers. Pie-dogs scavenged in rubbish bins both inside and out side the station, and the atmosphere was frenetic.

Keeping her balance with some difficulty amid the bustling throng, Minette stumbled and almost fell to her knees. Behind her, Lieutenant Crossley-Montague who had met them on arrival outside the station, now took it upon himself to support the distressed girl to the appropriate railway carriage.

Hiding his disapproval that Patrick O'Hara appeared indifferent to his wife's plight, the officer attempted to distract Minette. He pointed out an array of tin baths containing large blocks of ice, explaining that the ice would be loaded into the carriages. It was thought to be effective in cooling down the temperature inside.

But Minette had noticed.

Inwardly raging at the blatant discourtesy of her husband, she accepted the lieutenant's helping hand and climbed up the step into the carriage. Shuffling round the huge ice block in its tin bath, she sat down on the velveteen banquette. Flustered, Minette thanked the young officer for his kindness and consideration. The lieutenant smiled, bid her goodbye, and left the carriage.

Minette moved her skirts aside to examine her ankles, which felt unusually tight for some reason. Grimacing, she saw how swollen they had become in the rising temperature, doubtless contributing to her lack of balance. Miserably, she wondered how on earth she was to survive the hours of travel ahead in such claustrophobic heat.

With a sense of enormous relief, she noticed a distinct cooling sensation coming from the ice block on the carriage floor. So it did really work! Perhaps the journey ahead would be easier to bear after all.

Carriage doors banged shut, the guard waved his green flag, and the train driver sounded the engine's shrill whistle. Amid clouds of steam and much clanking of heavy metal wheels, the engine moved slowly forward along the tracks.

Looking out of the window, Minette saw a countryside crisscrossed by paddy fields of rice, where dark skinned workers bent double as they toiled ankle deep in water. Scrawny ponies hauling overloaded carts stumbled along dusty roads, their drivers wielding a lash to encourage the unfortunate animals to further effort.

Hordes of half-naked, skinny children of varying age scampered beside the slowly advancing train. Runny eyes and noses attracting clouds of flies, small children carrying the burden of an even younger child, outstretched hands begging for *baksheesh* in the hope that a few coins were tossed their way.

Horrified by the poverty, Minette turned away and closed her eyes. It had never occurred to her that people could live under such miserable conditions, dependent on what they could beg—or steal. Maybe one day, she could somehow help poor creatures such as these ...

Sitting opposite, Patrick O'Hara sighed, his eyes resting on the dozing girl, her bulky body slumped uncomfortably to one side. Despite his efforts to look on the brighter side of things, he was unable to shake off the resentment of being locked into a situation over which he had no control.

All the more galling was the undeniable fact that this banishment was entirely due to that damned baby Minette was carrying so joyfully. With a faint prickling of shame, Patrick knew he had been hoping the stress of travelling would induce a miscarriage. That would have resolved a major part of his dilemma. Minette, however, was made of sterner stuff, and had undertaken every stage of the irksome journey without complaint.

The weeks at sea had done nothing to improve his state of mind—forced to watch the lovely girl he had married turn into something gross and unattractive. Thank God for the ship's doctor, who had been more than generous with his bottles of scotch and a cask of good cognac! Just as well Minette had never suspected. She became entirely unreasonable should she notice him having an occasional drink to keep up his spirits. If she imagined he would allow her to dictate to him in future—she could think again.

Patrick's expression was grim. He had no doubt that with the arrival of her baby, Minette would be transformed into an obsessive mother-figure, ready to regale him with sickening details of its progress. Intolerable, when he recalled how much he had forfeited for her sake. He would ensure a nursemaid was employed from the start, that he might at least retain exclusive entitlement to his wife's company. Any objections from her, he would stamp on at once.

Minette awoke from her sleep two hours later, unaware of her husband's hostile reflections. Slightly more refreshed, she tried to talk to a monosyllabic Patrick, but soon gave it up and returned to reading her book. Frowning, she wondered what the reason could be this time for his surliness.

As the hours went by, Minette was conscious of her ankles beginning to swell once again. Dismayed, she noticed the ice block was in need of replacement, as the tin bath now contained a quantity of opaque water. Unable to wedge herself comfortably on the banquette, Minette wondered how much longer she would be able to endure the ordeal without dissolving into tears!

As if he had read her thoughts, their steward knocked at the door. Entering the carriage, he set about lowering full-sized bunks from their place of concealment, the mattresses already made up with spotless sheets and pillows.

Kicking off her now too-tight shoes, Minette staggered on puffy feet over to a bunk. Lying back, she stretched out her legs with a thankful sigh. She would ask that the bunk should remain down for the remainder of the journey. Half an hour later, the ice block was replaced during a brief halt at a station—to Minette's gratitude.

The seemingly endless journey came to an end as the train puffed its way into the station at Lucknow. A Sergeant from the cantonment was waiting to meet the O'Haras, who then set about locating their vast quantity of luggage. Three extra grooms had also come to assist those in charge of the horses, which by all accounts, had travelled very well.

A short carriage ride to the cantonment followed, and deposited on the pavement outside the doctor's residence, Minette saw her future home for the first time. The bungalow was a good size, encircled by well-tended flower beds filled with frangipani of differing shades, hibiscus, and scarlet cannas lilies. Prolific pink and purple wisteria wound its way up and over the railings of a covered veranda.

Entering the bungalow, Minette was impressed by the cleanliness of the interior, the work of servants Patrick was inheriting from his predecessor. Central to the house was a spacious living room, the four bedrooms leading off a corridor to the back of the house, where the kitchen and servants quarters were located.

Emotion swamped the tired young woman. Here she was at last in her very own home! She would create a comfortable haven for Patrick, to which he could look forward to returning after work. All the hideous dramas culminating in an ignominious flight from England must be firmly relegated to the past.

It was here, in this pleasant house, that the two of them would rekindle their love, and so find peace and happiness—of that Minette was sure.

CHAPTER SEVENTEEN

Ten days after her arrival in Lucknow, Minette was sitting at her desk writing a letter to her father. Although she had regularly written to him and to her beloved grandparents, she never received a reply to any of her letters. She must assume the Marquise was still ensuring her daughter was effectively cut off from the family. Despondent, Minette nevertheless resolved to continue writing in the hope that one or two might slip through her mother's net.

"Excuse me *Memsahib*." The *bearer* entered the sitting room on silent feet. "I am having one *ayah* coming to back door, she wanting work with *babas*."

"*Babas?*" Minette repeated, then her face cleared. "Ah, yes, children! I will need a nanny of sorts, so please send her in."

A tapping at the door announced the presence of a diminutive Indian woman who came forward with a shy smile. Eyeing Minette's substantial bump, she nodded, her eyes twinkling.

"Good morning, *Memsahib*! My name Mailie, and I am veree good with looking after *babas*! I also do everything for *Memsahib*."

Liking the little woman at once, Minette employed her on the spot. Throughout the years that followed, she had cause to thank God for giving way to that impulse. In passable English, Mailie explained she was originally from Tibet. Her old employer had returned to England, so she was free to start work at once.

Unlike most other Indian women Minette had seen, Mailie was dressed quite differently. A snowy white sari was wound about her waist, and then taken up over her head like a veil. She wore a blue cotton jacket with long sleeves and a tiny, rather feminine frill around each wrist. A fine chain was attached from her nostril to an ornate earring on the same side of her face.

Glancing at it, Minette winced, imagining how easily a baby could grasp the attractive jewellery … and pull! She said as much to Mailie, but the *ayah* dismissed her concerns with a flashing smile.

"Not to worrying, Memsahib! I be looking after many, many *babas*, and nobody hurting me yet!"

From the moment she was employed, Mailie took charge of her memsahib with authority and enthusiasm. Minette found herself cosseted in a manner she had never known, the little ayah anticipating her every need. Her existing wardrobe was washed and ironed back to its original freshness, her shoes cleaned to a brightness they had rarely seen. The young mother-to-be revelled in the attention.

With great diplomacy, the *ayah* advised Minette to have a few loose gowns made up. It would not only be cooler, but very much more comfortable during the final weeks of her pregnancy. Far more practical than sewing inserts into garments which were in any case unsuitable for the intense heat of the Lucknow climate.

No sooner had Minette assented to such an attractive suggestion, a *durzi* appeared at the bungalow. A chubby white-turbaned Sikh, he carried an ancient sewing machine under one arm, a tape measure round his neck, and a large bundle over a shoulder. With a wide smile, he bowed to Minette, his palms together in courteous greeting.

A lively argument ensued between the *durzi* and Mailie, transpiring to be an amicable discussion of the tailor's fees. "No *badmashi durzi* should try too much charging my *Memsahib!*" the *ayah* declared, giving the man a hard stare.

As time went by, it became clear that Mailie held sway over all the household servants. Even the dignified *bearer*—ostensibly the head servant—found it easier to give way over most issues. Amused, Minette noticed the other servants avoided confrontation with the little *ayah*, making sure their work merited no criticism!

Her domestic arrangements more on an even keel, Minette found there were certain aspects of Regimental social life she found irritating. In particular, the inverted sense of snobbery that seemed to exist among certain officers' wives. Assuming the mantle of their husbands' rank, these ladies believed it endowed them with the right to look down upon others as lesser mortals.

Exercising unusual self-control, Minette generally managed to keep her mouth shut and her opinions to herself. However, the occasion arrived when the Colonel's wife invited her for afternoon tea. Mrs Briggs-Gregory turned out to be a rather over-blown lady, possessed of a fine sense of her own importance.

Within minutes of her arrival, Minette was introduced to several of the lady's sycophantic friends—doubtless to cast an eye over the new doctor's wife—Minette cynically presumed. Judgement would then be passed as to whether the newcomer was worthy of being included in their elite clique.

"My dear Mrs O'Hara, welcome to our little society," the hostess grandly intoned, handing Minette a cup of tepid tea. "I thought to render you a service through introduction to a few ladies of note in our community. It will save you the embarrassment of rubbing shoulders with riffraff without realising it!"

"*Riff-raff?*" Minette repeated with raised eyebrows, concealing her irritation with an effort. "What is that? I'm French, you see, so please excuse my ignorance. Tell me, is this "riff-raff" a horrid disease to be avoided at all costs?"

"Disease?" The lady was clearly flustered over Minette's question. "Well no, it's just that one cannot be too careful about whom one associates, Mrs O'Hara. It's a question of good breeding together with an unblemished reputation."

Oblivious to Minette's not-so-subtle sarcasm, Mrs Briggs-Gregory warmed to her theme. "Dear lady, despite you being a French person, I imagine you will have come across the importance of high standards through association with your husband. Why, in England one simply doesn't acknowledge a member of the vulgar masses, let alone address such a person," she finished in a lofty tone.

A slow smile crept over Minette's face, her eyes glittering like chips of blue glass. "Despite me being French? Heavens, we are not entirely uncivilised in France, you know. To be frank, I was brought up to understand that people of a lesser class deserved to be shown common courtesy. It was emphasised that to do anything else would be considered vulgar arrogance."

Minette rose to her feet and faced her empurpled hostess. "I beg your pardon if it offends you, Ma'am, but I must beg leave to choose my own friends. Thank you for asking me to tea. Regretfully, I must take my leave of you as I begin to feel a trifle nauseous … perhaps due to my condition?"

Returning home, Minette reflected on the scene in the Briggs-Gregory sitting room. During the altercation between herself and the Colonel's lady, the other women had sat silently, agog, a forgotten cup of tea half way to their lips. She supposed she should not have lost her temper, but the pretentious woman had been damned rude! Minette shrugged. *Tant pis!*

That evening, Minette recounted the incident to her husband over dinner. She was astounded to note a heavy frown settling over Patrick's features as he listened to the sorry tale.

"For Christ's sake, Minette, we've only just arrived here, and you are already making enemies!" he exclaimed in obvious irritation.

"Don't you realise how close you came to insulting that woman … who just happens to be my Colonel's wife? Have you no sense? You cannot get away with bluntly speaking your mind in a close community such as this."

"You cannot seriously expect me to put up with that female's ignorant remarks about my being French … as though it's some ghastly affliction?" Minette angrily demanded. "Or that she should be free to dictate whom I may befriend, and whom I must ignore? The woman is vulgar and obsessed with her own importance."

"Frankly, it doesn't matter what you think she is," Patrick threw down his cutlery to glare at Minette. "She is the Colonel's lady, and you are obliged to respect that. I only hope she hasn't thought to inform her husband of your bad manners. Perhaps if you apologise—"

"*What?*" Minette got to her feet in fury. "Apologise to that imbecilic female? Creep on your belly to your Army Overlords and their beastly wives if you must. But don't expect me to do the same!" Flinging down her napkin, Minette stormed from the dining room.

Subsequent to the angry exchange with Patrick, Minette abandoned all efforts to socialise with most of the army wives. She spent an hour or two each day in the stables visiting the new mare she had named Fantastique. Unable to ride, she built up a relationship with the horse by spending a great deal of time in the loose box with her. She also liked to supervise the mare being exercised by one of the grooms during the relative cool of evening.

On occasion, Minette accompanied Mailie to the local *bazaar*, where a conglomeration of wares was on offer. Stacks of watering cans, cooking utensils and brooms were incongruously piled up next to bolts of beautiful material. Silks, richly embossed brocades, pretty cottons and cool muslin were set out attractively to tempt the shopper.

Bearing the *ayah's* earlier suggestion in mind, Minette purchased lengths of blue and white gingham, and pink and white pinstripe. The *durzi* would make up loose garments for her to wear around the house. Turning away with difficulty from the more glamorous materials, Minette also bought soft muslin to be sewn into square napkins for the coming baby.

The covered market where rather grander shops were located was next on Minette's agenda to explore. Goldsmiths and silversmiths huddled next to shops selling intricate ivory or aromatic sandalwood carvings. Jewellers were in abundance, their ornate creations of gold and precious stones displayed against a backdrop of black or scarlet velvet. Graded poles stretched upward, encircled by innumerable gold bangles sparkling expensively in the light of flickering lamps.

Never having seen anything like it in her life, Minette thoroughly enjoyed her excursions to the *bazaar*. It afforded a temporary distraction from the shadowy discord affecting her private life. Neither she nor Patrick had referred to the friction over her supposed discourtesy to the Colonel's wife, but it lay between them, precluding even the remotest form of intimacy.

The continuing chill in the atmosphere began dredging up disturbing memories and unanswered questions for the young woman. They seemed to lend credence to the otherwise inexplicable change in her husband's attitude towards her. Occasionally, Minette wondered how her life might have turned out if...

No! She would not allow her mind to dwell on useless supposition. Once the baby was born, she would be less tired, her body would regain its slenderness, and everything would change for the better.

It wasn't long before Minette was given to understand her enjoyable jaunts to the *bazaar* with Mailie were the subject of heavy criticism by the female hierarchy. A handful of well-meaning ladies attempted to let Minette know—warnings she chose to ignore. However, it came to a head one morning on her way home from a trip to the *bazaar*. Minette was dismayed to find herself confronted by none other than Mrs Briggs-Gregory—spokeswoman-elect.

"Mrs O'Hara, most reluctantly I am taking it upon myself to warn you about over-familiarity with servants," the lady began with all due pomposity. "You are seen laughing and conversing with your *ayah*, just as though you considered her your equal. I'm afraid it simply will not do, Mrs O'Hara! Especially in your condition, such behaviour cannot … "

"Just a moment, Mrs Briggs-Gregory," Minette interrupted the flow, holding her rising temper in check. "Please understand I do not care to be spied upon by busy-bodies who obviously have too little to occupy them. I am more than capable of deciding for myself with whom I wish to associate. I thought to have already made myself clear on this point?"

"Spied upon? My dear Mrs O'Hara, what a very unpleasant term to use with regard to well-meaning advice! It was intended for your own good. In the event that you choose to ignore my warning, I shall have no option but to report the matter to my husband. The Colonel is very conscious of maintaining standards in our society, and I am sure he will be interested in what *your* husband has to say."

Minette stared silently at the woman, whose expression was that of a satisfied, over-fed cat. She was acutely aware that Patrick would react badly to being hauled over the coals by his Colonel on account of his wife's behaviour. But how in God's name could she allow this frightful woman the satisfaction of dictating how she should lead her life?

"Mrs Briggs-Gregory, naturally I shall bear your advice in mind," Minette prevaricated. "But please do not threaten me as if I were a naughty child. I find it very upsetting, and my doctor is against me being exposed to undue stress … bad for the baby, as I'm sure you will understand."

The older woman took a step backward, finding herself

unexpectedly at a disadvantage. "I most certainly do not intend to upset you, my dear ... nor do I wish to endanger your infant. My advice was meant only for your personal edification."

"I understand," Minette raised a weary hand to her temple. "Would you be so kind as to excuse me, Mrs Briggs-Gregory? I'm feeling a trifle faint, so I had better go straight home. I bid you good-day."

Once out of the Colonel's wife's sight, Minette's pace increased, her face flushed with anger. She would do exactly as she wished, and those who didn't like it could go to hell ... including her bloody husband!

Sitting on her veranda, sipping a cool drink, Minette's fury began to subside. It simply wasn't worth triggering another hideous row between herself and Patrick over her perceived conduct. The last occasion still rankled.

Perhaps it would be wiser to stop the excursions to the *bazaar*. In any event, her increasing girth made the effort of walking in the heat quite exhausting. That should satisfy those snooping females who pretended shock over the doctor's wife hobnobbing with her *ayah*— thought the disgruntled young woman.

Over the next few weeks, a bored Minette chafed against her increasingly restrictive lifestyle. She was also lonely, for Patrick had taken to visiting the Officers' Mess after work almost every evening, missing dinner with his wife, and often remaining there until the early hours.

Sometimes Minette's mind would wander back to her childhood home in France. Would her father ever forgive her transgressions? She still had no word from him, or from her beloved grandparents. Trying to avoid painful brooding, Minette began writing at length in her Journal. She wrote in retrospect, always frankly, revealing her innermost thoughts from the days of her childhood. The exercise proved cathartic, and she felt more at peace with herself whilst she waited for the arrival of her child.

Early one morning, Minette was seated in the veranda, breakfasting on her usual slice of papaya and lime. Leaning forward to brush away a tiresome fly, she froze, conscious of a sudden gush of liquid from between her legs soaking the chair cushion beneath her.

"Mailie!" Minette called, apprehensive of what was to come. "Come quickly, I think the baby might be on the way!"

Without delay, Mailie sent off the hovering bearer with a message for the midwife to come as quickly as possible. He was also to go to the hospital to give doctor-sahib the news. Turning back to the shocked girl, the *ayah* gently steered her back to the bedroom. Settling Minette on the bed, she propped her up as comfortably as possible with several pillows.

"Armee laydee helping memsahibs to be having *babas*, she now coming quicklee," the little *ayah* told her as she bustled about, fetching clean linen and boiling up water. "Soon-soon, *Memsahib* have *baba* in her arms!"

Mrs Symes, the army midwife, arrived at the bungalow within the hour and took the situation in hand. Her competent presence was reassuring to the young woman as her labour inexorably progressed over the next hours.

"Come now, young Missis ... one more big push and it'll all be over!" exhorted the midwife to the sweat-soaked girl on the bed. It had not been a difficult delivery, but it was now nearing the middle of the day. The increasing temperature was not only wearing for the midwife, but it was unbearable for an exhausted Minette.

Resting a moment, she brushed tendrils of damp hair back from her face. Then taking a deep breath, she clenched her teeth and heaved with all of her remaining strength. Her mighty effort was rewarded by the baby's rapid arrival into the world ... a boy! Held up by his feet, he received a smart smack on his little bottom from Mrs Symes. With a gasp of outrage, the infant released a piercing howl.

Exhaustion forgotten, Minette propped herself on an elbow to inspect her new son. Bald, except for a damp fringe of auburn fluff encircling his head, the baby had been spared the newborn's wrinkled skin—thanks to his late arrival. Having stopped howling, he now attempted to ram a tiny fist into his mouth.

"Ee's a luvly li'll lad, int'ee!" Mrs Symes stood back with a smile. "An' ah kin see 'ee won't be givin' yer strife wiv 'is feedin'! Look at 'im wantin' 'is grub oready! Better put 'im to the breast, m'dear ... he needs 'is colostrum. Yer milk prob'ly won't be cumin in b'fore termorrer."

The midwife moved forward to show the new mother how to place the baby in the correct feeding position. But Minette had forestalled her, for the infant was resting on a pillow close to her breast and nuzzling the soft flesh. Fastening his mouth over the nipple, he began to suck with enthusiasm.

"Thank you so much for all your help, Mrs Symes." Minette laughed at the puzzled expression on the midwife's face. "I used to help out in the maternity ward of a cottage hospital in England," she explained. "I'm sure it will be an advantage in coping with my own baby."

"Ah'm sure it will," The midwife agreed with a grin. "An' if yer don' mind ma sayin' so, yer looks far too young to be a muvver, Missis. Jes' comin' out'v a schoolroom, more like!"

Minette smiled pleasantly, knowing the woman meant well. She wondered if Patrick had come home from the hospital, and asked the departing midwife to send in her ayah.

"*Memsahib?*" Mailie peeped round the door. "Can I come see new *baba?*"

"Of course you may! Is my husband home yet?"

"Not yet, *mem*." Mailie avoided Minette's gaze. "Mebbe him veree busy in hospital, but him coming soon-soon to see new *baba!*"

Patrick did not return until after eight o'clock that evening. Swallowing intense disappointment, Minette managed to smile at her husband standing in the doorway of the bedroom.

"Darling, come and meet our baby son," she beamed down at the sleeping infant at her side. "Isn't he utterly gorgeous?"

"Hmm, only a doting mother could call *that* gorgeous, for God's sake," Patrick exclaimed, his tone disparaging. "Healthy perhaps, but newborns can hardly be classified as "gorgeous."

In her highly emotional state, Minette could not prevent tears from rolling down her cheeks. She was already upset that Patrick hadn't bothered to return earlier in the day. But this unvarnished meanness was the final straw.

"Er ... didn't mean to upset you, sweetie." Too late, Patrick realised he had overstepped the mark. "Just a joke, um ... he looks a lusty enough fellow. Hope he didn't give you too much trouble coming into this world of ours?"

"It was worth it … to me, anyway, and I shall call him James." Minette kissed the top of her baby's head. Devastated by Patrick's disinterest in the baby, she decided it would be in her interests to suppress it. Perhaps James would become more interesting to his father when he was a little older?

Shortly after James' birth, Minette settled into a pleasant routine of riding her mare each morning, accompanied by one of the grooms. Having fed her baby and handed him over to Mailie, she made her way to the stables before sun-up whilst the temperature was still relatively cool.

After months of forced inactivity, Minette revelled in her relationship with the mare. Nick-named "Fanny" by the groom looking after her, the diminutive was immediately adopted by her mistress. Cantering along misty hedgerows outside the cantonment, Minette re-discovered a half-forgotten sense of freedom.

Mailie proved to be a god-send, unobtrusively taking over the baby's care should Patrick come home before he was put down for the night. Despite this measure, should he come upon Minette with the baby in her arms, he would retreat into glowering silence with a glass of whisky.

As time went by, the happy illusion Minette was nurturing that Patrick would come to terms with the baby's existence gradually faded. To the contrary, he seemed to view him with increasing hostility. The strain of coping with the situation stretched the young mother's nerves to breaking point.

As the months passed, little James became less willing to be carted off to the nursery when his father happened to be in the house. The child was carried off kicking and screaming, Patrick would bellow with rage and storm out of the house, slamming the front door behind him.

Subsequently, it became the favoured excuse for Patrick to prolong his sessions in the Officers' Mess. There he could drink in the congenial company of fellow officers … without the irritation of reproachful looks from his wife. Maybe play cards in peace—well away from the screams of that revolting little termagant!

At her wits end, Minette was desperate to claw Patrick back from the attractions of the Officers' Mess. She resolved to make a determined effort to share her husband's interests, and lose more of the weight she had gained during pregnancy. She would also take care not let her husband see her with James. Closing her mind to the inevitable deprivation of her baby boy, Minette set out on a strict *régime* of diet and exercise.

In only a few weeks, Patrick noticed his wife's figure had returned to its former glory, and her engaging personality restored. Best of all, she no longer inflicted the brat on him, nor did she regale him with dull anecdotes of its progress. It seemed to live with the *ayah* these days—well out of his sight, thank Christ!

For the young mother, however, the neglect of her baby was a high price to pay in order to regain a modicum of attention from her husband. In the privacy of her bedroom she wept bitter tears, and tried to bolster her resolve by telling herself how very necessary it was.

Not merely for keeping the peace, but to discourage her husband from excessive drinking sessions. Worse still, there was the danger of him joining others in visiting whore-houses in the district. God alone knew what filthy diseases he might bring home.

For his part, Patrick was pleased to have his attractive wife's undivided attention. He enjoyed intercepting envious looks directed at her from fellow officers, her looks and vivacious personality overshadowing most other women on social occasions.

His pleasure was transient, however, in no way offsetting his loathing of India in general. Dealing with horrors brought back to the cantonment in carts from battlefields, there were times he felt his existence to be perpetually filled with screams of hardened soldiers going under the knife. And far too often with little hope of recovery. Dreadful wounds, suppurating due to unavoidable neglect resisted efforts to control infection, the stench of putrefaction remaining in Patrick's nostrils long afterwards.

Filled with terrible despair, it unleashed a suppressed longing in the young doctor to return to civilisation. At least there he could take up a career of medical research in the blessed quiet of a laboratory. He would leave this God-forsaken part of the world to those who were better able to adapt to it than he.

Cold reality would then hit Patrick like a bucket of ice-cold water. Such a dream was hopelessly out of the question. A return to the western world could result in facing prosecution—even a jail sentence.

The reason? His wife, and that blasted brat of hers.

Hefty doses of whisky helped dull Patrick's disillusionment. In the beginning it was after he had finished work at the hospital for the day. Slowly, insidiously, the drinking extended until late at night, and even into the early hours of the morning. Patrick had struggled with insomnia since his arrival in Lucknow. In a desperate attempt to promote sleep, he persuaded himself that whisky was the answer. In which case he could blot out the awfulness of his day, if only for a few hours.

It was not long before Patrick felt the need for a stiff whisky to face his day with the maimed and the dying. Assuring himself that a tot of alcohol would not affect the precision of his work, one whisky became two.

CHAPTER EIGHTEEN

Unaware of the nature of her husband's private hell, Minette made the dismaying discovery that she was pregnant once again. Riding each morning and busy with the running of her home, she had failed to notice the absence of her monthly period. It was not certain, but she suspected that she must be three, possibly four months into her pregnancy.

Minette ground her teeth with frustration. It was only a few months since James' birth. Not long enough to dispel the constraints and discomfort of pregnancy from her mind! Not to mention the pleasure of wearing normal-sized clothes after months of voluminous "tents."

With a jolt, the young woman recalled she had agreed to compete in a Point-to-Point in Darjeeling, due to take place in only a few weeks time. Patrick had shown an interest in her decision to race, so a withdrawal would invite immediate and unpleasant recrimination.

Minette was already riddled with guilt to be neglecting her small son in order to please her husband. The announcement of another infant on the way was certain to provoke a hellish row. And that was more than she could bear to contemplate.

Against her better judgement, Minette decided to go ahead with plans to ride in the Point-to-Point. Dismissing a feeling that it was irresponsible to a degree, she reasoned the risk was negligible—she being an experienced rider. Yes, she would ride in the damned race, and nobody would be any the wiser.

Meanwhile, little James was growing into a miniature version of his father. His head was a mass of burnished curls, the identical colour of his father's hair. Not yet two years old, a wilful child, he yelled with fury if thwarted or was deprived of something he wanted.

Should Patrick be at home during one of his tantrums, he would bellow at the child. Howling in genuine fright, James scuttled to his hovering ayah as fast as his chubby legs would carry him. The situation was fast becoming a vicious circle over which Minette felt she had little control. She watched from the sidelines in a quandary of helplessness, knowing Patrick hated to see her handling the child.

Galling though it was, Minette recognised the inevitability of her small son becoming firmly attached to Mailie. James obviously associated the *ayah* with emotional security—instead of his mother who always seemed anxious to send him away. A high price to pay for pleasing her husband. Was it worth it? Minette's lips tightened. Probably not, but it was not her immediate concern.

Minette turned her mind to Patrick's increasing dependency on alcohol. Not long ago, she had unwisely commented on substantial quantities of whisky being delivered to the house. Not to mention empty bottles taken away by the score. Patrick's reaction had been explosive.

"Will you stop your constant bloody nagging?" he had snarled. "I've told you repeatedly how a snifter or two helps me to sleep at night. There's nothing wrong in that, for Christ's sake!"

"It's not only what you drink at home," Minette had struggled to keep her tone neutral. "But together with the quantities you get through at the Officers' Mess every evening—that *is* a lot of whisky."

"Oh, I see. Burning with resentment because I choose to relax for an hour or two after work with fellow officers? My God ... you really do take the biscuit."

"Patrick, as I recall we planned to spend pleasant evenings together!" snapped the young woman, annoyed by her husband's aggressive stance. "It is difficult for me to accept that you prefer the company of your friends in that smoke-filled den."

"What is there for me to come home to, might I ask? Whining, if I so much as ask the bearer for a tot of scotch ... "

"You have a little boy who needs his father!" Minette's patience cracked. "He's afraid of you—can't you see that? If you would only spend time with James, it would make such a difference."

"I don't give a damn about seeing anything of that snivelling brat!" Patrick had retorted furiously. "At least by coming home late, I am spared his tedious tantrums."

Minette sighed. These outbursts of temper were becoming more frequent every day, more often than not triggered by inconsequential events. Sometimes it was against the perceived inadequacies of senior officers—or a servant was bellowed at over a minor infringement. Nowadays, her husband seemed to take exception to the expression on her face. It was unwise to mention James at all.

It had also become obvious Patrick wanted little to do with the running of the house. Even the stately *bearer* wearied of waiting for sahib's daily orders, and now came to Minette for consultation each morning. A further aggravation was that she had to beg for money to pay the servants ... invariably in arrears.

Patrick's irritable claim for this abdication of responsibility was lack of time, due to many hours spent at the hospital. Then there were minor skirmishes when he was sent out as Medical Officer, allowing even less time to deal with mundane matters at home. Money was tight—Patrick declared—so Minette must find a way of coping. God knows, she had little else to do.

Yet you still manage to spend money swigging countless glasses of whisky in that damned Mess—thought Minette resentfully. And if money is tight, it is hardly surprising since you gamble away chunks of your salary playing cards. But to keep the peace, she thought it better to refrain from comment.

One hot afternoon, Minette was sitting in the veranda with a cool drink. A sleepy boy sat in a corner, operating the *punkah* with a string tied to his big toe. She had been reading a book, but now it lay forgotten in her lap.

Time had flown by, and the date for the Darjeeling Point-to-Point was only days away. Earlier in the pregnancy, Minette's decision to go ahead and compete had seemed simple. But now it was a different story. Her breasts were tender, and she had even felt the unborn infant's first fluttering of life. Time to make a final decision!

The embattled young woman vacillated this way and that. Should she weather the storm a withdrawal from the race would provoke? Or should she follow through with her plan to ride in the race, but avoid foolish risks? The last really did seem the easier option.

Sighing, Minette rose from her chair and went to see if James had awakened from his nap, a new toy in her hand. She was uncomfortably aware she often over-compensated the child for his father's animosity … and her own neglect.

Today's gift was to assuage guilty feelings about leaving him at home with his *ayah* in Lucknow. The trip to Darjeeling would be disruptive to the toddler, who would undoubtedly scream and enrage his father. He would be happier at home, and Minette knew Mailie would protect James with her life.

Patrick and Minette left for Darjeeling two days before the Point-to-Point race. The hill station was situated in the lower reaches of the Himalayas, but sufficiently high up the mountain to necessitate a mountain train. Hauling its burden of narrow carriages and running on a single rail, the sturdy little engine huffed and puffed its way up steep slopes and round sharp bends with ease.

Looking out of the window, Minette was amazed to see wild flowers growing prolifically on either side of the track. Chugging through curtains of overhanging foliage, everything seemed green and lush as that of the English countryside in springtime. As they climbed higher and higher up the mountain, a significant drop in air temperature became noticeable, in pleasant contrast to the dust and heat of the plains far below.

Upon arrival at their hotel, the travel-weary young woman went directly up to the bedroom. Kicking off her shoes, she lay back against a heap of pillows on the bed with a thankful sigh. What beggared belief was that Patrick had already abandoned her for the hotel bar. His throwaway line was that he was in need of a restorative drink after such a gruelling journey.

Tcha! Minette's lips twisted in self-mockery. To think she had been hoping this trip away together would go some way towards refreshing their relationship. Sad to say, the call of the whisky bottle had been too strong. Closing her eyes, she drifted into a dreamless sleep.

An hour later, Minette awoke, refreshed and filled with unusual energy. She was alone in the room, so it must be assumed Patrick was still ensconced in the hotel bar. Unwilling to wait about on the off chance her husband might appear, Minette washed and changed into fresh clothes. She would locate the stabling, and identify the horse she would ride in three days time.

The stables were easy to find, being only a short distance from the hotel. In the empty Stable Office, Minette discovered a list of entries tacked to a notice board. Running a finger down the list, she found her own name alongside that of her mount—Turka. An odd name, she thought, making a note of the owner's name in brackets after it.

Leaving the Office, Minette wandered down the line of horses standing in narrow stalls, the name and age of the animal roughly chalked on a board beside each one. At the very end of the stabling, Minette found her horse—a small bay Arabian stallion, only three years old. Its head was twisted up at an unnatural angle by a ridiculously short length of rope attached to a ring in the wall. Why, the poor creature was unable to eat or even drink, Minette realised in horror.

Speaking softly, Minette stroked the horse's sweating neck. Unused to kindness, the animal jerked away from her hand, eyes rolling in fear. Saddened but unafraid, Minette continued to move her fingers gently under the cringing creature's chin.

Enraged that this poor abused animal should fail to recognise a caress, Minette was pragmatic enough to realise she would be unable to undo this kind of damage to a horse's psyche in days. What she could do, however, was to ensure the animal was properly fed and watered during her association with it. One could only hope he would accept her as a rider without too much drama. Filling a nearby bucket with water, Minette also loosened the rope tying the horse's head to the wall. Bending his head, he drank thirstily until the bucket was empty.

After refilling the bucket, Minette went in search of the owner, who turned out to be a Sikh gentleman. Obviously wealthy, he was all flashing white teeth and quantities of gold jewellery. Delighted to have such an attractive lady delegated to ride his horse, the owner was ready to provide Minette with information about the animal's origins.

"This *ghora* veree good, much money from Afghanistan, Madam!" the man enthused. "He jumping nicely big, big, fence. But I am telling you, Madam, he sometime be veree *badmash!*"

The gentleman looked askance at Minette's slight figure, privately wondering if she was capable of controlling his notoriously unmanageable animal. "He needing big beating before running nicely."

"Don't worry, Mr Shah, I have ridden naughty horses all my life," Minette managed to conceal her anger over the man's gratuitous advice. "I'm sure Turka and I will get on very well."

Back at the hotel, Minette asked the manager for some raw carrots sliced lengthways. Bemused, the man complied and the young woman set off once more for the stables with her booty.

Turka had drunk most of the second bucket of water. Taking a slice of carrot from the paper bag, she offered it to the little horse. His ears flattening, he jerked against his rope, baring his teeth aggressively ... but the hand holding the carrot did not waver. Puzzled, the horse stretched out his nose to investigate. After a long hesitation, Minette felt velvet lips move against the palm of her hand as Turka accepted her offering. The rest of the carrots vanished without further ado.

Returning to the Stable Office, Minette delivered a few basic instructions to the manager regarding the horse's feed and general care. She also mentioned her horror about how the *syce* had left the horse to suffer. To ensure his cooperation, Minette pressed a generous sum of rupees into the man's willing hand. Satisfied that she had done all she could, Minette hurried back to the hotel. Patrick was probably wondering where she was.

Patrick was still conspicuous by his absence.

After a lonely dinner that evening, Minette returned to the stabling. It was still light outside, so it would be as well to check her instructions had been carried out. Turka now stood in a deep bed of straw, and his rope was sufficiently long to allow him to eat from a manger filled with feed. His bucket had also been replenished with fresh water.

Stroking the horse's neck, Minette was rewarded by a soft nicker—barely audible, but a compliment nevertheless. Pleased that a fragile bond seemed to be forming between them, the young woman felt a glimmer of hope. She made up her mind the little horse should not be returned to a cruel fate after the race. In fact, she would ask Patrick to buy Turka for her.

Her mouth stretching in a cynical smile, Minette reflected her absentee husband would be suffering from guilt having abandoned her for an entire day. Excellent! She intended to profit from that!.

The following morning, the young woman awoke to find Patrick snoring on the other bed—still in his clothes. The room smelled rank, and wrinkling her nose in disgust Minette hastened to open a window. Leaning out to breathe in fresh air, she glanced back at her unconscious husband, glad of his inebriated condition for once. It made her mission to purchase Turka that much easier to achieve.

Dressed in riding clothes, Minette set off for the stables. She found Turka's *syce* loitering in front of his stall, his expression sullen. The man was still burning with resentment over the Stable Manager's bellowed orders that the horse was fed, watered, and bedded down correctly. And Minette's directive to make himself scarce whilst she tacked up the horse did nothing to improve his humour.

"*Memsahib*, this *ghora* is veree badlee temper! *Bhot badmash* … even for brushings. I touching feets onlee after good beatings! *Kabadarh, Memsahib!*"

Minette's lips tightened, guessing this individual was responsible for the horse's misery of the previous day. Ignoring his annoying bluster, she entered the stall and placed a hand on Turka's neck. He turned towards her, ears pricked engagingly.

Astounded, the *syce* stepped forward to see what the crazy young memsahib was doing to elicit such a response in the awful animal. With a shrill squeal, the horse whipped round to glare at the man, a hind foot threateningly raised. Reeling back with an oath, the *syce* reached for his preferred weapon—a pitch-fork. Angrily wrenching it from his grasp, Minette ordered the man out of her sight. Sniggers from interested onlookers followed the *syce* as he slunk away, vowing vengeance on the culprit for his loss of face—that accursed *sala* of an animal!

Minette took her time over fitting the saddle comfortably on Turka's back, with no sign of resentment from the horse. The bridle was slipped on and she led him out of the stable block, positioning him beside a mounting block. It was only now that the horse began to tremble in expectation of unpleasantness—or pain. Minette spoke softly to him, and the trembling lessened as the animal relaxed.

Placing her foot in the stirrup iron, she eased herself into the saddle and rested a comforting hand on the horse's glossy neck. When the trembling had stopped altogether, she closed her legs against Turka's sides, inviting him to move forward.

Tensing, the horse took a step, and then another—in clear expectation of a punitive whip to descend at any moment. Asking nothing of him, the young woman sat still, her hand still resting on his neck … and waited.

Without warning the little horse danced forward, Minette easily sitting him on a loose rein. Her attention nevertheless sharpened, aware that violent bucking so darkly prophesied by the Sikh owner might be next on Turka's agenda.

Showing no sign of wanting to dislodge his rider, the horse broke into a flowing canter. Minette gasped with pleasure, thrilled by the floating sensation beneath her. She allowed Turka his head, and they flew along the grassy bridle way for a mile or two without the horse showing any sign of fatigue. Minette brought him back to a walk, and the two of them returned to the stables, exhilarated by the exercise.

Slipping from the saddle, Minette groped in her pocket for carrot pieces which the horse accepted at once. With deep reluctance, she handed Turka over to the hovering *syce*—with a warning that he had better not entertain any idea of being cruel to the horse. Should she discover he had, she would see to it that he lost his job. Eyes lowered to conceal his inner rage, the *syce* led the horse away.

Minette was revelling in the cool of the Darjeeling climate. During her early morning ride, she had watched her breath misting in the cool crisp air—a far cry from the sweltering heat of the Lucknow summer. Filled with renewed energy, she made her way back to the hotel for breakfast.

Patrick had shaved and was dressed in clean clothes upon his wife's return to the bedroom. Not a trace remained of his prolonged session in the hotel bar. To her secret satisfaction, Minette detected a slightly shamed expression in his eyes as he bent to kiss her.

"Darling, so sorry about vanishing yesterday," Patrick was contrite. "Saw some old chums, and one thing led to another—you know how it is."

"Oh yes, Patrick, I most certainly do know how it is," Minette replied, her tone dry. "After all, it happens often enough!"

"Sweetie, I'll make it up to you, I promise. Been out riding on your allocated horse, I imagine? Any good?"

"Turka is gorgeous, Patrick," Minette enthused. "He's a little Arab stallion with fantastic paces and an unusual turn of speed. I stand a good chance of placing with him—all things being equal."

"What do you mean by that? Is there something the matter with the animal?"

"No ... not with the horse, he's a sweet fellow. The problem is with the *syce* supposed to be looking after him. He's an absolute rotter, and terribly cruel to the poor animal."

"Surely something can be done about that?" Patrick frowned. "Have you complained to the owner about the fellow?"

"Indeed I have," Minette smiled without humour. "And he recommended giving Turka a good beating just before the start of the race."

"For God's sake, the man must be mad!"

"Patrick, I really love this little horse," Minette placed a supplicating hand on her husband's arm. "I seem to have a connection with him that I haven't known since my Ariadne in France. Would you consider buying him for me?" Minette gazed up at Patrick, her vivid eyes guileless. "I would be so grateful to you."

"Buy him?" Patrick stepped back with a frown. "What about your mare in Lucknow? Surely you haven't tired of her?"

"No, of course not. You know I love Fanny. But being a Thoroughbred from England, she feels the heat dreadfully. I cannot ride her at all during the summer months."

"I see, but why this particular horse, Minette? It seems such a palaver to arrange transport for it all the way back to Lucknow. Makes more sense to look for something suitable nearer home, don't you think?"

"Turka is the horse I want, Patrick—none other," Minette's

voice lost some of its warmth. "When have I ever asked you for anything? If I had my own money, I wouldn't need your permission."

"Look, Minette, I only thought ... "

"Forget I asked." Minette turned away. "It's clear you think my request to be just a foolish whim. Are we to have breakfast together ... or will you be rejoining your friends of yesterday?"

Wincing at the oblique reference to the hours he had spent drinking, Patrick sighed. "Very well, you may have the horse, provided the Sikh fellow is prepared to sell. Doubtless, the asking price will be well above the animal's actual value!"

"Thank you, darling!" Minette was radiant. "I shall always remember your generosity."

With the intention of pleasing his wife, Patrick kept his distance from the hotel bar. With considerable ostentation for Minette's benefit, he refused invitations from erstwhile drinking companions to join them for pre-lunch "snifters." Instead, he accompanied his wife to the stables, curious to see the horse that had so taken her fancy.

Looking over the clean tendons, dished little face and dainty body, Patrick privately thought him too small to be anything of a threat to other race contenders. The flattened ears and fiery eye rolling in his direction did nothing to improve his opinion of the animal. But with unusual wisdom, Patrick kept his thoughts to himself, resigned to purchasing the bad-tempered little beast.

The day before the race, Minette was on her way back to the hotel to change after her morning ride. Cheeks pink with exhilaration, dark curls wild about her face, she was wondering if there had been any news on the purchase of Turka. Although the present owner had told Patrick he would consider his offer, so far there had been no word.

"Ah, there you are, darling," Patrick came down the hotel steps in the company of a fellow officer from Lucknow, whom Minette knew only by sight. "I would like to introduce Frederick de Barre, a fellow countryman of yours—if somewhat anglicised these days.

"*Enchanté, Madame,*" Frederick took Minette's rather grubby hand and raised it to his lips. Warm brown eyes twinkled in amusement as he resisted the young woman's embarrassed efforts to withdraw her hand from his grasp.

Conscious of her dilapidated state, Minette smiled weakly, wondering if this man was one of Patrick's regular drinking companions. A second glance at Frederick dismissed the possibility. The man's clear eyes and healthy complexion was devoid of the tell-tale ruddiness of thread veins—increasingly apparent on her husband's cheeks and nose.

"How lucky you are to have such a talented wife … as well as being very beautiful," Frederick smiled in open admiration. "I believe you are to ride in the Point-to-Point tomorrow morning, Madame? May I know the name of your horse, so that I am able to place a small wager on him to win?"

"Don't waste your money, Monsieur! My horse and I are virtual strangers to each other, so the combination is likely to be an unknown quantity."

"I wouldn't believe a word of it, Freddie," Patrick broke in. "Minette is fiercely competitive. She is riding an Arab by the name of Turka. Seems a trifle on the small side, but I am assured he is fast and jumps like a stag."

"Your husband's recommendation is very convincing, Madame," Frederick declared straight-faced. "It seems I cannot fail to make myself a tidy sum from the bookmaker."

"When you find yourself the poorer for your bet … do remember you were warned!" Minette grinned. "Please excuse me now, gentlemen, but I really must go and change."

On her way upstairs, Minette reflected that Frederick spoke English as well as she did herself, with only the tiniest hint of a French accent. Nice looking fellow, too, all that curly fair hair, and easy to talk to. A good enough influence to keep Patrick out of that damned bar? Minette fervently hoped so.

CHAPTER NINETEEN

The following day dawned cool, but fine. Dew laced the hedgerows where bejewelled spiders' webs sparkled in the early morning sunshine. A light morning mist floated between clumps of pine trees on the surrounding hills.

Leaning out of her bedroom window, Minette was confident it would vanish within the hour as the sun rose higher in the sky. Perfect for a Point-to-Point race! Dressing quickly, Minette glanced over at the bed where her husband lay snoring, his mouth open. At least he had managed to undress before getting into bed last night, she thought dryly. And neither had he noticed the window had been left open—praise the Lord!

First visiting Turka to ensure he had been fed and watered, Minette went in search of the *syce*. She discovered him behind the stable block, squatting with other *syces*, all of them puffing on *beedies*. Seeing Minette approaching, the *syce* reluctantly got to his feet, hiding the cigarette behind his back.

"*Namaste, syce*." Minette smiled at the man. "Whilst the horse is finishing his hay, please would you take the saddle, numnah and girth and put them to one side by the Start Line for me. After that, I would like you to walk Turka for half an hour before I saddle him up."

"Yes, *Memsahib*," muttered the man, seething that he was obliged to take orders from this stupid white woman. But he had no wish to receive a cuff round the ear and another strident upbraiding from the Stable Manager.

"Thank you," Minette hesitated, uneasy about the unaccountable glower on the *syce's* face. Might he dare to defy her ... when she had already reported him to the Stable Manager? No, it would be more than his job was worth.

Returning to the hotel, Minette joined her husband for a swift breakfast of toast and tea. Glancing at the clock on the dining room wall, she dropped Patrick a quick kiss and departed in search of her horse and the *syce*.

Turka was nowhere to be seen. Perplexed, the young woman searched down the line of horses waiting to compete. Their *syces* squatted beside them, chatting amongst themselves and smoking *beedies*. All of them shook their heads at her enquiry. Neither was Turka in the exercise paddock where horses were walked prior to the race. Minette hesitated. Should she inform the authorities her horse seemed to have vanished?

A piercing scream from an animal in agony rent the air! Skin prickling in apprehension, Minette hurried towards a huddled group, from where she could hear further high-pitched screams. Elbowing her way closer, she was horrified to see a maddened horse struggling in the midst of curious onlookers.

Turka!

Eyes wide and rolling in an extreme state of terror, blood-flecked foam gushing from the curbed bit in his mouth, the little horse was plunging wildly at the end of a rein. Clutching it was the grinning *syce*, viciously yanking it in clear delight to see the animal's agony. In the man's other hand was a pitchfork, with which he sought to stab the terrified creature in his soft underbelly. Every time blood was drawn and the horse screamed, the *syce* burst into maniacal laughter.

So engrossed was he in punishing the *badmashi ghora*—responsible for his loss of face—the *syce* failed to notice Minette's appearance at his side. Shocked, he found himself dragged backwards by the scruff of his neck, and flung to the ground. A booted foot kicked the pitchfork from his loosening grasp.

Ignominiously sprawled on his back, the man stared up into the pale face of the young memsahib, her lips drawn back in fury. As fast as he was able, the *syce* scrambled to his feet and lost himself in the mass of people jostling for a better view of the entertaining fracas.

Minette now turned her attention to the traumatised horse, standing and shuddering in dazed shock. Approaching him one step at a time, she bent to pick up the trailing reins. Snorting with fear, the crazed animal almost jerked the young woman off her feet—but she held fast. He reared violently, hooves thrashing only a fraction from her head. Thanks to the experience she had gained when dealing with her father's young stock, Minette stood firm and unafraid.

Sadly, she recognised that only one realistic option existed now—to withdraw from the race. Feeling in her pocket for slices of carrot, Minette wondered if the poor little animal was too far gone to even register the offering. To her amazement, Turka turned to hide his face against her ... as if seeking comfort. Moments later, he accepted the carrot, crunching it with evident pleasure despite his wounded mouth.

On the verge of tears over the wanton brutality she had witnessed, Minette leaned her face against the horse's sweat-sodden neck. Turka nickered and turned to place his bleeding muzzle in her hand.

A sign of trust.

Unsure if she was about to make a grave mistake, the young woman led Turka over to where her tack had been placed. First checking his back to ensure there were no wounds, she eased the saddle into place and did up the girth. Placing her foot in the stirrup, Minette paused in case the horse reacted badly. But Turka remained calm and allowed her to mount. There was no question of racing, but if she rode him quietly for half an hour, it might help restore his confidence in man.

So far ... so good!

Minette gathered up the reins, taking care to avoid unnecessary contact with his mouth, and the horse moved forward. The occasional shudder ran through his body, but within minutes that ceased altogether. Leaning forward in the saddle, Minette fondled Turka's ears, and he responded by fluttering his nostrils.

The sheer stoicism of the little horse was astounding! When taken into an exercise paddock, he further surprised Minette by his calm and lack of residual stiffness—despite his wounds. Might he be able to cope with the race after all ... mentally as well as physically? Minette decided to take a chance. How providential that she had decided to walk the course the day before, since there was no time to do so now.

Making her way towards the Start Line where crowds of spectators were gathered, Minette noticed her husband waving a cloth marked with a number. Ignoring Turka's clear objection to his presence, Patrick affixed it to her back, with the information that the Sikh gentleman had agreed to sell Turka. Money had already changed hands, so Minette was now the owner of this horse ... of which she thought so much!

Overcome with gratitude and relief, Minette took her husband's hand and for a fleeting moment, laid her hot cheek against it. Straightening, she gathered up the reins and re-mounted to line up by the Start Line, waiting for a whistle blast to signal her turn on the course.

During these final few minutes, she could feel tension building in Turka's body beneath her. Of course! Although young, he had already raced and he was now sensing a competitive atmosphere!

At the sound of the whistle, Turka surged into his wonderful flowing gallop towards the first fence. Collecting himself, he sailed effortlessly over the obstacle, and followed Minette's indication towards the next. Enthralled anew by the little horse's evident talent, she realised her only requirement was to sit still and ride on a light contact. Turka had no need of interference with his approach to obstacles.

Safely over the final jump, Minette was certain they had made good time round the course. Confirmation came from wild cheering by spectators as Turka sped past the Finishing Post. Bringing him back to a walk, Minette dropped the reins and leaned forward to pat the horse's sweating neck. She did not notice a figure shoving his way to the front of the shouting onlookers.

But Turka had.

Confronted by the man responsible for tormenting him earlier, the horse swerved violently, fearful of being attacked again. Unexpectedly thrown off balance, Minette slipped from the saddle to fall heavily to the ground. From long experience, she hung on to the reins and scrambled to her feet—unhurt but alight with incandescent rage.

"*Get out* ... get out of my sight," she yelled at the nonplussed *syce*, "and get away from my horse, you cowardly imbecile!"

Staggering backwards in the face of the young woman's fury, the *syce* whirled and vanished into the milling crowds.

"Good God, Minette ... are you hurt?" Patrick arrived at his wife's side. "What on earth made the stupid animal shy like that?"

"It wasn't Turka's fault, Patrick!" Minette was shaking with rage. "He caught sight of that damned *syce* who had been torturing him just before the race ... take a look at the poor little thing's mouth! And see those open wounds under his belly ... and in his quarters? Those were inflicted with a bloody pitchfork."

"Christ!" Patrick peered under Turka's belly, then stood back as the horse's ears flattened with resentment at his proximity. "You can rest assured the little bastard will get his come-uppance from *Subedar-Major* in charge of stable staff. I'll ask him to arrange a decent *syce* for the horse. By the way, your time on the course is the best so far ... but there are more competitors still to go."

Removing the saddle, Minette led Turka round for twenty minutes to allow him to cool down. She then returned to the stables where she found a new *syce* already waiting. After a few cursory snorts of suspicion at the unknown individual, Turka allowed himself to be washed, his wounds attended to, and then bedded down. His nose buried in a bucket of feed, the little horse seemed none the worse for his terrible experience. Pleased to see Turka relaxed and content, Minette made her way back to the hotel.

Showered and changed from her riding clothes, Minette ran downstairs to the dining room. It had been arranged earlier that morning that she would join her husband and Frederick de Barre for late *tiffin*. Looking round the mostly empty dining room, she saw Frederick at a table by the window. He rose to his feet with a smile as she came over to join him.

Of Patrick—there was no sign.

"In case you haven't heard, your little Arab has come first in the race, and by a respectable margin!" Frederick grinned. "Thanks to the pair of you, I have won a goodly sum from the bookmaker."

Minette clasped her hands in delight. "I just knew he could do it, Frederick! It was entirely him, you know. All I had to do was steer."

"Well, this lunch is on me, and I've ordered a bottle of champagne to toast our respective successes."

"How sweet of you Frederick … but where's Patrick?" Minette glanced towards the door with a frown. "I would have thought he'd be here by now?"

"He … um … popped into the bar to see someone he knew. I imagine he will soon be joining us. Of course, he's delighted about your win."

Minette's heart sank. The bar. That blasted booze-swilling den that attracted her husband like a magnet. Surely he wasn't abandoning her again—today of all days? No. He wouldn't dare do such a thing, knowing Frederick was waiting …

But Patrick did not come.

Trying to avoid undue awkwardness, Frederick ordered lunch for them both. He told the dining room bearer that the other sahib would be along soon, and reached for the champagne bottle. Deflated, Minette sipped at the fizzing champagne.

Glancing at Frederick's concerned face, she was brought up short. Just because Patrick chose to be unmannerly, by no means did that give *her* leave to be churlish. After all, Frederick had bought champagne to celebrate their win! Pasting on a brilliant smile, Minette addressed her companion in French. Such a pleasure, she declared, to have the opportunity of speaking her mother tongue.

Tiffin came to an end with still no sign of Patrick. Minette thanked Frederick for the splendid meal, and went upstairs to her room. She had been conscious of vague backache throughout lunch—doubtless a legacy of her fall. Nothing that a good soak in a warm bath couldn't put right.

Having rung Room Service, hot water duly arrived with a hotel bearer who poured it into a zinc tub in the bathroom. After the servant had left, Minette undressed and pulled down her knickers—then froze—staring horrified at a spreading stain of bright blood. Light-headed with shock, she realised a bath was now out of the question. She must lie as still as possible on her bed, a rolled up towel between her thighs, praying the portentous bleeding had little significance.

Two hours later, the door opened and a penitent Patrick entered the bedroom. Divesting himself of his coat, he looked over at his wife lying on the bed, her back towards him.

"Darling, sorry to have missed you at lunch. Met up with some fellows who twisted my arm to join them for a snort or two. Time just got away from me, I'm afraid, but I'm sure Freddie looked after you admirably."

Frowning over the lack of response to his apology, Patrick stiffened, preparing for an angry confrontation with his wife. "For Christ's sake, I hope you don't mean to give me the silent treatment, Minette? I won't stand for it! You've got the bloody horse you wanted, so don't begrudge me a moment or two with chums."

The only answer his words elicited from the young woman on the bed was a gasp, followed by a deep groan. Bending over her, Patrick saw at a glance that his wife was perspiring and appeared to be in considerable pain. In between gasps, he came to understand she was pregnant, and was now in terror of losing her baby.

With immense difficulty, Patrick restrained himself from bellowing his rage. Not only had the business been kept secret from him, but Minette had also risked her life in the most foolhardy manner imaginable.

It was clear a miscarriage was now in inexorable progress. His own medical expertise was going to be necessary, since finding another doctor in time was out of the question. No possibility of saving the foetus, but steps had to be taken to prevent a haemorrhage. Grim faced, Patrick fetched his medical bag from the cupboard.

Minette turned her face into the sodden pillow beneath her head, eyes swollen with weeping. It had been two days since she had been delivered of not one tiny stillborn infant ... but two! Two dead little faces, to be forever imprinted on her memory. Raw with grief—and guilt—Minette had reacted violently to her husband's accusation of extraordinary irresponsibility.

"Don't *dare* to swear at me, Patrick O'Hara!" she spat at the man standing by the bed, hands on his hips, a hostile expression on his face. "I rode in that damned race because I was afraid—yes, afraid—to tell you about the coming baby."

"Afraid? Since when have you been afraid of me, Minette? Stop trying to infer I am some kind of monster."

"Ah, but that is exactly what you have become, Patrick. A beast who doesn't hesitate to terrify his little son so that he wets himself with fright. Is it really so strange I was apprehensive of telling you a second child was on the way?"

"The hell it is!" Patrick snarled. "You know bloody well I never wanted children. Obviously not satisfied with the one you have—you go ahead and get yourself pregnant again."

Minette had gasped at the rank injustice of her husband's accusation. "My God, what an arrogant pig you are, Patrick! So I became pregnant all by myself, did I? If you had nothing to do with it … I must have been inseminated by the Holy Ghost."

Bolstered by an earlier consumption of two stiff whiskies, Patrick slammed from the bedroom. Minette was left to sob in shocked rage, but also in genuine sorrow over the loss of her babies.

The following day, the young woman was feeling more herself. Still stunned over her husband's insensitivity, she was inclined to withdraw into a prolonged icy silence. However, she was pragmatic enough to realise it would merely provide Patrick with an excuse to rejoin his drinking companions. She was therefore obliged to pretend normality—much as it would go against the grain.

Minette thoughts touched upon the continuing lack of a Blessing on their marriage within the Catholic Church. Worrying through it was, the thought of approaching the over-zealous Catholic priest in the cantonment was enough to make anyone quail. Given to prognostications of hell-fire over the most minor infringements of his personal interpretation of the Catholic Faith—how would he view a lack of religious marriage ceremony? In particular when a child of their union had already been born? Minette shook her head. Perhaps a less formidable churchman might be found later on.

In any event, she intended to seek advice over how to avoid conceiving in future—regardless of Catholic dictates. However ridiculous, it was clear her husband held her solely accountable, making no effort of his own. Besides which, it was out of the question that she became pregnant every year of her life.

Without warning, Minette's eyes swam with nostalgic tears for her old home in France. It was where she had spent a happy carefree girlhood, marred only by her mother's antagonism—but from which she had been largely protected by her grandparents. Problems seeming of immense proportion at the time—she could now review in a realistic perspective.

And those accusations of spoiled behaviour, and a grim determination to have her way in all things ... perhaps that hadn't been too far from the truth? Minette pressed the back of a hand against her trembling mouth.

Well, she was paying for it now—in spades.

An insidious dark cloud of depression settled on the young woman's spirits, swamping her like damp fog. Gone forever was that adoring beau she had known in far off Convent days. Patrick needed little justification to lose his temper with her. Sometimes he could scarcely keep a civil tongue in his head.

Fresh tears of disappointment and bewilderment sprang into Minette's eyes. Much of his ill humour could be attributed to the whisky bottle, perhaps. But why, *why* did he need to drink himself to a standstill in the first place? She simply did not know.

Thrusting the impossible conundrum from her mind, Minette sat up straight. She mustn't allow herself to wallow in a sea of self-pity. Yes, the loss of her babies was a personal tragedy, and the guilt weighed heavily on her spirits. But she must remember she already had a little boy—and James was very much alive.

A trip to the stables to see Turka would do wonders for her morale, she knew. All her life she had sought comfort—and received it—from close proximity to horses. Rising to her feet, Minette washed away her tears, lifted her chin, and walked out of the bedroom.

Patrick was conspicuous by his absence during the whole of that day—and the next. On the morning of their intended return to Lucknow, a worried Minette was in the hotel bedroom, packing their possessions into valises. Turka's loading into the train was still to be overseen, as well as affairs requiring attention before their departure in the early afternoon—such as the hotel bill. Minette paused with a frown, the garment she was folding forgotten for a moment.

What if Patrick failed to materialise in time? Perhaps she should ask Frederick de Barre for his help in loading her little horse, and borrow funds from him to settle the various accounts. Assuming he also intended returning to the cantonment, she would also ask to travel under his protection.

The door to the bedroom suddenly opened to reveal Patrick, a sheepish grin on his face. Although somewhat pallid, he appeared more or less sober. Advancing into the room without a word, he took his wife in his arms.

"Sorry to have been a bit of a beast to you, darling," Patrick whispered into her hair. "I was petrified over how easily you might have died, and it made me over-sharp. Can you forgive me?"

"Of course I will," Minette's eyes filled with easy tears. "I can't tell you how dreadful it feels to have directly caused the death of those two tiny babies."

"You will feel better in time, sweetie. The main thing is that you regain your health and spirits. And don't ever feel afraid to tell me anything in future."

With a sigh, Minette leaned her face against her husband's chest—unwilling that he should notice a trace of cynicism reflected in her eyes. Patrick meant what he was saying now—but for how long? She was beginning to understand her husband's bonhomie was usually a transient affair.

With little fuss, Turka was loaded into his special stall on the train, and tucked into a bulging hay net with enthusiasm. Patrick, Minette and Frederick settled themselves in a compartment as close to the little horse as possible. Making sure all the carriage doors were shut, the guard blew his whistle and waved a green flag to the engine driver. Huffing and puffing amid clouds of steam, the little train started downhill on its single track to the plains far below.

CHAPTER TWENTY

Upon their return to Lucknow, Patrick made a visible effort to control his drinking. He even began taking an interest—largely adverse—in his small son. He made no secret that he thought the child a spoiled brat—unsurprising since he was waited on hand and foot by doting women.

But after James' fourth birthday, Patrick informed his wife he intended to take an active hand in the boy's upbringing. He would put a stop to those tiresome rages, and instil much needed discipline in his son. Far from being pleased to hear this, all Minette felt was a sense of trepidation ...

Only a few months after her return from Darjeeling, Minette discovered herself to be pregnant once again. When informed of this fact, Patrick said little ... but refrained from accusing his wife of deliberate conception. A definite improvement.

For Minette—obliged to stop riding even in the most sedate manner—the subsequent months became mind-numbingly tedious. Taking advantage of her forced inactivity, she taught James his alphabet, French nursery rhymes, and to count. From the outset she had spoken to the child in both French and English, so the little boy was equally comfortable in both languages.

Late, and with little warning, Charles O'Hara came yelling into the world. Like James, he was a redhead, but that was where the resemblance ended. Little Charlie was a delight to everyone, drank his milk and slept for hours, on occasion lying awake in his pram gurgling contentedly. Even the stately *bearer* was moved to fashion a crude mobile suspended from a branch above the pram. Gazing up in fascination at the fragile straw birds twirling above him, the baby was provided with endless amusement.

From the moment of Charlie's birth, James made it clear that he took the newcomer's arrival as a personal affront. No amount of explanation or hugs from his mother or *ayah* seemed to reassure the jealous little boy. He would sneak into the baby's environment and inflict sly pinches on his brother's delicate flesh. The unfortunate baby would howl in anguish, but when someone came running in alarm—the culprit was nowhere to be seen. Just an ugly bruise on the baby's body bore witness to the fact that James had been there.

With great reluctance, Minette was forced to accept that James was not to be trusted. A close watch was kept to ensure the older child was unable wreak his spite on the baby. Deprived of venting his anger on the newcomer, James broke whatever toys he could lay his hands on.

The only person able to exact a modicum of obedience from James was his father. Although fearful of his loud voice, the boy nevertheless sought his father's approval. Failing to achieve that, James would take out his frustration through screaming and kicking poor gentle Mailie. Minette was at her wits end to know how to handle this difficult child of hers.

Two years seemed to flash past for Minette, during which she gave birth to a little girl. Dark haired, and with her mother's vivid blue eyes, Claire grew into an enchanting if mischievous imp. To her, it was treat to be to taken in her wicker pushchair to watch her brothers riding their ponies on the maidan. Bouncing up and down in her pram harness, she would shout, "—me wanta ride horsey … me wanta ride horsey!"

Minette adored her effervescent little girl, and even Patrick seemed to soften in the face of Claire's insouciance. Unafraid of her father's hectoring voice, the child would dimple saucily up at him, and Patrick's face would relax into an answering smile. Minette looked on, filled with renewed hope that perhaps this little girl possessed the key to Patrick's elusive sense of fatherhood.

Something his sons had signally failed to do.

Despite Mailie's contraceptive potions, Minette fell pregnant only a year after Claire's birth. She was deeply annoyed, having only recently regained her figure to its former trimness. She was also enjoying riding her two horses on alternate early mornings, taking advantage of the relative coolness before sun-up.

Now her freedom was to be curtailed yet again during the wait for this new infant's arrival! Minette ground her teeth with frustration. It was sickening! Destined to be pregnant almost every year? The very idea was intolerable! But unless a reliable method of contraception could be found, the only way she could see clear was to not allow Patrick into her bed. Minette grimaced, thinking of the explosive row *that* would ignite!

But she was also tired of those unfair accusations of engineering pregnancy against her husband's express wish. Ridiculous, in particular, coming from a damned doctor of all people.

At least she would still be able to enjoy watching evening Polo now and again—Minette tried to console herself. Polo was always a social occasion when entire families brought stools and canvas chairs to watch the game from the sidelines.

Aside from the excitement and inherent danger of the game, a gargantuan afternoon tea always followed the end of chukkas. Laid out under striped canvas awnings, plates were piled high with sandwiches and a variety of cakes and biscuits, in addition to dishes of popular Indian delicacies. It was one of the few Regimental social occasions that the young Frenchwoman really enjoyed.

As time passed, the weather turned hotter and more humid, the slightest movement causing a rush of perspiration. Minette's clothing clung unpleasantly to her increasing bulk, and her temper ignited over incidents she generally took in her stride. The children were fractious, and Patrick's drinking was on the increase.

Subsequent to yet another horrendous row over her pregnancy, Minette found herself fighting against an all-too-familiar depression. She retreated into an enduring silence, remaining in her bedroom for much of the day. Aware he had badly over-stepped the mark, Patrick sought to reinstate himself in his wife's favour. He would take her away on a short holiday.

He requested ten days local leave which was granted without hesitation. On a colleague's advice, Patrick decided upon Kashmir, high up in the Himalayas. Without the children.

Minette was delighted over her husband's thoughtfulness, and thrust aside lingering feelings of guilt over leaving the children in Lucknow. After this suffocating heat, what a pleasure it would be breathe fresh air! Why, from what she had heard, it was sometimes necessary to have a brazier filled with glowing coals to offset the chill of Kashmir evenings.

Leaving their noisy family in the care of Mailie and her recently employed cousin, Seenta, Patrick and Minette set off up-country to Kashmir. A comfortable houseboat had been booked for ten days, moored in the midst of a carpet of water lilies on Srinagar, one of Kashmir's two beautiful lakes.

Minette caught her breath, thrilled by the beauty and lushness of the countryside against a misty background of snow-capped mountain peaks. The air was fresh and clean, and in such pleasant conditions she would sleep through the night … at last.

The cooler climate and tranquillity of the lakeside residence went a long way towards restoring Minette's natural good humour. The cook-boy on the houseboat proved excellent, and for the first time in months, she was enjoying her meals.

The only disturbing element was that Patrick evidently still felt the need to imbibe large quantities of whisky each night. It was rare that he sat down to dinner with his wife, preferring to remain on the after-deck with his bottle of scotch and a glass. Minette had hoped the mountain air and stress-free environment might help him to relax. Maybe even enjoy the company of his wife?

Apparently not.

Determined not to think about this jarring element of an otherwise delightful life-style, Minette thoughts went to her children. The arrival of Mailie's cousin had proved such a boon! Unfazed by the boy's tantrums, Seenta would casually pick up a scarlet-faced James, kicking and screaming with rage, and cart him off to the nursery to be deposited on his bed. She made sure the boy remained there until he had controlled himself. Minette grinned, thinking that James had finally met his match in the new ayah! Seenta also watched over little Charlie, making sure his brother did not make his life a misery.

Mailie must be heartily relieved to leave the troublesome child to her unflappable cousin—Minette thought ruefully. She was beginning to recognise the unpalatable fact that aspects of her elder son's personality seemed to bear an uncanny resemblance to her own brother, Jérome—heaven forbid.

One evening, Minette and Patrick were sitting together in the cushioned stern of the houseboat, watching a spectacular sunset reflected in the still dark waters of the lake. Inexplicably morose, Patrick stared into the bottom of glass he was clutching to his chest. Draining the last dregs of whisky, he shouted for the houseboy.

"*Quoi hai*? Whisky bottle *lao … jaldi!*"

"Darling, don't you think we should have dinner now?" Minette ventured, attempting to stifle her anxiety. "It's a bit mean to keep the servants waiting around until late at night. And all that alcohol can't be a good thing on an empty stomach."

"For Christ's sake, you aren't going to start your usual bloody nagging, are you?" Patrick barked, immediately aggressive. Scowling, he refilled his glass from the bottle the servant had placed on a small table between them. "Believe me, I need more than a few pegs to forget the disgusting scene I witnessed on the way to the station in Lucknow."

"What scene?" Minette frowned. "I don't recall any scene?"

"My dear girl, I doubt you would have noticed anything amiss," Patrick's tone was patronising, to his wife's intense irritation.

"But in the event you had, I imagine you would have averted your eyes, lifted your skirts, and passed by on the other side of the road … much as your coterie of memsahibs would have done," he finished loftily.

"Don't you dare classify me with those vapid females married to your regimental brethren," Minette retorted with spirit. "I do happen to possess independent thought, you know. Are you going to tell me what you saw—or not?"

"I saw an infant girl flung naked on a dung heap to die," Patrick exploded. "Yet another example of unmitigated cruelty in this accursed country! How does *that* fit in with your unfailing enthusiasm for India and its charming customs?"

Minette lowered her eyes to her hands folded in her lap. Unbeknown to her husband, she had involved herself with a body of nuns from the Loretto Order several months ago. She was fully aware of the hideous practice regarding the disposal of unwanted girl babies in gutters or on dung heaps.

These good women set out to rescue infants such as these. Placed in a safe environment, the children would be given an appropriate education towards future employment as nannies or teachers. Minette had been helping with the search.

She had gone out of her way to keep these activities secret from her husband. He was certain to be appalled by the possibility that his colleagues or their wives might discover the unsavoury occupation in which their doctor's wife was embroiled! And now was not the time to mention it!

"Yes, I agree it is a terrible practice," Minette said at last. "Perhaps someone could begin rescuing the poor little things. Given an education, they might end up having some kind of life."

"Huh!" Patrick grunted, "pipe-dreams, dear girl just pipe-dreams. Who the hell would give up their time to such a joyless venture?" Throwing the contents of the glass down his throat, he poured himself another hefty measure of whisky. "Nobody in their right mind, in any event."

"Darling, I beg you not to drink any more tonight," Minette stood up to massage a cramp in her lower back. "Let me call for dinner … or at least some sandwiches."

"*Christ Almighty!*" Patrick slopped the contents of his glass down his front in anger. "Will you stop your bloody preaching? Holier than thou, you watch my every blasted move like some kind of repressed schoolmarm."

"If you imagine I am going to sit here and watch you becoming progressively more and more drunk—you have another think coming, Patrick O'Hara!" Minette flared. "Where is your self-respect? Horrid stains all down your clothes, and when did you last bother to shave? Yes, take a good look at yourself in the mirror and you'll see how repulsive you have become."

"Shut your goddamned mouth, you stupid bitch!" snarled the man, eyes red-rimmed and bulging with fury. "Nag, bloody nag, that's all you are capable of these days. Christ, I'm sick to bloody death of you and your prissy face!"

Minette stepped back, shocked that Patrick should used such abusive language to her. Eyes burning with unshed tears, she lifted her chin and withdrew to the bedroom with as much dignity as her heavy body would allow. Slamming the door behind her, she turned the key in the lock. Tonight, at least, she would not be subjected to foul alcohol-laden halitosis blasted into her face whilst trying to sleep.

Lying on her bed, Minette cursed herself for not having handled the situation with rather more diplomacy. She had been hoping to raise a matter distressing to her during this holiday, whilst Patrick was relatively sober. Minette sighed wearily. Unfortunately there hadn't been a "right time."

It was to do with riding lessons he had undertaken to give the boys ... and lately to little Claire. Out of the blue, Patrick had declared his intention to take over James and Charlie's riding lessons. A wonderful idea on the face of it, and the boys were thrilled to be having their usually distant father's undivided attention.

Their excitement was destined to come to an abrupt end.

Patrick decreed that all the namby-pamby toddling about on the *maidan* with grooms in attendance was to stop. He intended to see to it that his sons became "proper riders." On Patrick's orders, the two ponies were brought out into an arena wearing only a head-collar and a lead rope. No saddle. The mystified boys were lifted on to the ponies' backs, and the end of the lead rope handed to them.

They were ordered to remain on their ponies—come what may. Falling off would be seen as clear disobedience, which would earn them an immediate thrashing. Unsure if their father was perhaps joking, the two little boys looked wide-eyed at their mother, who had come to watch the riding lesson.

Without warning, Patrick's riding whip whistled down on the haunches of both ponies. Startled, the animals bounded abruptly forward, immediately unseating the children who slithered off their backs into the sand. Stupefied, the little boys remained sprawled on the ground whilst grooms caught the frantic ponies.

Hoisted to their feet, their backsides stinging from their father's whip, James and Charlie were set back on the ponies ... and the exercise repeated. Within half an hour, both children were grovelling in the dirt, howling in earnest, and begging to be let off riding.

Minette looked on in horror. She had been taught to ride by her own father, who had emphasised respect for a living animal. Whips had been discouraged, and she had learned to ride without being terrorised.

Unlike this…this *fiasco!*

Minette closed her eyes, thinking of the distress of those two terrified little boys. Of course, she had attempted to remonstrate with her husband on their behalf, and Patrick had retaliated in fury.

"Damn it, don't presume to tell me how to handle my own sons! You and that bloody *ayah* have made the pair of them into whining little milksops, always trying to hide behind their mother's skirts. Discipline is what those two badly need—and I intend to see that they get it. If you do not care for my methods, I suggest you clear off!"

Three weeks before leaving for Kashmir, Patrick had arbitrarily dismissed the groom who took three-year-old Claire for a riding lesson each morning. The little girl was devoted to her pony, Tom, and looked forward to her daily ride.

One morning, Patrick had moodily watched his little daughter laughing with delight over her recent success with rising trot. In his opinion, her progress was not swift enough, and therefore unsatisfactory. He announced he would teach her to ride himself. Subjected to the same rough methods as her brothers, half an hour into her ride Claire lay in the sand, screaming for her mother. She had fallen off the pony four times to be beaten by her father.

Sickened, Minette had ducked under the railing and gathered up the bruised little body in her arms. Turning her back on Patrick's thunderous commands to leave Claire to him, Minette carried her howling daughter home.

Two days later, Patrick demanded that Claire should be returned to him for further tuition. Ignoring Minette's pleas to be gentle with the child, it wasn't long before the child had fallen to the ground for the second time, her little bottom crisscrossed from her father's riding whip. This time she remained lying in the dust, screaming hysterically and refusing to get up.

That same night, Claire began to wet her bed … something she hadn't done for over a year. She was also waking up several times during the night to beg her mother not to make her ride in the morning.

Outraged, Minette had resisted Patrick's determination that Claire resume riding lessons with him. He had given up in a fury, declaring the child to be cowardly and "a lost cause." His sons, however, were a different matter, and Minette would be advised to mind her own business.

It had been Minette's intention during their time in Kashmir, to beg Patrick not to make riding such a miserable experience for poor James and Charlie ...

A tap on the door broke through Minette's unhappy reverie. Certain it wasn't her drunken husband, she dragged herself to her feet and unlocked the door.

"*Memsahib*, is you coming for *makan* ?" the houseboy was tentative. "*Sahib*, he ... er ... no wanting any."

"Just a little on a tray, please." Suddenly feeling bone-weary, Minette forced a smile. Probably just delayed reaction to the row with Patrick. "I'm not very hungry this evening."

The servant disappeared, and Minette returned to her bed, conscious of a sudden headache lurking on the edge of her consciousness. Perhaps she was hungry and hadn't realised it. But when the beautifully presented meal arrived a few minutes later, Minette found her usually robust appetite had vanished. She toyed with the food until it lay congealed on the plate.

Putting the tray outside the door, she turned the key in the lock once again. She slowly undressed, taking care not to suddenly bend and make her headache worse. Climbing into bed, she fell asleep almost at once.

As dawn was breaking, Minette awoke in a pool of perspiration. Her headache was much worse, and her throat unbearably sore. Attempting to sit up, she was forced to abandon the effort with a groan, every joint in her body screaming in agonised protest. A reddened rash was spreading up her arms and lower limbs, and with vague surprise, Minette realised she must be ill.

Mustering her dwindling strength, she dragged herself from the bed to the door. Pulling it open with an effort, she saw one of the houseboat servants dusting some furniture. Startled to see the memsahib clad in night attire, the man backed away salaaming politely.

"No! Please don't go!" Minette croaked. "Fetch *Doctor-Sahib* ... *jaldi! jaldi!*"

The servant sped away, leaving her clinging to the door, giddy and nauseous. Staggering back to bed, she collapsed on crumpled sheets become damp and rubbery with sweat. Tears of helplessness trickling down her burning cheeks, she lapsed into unconsciousness.

Summoned by the agitated servant, Patrick rushed to the bedroom and stared with horror at his wife thrashing restlessly on the bed. Sobering, he realised with a shock that Minette was not just unwell, but very ill indeed.

Examining the angry rash spreading all over his wife's body, he stood back in alarm. Unless he was grossly mistaken, it looked as though Minette was in the early stages of smallpox! The survival rate of the disease Patrick knew to be poor. Even should she live, the pustules would scar her for life.

Sick at heart, Patrick instructed a servant to fetch a *gharri*, a horse-drawn vehicle used locally for transport. He would take her to the small military hospital he recalled being on the outskirts of the town. Wrapping up the unconscious figure on the bed as warmly as possible, Patrick was aware of a dim recollection of having yelled at her over something he could not quite recall.

For eight days, Minette hovered in a twilight world between life—and death. Suppurating blisters covered most of her body, face, and even her scalp. Her wrists were bound to the bed with bandages to prevent her from raking the blisters open with her nails. Twisting and turning in delirium, she repeatedly pleaded with her father to forgive her, or she begged someone she called "Nou-nou" not to leave her ... then to lie as if lifeless on the narrow hospital bed.

Filled with dread, Patrick sat with her in an agony of self-recrimination. If only she would live! He would change—stop drinking—do anything if she would only survive. If Minette died, the fault would his for not recognising how ill she was that last evening. And how was he to manage those children by himself?

Early one morning, Patrick was slumped, dozing in an armchair beside Minette's hospital bed.

A sound.

Frowning, Patrick sat up and glanced over at the still figure in the bed, No, he had only imagined she had spoken. But Minette's eyes were open and—incredibly—she was attempting to smile.

"Patrick? What ... where on earth am I?" Minette strained to lift her head.

"Sweetie, you've been terribly ill," Patrick bent over his wife. "Rest a moment, while I call the nurse who is looking after you."

"Nurse?" Minette wrinkled her forehead in bewilderment. "Am I in hospital? The smell does seem familiar ... "

Slowly, very slowly, Minette fought her way to recovery. Learning the nature of her illness, she was sickened by the thought that she might have infected her own children before leaving Lucknow. Tears of remorse trickled down her cheeks upon the realisation that the source of infection must have come from the Children's Refuge she visited in the course of her work.

On Patrick's next visit to her bedside, Minette begged him to ascertain through the telegraph system that their family remained fit and healthy. This he did without argument, concerned that Minette's progress might be hindered by worry. Weak with relief, the young woman turned her attention to her appearance.

It seemed weeks since her hair had been washed, and her scalp was driving her mad with itching. Putting a hand up to her head, she was astounded to discover her mass of hair had been cut very short indeed. Presumably to make the task easier for the nurse to apply that rather strong-smelling medication to her scabs twice a day. *Ugh!* What must she look like?

"Nurse, please may I have my hairbrush and a mirror?" Minette asked the bustling British nurse who had just given her a refreshing blanket-bath. "I'd also love to have a hair wash if possible."

"Sorry, m'dear! No can do ... doctor's orders y'know!" replied the nurse, tucking the bedclothes round her patient. "You have been very ill, and Doctor Saunders recommends that you do not move from that bed for another week at least."

"I suppose I may at least brush my hair? God, I must look like a witch! If you would please pass me my handbag from the cupboard?"

"Here you are." The nurse handed the bag to Minette. "Do try and sleep a little after lunch, so you aren't too tired when your husband visits later in the afternoon."

"Er … my compact seems to be missing." Minette was rummaging inside her bag. "Everything else is here, except that."

"Really? It must have fallen out somewhere. Don't worry m'dear, I'll ask around for you." The nurse left the room, knowing the doctor had decreed his patient must be denied access to mirrors for the time being. Including the tiny one in her compact. She was simply not yet strong enough to cope with the scarring.

Later that afternoon, Minette gingerly got out of bed to visit the lavatory. After a few wobbly-kneed steps, she stiffened as a rush of warm liquid streamed down her legs to pool on the floor. Cold with fear that this signalled the premature delivery of her baby, Minette burst into tears. Tottering back to bed, she frantically rang the call-bell for help.

In answer to the bell, the nurse looked round the door in enquiry, taking in the situation at a glance. First settling the distraught young woman back on the bed, she went in search of clean linen—and a midwife.

Several hours later, Minette lay on her back staring at the ceiling in abject misery. What had she done to merit being overtaken by such terrible events? Surviving a disgusting disease by the skin of her teeth … only to miscarry another set of twin boys, this time through no fault of hers. Weak tears rolled down Minette's face as she thought of those little bodies hideously blotched by smallpox pustules. Turning her face into the pillow, she wept as if her heart was breaking.

In the hospital mortuary, Patrick gazed morosely at his two dead sons, their tiny bodies suspended in a jar of formalin. The hospital had been anxious to retain them, it being a phenomenon that unborn twins had been infected by their mother's disease. Patrick had hesitated, vaguely conscious of something distasteful about it. Convincing himself of its scientific benefit, he finally agreed to release them.

Patrick turned away from the tragic sight, struck by a desperate need for a drink to help him through the series of disastrous events overtaking him. Avoiding his wife's bedside, he took a rickshaw back to the houseboat. A couple of good snifters would prop him up. And Christ, he still had to face the business of Minette seeing her scarred face for the first time later in the day. Today of all days, did he not deserve assistance to get through the miserable affair? His wife need never know ...

Minette smelled alcohol on her husband's breath within minutes of his arrival. Disgusted, she shrank away from him.

"So much for your promise not to drink, Patrick O'Hara! Broken—like every promise you ever make."

"Just a moment, I promised not to drink too much ... and a couple of pegs hardly qualifies as excessive, don't you think?" Patrick retaliated, reddening with alcohol-fuelled annoyance. "Catching smallpox caught from trips made behind my back to that damned *bazaar* is a great deal worse, in my opinion!"

"What? I haven't been near a *bazaar* in months. I must have caught it from someone in the cantonment ... "

"There is no smallpox in the cantonment, "Patrick interrupted. "None of the other women show any sign of it, so where the hell did you go to catch something so disgusting?"

"None of the other women have it because all they ever do is play Mahjong and Bridge!" Minette snapped, casting caution to the winds. "I, at least, do something worthwhile with my time. Remember what you thought about girl babies being thrown away like so much refuse? I help to find the poor little things, and take them to nuns who run a Children's Refuge outside the cantonment!"

"My God!" Patrick stepped back, his lip curling. "In that case, consider yourself directly responsible for the condition and subsequent death of the twins—thanks to your "good works."

"Patrick!" Minette blanched. "How can you be so...so cruel? I don't think I deserve that beastly remark."

"Well, you asked for it!" Patrick blustered, a little ashamed despite being bemused by his intake of whisky. "Why do you have to attack me for nothing? Come now, darling—don't let's fight."

"Don't!" Minette leaned away from her husband's attempted embrace. "I want to talk about our babies' funeral, Patrick. I think they should be buried here in Kashmir, where they were born. I imagine there must be a church in the area where a service could be held for them?"

"I…I've allowed the hospital to keep them. Unborn infants with their mother's smallpox—for the advancement of science, you understand."

Minette stared at her husband in horror. "What can you mean, Patrick? Where are they? Tell me at once!"

"For Christ's sake, the babies are preserved forever in a glass jar of formalin! Better than digging a hole in the ground, surely?"

"Without asking me first?" The young woman burst into tears. "How dare you, Patrick! My dead babies to be specimens for the curious? Couldn't you have shown them some respect you beastly man? They don't even have names—"

Turned on his heel, Patrick stalked to the door. "You are conveniently forgetting they are *my* infants, to do with as I choose. You are in no fit state to decide anything. I trust you will be in a better humour the next time I visit."

Having overheard shouting, the nurse entered the room, horrified to see Minette in a distraught state. Without a word of explanation, Patrick pushed past her and left without a backward glance at the sobbing figure of his wife.

A week later, Patrick and Minette travelled back to Lucknow, both in a dismal fame of mind. Almost sober, Patrick had attempted to cajole his wife from her icy demeanour towards him—with scant success.

Stung by her rejection, Patrick lapsed into glowering silence. He had thought himself generous to be overlooking Minette's bizarre searching of gutters and dung heaps for newborns. Unthinkable that his own wife had been engaged in such gross deceit! He hoped to God that nobody in the cantonment was aware of her activities. And she had the damned nerve to ignore his magnanimous overtures.

Stony-faced, Minette sat as far away from her husband as the railway carriage banquette allowed. Her guilt over the death of her babies was ever-present in her mind, but she could never forgive Patrick for his disrespectful disposal of them. It had also been a dreadful shock to see how the healing scabs had disfigured her face. She was ugly, and would probably remain so for the rest of her life.

Minette was in for a further shock.

Upon her arrival home, she had to endure the three children staring goggle-eyed at her scarred face. Attempting to give Claire a reassuring cuddle, she saw her daughter's mouth begin to tremble. With a sob of fright, the child tore herself free from her mother's arms and ran to Mailie, burying her face in the *ayah's* sari. Embarrassed, the two boys tried not to stare at their mother. Minutes later they thankfully escaped to play out on the *maidan*.

Depressed by her children's reaction, Minette retired to her bedroom. She had a burning desire to be away from everyone's gaze. Maybe she could think of a way to alleviate the horror of her appearance, that she might feel less of a pariah ...

CHAPTER TWENTY-ONE

A few days later, a disconsolate Minette was sitting at her dressing table, gazing at the pits in her face. Would they *ever* fade? Was she destined to remain some kind of horrid hobgoblin to her own children? Would she ever dare to leave her house and endure inevitable staring from the curious? The depressed young woman's spirits sank ever lower.

A light tapping at her door, and Minette glanced round to see Mailie's cousin, Seenta sidle in. Closing the door behind her, the *ayah* padded over and took the dejected young woman's face between her hands. She examined the lesions first on one side, and then on the other. Gently removing Minette's cotton *peignoir*, she looked over the pits on her legs, arms, and back. Apparently satisfied, Seenta's round face split into a flashing smile as she helped Minette back into her robe.

"You not be worry any more, *Memsahib*! Three, four months and you be veree beautiful like before—Seenta knows! I bring magic cream for skin. Veree, veree good cream! Everyday we putting cream. You see then what happen, *Memsahib*!"

Tilting her head to one side, the *ayah* gave her mistress a searching look. "Is important *Memsahib's* spirit happy. No more worry how naughty *babas* be to you … they frightened for mummy, is all."

In spite of herself, Minette felt rather more cheerful after the *ayah's* visit. Seenta followed it up by reappearing with an earthenware pot in her hand. Indicating to Minette she should lie down on the bed, the *ayah* began a gentle massage of her face and then her limbs.

The unguent felt fresh and soothing on the skin, and in no time Minette had fallen fast asleep whilst the *ayah* worked on.

As always, it was her horses that restored the afflicted young woman's flagging morale. Neither Turka nor Fanny could have cared less about their mistress's scarred face, setting up loud nickering when she crept into their stable at dawn one morning. Joyfully snuffling in her hair, they then strained to investigate the contents of the paper bag in her hand—never a disappointment!

In time, Minette regained sufficient strength to ride out in the early mornings. Few people were about at that time, and the groom who was to accompany her behaved normally, and without undue staring. Cantering along the familiar pathways against a skyline suffused by the glory of an Indian sunrise, Minette's disfigurement could be pushed to the back of her mind.

The young Frenchwoman went out of her way to avoid contact with other wives, aware of being the subject of a barrage of criticism. Stories circulated about the doctor's crazed wife participating in a horse race whilst pregnant. Of course she had miscarried— whispered the gossips—twin boys, apparently. And have you seen her horridly scarred face! Poor, poor Doctor O'Hara having to put up with all that!

Minette found the spiteful tittle-tattle easy to ignore, although it did cross her mind to wonder about the source of their information. Patrick in his cups, without a doubt. She openly transgressed the boundaries of convention at times– without apology—and refused invitations recognisable as being extended from rank curiosity.

Mustering her courage, her chin held high, she eventually attended evening Polo. The whispering began at once, and losing her patience Minette decided to give them something else to prattle about. Within earshot of the muttering memsahibs, she commented that after her baby was born, she had every intention of joining in a chukka or two on her Arab horse. Maybe on a regular basis ...

Disgraceful—spluttered the gossips—that Frenchie has no sense of decency! So difficult for poor Doctor O'Hara.

Patrick's drink problem continued to escalate, a source of continuing anxiety for Minette. His general appearance was visibly deteriorating—the once-thick coppery head of hair becoming sandy and prematurely thin. Thread veins lent a ruddy glow to his nose and cheeks, and a well-defined paunch stretched the buttons on his uniform.

More often than not, Patrick would remain in the Officers' Mess until well after midnight. Arriving back at the bungalow, he would curse volubly as he staggered against furniture or tripped over rugs. Minette would pretend sleep, unable to bear the thought of his unwashed body near her after a day in the heat—often making clumsy and unwanted amorous overtures. Not to mention the stale breath that made her gag …

One advantage of Patrick's daily absence from the house was that the children rarely witnessed their father's erratic behaviour. Neither were they banished to the nursery for hours. The two boys were still obliged to have riding lessons with their father—when he remembered—and which they continued to dread. Both had become strong riders, in order to avoid their father's riding whip. In general, Minette felt the atmosphere within their home to be a less of a strain.

One morning, Minette was sitting at the breakfast table on the veranda with the children. About to take a sip of her tea, she became aware her face was under close scrutiny by her small daughter standing beside her.

"*Maman*, those horrid marks on your face have all gone!" Claire remarked, leaning against her mother. "You are pretty again!"

"Have they really?" Minette put an astonished hand to her cheek. "I suppose I haven't looked lately. Thank you for saying such a sweet thing, darling!"

"Yes, you do look better," conceded James through a mouthful of toast. "Don't you look in the mirror when you brush your teeth every morning?" he demanded in sudden suspicion. "After all, you make us do it every day!"

"Not everybody stares at themselves for ages like you do, James," Charlie dared to comment. "Anyway, *Maman* has always looked pretty to me."

"*Yuk!* Sickening baby boy sucking up as usual!" James sneered. "You know perfectly well *Maman* looked ugly with all those scars— you just won't admit it!"

"You're ugly, James," Claire frowned ferociously at her elder brother, sticking out her tongue. "James is a beast … ugly-bugly beast!" she chanted, "and anyway, *Maman* is even prettier now than Mrs Phillips!"

"Shut your mouth, you little twerp!" James snarled, "and Charlie, you are asking for a good duffing up if you aren't more careful!"

"Right, that is quite enough from all of you!" Minette hid a grin, having been favourably compared by her daughter with her rotund neighbour of fifty-odd years. "Boys, don't be late for your ride," she instructed, "and Claire, go and help Mailie to tidy the toys away in the nursery."

Back in her own bedroom, Minette sat at her dressing table and leaned forward to examine her face. It was true! Her complexion was as unblemished as it had been before her illness! Gathering up her skirts, she looked down at her legs, and they too were devoid of scarring. Elated, the young woman hugged herself.

As time passed, Seenta had continued giving her a daily massage all over her body with the special ointment. And on the *ayah's* recommendation, Minette had not bothered to examine the upsetting pock-marks on her face! The astonishing clarity of her complexion now came as a wonderful surprise, and she felt a surge of gratitude towards little Seenta.

Filled with sudden energy, Minette went in search of her small daughter. Perhaps she could persuade Claire to at least sit on her pony for a few minutes this morning. Since the last disastrous "lesson" with her father—now four months ago—the child had refused to ride, even with her mother. Just the suggestion resulted in hysterical crying. Perhaps today, Minette might manage to persuade her?

"No, *Maman*, no!" Claire implored her mother, her voice rising in distress. "Please don't make me! I hate riding, I'm frightened—please don't make me."

Sighing, Minette sadly gathered the child to her and stroked her hair. It did seem that Claire's riding days were well and truly over. Thanks to Patrick O'Hara's brutality, her own dream of one day riding out with her daughter had dissolved into thin air. She was sure the person Patrick had once been would never have petrified a little girl of three. A tragedy for his small daughter who had loved riding her pony.

Despite his ability to consume vast quantities of alcohol, Patrick's reputation as a superb surgeon remained intact. He was much in demand for the more refined aspects of surgery, not only within the cantonment, but he also attended Maharajahs or local Chieftains at their request. Upon learning of her husband's popularity, Minette's dry reflection was that surely these accolades must count as one less reason to drink?

Over the past few months, Frederick de Barre, the Anglo-French officer Minette had met in Darjeeling, had become a valued friend to the lonely young woman. Seeking her out that they might speak French together, he often accompanied her on early morning rides instead of the groom. In Frederick's company, Minette's spirits lifted, and she even found herself laughing out loud at his sense of the ridiculous.

He frequently joined James and Charlie on the *maidan* for a game of cricket, or sat under the trees telling the boys tales of adventure. Frederick very soon became a hero in their eyes. Watching her boisterous boys laughing and play-fighting with her French friend, she couldn't help feeling a twinge of regret that their father seemed disinterested, and unable to unbend in the same way.

Out of the blue, Patrick informed Minette that he was over-due for Home Leave. They were to spend six months in England, sailing from Bombay at the end of the month. It was an exciting thought, and the young woman was delighted her children would soon be seeing something of their own country.

Since she was now twenty-six years old, Minette imagined there was no longer a danger that the English police would prosecute Patrick. It might even be possible for him to investigate the possibility of a career in England ...

Over the years, she had heard nothing from her family. Even letters giving news of her children had been ignored. Minette shook her head in sad disbelief. They were her father's *grandchildren*, for God's sake! But perhaps her mother had succeeded in purloining every letter sent—or received. She supposed she would never know.

It would be high summer when they arrived in England. Not too drastic a change in temperature for the children, it would be sunny and warm without the unpleasantness of humidity. Of course, they would meet Belinda and Oliver's children who were of a similar age. The change of scene would do everyone good—including Patrick.

One evening, Minette was sitting in the veranda, a cool drink on the table in front of her. The children were in bed, and she was absorbed in writing letters to Belinda O'Hara and to Jane Ogilvy. She knew she would be seeing Belinda and her family, but also hoped to see something of Jane who had recently returned to Scotland from nursing in Africa.

Her eyes filling with tears, Minette's pen hovered above the flimsy notepaper as re-read Jane's last letter. It contained the most terrible news imaginable. Marauding bandits from a township inland from Johannesburg had killed several nuns running a popular Mission. Amongst the casualties was Alice, their dearest friend from Convent days. The gentle missionary who had never harmed a soul was dead.

Distraught, Minette could find nothing adequate to say to Jane who had been so close to sweet Alice. The pain of losing her friend must be unimaginable.

The slamming of the front door broke through Minette's saddened thoughts, and she started to her feet. God, surely that couldn't be her husband so early in the evening? As it turned out, it was indeed Patrick stalking into the veranda, a heavy scowl distorting his features. Her heart sank. Now what?

"Darling, how lovely to see you home so early," Minette forced a pleasant smile in the hope of deflecting a row. "Would you like tea, or perhaps a glass of *nimbu pani?*"

"Tea? No thanks! Tell the bearer to bring me a bottle of scotch and a decent glass, not one of those ridiculous thimbles you think to fob off on me."

Sprawled in a rattan chair, Patrick waited for the bottle to arrive. Pouring out half a tumbler of whisky, he took a large swig, and then sat back with a sigh. "It's bad news, I'm afraid. Squadrons are being detailed to the Chinese border to quash an uprising of sorts. It seems I am to go with them as Medical Officer. Let me tell you, I was far from happy to learn the overall commander is to be Wellesley—that over-zealous, straight-laced buffoon who rules the bloody roost here!"

Minette hid a smile. The Brigadier was known to be an ardent supporter of the Temperance Society. On his express order, no alcohol was to be consumed whilst on active service. Anybody disobeying would be put on a serious charge. No wonder Patrick was unimpressed. Perhaps it was not inconceivable that her husband's enforced sobriety might allow him to see the destructiveness of excessive drinking? She fervently hoped so.

It suddenly dawned on Minette what the Chinese venture meant to her, personally. Home leave would have to be cancelled. Those pleasant dreams of spending a few months in England were evaporating into thin air. The disappointment was crushing.

"I take it that we won't be going on Home Leave after all?" Minette said at last. "I was so looking forward to seeing Belinda and her family. I had also thought how lovely it would be to take the children to meet their grandparents in Ireland."

"Why don't you go on your own?" Patrick refilled his glass with a hefty measure of whisky. "Better than staying around here in the filthy heat on your own."

Minette was silent for a moment. Her husband's suggestion did seem to make sense on the face of it. They would all benefit from the cooler climate, and Charlie's awful prickly heat might clear up.

"I suppose you are right, although it's disappointing we can't be together for our first Home Leave," she said at last. "It's also rather a daunting prospect to be travelling on my own with the children. Do you happen to know anyone who might be going back to England around the same time?"

Patrick grinned mischievously, and for a brief moment Minette caught a flash of the man she had once adored to distraction.

"Perhaps I should persuade Frederick to accompany you, darling—he seems so much part of the family these days … *hey!*" Patrick ducked to avoid the cushion his wife aimed at his head. "Joking … just joking!"

Minette and the three children sailed for England at the end of the month. It was the first time she had coped with the children without the help of her *ayahs*, and the frazzled young woman often thought of them with longing. The efficient service of a First Class steward was available to her, but Minette still managed to forget handing over an ever-increasing pile of dirty clothes for laundering.

A daily problem was to think up suitable occupations for the children, in the hope of passing the time without fierce arguments or tantrums. No easy task—was her glum thought—especially with all those weeks at sea stretching ahead.

James' aggressive behaviour towards his younger brother was already noticeable. A certain amount of friction was to be expected, but never to this degree. Should Charlie not jump to his demands, James would secretly inflict painful retribution on the little boy and make him howl. Not satisfied with that, the older boy would then jeer at him for being a cry-baby.

In abject fear of his brother, Charlie had developed a stammer as a direct result. Seeing the distress of her younger son at close quarters, Minette gritted her teeth and forced a confrontation with James. Ignoring the boy's surly face, she threatened him with immediate suspension of pocket money should he continue bullying his brother. Money carried much weight with James, so it had the desired effect ... to Charlie's evident relief.

Claire, on the other hand, was rediscovering much of her natural *joie de vivre*. The nocturnal bed-wetting stopped, and a healthy colour appeared in her cheeks. In the absence of her father's intimidating presence, the child was positively blooming, Minette reflected with regret.

Expecting to miss Patrick terribly, the young woman made the uncomfortable discovery that she did not. To the contrary, it was blissful to be free from worrying each day about what condition her husband might be in, or trying to prevent the children from annoying him. She was sleeping better, and her energy level rose accordingly.

There was, however, a drawback to Minette's contentment— the suspicion that she might be pregnant again. In which case, the new baby would be due around the time she would be planning a return to India. Perhaps she should consider remaining in England until after the birth? A decided advantage of doing so, was that it would put off the inevitable accusation that she had engineered yet another pregnancy.

Peering critically at herself in the rather dim bathroom mirror, Minette wondered how Belinda would view her after so long? A slightly angular face gazed back, framed by a mass of dark curly hair now grown down to her shoulders. A faint crease between the eyebrows lent her a vaguely anxious air.

Leaning forward for a closer inspection, Minette was gratified that not a trace remained from the horror of smallpox. Her figure was as trim as ever, due to a careful diet and regular exercise. Not too bad, she decided—all things considered.

Tedious weeks at sea dragged by, and Minette longed for the end of the voyage. Her nerves were frayed with the strain of having to cope with bored and fractious children, not to mention relative inactivity. Heavens, what she would give for Mailie and Seenta's help!

At last, a dark smudge on the horizon was identifiable as the coast of England, and the young woman breathed a heart-felt sigh of relief. They were to stay with Belinda and her family for a few weeks at first. After which she was free to decide what came next. Dare she ask her father for permission to visit her old home? She must give it serious thought.

An hour later, the ship edged towards Southampton's wharf, eventually docking with a scream of its siren. Crewmen hurried to throw heavy ropes to those on the quayside, swiftly securing the liner to huge iron bollards. A tide of people on the quayside surged towards the newly arrived ship in anticipation of meeting those soon to disembark.

A watery sun peeping from behind fluffy white clouds did little to offset the chill of an early English morning. Groups of passengers waiting on deck were huddled into great coats and extra shawls, trying not to shiver in the unaccustomed cold. Standing at a railing above the cobbled quayside, the three children were bouncing with excitement, asking their mother to point out the new cousins from the milling throng below.

A flash of copper caught Minette's eye, and Belinda burst through the throng, her burnished halo of hair tossing about her face in its usual wild disorder. A young boy accompanied her, also a redhead, who appeared to be a replica of her own James!

With considerable difficulty, Minette managed to engineer herself to the front of a straggling group of women and children queuing to disembark. Holding Charlie and Claire by the hand, James following close behind, she negotiated the swaying gangway down to the cobbles below. Belinda waited at the bottom, her freckled face alight with joy. The two young women tearfully hugged each other, the emotional greeting regarded with curiosity by their respective children.

"Why, you must be Rob," Minette turned to the boy beside Belinda. "Good gracious, how alike you and James are ... but I suppose you *are* first cousins!"

"Yes, this is Rob," Belinda answered for her son, who was shyly hanging back from the lady with a funny-sounding accent. "Rosie is at home with Nanny, because Miss Mischief couldn't be trusted to stay by my side!"

"No prizes for guessing who you are, young man!" Belinda grinned at Minette's older boy. "You and Rob could pass for twins!"

Taking Belinda's gloved hand, James bent over to kiss it. "*Enchanté Madame*," he murmured to his mother's astonishment. "*Je m'appelle James O'Hara*." Repressing a smile, Minette brought her other two children forward.

"Do I call you Aunty?" Claire wanted to know. "*Maman* says you're my aunty."

"Of course you may, sweetie ... Aunty Belinda will do nicely." Belinda looked at Charlie, who blushed scarlet under her gaze. "And you must be ... ?"

"M-m my n-name is Ch-Charles, Robert O'Hara," pronounced the little boy holding out a sticky hand. "But you c-can call m-me Charlie, because I think I'm g-going to like you."

Without missing a beat, Belinda took the small hand. "How do you do, Charlie. I'm pleased you are going like me because I like you already!"

Charlie smiled ... then his face suddenly crumpled. "Ow ... *ow!*" The child made a valiant effort not to cry. "*Don't* James, that really h-hurts!"

Annoyed that attention should be diverted away from him, the older boy had surreptitiously ground his heel into Charlie's instep.

"Don't be so wet, Charlie," James said with a wolfish grin. "It was an accident."

"No! I know you d-did it on p-purpose—*ow!*" Charlie began to cry in earnest.

"*Maman*, I just saw James giving Charlie a great big pinch!" Claire declared in outrage. "Look at what he's done!" Claire pointed to a mauve bruise appearing on the boy's leg just below his short pants. "Nasty, horrid James!"

"You deserve a good slap, James O'Hara!" hissed a mortified Minette, rounding on her elder son. "No pocket-money for a week. Do something like that again, and you'll bitterly regret it!"

Sensing a storm was brewing, Belinda suggested they identify the luggage and go through Customs. They would then catch the next train to London, after which it was only a short carriage ride to Belinda and Oliver's home in Belgravia.

Oliver was at home when they arrived, and emerged to welcome Minette with genuine warmth. He expressed his regret that Patrick had been unable to accompany his family, for that would have been perfect! Beside him stood Rosie, a little *gamine* with the same wild profusion of red curls as her mother. The two little girls eyed each other for a moment. Clearly liking what they saw, Claire and Rosie went off hand in hand into the house, the others following behind.

Minette relinquished her children to Belinda's Nanny Wilson, whose motherly appearance belied a lady who brooked no nonsense. Nothing further was seen of the five children until bedtime! Nanny Wilson had whisked them off to a local park, where they met up with other children and their nannies, and an exciting game of "rounders" was soon under way.

After an early dinner that evening, the children were tucked up in bed, and Oliver excused himself to work in his study. Belinda and Minette sat together by the fire in the sitting room nursing a cup of hot chocolate, much as in days gone by.

Suddenly unaccountably washed-out and tearful, Minette tried to conceal it by staring at the dregs in her cup. A moment later, she felt a warm arm steal about her shoulders as Belinda edged closer, a look of concern on her face.

"Sweetie, what's the matter? Are you missing your Patrick so very much?"

"Far from it," Minette exclaimed, helpless tears running down her cheeks. "I wish to God that I did." She looked up into Belinda's face, unable to check her outburst.

"Belinda, I can hardly bear to tell you how Patrick has changed over the years. He drinks heavily and gambles his salary away … yelling unforgivable things at me if I dare mention it. I sometimes think he actually hates me."

"But why, Minette? What on earth has happened to make him behave in this way?"

"I just don't know," The young French woman admitted miserably. "He flies into a rage if I try and talk about it. Patrick blames me for everything—even the existence of our children whom he says he never wanted. On would think I somehow managed to fabricate a baby all by myself!"

"But surely he must love them now?" Belinda frowned. "His own children?"

"No. When Patrick is home, I've always had to make sure they are nowhere to be seen. All three are terrified of their father. My God, you should see his method of teaching the boys to ride! *Brutal* is not too strong a word to describe it. Even my little Claire who adored riding her pony … she was subjected to the same thing. She has hysterics if riding is even suggested."

Belinda was silent, her mind whirling. It seemed unbelievable that her attractive, debonair cousin had degenerated into a violent drunk. Brutal with his own children? She couldn't begin to imagine her own husband behaving in such a disgraceful way. Oliver loved his two children, and spent as much time with them as his busy Law Practice allowed. He would be appalled to hear of Patrick O'Hara's degeneration.

Belinda's generous heart contracted, envisaging the misery and stress her French friend must have been experiencing on a daily basis over the years. Her loneliness and lack of emotional security was evident in every word she spoke.

"Minette, try to forget I'm Patrick's cousin, and tell me everything from the very beginning," Belinda encouraged. "Then we'll think about what to do for the best."

Minette talked for two hours. Her exhaustion was forgotten in the sheer relief of confiding to a sympathetic listener. Gripping her hands together, she spoke of Kashmir, the nightmare of smallpox, and subsequent loss of her twin boys. She told a shocked Belinda of Patrick's donation to the hospital of the dead pock-marked infant twins, preserved forever in a jar of formalin as some kind of macabre curiosity. Her own hysterical objection having been brushed aside.

With infinite regret, Minette went on to describe her husband's bloated appearance, the once-handsome features marred by the ravages of alcohol abuse. Both women were crying by this time. Belinda wept to have lost a much-loved and kindly cousin, once so familiar to her. Minette, because she envisaged a future as desolate and emotionally barren as the past few years had been.

"Come, let's go to bed now," Belinda said at last. "No more brooding, and we'll talk again tomorrow." Arms about each other, the two old friends slowly climbed the stairs.

Breakfast the following morning was a relaxed affair. Nanny Wilson departed with the children to London Zoo, whilst Belinda and Minette remained sitting at the table in their dressing gowns.

"God, this is heaven having you here at last," Belinda declared, lacing her hot chocolate with several spoonfuls of sugar. "Oliver goes off so early each morning, it's sometimes hard to think up things to do. I've been so damned bored at times, I even contemplated having another baby—no, just a joke! Rosie is most definitely my swan-song."

"I wish Claire was mine," Minette grimaced. "Unfortunately, I've a nasty suspicion I may be pregnant again. All the signs are there."

"Oh, you poor thing!" Belinda was genuinely sympathetic. "But why are you caught so many times, sweetie? Doesn't Patrick do anything about preventing it, since he's against having children in the first place?"

"No, he steams right ahead to the bitter end ... and then has the gall to accuse me of deliberately conceiving," Minette's tone was dry.

"Can't say I understand it since he's a blooming doctor for heaven's sake!" Belinda shook her head. "Oliver takes care of all that sort of thing ... doesn't quite finish the job, if you know what I mean."

"After this baby, I intend to move heaven and earth to find a preventative measure—something that does really work. I cannot just go on breeding until I'm worn out."

"In view of all those pregnancies, it's amazing how slim you still are," Belinda sighed, patting her own rounded stomach. "My downfall is hot chocolate with rounds of yummy buttered toast and strawberry jam ... preferably several times a day."

Minette laughed. "I don't starve myself, believe me! But I do ride both horses every day, unless it's too hot for Fanny, my English mare."

"I don't ride much these days. Such a business getting on and off, I find." Belinda stretched out plump arms with a sigh. "I suppose we should be getting ourselves dressed." Struck by an idea, she turned to Minette.

"Why don't we take the children to Ireland for a couple of weeks? We'll see Mama and Papa, and you can show off your little darlings to John and Serena—who are their grandparents after all. God, Aunt Serena will swoon when she claps eyes on darling Patrick's children! James in particular, who happens to be the spit of his Pa!"

"But we've only just arrived," Minette said doubtfully. "I don't know if it's too much travelling for the children ... "

"Nonsense! The children would love it there," Belinda interrupted briskly, "lots of animals and clean air after stinky old London! Why, you might even tempt me back in the saddle, and we could go riding together like we did in the old days."

Caught up in her friend's enthusiasm, Minette nodded. Just the thought of riding out in the fresh air of the Irish countryside was temptation indeed!

"Good! That's sorted out then," Belinda said with satisfaction. "Did I tell you that Sean gave in to his mother's harping to marry that awful Bridget female? Silly fellow! Do you remember her? Aunt Serena's bosom friend's scrawny, flat-chested daughter, who possesses the most frightful buck-teeth?"

"Yes, I do! Didn't we call her *'Frigid-Bridget'* because she was always so *pi* and inclined to flounce? I bet she's leading poor Sean a merry dance."

"I'll say ... and backed to the hilt by her mother-in-law."

"You know, Serena never answered any of the letters I've been sending for years," Minette told her friend. "Not even when the children were born."

"You know what a poisonous old bat she can be, Minette— furious because you bagged her darling son! She'll thaw when she sees her grandchildren for the first time. She must realise by now they are the only ones she'll ever have, since it's doubtful the gorgeous Bridget allows Sean into her virginal bed that often."

Helpless with laughter, the two young women went upstairs to dress, and then plan their forthcoming visit to beautiful County Kildare.

CHAPTER TWENTY-TWO

The journey to Dublin dredged up many memories for Minette. Some of them good—others less so. The weather remained fine and the sea calm, so at least there was no sea-sickness to cope with. Nevertheless, both young mothers were thankful for the presence of Nanny Wilson, who had a knack of controlling five lively children!

Upon a return to the cabin after a stroll on deck, Belinda and Minette were astounded to find the children lying on their bunks, reading comic papers and books! Even in the short time that James had been under Nanny Wilson's care, Minette noticed his manners and general demeanour were improved. He rarely bullied his brother, and as a result Charlie's self-confidence was growing and his stammer showed signs of improving. Claire had little time to think of thumb-sucking, so engrossed was she in playing games with Rosie.

On arrival at the docks in Dublin, the disembarking passengers filed down a gangway to the quayside. In minutes Jennifer and Robert could be seen pushing their way towards them through the crowds, their faces alight with pleasure. Ecstatic to be seeing her daughter, Jennifer hugged Belinda and her grandchildren. Then, with a wide smile she turned to Minette who was waiting to one side.

"My dearest Minette, what a lovely, lovely surprise!" she exclaimed, "I've been so excited since Belinda let me know you were all coming to Ireland on a visit. Now, introduce me to your children. James is it? Good heavens, you could be Rob's twin—but I'm sure you must be tired of hearing that."

"You must be Charlie and you are little Claire. Goodness me, you're the image of your mother but in miniature," Jennifer bent to kiss each child in turn.

Over the days that followed, Minette enjoyed considerable freedom from the supervision of her children—thanks to the presence of Nanny Wilson. It allowed her to relax, and find time to consider her personal situation. Before departing from Belinda's home, she had received a letter from Patrick filled with enraged railing against tedious strictures imposed by the hated Brigadier. A post-script mentioned he was missing her.

Not a word about the children.

Minette was now certain about her condition, and dreaded having to inform her husband that another baby was on the way. The more she thought about it, the more she was inclined to remain in England for the birth. It would give her time to recover in order to deal with the inevitable harangue. She would write to Patrick in a day or so, after she had given some thought to what she should say. Meanwhile, there was the present moment to enjoy—she was riding every day whilst she could—and the future could take care of itself for the time being.

A few days later, Robert and Jennifer were arranging a family Champagne party. It was not only to celebrate Belinda's birthday, but it was also a surprise for John and Serena to meet their grandchildren for the first time. Jennifer was keenly aware that her sister-in-law was desperately hoping her younger son and his wife might provide her with a grandchild. None had been forthcoming, but now she would have three. Her favourite son's little children had come all the way from India to see her in Ireland ... Serena would be ecstatic!

On the evening of the party, Minette made time for the luxury of a bath. Nanny Wilson would ensure the children remained moderately clean, so she was able to lie in the warm scented water without interruption. Her mind touched upon that other set of grandparents, far away in France. Why was it that they continued to maintain such an enduring silence? Never a reply to any letter she had sent.

Again, she wondered about contacting her father to ask if she might bring her children home? How she would love to see her father's face when he met his own grandchildren! Claire, who resembled her as a child so closely, was bound to be his favourite. She would take the boys riding through the woods and show them her old hiding places … Minette sat up abruptly in the bath with a frown. Silly to indulge in foolish fantasies without the slightest substance behind them.

Minette dressed with great care that evening. Avoiding uncomfortable corsetry as always, she wore a blue silk gown in her favourite Empire line, the exact colour of her eyes. Several gold bangles adorned her arms, and gold filigree drop earrings fell from her ears, glistening against the riot of dark curls framing her face.

Standing back from the mirror behind the bedroom door, Minette cast a critical eye at her reflection. Her skin was tanned to an unfashionable pale gold from exposure to the Indian sun, nevertheless an attractive contrast against the vivid hue of her silk gown. Her figure remained slender, with no sign as yet of a baby on the way. Pleased that she had done what she could with her appearance, the young woman went downstairs to join the family.

"Ah, there you are, Minette" smiled Robert O'Hara, handing her a glass of bubbling champagne. "You are looking very lovely if I may say so, my dear."

Jennifer came bustling over, elegant in dove grey velvet. "I've told Nanny to keep the children outside in the garden until John and Serena arrive," she told Minette, "then we can call them in to surprise their grandparents."

"Cheer up old thing!" Belinda came to join her friend. "I can tell from the look on your face that you are worrying about the old dragon! Once she claps eyes on young James, believe me, she'll be over the moon!"

"She … she hated the idea of a "foreign" daughter-in-law, Belinda, and I'm still that," Minette said doubtfully. "But I suppose that was long ago now … "

"Sean is also coming this evening, no doubt dragging the delightful Bridget with him," Belinda grinned. "Let's be thankful she has no children. God, can you imagine it? Lots of Midget Bridgets complete with rabbit teeth, scurrying like ants underfoot? What a ghastly thought!"

Amused by her friend's sense of the ridiculous, Minette was

about to reply when there was the sound of carriage wheels arriving in front of the house. Jennifer and Robert went to greet the guests, whilst Belinda and Minette summoned their brood from under the watchful eye of Nanny Wilson.

Returning to the sitting room with her children, Minette saw John and Serena O'Hara standing in a group with an unchanged Sean, accompanied by a skinny young woman. Correctly surmising her to be Bridget, Sean's wife, Minette stifled a giggle thinking of Belinda's earlier remarks.

A swift glance at John confirmed his heart attack of a few months ago had aged him significantly. Her mother-in-law, however, had scarcely changed—still tightly corseted, her silver hair immaculate. Bridget, unsuitably clad in puce satin, edged closer to Serena, and fixed the Frenchwoman with an unblinking stare.

Seeing Minette enter the room, Serena was clearly startled, but recovered her composure at once. Gathering up her skirts, she swept over to Jennifer and addressed her in peremptory and over-loud tones.

"Jennifer, why did you not mention that persons other than family had been invited to Belinda's birthday party this evening? In the existing circumstances, I would have preferred to have been told."

"What? For heaven's sake, Minette happens to be your elder son's wife, so she can hardly be classified as anything other than family," Jennifer retorted with an irritable frown. "Minette dear, do bring the children over to meet their grandparents."

"*Grandparents?*" Serena stepped back in apparent outrage. "Oh, how dare you, Jennifer! As you very well know, I have never recognised that ridiculous cow-shed charade of a wedding, into which my unfortunate son was inveigled."

"Aunt!" Belinda stepped forward in disbelief. "How can you say such an awful thing? Of course they are ... "

"Just be quiet for once, Belinda!" interrupted the woman coldly, never taking her eyes from Minette's stunned face. "It's high time someone in this family had the courage to tell this...this hussy of the damage she has done to my Patrick, as well as to our entire family."

Taking advantage of the appalled silence that followed her words, Serena turned to glare at Minette, who was standing as if turned to stone. "I want you to know—*Miss*—that I hold you responsible for the loss of my son," she stated with chilly deliberation.

"Because of you, Patrick has been forced to hide away in a far corner of the uncivilised world. Not only have you ruined the career of a gifted surgeon, but you have also dashed all hope of pursuing his dream of medical research. He is painfully aware that he has been robbed of his life—both professional and personal."

The infuriated woman venomously sucked in thin lips. "Saddled with an ever-increasing tidal wave of illegitimate brats, it is of little wonder that Patrick is so very miserable with how his life has turned out. You have brought great shame on this family, and on your own if my memory serves me correctly. We are both good Catholic families, so in the eyes of our Church you have never been married to my son. To us, you are nothing other than a concubine. Therefore, you have no right to the name of O'Hara ... and neither does your litter of little bastards." Serena's scornful gaze swept over the three bewildered children standing beside their mother.

"Frankly, I cannot but marvel that my sister-in-law has seen fit to receive you—but Jennifer has too soft a heart. Of course, had I known that you and your brood of illegitimate progeny were installing yourselves in her home, I would have never accepted her invitation this evening."

Jennifer and Belinda were frozen in stricken silence, whilst John O'Hara stared fixedly at the floor. Robert and Sean were returning to the sitting room with more bottles of champagne—in time to overhear the last of Serena's vicious attack against the young Frenchwoman. Both men's mouths fell open in embarrassment and horror.

Suddenly galvanised, Jennifer started forward, holding out her arms to Minette in unconscious supplication. But the young woman drew herself up, her sapphire eyes blazing in a face pale with fury. Defeated, Jennifer's hands dropped to her sides.

"*Stop!*" Everyone in the room turned to look at Minette. Never had she looked so magnificent, the dignity and nobility of her ancient lineage suddenly apparent in the very hauteur of her bearing.

"Madame, I will not listen to another word of your ignorant, foul-mouthed ranting! You are in no position to speak of matters about which you know nothing, absolutely nothing. Furthermore, how dare you use insulting and abusive terms in the hearing of my innocent children?"

Every word Minette spoke fell like a drop of icy water into the silence as she advanced on the older woman. Forced to take a nervous step backward, Serena O'Hara stared, mesmerised, into her victim's face now taut with rage.

"Spewing your ridiculous bigotry and filth … a woman of your age and supposed standing should be deeply ashamed," Minette continued inexorably. "I was brought up never to resort to gutter language—sadly not the case where you are concerned, Madame. I suggest you return home to wash out your mouth with carbolic soap!"

Casting a disdainful glance at the apoplectic woman, Minette took her two younger children by the hand and left the room, James trailing behind, his eyes like saucers.

Nobody in the room spoke or moved for a long moment.

"Serena, this time you have gone too far!" Robert told his brother's wife, his face flushed with anger. "You've got a damned nerve insulting a guest in my house. Of course, you will apologise —"

"*Apologise?*" Serena shrilled, her cheeks flaring an unattractive red. "To that immoral French creature? Not in this lifetime! And you can stop being two-faced, Robert O'Hara—since you know perfectly well that I was merely voicing what the rest of us have thought for years. Admit it!"

"Speak for yourself, Serena!" Robert retorted through clenched teeth. "And by the way, I thought Minette dealt with you with singular accuracy!"

"Well, *I* think you are being very unfair on poor Mother," broke in Bridget with an air of importance. "Remember she has lost a son to that conniving Frenchwoman. In my book, that's—"

"Bridget, I'll thank you to keep quiet about matters which do not concern you!" Sean barked at his outraged wife. "It is not fitting that you criticise Minette, so mind your own business, if you please."

Shocked, that her generally acquiescent husband should speak to her in such a manner, Bridget sank her protruding teeth into her lower lip and flounced from the room. A departure that perturbed nobody.

"Belinda, go after Minette and apologise on our behalf for Serena's appalling behaviour," Jennifer appealed to her daughter who was standing beside her, every freckle apparent on her blanched face. "Convince her that we do not share her views, regardless of what the Church might stipulate. Oh my God, I hope and pray those disgraceful remarks went over the little ones' heads."

Belinda found Minette alone in her bedroom, standing by the window. Hearing her enter, the young Frenchwoman glanced round, dry-eyed and unsmiling.

"Dearest Minette, I just want to say—"

"You know, I never realised the extent of your aunt's hatred of me," Minette interrupted her friend. "Of course, I knew she was furious over our rather clandestine marriage. But I imagined she would have mellowed by now, especially where the children were concerned. How terribly wrong I was."

"The woman's gone round the bend, Minette! Mama and Papa are absolutely furious, and they hope you will know they don't share her horrid views."

"Belinda, I don't care a damn what the woman says to me, personally. But to use foul and despicable terms in relation to my children ... *in their hearing?* By anyone's standards that is utterly unforgivable! God only knows what damage has been done."

Minette's expression hardened. "At least, I now know the reason for my husband's hostile attitude towards me, his disgusting drinking, and his obscure hatred of our children. Evidently, he managed to write as much to his parents."

"Sweetie, I don't know what to say—" Belinda began.

"There is nothing left to say, don't you think?" Minette's voice was flat. "But I will not be held responsible for a split within your family, Belinda. I am very fond of your parents who have always been so kind to me, and you and I are close. Sadly, it must come at an end when I leave Ireland tomorrow. In the circumstances, I have decided that Patrick's family must be excluded from my life, and from the lives of my children. Permanently."

Belinda's mouth fell open with shock. Appalled though she had been to see her French friend so humiliated by her aunt, it had not occurred to her that Minette would react in such a drastic way. Was she to lose her dearest friend?

It now crossed Belinda's mind that Minette was convinced Serena was telling the truth saying she merely voiced the private opinion of the entire O'Hara family. It stood to reason that in their eyes, the status of her children would be viewed as questionable. Belinda's eyes swam with tears of regret. No wonder Minette wished to cut all ties. With a muffled sob, she turned and left the room.

Dinner that evening was a subdued affair. Pale but composed, Minette accepted Jennifer's apology with cool dignity, changing the subject as soon as it was polite to do so. Directly afterwards, she requested a carriage the following morning to take her and the children to catch the boat back to the mainland. Her immediate departure was better for everybody, the young Frenchwoman explained with grim finality—cutting across Belinda's tearful protest. Excusing herself, she went upstairs to her room.

Lying sleepless in bed, Minette watched the shadowy branches of an oak tree gently moving in the night breeze outside the window, an acute reminder of her old bedroom in France. Blinking back hot tears of sudden homesickness, she was unexpectedly seized by a sense of terrible grief and isolation.

Once the adored daughter of her father, she had impulsively abandoned a relatively carefree life to run off with a man she scarcely knew. A man, who even now was not only spiralling into alcoholism, but caught up in a vortex of self-pity over his "ruined" career. For which he held his wife directly responsible.

How naïve she had been, sacrificing all she held dear to escape marriage to a man of her father's choice. Jacques Briand, a kind enough man, if not exciting to the foolish girl she had been, would have given her the security she now so desperately lacked. Instead, she was viewed as a *pariah*—a *concubine*—the mother of *bastards!*

Gasping in an agony of humiliation, Minette was struck by the terrifying thought that she was alone in the world. There was simply nobody to whom she could turn for advice or comfort. Had she been too hasty in dismissing Belinda's suggestion that they all return to London together? No! Let it not be said that she and her children were parasites on Oliver and Belinda's generosity—she thought grimly.

It was all she could expect from this judgemental Irish clan.

Minette slept little that night.

The following morning, it was clear that Jennifer was deeply upset by Minette's decision to leave, but the young woman remained adamant. In tears, Belinda left the breakfast table whilst Minette excused herself that she might prepare her children for the journey back to England.

Bewildered by the sudden change in plan, Minette's children regarded their mother with resentful eyes. But why did they have to go? They were having such fun with their cousins! The two older children were dimly aware that something was badly wrong. Was it to do with that old lady shouting horrid things yesterday? But one look at their mother's stony expression deterred further argument.

It wasn't long before James' face took on its familiar mulish scowl, whilst a sulky Claire resumed ardent thumb-sucking. Charlie was the only child to take matters he didn't understand in his stride, assuming his mother knew what was best. Minette briefly hesitated, unhappy to see how upset her children were to be losing the cousins to whom they had become close. But the image of Serena O'Hara's sneering face sprang to mind, and her resolve hardened.

No question of a change of plan.

Three hours later, Minette and the children were standing in the stern of the little steamer taking them back to England. Robert O'Hara stood alone on the quayside, having escorted the little family to the docks in his carriage. Jennifer and Belinda were too upset to go. Waving goodbye to Robert, Minette was painfully certain she would never see him again. He had always been kind, even affectionate, and she would miss his quiet presence. But it also underlined the rightness of her departure, that his close family was not split apart in acrimony.

Returning to the saloon, Minette knew she had made a definitive decision to turn a page in her life. It was important now to look forward—not back. A couple of days in a London hotel, a few trips to the park or zoo would help settle the children. In the meanwhile, she would send a telegram to Jane Ogilvy in Scotland.

CHAPTER TWENTY-THREE

Jane was thrilled to receive a telegram from her old friend, asking if she and her family might visit her in Edinburgh for a few days? Jane lost no time in replying with a warm invitation to stay for as long as they could spare.

Minette and the children were now due to arrive late afternoon the following day, and Jane could hardly contain her excitement. They had so much catching up to do! After all, it was now several years since the auspicious day of Minette's marriage to Patrick O'Hara.

A few months ago, Jane had returned from Africa where she had been working as a British Army nurse for almost six years. Having seen enough blood and gore on a daily basis to last her a lifetime, she had made the decision to leave that beautiful, if troubled continent.

Back in Scotland, Jane had found employment at the big teaching hospital in Edinburgh where she had originally trained. It wasn't long before the efficient nurse was promoted to Theatre Sister, a position she enjoyed. The shift work was less arduous, leaving more time for leisure activities—something that had been lacking in Jane's life for a considerable time.

Left a sizeable legacy by her grandmother, Jane had purchased a large three-bedroom apartment in an old country mansion situated in a quiet sought-after area on the outskirts of the town. The gracious house stood at the end of a drive winding its way through sweeping lawns shaded by old oak trees. Subsequently, she had amused herself by furnishing her new home, which included the delightful scouring of antique shops in search of hidden treasures.

Many years ago, Jane had made a conscious decision not to marry. She had seen enough of her friends' marriages to form an opinion that the married state for a woman was tantamount to becoming an unpaid housekeeper. She did exactly what she wanted, led a busy life, and there was no room for a man in it. Of course, it meant she would be childless—Jane's only regret.

But now Minette was coming with her children, and she would enjoy having them around for a decent chunk of their Home Leave. The three children were young enough to share the larger guest bedroom, so Minette would have the other to herself. Jane remembered a young couple living in one of the other apartments had children of a similar age. She would mention that she was soon to have three more coming to stay, and of course they could all play outside on the lawns in perfect safety. What fun it was going to be!

The following day dawned crisp but fine, promising to remain so for the rest of the day. At five o'clock in the afternoon, Jane waited with impatience behind the barrier at the railway station. She thought to have heard the scream of a whistle in the distance, an indication of the train's imminent arrival. Ten minutes later, the huge engine hauling a long line of carriages clanked its way into the station precincts, juddering to a halt with a final hiss of steam.

Carriage doors were thrown open, and travel-weary passengers descended to the platform. Scanning the new arrivals, Jane wondered if her French friend's general appearance might have changed? Was she perhaps a little heavier after all those pregnancies? Had that awful bout of smallpox disfigured her? Jane chewed her bottom lip with anxiety.

The crowd suddenly parted to reveal Minette, her figure astonishingly slender, and in possession of enviable cheekbones in a clear honey-coloured complexion. She was holding the hands of two small children, a slightly older red-headed boy following close behind.

Ecstatic, Jane pushed her way forward and threw her arms about her friend. The two young women hugged each other, watched by three silent children visibly drooping with tiredness. Squatting inelegantly on her heels, Jane introduced herself as Aunty Jane—their self-appointed Godmother.

Arriving back at the house, the children tumbled out of the hired hackney cab to find themselves taken over by Jane's housemaid. Mary, a rosy-cheeked Scots girl with a jolly attitude to life, bundled the children off to the kitchen for something to eat. A scrubbed oak table had been laid with a high tea of cheese toast, pancakes and syrup, egg sandwiches and fingers of buttery shortbread. A glass of milk stood beside each plate. In spite of themselves, the children's eyes lit up at the sight of the appetising spread.

"Och, but aren't ye the bonniest wee bairns this side o' Scotland, now!" Mary exclaimed as she sat them down at the table. "Now, me darlin's, eat up a guid supper afore goin' tae yer bed." Needing no further encouragement, the children fell on the food with alacrity. Soon after, Mary saw them into warmed beds where they immediately fell fast asleep.

Minette was equally as exhausted as her children, the train journey having seemed both endless and tedious to a degree. The children had been fractious, whining, and pushing their mother's patience to the limit. Especially James, who amused himself by teasing Charlie until the younger boy was bawling.

However, it was easy to relax with Jane. She was evinced such joy to be having Minette and her children to stay, that her flagging self-esteem received a welcome boost. Of course, she would tell Jane what had transpired during her ill-fated trip to Ireland ... but not just yet. The whole ghastly episode was still too raw in her mind. Meanwhile, she would try to come to terms with what she had learned about her husband's betrayal of her to his vile mother ...

It wasn't long before Jane sensed there was something very, very wrong with Minette. Her friend's natural insouciance was lacking, and she would sometimes just stare into space, unheeding of being spoken to. Jane was sensible enough not to probe. She would allow Minette to tell her what was troubling her—or not. This lack of pressure was what the traumatised young Frenchwoman needed most. A close friend who respected her privacy, whilst she tried to make sense of her life.

To Minette's infinite relief, the children adjusted well to their new environment, playing outside in the gardens for much of the day. No mention had been made of the unpleasant scene they had been subjected to, and Minette felt heart-felt relief that the significance of Serena's appalling remarks seemed to have passed them by.

Children from the other apartment came out to play with them, and lively games of cricket or rounders were soon under way. Mary was delegated to keep an eye on them, sitting on a bench and knitting some unrecognisable garment. Subsequently, Minette felt no guilt in having little to do with the children for the time being.

Ten days flashed by, and the young Frenchwoman' battered morale began to rise, due to the restful and uncomplicated life she was now leading. The children were rosy-cheeked and happy. James' sulky glower vanished, and Claire once again abandoned thumb-sucking. Even Charlie's stammer lessened as the boy relaxed into the pleasant atmosphere of Jane's home.

Minette had already written to Patrick, informing him of the eventual arrival of another infant. Unable to write in affectionate terms to her husband, she merely stated it would be best if she remained in England until after the birth. There had been no reply to her letter as yet. Minette mentally shrugged. To be rid of the children for an extended period would in all probability be an attractive suggestion to their father, she thought wryly.

One morning, Minette and Jane were at the breakfast table with the children. Aware that their friends were already waiting outside, they hurried to drink their milk and eat an obligatory slice of toast before leaving the table.

"Aunty Jane, what's a bastard?" enquired Charlie through a mouthful of toast.

"What? Oh … a bastard," Jane hurriedly replied, before the child could repeat the word. "Why, it's somebody whose parents haven't been married, Charlie."

James froze, a piece of toast halfway to his mouth. "*Maman*, why did that horrid lady in Aunt Jennifer's house call us bastards?" he demanded looking hard at his mother. "Everyone knows our parents are married, don't they?"

"I've no idea, James," Minette prevaricated. "It may be that she doesn't like me, and just wanted to be very rude."

"Is that why we had to leave—"

"Hurry up now and finish your toast," Minette interrupted. "Remember your friends are waiting for you outside."

With a last considering look at his mother, James followed his brother and sister to the front door, where Mary was waiting for them.

With raised eyebrows, Jane glanced at Minette whose cheeks were on fire with mortification. "Well! What was that all about then?"

"I rather think you deserve an explanation, Jane. I'm so sorry if you were embarrassed! Poor little Charlie had no idea what he was saying."

"For heaven's sake, I think I'm old enough to have heard that word before!" Jane retorted without rancour. "It was just surprising to hear it on the lips of an innocent child!"

"It's high time I told you about the whole ghastly business, Jane." Minette licked dry lips. "Oh God, I was praying the children hadn't absorbed the gist of that dreadful scene."

Jane listened intently as the unfortunate sequence of events unfolded. Privately, she was horrified that Patrick and Minette had failed to solemnise their union within the Catholic Church. Should they continue procrastinating the issue, might there not be dire problems ahead with regard to their children? But now was not the moment to harp on that possibility.

Crying unrestrainedly for the first time since the confrontation with her mother-in-law, Minette came to the end of the sorry tale. Not only was she pregnant again, but she couldn't bear the thought of returning to her miserable existence in India.

Or to Patrick O'Hara … who had betrayed her trust so abominably.

"Dearest Jane, could you bear to put up with us all until the new baby is born?" Minette begged, her sapphire eyes awash with tears. "I don't think I can face Patrick's predictable reaction to another child. Having a few extra months here would allow me time to think of the possibility of an alternative future for myself and the children."

"Of course you may stay!" Jane leaned forward to put an affectionate arm round Minette's shoulders. "You are more than welcome, sweetie, you must know that? I'll book you in to our new Maternity Ward at the hospital—it's excellent. But have you thought about Patrick? Might he order you back to India—regardless?"

Minette's mouth tightened. "In this instance, I shall do as I think fit. I have already written to him with the suggestion, but there has been no reply as yet. I daresay the prospect of the continued absence of his children will prove an excellent inducement for him to agree!"

Watching the changing expressions on her friend's face, Jane could make an intelligent guess as to what was passing through her mind. It was clear that Minette wanted to leave her husband for good. In light of what she had just heard, Jane could well understand why.

But the stark realities of her existing situation could not be avoided. Should Patrick prove parsimonious, Minette might find herself obliged to assume sole financial responsibility for three children ... soon to be four.

Not an easy path to tread for a woman on her own.

Jane shook her head decisively. Now was not the time to point out to the poor girl that she might have no choice but to return to her husband. Better to deflect the issue for the moment. It could always be reassessed after the birth, when perhaps Minette might see things in a more realistic light.

"In that case, sweetie, we are going to have such fun choosing gorgeous baby clothes," Jane grinned at her friend.

A letter from Patrick arrived within the month. In principle, he agreed to allow Minette to remain in England until after the birth of her baby. However, he wished to be given an idea of how long she intended to remain thereafter, presumably a question of a week or two.

No mention of his children.

Of interest, however, was Patrick's description of a memorable incident on the Chinese border. An important Mandarin hearing of the surgical skills of the British Major-doctor requested that he attend his eldest son as a gesture of good will. The young man had been wounded during a skirmish some weeks earlier, but the wound continued to fester despite the attentions of Chinese healers.

With the agreement of the British Commander, and under the protection of four of the Mandarin's personal bodyguard, Patrick rode over to the palace set high up in the hills, a dusty and difficult trek that took some three hours.

Upon examination of the unconscious young man, Patrick had seen at a glance that his condition was serious. The wound was jagged, suppurating and stinking with infection. Without immediate medical attention the Mandarin's son would die. Patrick had cleaned the area with disinfectant, tidied the wound and applied specially prepared poultices to draw out the poisons.

Two days later, the now sterile wound was stitched, and the following day the young man woke from his comatose state—weak— but on the road to recovery.

Beside himself with gratitude, the Mandarin had offered Patrick a substantial quantity of gold coin, which he was obliged to refuse with regret. Determined the doctor should be rewarded in some way, the Mandarin presented Patrick with a beautiful ceremonial sword, its scabbard heavily embossed and hung with silken scarlet tassels.

Also pressed into his hand was an unusual ring of priceless jade, surrounded by rubies set in rose gold. Patrick indicated the ring was destined to adorn his wife's hand upon her return to India. His letter closed with a mention of missing her.

Folding the flimsy letter paper, Minette's lips twisted in cynicism. That she should even see this wondrous ring was doubtful! Patrick would probably sell the thing to fuel his blasted gambling ...

Interrupting her sombre reflections, Jane entered the room, a bundle of white fluff in her arms. Two bright eyes peeped from the cloud of hair, and a busy pink tongue flicked in and out. The wriggling bundle turned out to be a puppy, and Minette fell on her knees with delight to fondle the silky little ears. Sensing a loving human being, the puppy clumsily attempted to clamber into her lap, his tail wagging in ecstasy.

Having grown up with her father's hounds and her grandmother's spaniels, she would have loved to have a dog in Lucknow. So would the children. But Patrick had never allowed it for reasons that escaped her.

"Meet Jasper, recently arrived from a friend's farm in the country,' Jane sat back on her heels with a grin. "I've always wanted a dog, and when the possibility presented itself, of course I leaped at the chance. Especially since the children are here to help me with him. Now, tell me what Patrick has to say about remaining in Scotland to have your baby?"

"I have his express permission to do so." Minette's infectious smile flashed, and for a brief moment, Jane glimpsed the effervescent girl she had once known. "So, I'm afraid you are stuck with us for the duration. But I insist that we pay our way, and no arguments, if you please."

The arrival of Jasper provided the children with a delightful occupation. Every morning, fierce arguments broke out over whose turn it was to hold the puppy's leash whilst walking in the gardens. The daily rumpus resulted in Jane making out a roster to pin on the kitchen notice board. Now each child could see whose turn it was to take Jasper out to do his business—and the rows ceased.

Feeling washed out and listless, Minette was more than happy for Jane to organise the children's activities. Guiltily, she mentioned the fact to her friend after the children had been put to bed one evening.

"Dear girl, you must know by now how I love bossing your brood about!" Jane returned. "Had I not forsworn the married state, I might find myself tempted if the arrival of a little girl like yours could be guaranteed."

"Yes, Claire's a poppet, isn't she?" Minette answered. "Now that she is away from her father's bullying, it's incredible how she has blossomed."

"Yes, I seem to recall you mentioned something of the sort in a letter. Wasn't Patrick giving her hideous riding lessons? Honestly, Minette, it's so difficult to equate the sweet man you married ... with this monstrous person, capable of persecuting a small child! Have you any idea as to what might have caused such a change in him?"

Minette hesitated for a long moment. "According to my mother-in-law, Patrick holds me personally responsible for his misery," she answered. "He chooses to perceive that I forced him into marriage, effectively ruining any prospect of taking up the career he had set his heart on." Her voice shook from the humiliation of such an admission. "I have therefore robbed him of a decent life."

Jane stared at her friend—aghast. She, of all people, knew the circumstances of that marriage! There had never been any question of Patrick being forced into it. What a *beastly* accusation.

"Now you know every sorry detail of my marriage, Jane,'

Minette said quietly. "Maybe you can now understand why I am reluctant to continue living with a man who blames me for my very existence? How can he be allowed to continue his reign of terror over my children?"

"Don't upset yourself by trying to make life-changing decisions now, my sweet," Jane advised her friend. "You still have several months ahead in which to reflect, and by then things will have clarified in your mind. Right now, you and I have some planning to do regarding the arrival of a little newcomer."

The next months flew by in a pleasant and relaxed atmosphere, and in the fullness of time a baby girl was born to Minette. The delivery was swift and uncomplicated, the infant small but perfect. Appointed Godmother to the baby, Jane chose her name—*Christina*.

The following day, Jane brought the children to see their mother and new sister at the hospital. Charlie and Claire gazed down entranced at the infant, grinning with delight when a tentative finger was gripped with surprising strength by a tiny hand! James, however, made a point of demonstrating disinterest by looking bored and standing as far away from the baby as possible. Minette sighed. Nothing really changed where her elder son was concerned.

A week later, Minette returned to Jane's home with her new baby, mentally braced for sleepless nights and bouts of colicky screaming. To her delighted surprise, Christina turned out to be a peaceful little soul, feeding, sleeping and rarely crying. Even when her pram was placed under a tree in the gardens, the baby slept on—oblivious to the shrieking of the older children playing nearby.

With an air of importance, Claire insisted on helping to look after her new baby sister. At her bath-time, she would sponge down the slippery little body. Then she would then wait for her mother to lift the baby out of the water, and carefully pat her dry with a muslin towel. Sitting in an armchair, the baby lying comfortably on a pillow across her knees, Claire would feed Christina her bottle of milk.

Despite having been the youngest of the three children, there was not even the slightest sign of jealousy—thought Minette with relief. To the contrary, Claire seemed determined her new sister should look to her for all of her needs.

A joyous Christmas came and went, the children excitedly

playing in the snow, their cheeks rosy with health. With considerable reluctance, Minette realised she must soon come to a decision with regard to the future. Occasional letters from Patrick had arrived— sensible letters on the whole. Nevertheless, they invariably ended with a demand to know when she intended returning to India.

Receiving these missives prompted a feeling of near panic in Minette. There must be another way forward, for God's sake? How could she take up that unhappy life she had left behind in Lucknow? Subject these happy children of hers to their father's brutality once again? It simply did not bear thinking about !

Jane categorically refused to be drawn over Minette's indecision. Only she could decide what was right for herself and her family. Privately, Jane imagined her friend would come to the conclusion that no real alternative existed but to return to her husband. Far from ideal, but from a financial and social aspect it was the only realistic option for a woman with four children.

However, Jane advised Minette in the strongest terms to make arrangements for her marriage to be sanctified by the Catholic Church at the earliest opportunity. It was of enormous importance for the children's spiritual and social standing, as well as their future happiness.

Minette continued to vacillate over how to move forward.

Weeks went by, and then a letter arrived from Patrick with a peremptory demand that his wife return to India without further delay. The infant was old enough to travel at four months. Passages to Bombay had been arranged, and the tickets would await Minette at the P&O Offices at Southampton. The ship's date of sailing was set for the twenty-eighth of February.

But that's only in ten days time—thought Minette in panic. Reading on, her eyes fell on a cryptic paragraph at the end of Patrick's letter. He had received a letter from his father indicating Minette's visit to Ireland had been disastrous, inordinately upsetting his mother as a result. Patrick expected a full explanation from his wife upon her return to Lucknow.

The young Frenchwoman's lips tightened. It was obvious that John O'Hara had sought to mitigate his wife's disgraceful behaviour by the implication that Minette was somehow at fault. How very weak-kneed of him—she thought scornfully.

Much as Jane predicted, a forlorn Minette realised she had no realistic choice but to acquiesce to her husband's demand that she return to India. Bringing up four children in relative penury appalled her, and as for finding funds to finance the boys' education—quite impossible. In any event, she doubted she had the nerve to embark on such a risky and lonely venture.

As a precaution, however, Minette withdrew a substantial amount of money from the account at Lombard's Bank in London, and placed it in a Scottish bank. She also arranged for Jane to be given Power of Attorney—in the event that funds were required in an emergency. The sum would cover sea passages back to England for her family, and was sufficient to cover living expenses for six months. She intended to remit further funds to the account whenever possible.

A small insurance against her husband resuming unacceptable behaviour.

The day of departure to London finally arrived. At the Railway Station, Minette stood on the platform facing a tearful Jane. The three children had already been ensconced in the carriage. James sat on his own, his expression surly. Charlie and Claire sat opposite, leafing through comic-cuts. The baby was fast asleep in her carrycot beside Claire. Luggage and pram wheels had been safely stowed. Realising it was time to say goodbye, Minette threw her arms about her loyal friend in a fierce hug.

"Jane, I shall never be able to thank you enough for everything," she murmured, her voice shaking with emotion. "Your wonderful Scottish common sense has been a godsend, and the children are almost unrecognisable from the pallid little waifs who arrived on your doorstep. They've been so happy at their Aunty Jane's home and are reluctant to leave ... just look at James' face!" Minette grimaced. "I have a nasty feeling he is going to sulk all the way back to Lucknow."

"Sweetie, you must know what a pleasure it has been for me," Jane gave a watery smile. "The flat is going to sound like an empty drum without you. Thank goodness Jasper will still be at home," Jane hesitated briefly, and then plunged on.

"Minette, at risk of sounding a dead bore, I beg you not to

forget to solemnise your marriage within the church. It's frightfully important for the children."

"I promise!" Minette hugged her friend once more and then climbed into the carriage to join her children. The Guard waved a green flag and blew his whistle, carriage doors slammed, and the engine fired up with much squealing of metal and hissing steam.

Charlie and Claire looked up, their eyes wide, struck by a realisation they were about to leave Scotland. It was here that they had known normality and real happiness for the first time in their young lives. Staring fixedly out of the window, James' eyes swam with resentful tears over being dragged away from the dog—and the life he had grown to love.

With further blasts of billowing steam, the great engine jerked, then slowly rumbled from the dimness of the station and out into the blinding brightness of early morning Scottish sunlight. Minette and her family remained unnaturally quiet. Each of them wondered with varying degrees of apprehension what might be awaiting them upon their return to Lucknow, now only a question of a few weeks away …

Upon their arrival in London, Minette booked them into the same hotel where they had stayed before leaving for Scotland. She had ensured there were two days in hand before the liner was due to sail from Southampton, to allow the children time to recover from the exhaustion of their long train journey. And Minette was determined they should enjoy their stay in London.

The Hotel's receptionist recommended a walk in Hyde Park, where a "Punch and Judy Show" took place every afternoon. Then, there was always a visit to London Zoo, which Minette recalled had been popular with the children when Nanny Wilson had taken them there. For a brief moment, she hesitated, wondering if she should risk a visit to Belinda and her family? No. Rob and Rosie had been present during that atrocious scene in Ireland. They might ask awkward questions which her children were unable to answer. Maybe after a few years had passed …

Two enjoyable days passed in a flash. The following day, Minette and the children caught the Boat Train to Southampton, where they boarded the liner that was due to sail later that afternoon.

Following instructions from the Ship's Purser, Minette located their interconnecting cabins, where she found a smiling stewardess waiting to welcome them.

At her request, the stewardess took charge of the baby in her carrycot, whilst the children accompanied their mother on deck to watch the ship's departure. Standing by the stern railing as the ship made towards open sea, Minette removed her stylish hat to allow the sea breeze to blow through her hair.

She wished she could bring herself to look forward to seeing her husband again. It was not yet a year since she left India, but it felt like an eternity in light of all that had transpired during these last months.

Minette had received a final letter from Patrick before leaving Edinburgh. It contained a surprising change of tone from the aggressive stance of his last missive ordering her departure. Neither was there any further mention of having upset his mother. It seemed almost conciliatory.

Her own letter setting out the conditions of her return to India had made something of an impression on her husband. He promised a change of attitude towards the children, and declared an abiding love for his wife. He would no longer drink to excess, and they would spend time together. Everything would be different once they were together again.

Was it possible that this long separation had—at last—brought Patrick O'Hara to his senses? Well, she was now committed to finding out for herself. Pray God he truly meant every one of those facile words he wrote in his letter …

The abrupt bark of a loudhailer startled Minette from further introspection. It was getting late, so she had better take the children down to their cabin. Of course, she must relieve the stewardess of the baby, but Christina was usually no trouble.

Quietly opening the cabin door, Minette discovered the stewardess sitting in a chair, the lighting dimmed, an empty feeding bottle on the table beside her. The baby lay in her cot, replete, and fast asleep. Thanking the kindly woman for her thoughtfulness, Minette cautioned the children to be quiet.

Rising to her feet, the stewardess whispered that she would

organise a tray of sandwiches and hot chocolate for the older children's supper. Dinner would not be served in the dining room for two further hours—by which time the little ones would be exhausted. She would return to the cabin in time for Madam to go upstairs and enjoy her meal in peace. Seeing her benefactress to the door, Minette thanked her once again, and then set about organising the family's possessions in preparation for the weeks ahead.

In her heart, Minette had been more than a trifle concerned about how she was to manage looking after four children during the long sea voyage. But offered this unexpected and much appreciated assistance from the stewardess, she could look forward to the luxury of spending a few hours on her own each day.

By the time the ship docked in Bombay, Minette was sure she would be well rested, her mind clear, and ready to greet her husband with genuine warmth and optimism for their future together.

CHAPTER TWENTY-FOUR

Minette stood at the ship's railing along with a few remaining passengers, making a valiant attempt to breathe through her mouth. She had forgotten about the stench of the harbour's dark green waters that had assailed her nostrils upon emerging on deck! Shading her eyes with a hand, the young woman scanned the mass of humanity milling like ants on the quayside some distance from where the ship was anchored.

Patrick would have travelled down to Bombay to meet his family, but as yet there was no sign of him. For heaven's sake, where was he? Surely not lurking in the bar at the Taj Mahal Hotel? Minette began to worry. The disembarking passengers had reduced to a trickle, most having left the ship over the past hour. Unless her husband materialised soon, her presence would become a distinct embarrassment to the crew, whom she fancied were beginning to look askance.

Her searching eyes settled on a familiar face, if not the one she was expecting. *Frederick!* Her close friend and riding companion. He was waving to her from one of the ferry-boats chugging to and fro from the ship to the jetty. But, still no sign of Patrick. Acknowledging his wave, a perplexed Minette hurried down to the cabins to relieve the stewardess of the children, who were still clean if rather sweaty. It would not do for their father to greet a grubby tribe.

After the months spent in the bracing Scottish climate, they had become unused to the intense heat and humidity. James' red-gold fringe lay in damp spikes on his forehead, whilst Charlie had fingered his sweaty hair straight up, comically appearing to have had a fright! The stewardess had drawn Claire's dark hair up into a beribboned knot on the top of her head, and the baby lay in her carrycot, clad in only a cotton vest and muslin nappy. Grinning toothlessly up at her mother, Christina resumed an examination of her little fingers.

A knock at the cabin door rendered all three children silent in expectation of their father's appearance. The next moment, their faces were transformed with joy! Their beloved Uncle Freddie stood smiling in the doorway.

With a cry of delight, James hurled himself into his hero's arms, to be swiftly followed by Charlie. Grinning, Frederick tucked a boy under each arm as he advanced into the cabin. Watching Frederick handle her boys so easily and with apparent pleasure, Minette was struck by a pang of regret that their own father seemed incapable of unbending in the same way. Setting the boys back on their feet, Frederick kissed Minette soundly on both cheeks in the French manner.

"It's wonderful to see you looking so well, *ma chère!* Evidently the cooler climate suits you all rather better."

"Freddie, where's Patrick?" Minette wanted to know. "Don't tell me he's stuck in some Bombay bar or other?"

"*Chérie*, I'm afraid you will have to put up with me as an escort back to Lucknow," Frederick explained, his tone casual. "Patrick is unwell at present … a fever of sorts, I believe. He sends his love, and is looking forward to having his family home at last."

Avoiding Minette's eyes, Frederick moved across the cabin to look out of the porthole. "Perhaps we had better make a move to get off this boat, or they might have the impression we wish to return to England."

Minette said nothing during the short ferry ride to shore, her silence nevertheless speaking volumes. Although acutely conscious of his friend's suspicious stare, Frederick did not intend to reveal the true nature of Patrick O'Hara's "fever." But he was also aware that Minette was far from stupid.

The truth of the matter was Patrick had gone on an extended bender the previous week. Sick and unsteady, he was unable to pull himself together in time to meet his wife in Bombay. He had called upon Frederick to go in his stead, swearing to God he would put himself to rights before his wife arrived home.

It was only when they were on their way to the Army bungalow in Breach Candy, that Minette broke her silence. "So Patrick is sick, is he?" her voice was dry. "How fortunate for him that you happened to be free to resolve the problem of his family's arrival in Bombay."

"Well, I had a few days leave outstanding," Frederick shifted uncomfortably. "I expect you are familiar with the bungalow here." He was anxious to change the subject. "You and Patrick must have spent a couple of nights there when you first arrived in India?"

"Yes, we did, and I remember what a welcome break it was. But God, did we suffer with prickly heat! I was so grateful to the *ayah* there who had some kind of soothing if evil smelling potion to rub on. Charlie usually suffers badly, but he's been free of it for months now. I pray it doesn't start up again, poor lad."

Frederick was relieved he had managed to divert Minette to safer subjects of conversation. He only hoped the remainder of the long journey back to Lucknow would prove as easy!

Sitting in the bungalow's veranda that evening, Minette gazed thoughtfully at Frederick over the rim of her glass of *nimbu pani*. The children were already in bed, having been taken over by the bungalow's resident *ayah*. The young woman was tempted to air her suspicions as to the nature of her husband's supposed "illness," but decided against it. It would be unfair to place the poor man in such an invidious position, Frederick being Patrick's close friend and fellow officer.

Instead, Minette asked for news of her horses and snippets of scandalous gossip always rife in the cantonment. Relieved the subject of Patrick's welfare was not about to be resurrected, Frederick recounted a few amusing anecdotes.

Watching Minette giggle like a young girl, the man thought once more what a bloody waste of an attractive and intelligent woman it was. He wondered if he was in love with her—a question he had frequently asked of himself, but found quite unanswerable. Straightening in his chair, he banished the treacherous thought with a sharp mental reminder that Minette was Patrick's wife. Even if he did not deserve her. With a neutral smile, Frederick suggested a game of cards.

As dawn was breaking the following morning, Frederick,

Minette and the children left Bombay by train. Travelling through the changing countryside, Minette found it as fascinating as she always had.

Sometimes sad, often beautiful—always disturbing.

As the train slowed towards brief halts at various stations, small children appeared from nowhere and scuttled beside the still-moving carriages. Running noses attracting swarms of flies, a forest of grubby hands were held out begging for *baksheesh*. Food hawkers patrolling the platform pushed the small beggars aside with menacing shouts, anxious there should be no impediment to their sales.

Due to the benefit of an ice block in its tin bath, the temperature inside the carriage was relatively cool, so the children slept for hours at a time. Now and then, one or the other would wake for a drink or to eat sandwiches from a substantial picnic box supplied by the bungalow *kensama*. Occasionally, they would play a board game or read a book. Bored, they would fall asleep again, rocked by the rhythmic movement of the train.

And so the long wearisome hours of travelling passed ...

After a seeming eternity, the train pulled into the station at Lucknow. Once she had organised her possessions into various receptacles ready for arrival, Minette changed into a fresh blue and white sprigged muslin gown. Climbing down from the railway carriage, she looked expectantly up and down the platform for the familiar figure of her husband.

But Patrick O'Hara was nowhere to be seen.

After several minutes, it became clear that he had not come to the station. Frederick had no option but to hire vehicles to transport the family and their baggage to the cantonment, whilst making a mighty effort to conceal his foreboding. For Christ's sake, where was the man?

He had even gone to the trouble of cabling Patrick before leaving Bombay, giving him time to make appropriate arrangements. Could he not at least make the effort to meet his wife at the station? This poor girl whom he had not seen for months? Frederick's jaw tightened in anger.

The transport drew to a halt, and Minette accepted Frederick's helping hand to alight from the carriage. Standing in front of her home, the young woman's mouth fell open in appalled disbelief.

Not only was her once-beautiful garden now a mass of weeds and overgrown creeper, but the house itself appeared shabby, the paint blistered and peeling from the walls. What could have happened to her old *mali*, who for years had tended the garden with such pride? And where was the *chowkidar* who guarded the gates? Her heart sinking, Minette wondered what other horrors she was about to encounter upon entering the house?

Aware of Minette's distress, Frederick sighed. Obviously Patrick had ignored his suggestion to employ a few workmen to knock the place into a semblance of order. With an inward shrug, he reminded himself it was none of his business, and went to attend to the unloading of baggage.

Before Minette could move, the front door was flung open, and out flew her two diminutive *ayahs*. Falling on their knees before their astonished mistress, they seized her hands to cover them in kisses. Jumping to their feet, the *ayahs* turned to the children standing tiredly next to their mother, enveloping each of them in a delighted hug. All three children laughed and hugged their *ayahs* back, for they adored Mailie and Seenta who had brought them up.

A sudden bawl rent the air, startling by its unexpectedness. Christina was awake and demanding attention! Guessing the baby was thirsty, Minette rummaged in a bag for a feeding bottle of boiled water wrapped in a muslin nappy. Mailie had already picked up the baby, and squatting down on her haunches, lodged her in the soft folds of her sari. Taking the feeding bottle from Minette, the *ayah* offered it to Christina. Seizing the rubber teat in her mouth, Christina began sucking with enthusiasm whilst Mailie crooned to her.

Without further ado, Seenta swept up the older children and took them through the house to their old bedrooms. Mailie followed minutes later, with a now peaceful baby in her arms. Minette now had time to stake stock of the situation.

Glancing round the entrance hall, she was astonished that no *bearer* had come to greet her. However, there was no dust on the furniture, and the marble floor had been swabbed spotlessly clean.

Presumably, it was the work of the sweeper since the *bearer* was absent for whatever reason.

"*Chèrie*, I must be off now," Frederick spoke from behind her. "There is a great deal I need to attend to before tomorrow."

"Freddie, how can I thank you for everything you have done for us? I could never have managed without your help." Minette hugged her friend in gratitude. "Shall I call the children to say goodbye?"

"No, don't disturb them, they must be dead tired poor little things. I think you should also rest for an hour or two." Frederick bent to kiss her on each cheek.

The door of the bedroom crashed open, and Minette sprang back in shock. Her dishevelled husband stood unsteadily in the doorway, his chin covered by ginger stubble, an all-pervasive stench of unwashed body emanating from his person. Blood-shot eyes swivelled from his wife to Frederick.

"Well, Madam! Back at larsh … last after taking 'vantage of my good nature to sh … stay away for fucking months on end!" Patrick belched whilst glaring blearily at Minette. "Yesh, an' what ish … is the first thing I sh … see but my darlin' wife in the armsh of 'nother man—damn your eyes!"

"Don't be ridiculous, Patrick!" Minette quickly recovered herself. "You know quite well I was thanking Freddie for looking after us since our arrival back in India. Something I was expecting *you* to be doing. However, in view of your present … condition, I can see why you were unable to undertake responsibility for your own family."

Patrick's eyes bulged in drunken fury, his vomit-stained vest gaping open to reveal a mass of damp matted chest hair. "Don't you curl your lip at me, Madam Prissy-pants!" The man swung his head towards Frederick. "An' what have you been sh … saying to her, blast you?" he snarled. "Don' think I don' know what your bloody game is, my fine cockerel! Been in love with m'wife for years! G'wan … admit it, you bastard!"

"I choose to ignore your damnable accusations, Patrick O'Hara!" Frederick's tone was icy. "It's preferable to assume it's the booze you've been swilling that is doing the talking—not you. As regards your wife, I suggest you pull yourself together, before she decides to leave India on the next available ship."

His face tight with anger, Frederick nodded to Minette, and quickly left the house before he said—or did—anything he might later regret. For a brief instant, Patrick appeared bewildered as if he didn't quite understand what had just transpired. Then, ignoring his wife, he belched loudly and staggered back into the bedroom, banging the door closed behind him.

Minette walked into the sitting room and flopped into the nearest chair. Shocked to the core of her being, she despaired at her own naïve belief in her husband's promise to change. So much for those foolish dreams of starting afresh! Forcing back scalding tears, Minette went in search of the *ayahs*.

It was a priority to discover what had happened to the household servants. Her husband's activities required no guesswork—the young woman's mouth twisted in cynicism. Under their mistress's direct questioning, both ayahs looked decidedly uncomfortable. No servants in the house … so where were they? It was clear their tight-lipped memsahib intended to get to the bottom of the matter.

"*Bearer* gone long time," Mailie said at last. "He going after *Sahib* hit him on head in front of *jamadar*. Big, big loss of face for *bearer, Memsahib*! He leaving here straightaway to go to *mulloch. Sahib*, he taking new *bearer*, but this one also going after on-y two days."

Her face grim, Minette stared at the little *ayah*, aware of how difficult this was for her. After a moment, she asked why her husband had hit the man?

"*Doctor-sahib*, he forgetting to order whisky, then blaming *bearer* when he find no more bottles whisky in house."

"I see. So what about the other servants?" Minette persisted. Where is my old *mali*?

"*Mali*, he go away last year because *Sahib* not pay him, so no money for food. *Chowkidar*, he also gone from gate because *Sahib* all the time calling him lazy bugger," Seenta supplied. "*Kensama* saying *Sahib* never come to eat food when ready. After veree long time, food cold and no taste nice, so Sahib shouting *kensama* no damn good. He going straightaway to *mulloch*."

Minette closed her eyes to conceal her disgust. "But where is the sweeper? Surely my husband kept on the *jamadar* to swab floors and take out the rubbish?"

The *ayah* shook her head. "*Jamadar* ... ah ... he running away, *Memsahib*."

"Why?" Minette demanded. "Mailie, you must tell me why the sweeper ran off!" Seeing the little woman's clear distress, she softened her tone. "You see, I need to know everything so that I may put it right."

"Yes, *Memsahib*," the *ayah* nervously licked her lips. "When *Memsahib* in England, *Sahib* is drinking, drinking much whisky. Sometimes he sick in bedroom or bathroom. *Jamadar* not happy, but he anyway coming to clean up mess. One night time, *Sahib* asking friends for dinner. One more sahib ... and two miss-sahibs from town. Not too much eating, but plenty whisky drinking. Everyone then going to bedroom."

Mailie swallowed hard before continuing. "After three four hours, *doctor-sahib* shouting for jamadar to come cleaning plenty sick on bedroom floor and also bed. But he already sleeping on charpoy. *Doctor-sahib*, he kicking *jamadar's charpoy* with plenty bad words, and *jamadar* falling on floor. Knee hurt and veree angry, so he go straightaway."

"Thank you for telling me," Minette reassured the *ayahs*. "I'm home now, and I will take charge of everything. But the house is so clean, so it must be you and Seenta I have to thank for that?"

Bobbing their heads, the *ayahs* thankfully disappeared. Minette remained frozen to the spot, trying to absorb the disgraceful behaviour of her husband during her absence. "*Miss-sahibs*" indeed ... bloody whores, more like! No wonder the poor *ayahs* were reluctant to tell her anything about it.

Where was the man who wrote that last affectionate letter to her? A far cry from the drunken, ranting sot of half an hour ago! Who was too mean to pay his servants their meagre wage, but still managed to swill gallons of whisky and hire whores.

Just months ago, she had left a competent household running her immaculate home ... only to return to this ramshackle mess! Blinking back angry tears, Minette forced herself to concentrate on how best to handle the nightmare in which she now found herself. She was thankful the children had not witnessed their father's disgusting behaviour. However, she would tell the ayahs to keep them out of sight whilst her husband was in his present condition. Primarily, for their safety.

Next was the question of food. In the spotless kitchen, Minette discovered half a loaf of bread, two eggs and a few potatoes. Outside on the back veranda, she found a small plate of cold cooked rice and a few wilted vegetables contained in a *dhoolie*, its fine mesh keeping the food free from insects.

Minette grimaced with mortification. God alone knew how these two little ayahs had managed to feed themselves during her absence. Patrick must have neglected to pay even them for months on end—if at all. Their loyalty to the family was incredible in the circumstances.

Summoning Seenta, Minette sent her off to market with money and a list of basic foodstuffs and milk for the baby. Given time, she would employ other necessary servants for her household so it ran on oiled wheels once again.

Patrick did not emerge from the bedroom again that day. Minette's relief was intense, having no desire to lay eyes on such an unedifying sight! The children went out to play on the maidan for an hour late in the afternoon. But tired from the lengthy train journey, they went to bed early without grumbling.

Later that evening, Minette sat alone on the veranda reading a book, a mug of hot milk with two slices of bread and butter on a tray in front of her. Unable to concentrate, she went to bed in the spare room where she drifted into merciful oblivion.

The next morning, Minette was up at first light. She checked on the children who were still fast asleep, as were the *ayahs* snoring gently in an adjoining room. Quietly, she let herself out of the house and walked briskly towards the Cavalry Stabling. At this depressing time in her life, there was nothing her flagging esprit needed more than her horses. Wonderful to lean against their warm necks once again and breathe in that wonderful scent!

Upon entering the stable block, Minette saw two heads turn towards her, ears straining forward upon hearing the footfall they knew so well. Seeing their adored mistress appear out of the gloom, Turka and Fanny burst into delighted whinnying, stamping and whirling in their boxes. Burying her face first in one silky mane and then in the other, Minette's anxious expression relaxed, happy to be with these wonderful animals that loved her so unconditionally.

But who to ride? Leaving one of them behind would create mayhem! Perhaps she should defy convention for once, and ride Turka with Fanny on a lead rein? The tack was under lock and key, but Minette remembered where the spare key was kept and hurried to fetch what was required.

In minutes Turka was tacked up and Fanny bridled. About to lead them out of the stables, the sound of booted feet made Minette freeze. *Damn!* It was bound to be a groom who would prevent her from taking Fanny! He would also insist on accompanying her. Such a bore. Peering through the dimness of the stabling, she relaxed with a sigh of relief.

It was only Frederick.

"Good God, Minette ... how did you manage to be up this early?" Frederick grinned at his friend. "What's this? Don't tell me you intended to ride and lead, you wicked girl? You know how risky it can be ... especially on your own with no escort, I notice."

"Oh Freddie, don't lecture!" Minette begged. "I simply had to get out of the bungalow to see my horses, and there wasn't a groom around."

"Don't try to tell me you were disappointed not to find a groom to ride with you," Frederick told her. "I happen to know you rather well, remember. Come on, give me Fanny and we'll ride out together." Frederick took the mare's reins and went in search of a saddle, acknowledging sleepy salutes from stables' staff arriving for work.

Minutes later, Frederick and Minette left the stable yard, Turka dancing sideways and showing off as always. Fanny strode alongside of him, rather more circumspect, but with a definite spring in her step.

Dawn was only just breaking, and the temperature relatively cool, so Frederick and Minette allowed the horses their heads as soon as it was practical to do so. Half an hour later, two tired but satisfied horses were handed back to their grooms to be showered off and then fed. Also exhilarated after the exercise, Minette and Frederick went their separate ways, having first arranged to ride again the following morning.

Making her way home, Minette hoped Patrick had slept off his drunkenness overnight. She had no wish for a repeat of yesterday's unpleasantness. It was still very early, so it was likely the children would still be asleep. Mailie would be taking care of the baby, so she would be free to have her shower in peace and get dressed for the day. There was much still to do in straightening out her home.

Upon entering the bungalow, Minette became instantly aware of her husband's raised voice—followed by the piping tones of a child. Then came the sound of a blow, running feet followed by hysterical howling! Hurrying to the veranda where the altercation was taking place, Minette was horrified to find Charlie and Claire standing stiffly to attention in front of their father. Both children were white-faced, and still in their nightclothes.

James was nowhere to be seen.

Patrick sprawled in a rattan chair, unkempt, his stained vest hanging open over a substantial paunch, glowering at the two frightened children. Summoning every ounce of self-control to avoid physically attacking her husband, Minette struggled to keep her voice level.

"What on earth is going on here, Patrick? Have the children done something to upset you?"

The man lounging in the chair ignored the question. "And where has Milady been, might I ask? Gadding about the countryside with your paramour, no doubt! Since you didn't come to bed last night, maybe you spent the night together?"

"I slept in the spare room," Minette replied neutrally. "Yes, I did go riding this morning ... just as I have always done. You know that quite well, Patrick!"

"Y'place is *here*, Madam! Dealing with your lazy undisciplined brats who were still dead to the world at six o'clock! O'course I was obliged to wake 'em up, and that morose little tyke, James, had the bloody nerve to give me lip 'bout being tired. He got a clip round the ear for his trouble, and off he ran squealing like a stuck pig."

"For God's sake, Patrick, don't you realise these children have—"

"And *you* can shut y' mouth, Madam!" The man swung round to glare belligerently at Minette, "since it's due to your lackadaisical ways! As for these two slug-a-beds, they're to stay in their room for the day with nothing to eat 'cept bread and water. That should teach the lazy li'l sods the meaning of discipline!"

With a final glare at the shrinking children, Patrick O'Hara staggered back to the bedroom—and his bottle of whisky.

Goaded beyond endurance, Minette first told the two crying children to find Mailie and Seenta and ask for their breakfast to be given in the nursery.

"But *Maman*, must we stay in there all day?" Charlie sniffled.

"No, *chéri*, only for a little while," Minette soothed, "afterwards, you can go out on the *maidan* to play until it gets too hot."

"But, Papa said ... " Claire began to quaver.

"Don't worry about that, I'll explain to Papa why you are still tired."

Minette watched the dejected children trailing towards their room. Then she whirled and ran into the bedroom after her husband, swinging the door shut behind her with an echoing slam.

Patrick was half lying across the bed, about to refresh himself with a second swig of whisky. Incandescent with fury, Minette stalked over and wrenched the bottle from his grasp. His mouth went slack with horror as she flung the half-empty bottle against the wall, where it disintegrated into fragments of glass in a widening pool of amber liquid.

"Wha ... what the hell d'you—"

"How *dare* you allow yourself to degenerate into this condition—and in front of the children, Patrick O'Hara? Have you no sense of decency ... no shame?"

"Don' you—"

"Has it not penetrated that alcoholic fog in which you live that these small children have been travelling for days on end? For God's sake, they need to sleep for their very well-being. One might imagine that you—a blasted doctor—would understand that."

"Madam, I forbid you—"

"Oh, no you don't," flashed Minette, "don't try your beastly intimidating tactics on me. They won't work! Have you taken a look at yourself lately? How filthy and reeking you are? How on earth do you manage to go to work like this?"

"I took leave to meet m'wife" the man mumbled, "an' don' you dare speak—"

"I dare, Patrick O'Hara, I most certainly dare!' Minette yelled, tears of helpless fury trickling down her cheeks. "I've put up with your drinking and foul moods for years, not to mention all those false promises to change."

Minette paused briefly to catch her breath. "And when I think of what your appalling mother had to say in front of her grandchildren—it makes me sick to my stomach! Why, that bigoted old woman had the nerve to refer to me as your blasted *floozie*, our marriage being unrecognised by her Church. She went on to call our children *bastards*, Patrick! A litter of little bastards—she called them and in their hearing. My God, I hope that vile woman rots in hell!"

Minette's scornful gaze swept over the man sprawled over grubby sheets on the bed, and then looked around the bedroom. Score upon score of empty bottles littered the floor or had been flung into corners. Plates of fly-infested, rotting food lay about the place, cigar butts crushed into the remains. The exposed mattress displayed several burn holes, presumably through forgotten lighted cigars.

A disgusting sight.

The young woman mentally cringed to think she had credited this man with moral decency, and a genuine desire to mend bridges between them. Glancing down at her husband, she addressed him once again, her tone icy.

"With regard to your accusation of having remained in Scotland for a few more months, may I remind you I was having a baby—your baby. Furthermore, I had your express permission to do so. And as for your filthy allegation regarding Frederick's regard for me, I'll thank you to cast your mind back to how he dropped everything to help you out. Furthermore, he was steadfast in his loyalty to you— insufferable beast that you are—for he said nothing to me about your condition."

Patrick's eyes bulged angrily. "What d'you take me for, eh? I know th' fellow's in love with you! And your 'sterical claims about things m'mother s'posed to have said are outrageous! M'father was clear about—"

"Frankly, I don't care what your father said, Patrick!" snapped his wife. "And I no longer mean to endure your repulsive behaviour, either towards myself, or to the children. Either you pull yourself together and stop drinking ... or I shall leave you for good. Do you understand what I am saying? I shall leave you and return to England. Consider that well before you open another bottle of whisky—because you will discover I mean what I say."

Suddenly conscious of the stale foetid atmosphere, Minette turned on her heel and left the bedroom. She had one more thing to do now—find her missing son. The eldest and most difficult of her children.

Patrick lay frozen on the bed, shocked into a semblance of sobriety by his wife's tirade. Leave him? Minette? Nonsense, surely she loved him far too much to go that far? And what was that about his mother calling Minette a tart and her children bastards? Through the fog of his drink-soaked brain, Patrick began to recognise the gross and unforgivable insult his mother had dealt Minette. Clutching a head that had started to ache, difficult tears rolled unheeded down his cheeks.

James was eventually discovered hiding behind some hibiscus bushes in the garden. Still wearing his pyjamas, the boy looked up at his mother from reddened eyes, his tear-stained face streaked with mud. A swelling purple bruise from his father's blow was evident under one eye. After a lively argument over whether he would return to the house, Minette led her son back to join Charlie and Claire in the nursery. All three children remained subdued over their breakfast.

Minette spent the rest of the day interviewing servants, and spending time with her baby. Of Patrick there was no sign, for which she thanked God. The children came in from the *maidan*, and crept like small ghosts to their nursery quarters—terrified of being confronted by their father.

Minette was saddened to see how fearful the children had become, knowing it would take a long time to pass. And how different they had been whilst living with Jane in Scotland ... happy, healthy, and full of *joie de vivre*! Like children ought to be.

CHAPTER TWENTY-FIVE

The following morning, Minette went out riding with Frederick as arranged. Frederick rode his own horse, but he also took Fanny out on a lead rein. Taking an obvious fancy to Frederick's young stallion, the mare began a blatant flirtation, nuzzling his neck and rubbing up against him whenever possible. Turka, already unimpressed that another entire horse was present, expressed his displeasure by flattening his ears and dancing sideways with much squealing and snorting!

Although Minette laughed at her little horse's antics, Frederick's keen eyes detected a faintly distracted air in his friend.

"*Chèrie*, is all well at home?" he asked, putting a gentle hand on the young woman's sleeve. "If it's too painful or private to discuss, forget that I asked."

"Oh Freddie, you are the only one I can talk to, being aware of Patrick's disgusting condition," Minette's iron control began to crumble as hot tears sprang into her eyes. "I have the feeling you knew of it before coming to Bombay, but didn't want to tell me."

"Yes, I did know. But I wanted to give Patrick a chance to clean himself up, and maybe do something about the bungalow. It didn't seem right to unnecessarily prejudice you against your husband."

"You really are a good sort, Freddie. Patrick doesn't merit loyalty such as yours. Oh Lord, there was the most awful scene when I returned home after riding yesterday! Patrick was up to his old tricks of terrorising the unfortunate children." Minette swallowed convulsively. "They were stunned, not having been subjected to that kind of abusive treatment for months."

"He had already hit James across the face for no real reason just before I walked in—you should see the ugly bruise under his eye. He then wanted to confine the two younger ones to their bedroom with only bread and water to eat, just because they dared to sleep past six o'clock!" Minette paused to look at her friend, terrible disillusionment in her eyes.

Sensing all was not well with his beloved mistress, Turka began snorting and dancing sideways, until Minette laid a reassuring hand on his neck. "I have told Patrick that unless he stops drinking and brutalising the children, I shall leave him and return to England."

"But do you actually mean that, Minette?" Frederick asked neutrally. "Leaving your husband is a drastic step to take, in particular when you have four children to look after, n'est-ce pas? Have you thought about what you would do if Patrick refused you funds on which to live?"

Minette was silent. Frederick had brought up exactly the same argument as Jane had over the issue. It was true she had not really thought things through to the bitter end. Nevertheless, it was unthinkable to stand back and allow the children's drunken father to continue making their lives a misery.

"Freddie, I appreciate what you are saying, and I have no real idea what I would do in such circumstances," Minette said at last. "But you may be sure I would find a way of managing to keep our heads above water. As things stand, our lives are untenable. I cannot watch my children grow up in an atmosphere of fear and distrust."

It was now Frederick's turn to remain silent. Despite his concern that Minette might plunge into the unknown on impulse, he was unable to refute what she had said. Patrick O'Hara was treading on extremely thin ice—should he wish to retain his beautiful and intelligent wife at his side.

Wryly, Frederick was also aware this strong-minded and fiercely independent woman would never accept financial help from him. Help, which he would be only too pleased to offer her. All he could do at this point was to assure Minette of his friendship and moral support.

Half an hour later, Frederick and Minette returned to the stables before the sun was too high in the sky. Turning to the depressed young woman, Frederick took her hand and looked deep into her eyes.

"*Chérie*, I want you to always remember that whatever happens, I shall be here for you in the event you need my help. As for now, I must get a move on as there is an important meeting I must attend."

Watching Frederick stride away, Minette wondered how he managed to remain such a kind and well-balanced man? In sharp contrast to Patrick, who seemed unable to keep his head or wits about him in this exotic, if stressful country.

Sighing, Minette walked back to the bungalow, wondering what state her husband was likely to be in today. Since she had so thoroughly lost her temper with him the morning before, he had been conspicuous by his absence. She was profoundly relieved to have respite—however brief—from further domestic chaos.

Upon entering the house, Minette frowned, alert to a significant absence of children's chatter. She had arrived back a little later than usual, so the children should have been at the breakfast table by now.

Alarmed, Minette made her way quickly to the veranda to see the three children sitting at the table, bolt upright, and silent. The reason for the unnatural silence then became clear—Patrick sat at the head, casually stirring a cup of tea.

Little remained of the repulsive, belligerent individual of the previous day. Patrick was shaven, his hair clean and slicked back. Gone were the stained filthy garments, his clothing pristine and neat. With a charming smile, he pulled out a chair for his wife to sit down.

Minette was conscious of three pairs of eyes glued to her face, beseeching her for permission to leave the table ... and their father's presence. Without glancing at her husband, Minette nodded and allowed the children to go. She told the boys to ask Seenta to accompany them on the *maidan* to play for an hour before lessons began. Claire was to be included—and no arguments.

Patrick made no comment as the children rushed to do their mother's bidding. He merely buttered another slice of toast and took a sip of his tea. Once the children had vanished from sight, he glanced across the table at Minette from watery but relatively clear eyes.

"Can you find it in your heart to forgive me, my darling?"

Patrick rose from the table to cross over to his wife. Taking her hand, he kissed the inside of her wrist, much as he used to do in happier times. "I missed you so dreadfully, that a glass or two of whisky was the only way to dull the loneliness. I am so sorry!"

Sitting down in a chair next to Minette, he continued to hold her hand. "Darling, I must also apologise for my mother's unpleasantness towards you. But don't hold me to account for her insensitivity, I beg you!"

Insensitivity! Minette stared incredulously at her husband. The insults and accusations hurled by that vile old woman were not lies, nor poisonous allegations—just "insensitivity!" Dismissed entirely were the years of hellish rowing over his excessive drinking, his violence towards the children. Neither had he referred to the slur his mother had cast on the validity of their marriage.

Minette opened her mouth in a heated retort—but then closed it again. What was the point in recriminations? It was obvious Patrick was hell-bent on believing his own version of events. Both Jane and Frederick thought she had little choice in the matter but to make the best of a bad situation. Nevertheless, she would take advantage of her husband's penitent mood to barter an improved quality of life for her children.

"Darling?" Patrick's cajoling voice brought her back to the present. "What do you say? Shall we let bygones be bygones and start afresh?" Patrick raised Minette up from the table to take her in his arms, certain she would melt as she always had.

With a firm gesture, Minette extricated herself from her husband's embrace, and stood back with a distinctly unfriendly stare. Muffling an involuntary curse, Patrick hid his irritation in having his advances unexpectedly rebuffed.

"Before we go any further, Patrick, there are a few things I wish to make clear to you," Minette's voice was frosty. "First, I never wish to see nor hear you abusing the children again. Have you not noticed how petrified they are of you? With reason, I might add! If you cannot bring yourself to like your own children, then at least have the goodness to hide it from them."

"Sweetie, you really are exaggerating! All children need discipline, and I—"

"*Discipline?*" Minette interrupted vehemently. "You call reducing small children to a quaking wreck on a regular basis "discipline?" No, Patrick, "persecution" would be a more appropriate word."

"Dearest girl, you are forever demanding that I involve myself in family life. But when I do so, you resent me correcting the children when they step out of line. As their father, I must insist—"

"No, Patrick," Minette folded her arms repressively. "My condition is quite clear: you are not to hit any of them again. If a punishment is deserved, there are other effective methods of dealing with it."

Shrugging, Patrick agreed. Privately, he was restraining himself from exploding with tremendous difficulty. Had the damned woman not caught him out like she had, he wouldn't bother to even listen to the ridiculous drivel she was spouting. However, to keep the peace …

"Secondly, your habit of drinking in the Officers' Mess for half the night must stop. When you return home drunk, you are unpleasant and unrecognisable as the kind and gentle man I married."

"For God's sake, Minette, a snifter or two with colleagues after work is hardly a great sin," Patrick shook his head in disbelief. "How can you begrudge—"

"Are you not hearing me, Patrick? As you very well know, it is never a "snifter or two" but more like a bottle or three! So, no more drinking after work."

"This is outrageous—"

"These are my conditions, Patrick. Take it—or leave it."

Patrick stared at the frozen-faced woman in front of him. Where was the delightful girl who had only ever wanted to please him? Replaced by a harpy, it might seem! Unfortunately, he would have to toe her bloody line for the time being. He was already in enough hot water with the Brigadier over excessive days off. He most certainly did not want his wife badgering his office for a return ticket to England because her husband was a violent drunk!

"Darling girl, I will promise you anything to make you happy," Patrick was at his most persuasive. "I cannot bear it when you speak so coldly. I want my sweet wife back!"

"Do you agree to the two conditions I have set out?" Minette did not mean to accept her husband's ambiguous agreement.

"Yes, *yes*, I agree to them both," Patrick exclaimed impatiently, opening his arms wide in invitation. With a small sigh of resignation, Minette stepped into his embrace. That would have to do for the moment, but she would take one day at a time. Only then would it become clear if Patrick intended to keep his word.

Satisfied that he had succeeded what he had set out to achieve, Patrick kissed his wife and sat down again at the table. Reaching for the teapot, he filled a cup for Minette with a slightly unsteady hand.

"As a matter of fact, I have some exciting news," Patrick told his wife. "It's about the Durbar, an important ceremonial event to be held in Delhi towards the end of the year. It marks the coronation of King Edward VII. Representatives of British Regiments throughout India will be participating, and families are allowed to attend. I'm sure you will find such a historical event most enjoyable."

Minette brightened. "How exciting! But where are we to stay? Besides ourselves, remember the two *ayahs* will be going too."

"There's no need to worry on that score, darling," Patrick reassured his wife. "We will be living in tented accommodation— but tents the like of which you will never have seen before. Very grand indeed, and equally as good as bricks and mortar. It's likely to be chilly in Delhi at that time of year, so each tent will be equipped with a wood-burning stove."

"So, tell me what happens during this amazing Durbar? I imagine huge crowds will be coming to join in the festivities?"

"Indeed there will, but certain areas are to be reserved for army personnel, I'm told. There should be no difficulty in finding a good vantage point from which to watch the proceedings."

Patrick went on to explain the Durbar constituted a ceremonial meeting of the Viceroy of India with hosts of ruling Indian princes. Requests or complaints could be aired and ostensibly resolved. Displays of horsemanship, dancing and other forms of entertainment would take place for the benefit of Indian royalty and British representatives present. Elaborate banquets were to be held every night, but only men were invited to those events.

"The Viceroy will be holding a Ball at Vice-Regal Lodge marking the end of festivities, to which we are all invited," Patrick continued. "I have no doubt your unique elegance will stand out as always against the overdone finery of most other ladies present."

Groping in a pocket, Patrick produced a small scarlet leather box which he snapped open with a flourish. Minette gasped to see an oval stone of glowing jade surrounded by rubies, set in a ring of rose gold. Removing the jewel from its black velvet nest, Patrick took his wife's hand to slide it over her finger.

"This is the ring I mentioned in a letter to you, darling, do you remember? A gift from a grateful Mandarin whose son I successfully treated. I want to give it to you now, so that you have time to search out a silk for your ball-gown which will complement the beauty of the jade."

"It's beautiful, Patrick ... thank you!" Faintly ashamed, Minette recalled how she imagined her husband would sell the ring to subsidise his whisky and gambling. Perhaps it was the ceremonial sword that went, since it was nowhere to be seen in the house.

The next few months passed uneventfully enough. True to his word, Patrick refrained from frequenting the Officers' Mess after work each evening. In turn, Minette warmed towards her husband, and moved back into their bedroom.

The children, however, were not so pleased over this change of events. The moment their father's voice heralded his return home, the *ayahs* hustled them away to their quarters. Minette had issued these instructions to avoid the risk of an unpleasant scene upsetting the uneasy balance of Patrick's good humour.

It was now only a question of weeks until the Regiment was due to leave for Delhi, to attend the great Durbar. A great deal of drilling took place each day on the *maidan* involving both the cavalry and infantrymen. Despite his work at the hospital, Patrick was also expected to take part in drills on occasion. An atmosphere of great excitement permeated the entire cantonment.

New uniforms were ordered for Officers, *Sikh* Cavalrymen, and Indian sepoys who were taking part in the Great Parade. *Durzis* were run off their feet making up new and elaborate ball-gowns for ladies attending the Viceroy's Ball.

To Minette's incredulity and then disgust, self-elected Burrah-memsahibs upheld the all-important matter of "precedence" by vetting the attire of ladies they considered inferior to themselves. Probably to ensure they were not outshone by the so-called "nonentities"—she thought acidly.

Frustrated by the young Frenchwoman's vagueness over details of her own ball-gown, the memsahibs' hierarchy choose to ascribe it to "Frenchified" ignorance. With a private grin, Minette ignored the insult with a charming smile—as though she had just received a compliment.

The cooler weather arrived, and over weekends the usual rash of invitations were sent out for various receptions and garden parties. Patrick and Minette were obliged to attend most, it being a matter of Regimental protocol. For Minette, it was a welcome occasion to dress up!

Cricket matches and Polo took place late afternoons, after which a magnificent tea was set out for players and spectators alike. Platters of sandwiches and cake-laden trays were borne aloft by Mess *bearers*. Cummerbunds in claret and gold brocade encircled their immaculate white uniforms, a flash of which peeped from the muslin *pugri* on their heads.

As was her habit, Minette continued to ride out early each morning. Should a groom not be about, or Frederick was unable to accompany her, she didn't hesitate to flout convention by riding out into the countryside alone.

It was at this time that Minette made the unwelcome discovery that she was pregnant. Deeply frustrated that her freedom was to be curtailed yet again, she resolved that after the birth, she would seek the advice of an innovative doctor in Delhi. Apparently, the fellow specialised in successful methods of birth control.

Minette was determined not to conceive any more children. Especially, since her husband scarcely acknowledged the existence of the ones they already had.

Every other method she had tried had been a signal failure, so the only certain way of preventing pregnancy was to deny Patrick her bed. Minette wryly grimaced at the thought of the scene *that* would provoke. In the meanwhile, it was a comfort to know she would still be slender enough to fit into her gown for the Durbar Ball.

The morning of the O'Haras' departure to Delhi finally dawned. Awaiting the transport to the railway station, Minette stared in disbelief at the immense quantity of baggage piled on the pavement outside the bungalow. Of course, Patrick's accoutrements comprised a significant amount, but the remainder consisted of the family's personal requirements and basic foodstuffs. How on earth would it all fit inside these tents in which they were to stay?

The journey to Delhi proved less arduous than she imagined, but Minette was glad to arrive at last, and install her family in their new quarters. Looking about her, she marvelled to see the town of enormous tents erected for the occasion. Roomy and comfortably furnished, the chill of the Delhi winter was offset by efficient pot-bellied stoves in each tent, the flue rising through a hole in the top.

The O'Haras occupied four tents, the larger two sleeping quarters connected by a "bathroom" tent, also equipped with a pot-bellied stove. Minette was pleased to notice a full-length mirror in the bathroom tent. It would make her preparation for the Viceroy's Ball easier than she had envisaged.

Whilst Minette and the *ayahs* were unpacking and settling the foodstuffs on shelving in a small "kitchen" tent, James and Charlie rushed outside to play. A pouting Claire was delegated to keep an eye on her toddling baby sister, until such time as one of the *ayahs* was free to take over. It was good for the rather spoiled little girl to learn some responsibility, Minette decided.

Everything finally in its place, Minette sat down for a cup of tea in the company of Delia Woodward, another young Regimental wife. She and her family were also staying in tented accommodation next to the O'Haras, and her sons were presently outside playing with Minette's children. Slightly in awe of the Frenchwoman, Delia had brought over her Ball-gown for Minette's inspection, and to ask her advice. Pearls round her neck and wrists—or would diamonds be better?

Eyeing the voluminous pink satin affair, its skirts heavily ruched with fat pink roses, Minette tried not to wince. Rotund little Delia could not but look like an overblown rose herself in such a garment—even without the proposed huge quantity of jewellery.

Delia, on the other hand, was privately horrified that Minette intended to wear what appeared to be a sea-green silk rag she noticed hanging limply from a hanger. Watching her friend's transparent efforts to conceal her dismay, Minette grinned to herself. In Delia's book, more was very definitely more!

The following morning dawned bright and clear ... perfect weather for the opening ceremonies of the Great Durbar. By the time Minette sat down for breakfast with the children, Patrick had gone to join fellow officers for the Parade.

Anxious not to miss the opening ceremonies, Minette and Delia set off in good time with their respective families. A substantial picnic basket had been packed, that they could remain *in situ* once they had identified the area reserved for Army families. Being early on the scene, the two young women commandeered a small hillock close to the Parade Ground, ensuring their view of the proceedings would be unimpeded by a forest of other peoples' heads.

In an atmosphere charged with excitement and anticipation of what was to come, the Grand Parade began. First came a display by Indian dancers and musicians, their costumes bright in jewel colours and garnished with silver and gold tinsel. On galloping ponies, fierce-looking horsemen from the hills performed incredible acrobatic feats, applauded from all sides by delighted spectators.

The braying of trumpets heralded the arrival of Lord Curzon, Viceroy of India, resplendent in elaborate ceremonial uniform, his helmet adorned with white ostrich feathers. Lady Curzon was attired in a gown of rich peacock colours, her jewellery ablaze in the sunshine. The Viceroy and his wife were seated in a gilded *howdah* perched on the back of a magnificently caparisoned elephant guided by its *mahout*.

At the foot of steps leading up to a tall dais beneath a cupola, the elephant knelt to allow the Viceroy and his wife to alight. The couple then made their way slowly upward on a scarlet carpet towards the dais, upon which two gilt thrones had been placed. Uniformed aides and richly attired fan and parasol bearers clustered about the stately personages, with all the pomp and ceremony befitting a representative of the British Monarch.

Minette's eyes were drawn to a seemingly unending procession of Indian royalty, winding their way towards the Viceroy from afar. Their mission was to offer him their swords in an ancient gesture of homage to the British Crown.

Rajahs, Maharajas, Nawabs and other ruling princes arrived, mounted on fine Arabian horses, or in swaying *howdahs* on wondrously caparisoned elephants and camels. Some reclined in heavily bedecked golden litters carried by liveried bearers, all of them escorted by vast retinues of liveried servants. Awed crowds thronging each side of the Parade Ground were clearly dazzled by the magnificence and splendour of the spectacle.

The thunder of galloping hooves signalled the Charge of British Indian Cavalry Regiments. Resplendent in ornate uniforms, snowy ostrich feathers waving from dress helmets, all of them rode in perfect formation. Squadrons of bearded *Sikh* Cavalrymen came charging close behind, sumptuous in striking uniform and *pugri*, astride gleaming horses, lances adorned by fluttering pennants held proudly aloft.

A medley of differing parades followed the dust storm caused by the galloping horses. Dancers, jugglers and fire-eaters pranced past, and then came the British Military bands playing rousing well-known medleys. As dusk began to fall, a display of spectacular fireworks merited much amazed applause from spectators.

The excitement of the day at an end, the two young women and their tired children returned to their respective quarters. Handing the three older children over to Seenta and Mailie, Minette went to spend time with Christina. The toddler had been too young to manage without her nap, and had stayed behind with the *ayahs*.

Minutes later, a yell of pain followed by hysterical giggling was heard coming from the children's tent. Hurrying to investigate, Minette discovered that James still had the energy to tease his younger brother who lay sprawled on the floor, crying. The older boy had inveigled Charlie to sit on the end of his camp bed, whilst he jumped heavily on the other end. The unfortunate boy had been launched into the air to land painfully on an arm. Furious, Minette threatened James with confinement for the whole of the next day, and then went to comfort a sniffling Charlie.

Still irritated, Minette retired to bed with a book and a plate of sandwiches cut for her by a thoughtful ayiah. Patrick and other officers of his Regiment were attending the first of the evening banquets, so Minette knew he would not be back before the early hours of the morning. She only hoped he would be quiet about it! An hour later, her eyelids beginning to droop, Minette laid down her book and settled to sleep. As she drifted off, she thanked God that her life seemed—at last—to be on an even keel.

A piercing scream of agony startled Minette awake, her heart thudding in alarm. Further prolonged screaming brought her running into the children's tent. Holding a lantern aloft, she could just make out James and Charlie in the darkness, sitting bolt upright in their beds, eyes round with fright. Christina was also awake and standing up in her cot. Sensing an atmosphere of fear, her little face began to crumple.

One bed was empty. *Claire's!*

A sinking feeling in the pit of her stomach, Minette tore into the bathroom tent from where more terrible howls were coming. She found Claire lying in a pool of urine beside the pot-bellied stove, screaming uncontrollably. Eyes starting from her head, the small body arching in agony, the child seemed unaware of her mother's presence. Standing over Claire was her father, evidently the worse for drink, his face suffused and glowering.

"My God, Patrick, what have you *done* to her?" Minette whispered as she crouched over the hysterical little girl. Claire's muslin night shift had become a network of blackened tatters down one side, the singed threads seemingly glued to the delicate flesh on the small buttocks.

Minette gathered her daughter in her arms, the child struggling and fighting in mindless agony. It was then that Minette noticed a purpling bruise under the little girl's left eye. She looked up at her husband, disgust evident in her eyes.

"You hit the poor little thing across her face. Why, you utter, *utter* beast!"

"Don' tell me how to man ... manage m'own chil'ren!" the man blustered in drunken fury. "You forget yoursh ... yourself, Madam! I will not tol'rate impudence from thesh bloody brats you're fr'ever landing me with! Blasted child was bleating it wanted to pee ...

should'a thought of that b'fore going t'bed. Needed a lesson not t'argue with me—and got it, by God! An' if it doesn't stop that bloody racket soon, I'll give it a'nother clip … "

"*Get out!*" Minette hissed, her eyes glinting dangerously. "Get the hell out of my sight you vile individual! Lay one more finger on this child, and I'll … "

"Jus' you try, Madam … jus' you try!" Glaring belligerently at his wife from bloodshot eyes, the man pushed past the *ayahs* hovering anxiously nearby, and lurched into his sleeping quarters.

Tight-lipped, Minette carried the struggling, screaming child back to her bed. Placing her face down, she asked Seenta to fetch a bowl of warm water, lint and a wide bandage. It was imperative the wound was dealt with immediately to prevent possible infection. Mailie attended to Christina, whose howls were threatening to drown out those of her injured sister.

Sponging, and then gently peeling the burned night shift away from the child's skin gave rise to further high-pitched screams, the small body bucking and writhing in terrible pain. Her own tears not far away, Minette gritted her teeth and persisted in cleansing the area. Finally, the singed strands of material came away to reveal the enormity of a raw and blackened wound.

Seenta reappeared with a cooling poultice to apply to the appalling burn, its soothing qualities taking effect almost immediately. Slowly, the little girl's screams dwindled, and the frantic thrashing of her body became less violent. But the purple bruise on Claire's face swelled so such a degree that her eye had closed.

It did not require much intelligence to envisage the sequence of events leading to the incident. The blow Patrick had dealt her must have been of considerable force, sufficient to send the child reeling back against the burning stove.

An intense tide of fury suffused Minette. To think that a grown man—a doctor—could raise his hand in such a manner against a small child! That easy Irish charm had been brutally exposed as a thin veneer, unveiling all the old resentments still festering beneath.

Nothing had changed … and never would.

An inescapable fact.

Minette knew the time had come to put aside her fear of the

unknown, and leave the drink-sodden imbecile she was married to. The safety of her children was of paramount importance. She would take her family back to Lucknow, where Claire would receive the urgent medical attention she required. And then she would pay a visit to the Brigadier's Office to request arrangements be made for herself and the children for an immediate departure back to England. She would explain why.

The boys were still sitting up in bed, horrified to see their sister so dreadfully injured by their father. Forcing a reassuring smile, Minette told them to dress for they were going home. It was imperative Claire was seen by their family doctor in Lucknow without delay, for the burn was too deep to manage.

The two boys complied in unusual silence. Turning to her injured daughter, Minette was relieved to see that Claire had drifted into a restless sleep induced by a potion made up by the *ayahs*. Smoothing the damp hair back from the child's forehead, she saw a small hand unconsciously reach out seeking comfort from her mother. Taking care not to interfere with the dressing on her wound, Minette carefully wrapped Claire in a warmed blanket.

The two *ayahs* evinced no astonishment over their mistress' decision for an immediate departure. They packed only essentials for the journey, as the remainder of the baggage would be returned at the end of the Durbar. Bottles of drinking water, bread, biscuits and fruit would be sufficient until they arrived home.

Minette wrote a short note to Frederick, letting him know she was returning to Lucknow due to an unforeseen emergency. Knowing her friend would be worried, she mentioned she was travelling under the escort of two British grooms she knew well. Sealing the note, she gave it to a passing military guard with the request that it was handed personally to Major Frederick Le Barre.

Minette glanced into the tent where her husband lay sprawled across the bed, unconscious and snoring, drool oozing from his gaping mouth. Encountering the sourness of the atmosphere, she wrinkled her nose in disgust as she quickly placed a curt note on the table nearest the bed. It informed Patrick of her return home to Lucknow, that the injuries he had inflicted on his daughter could be attended to.

When he finally emerged from his alcoholic stupor, she hoped the bloody man felt abject shame of what he had done to that poor little girl. Her lip curling in revulsion, Minette turned on her heel and left.

CHAPTER TWENTY-SIX

The journey back to Lucknow was little short of a nightmare, Claire crying and screaming almost the entire way over every jolt and bump. But to Minette's surprise and gratitude, the two boys sat quietly, and without quarrelling.

It was with infinite relief that Minette arrived back at the bungalow. First ascertaining that Claire was comfortably installed, she pressed a generous quantity of rupees into the delighted, if embarrassed hands of the grooms who had escorted her home.

The sweeper was sent off to fetch Doctor MacElwee, who generally looked after the families within the cantonment. A wise, bluff old Scotsman, he could give an injection faster than a young patient could object! The doctor came at once, and exclaimed in concern at the gravity of Claire's burn, the child howling and fighting to prevent him from touching the wound. Examining the swelling of the purple bruise under her eye, the doctor shook his head, clearly perplexed.

"Weel lassie, I fear ye'll be carryin' a mark o'yer burn all yer life … but it's in a guid enough place, is it not? Tell me, ma wee one, how did ye do such a daft thing as ta fall agin'st a red-hot stove?" The doctor smiled at the sniffling, hiccoughing little girl. "An' hae'ye bin a-fightin' wi' yer brothers for a black eye?"

"Papa hit my face!" Claire swallowed convulsively. "I wanted to do wee-wee, but he said go back to bed. I told Papa I couldn't wait … an' he hitted my face hard so I fell on the stove an' burned my poor bottie!" The child stared glassily at the horrified doctor. "I hate Papa … I really, really *hate* him so much!"

Straightening, the old doctor signalled to Minette that he wished to have few words in private. Leaving Mailie with Claire, the young woman followed the old man out of the bedroom. Outside the closed door, Doctor MacElwee delved into his black bag and produced several sachets of analgesic powders.

"Ther'ye are, Mrs O'Hara ... one mornin' and evenin' in a spoon o'honey should control the wee gurl's pain." The old doctor's expression was sombre. "Ah hafta say, Ma'am, ah didn'a tek yer husband fer a violent mon! A verra bad business this is ... verra bad!"

"My husband drinks to excess, Doctor MacElwee," Minette stated badly. "And when he is drunk, he becomes aggressive towards the children–often violent."

"No, no, *no* ... he mustn'a hit yon wee gurl again, Mrs O'Hara!" the doctor exclaimed, shocked. "Have ye tried t'talk about this to yer husband afta the drink wears off and he's sensible?"

"Believe me, Doctor, I have tried every imaginable avenue to reason with him," Minette grimly retorted. "He makes all sorts of promises, but they never last long."

"Lassie, these days there's a bit o'thinkin' that excessive consumption o' alcohol should be viewed as an illness. Aye, ah ken it's a wee bit far fetched fer some, but there is mebbe somethin' in it?"

"Frankly, I don't care to think up feeble excuses for Patrick over a disgraceful attack on a five year old child," Minette's tone was bleak. "Who will be next? The baby? Me? No, Doctor, the risk is too great. I believe the best thing for us is to return to England—permanently."

"Och, lassie, lassie ... think on before doing anything rash! It's a harsh old world oot there fer a woman alone wi' four bairns—aye, an' another to come later this year, as ah recall!"

"Yes, I cannot say I'm happy to be bringing another child into an atmosphere of hatred within the home. But it is also another reason to remove myself and my children from being attacked by that drunken imbecile."

The old doctor shook his head. "Ah ken what you are sayin' Ma'am, but I dinna know the answer to it except to mebbe inform the Brigadier. Take yer time to think on it before ye act, ah beg o'you, Mrs O'Hara. Don't hesitate ta gi'e me a call if yon wee gurl isn'a right in a week's time. Now, ah hafta see to that nasty burn of hers, and ah'll need yer help to hold her fast."

The following days passed without incident, except that the two boys were obviously still upset over the incident with Claire. James threw tantrums when his demands were frustrated, and Charlie whined about not liking his food. Both boys were dreading their father's return—especially if he arrived at night.

"What if Papa comes home and we're not asleep?" worried Charlie. "He leans over to see if we blink, and then he beats us for being awake! If we cry, he says he'll beat us more."

"If he does that to me again, I shall tell him how much I hate him!" James stoutly declared, his bravado undermined by a trembling mouth.

Minette was shocked. She had thought Patrick was making an effort to be a family man by going in to say good night to the boys. Instead of which, he was merely seeking an excuse to wallop them! How could she not have realised?

Taking advantage of her delicate condition, Claire had also been testing her mother's resolve to keep her temper. Each day, she demanded only puddings for her meals, flatly refusing to eat anything that was not sugary. However, Minette could see the wound was healing in a satisfactory manner. She told her sulky little daughter the time for spoiled behaviour had now run out. She would eat what was prepared for her—or go without.

The Durbar at an end, Regimental personnel began to trickle back to Lucknow. Minette knew it was only a question of time before her husband walked through the front door. Despite his undoubted explosive reaction, she intended to inform him at once of her decision to leave India with the children.

She would make it clear that should he attempt to obstruct her departure, she would immediately appeal to the Brigadier. And she would tell the alcohol-abhorring commander exactly why she intended to leave her husband. Having a plan of sorts, the young woman's flagging courage received a necessary boost.

One evening, Minette and the children were having an early

supper on the veranda. Hearing the front door violently slammed shut, all conversation ceased.

He was back!

The crash of uniform accoutrements being flung to the floor was followed by a bellow for his wife's presence. The three children stopped eating, their eyes round with fright. To be on the safe side, Minette told them to take their plates of food to the nursery to finish their meal. Summoning a calm she was far from feeling, Minette went to confront her husband.

"So, Madam!" It was apparent that Patrick was still inebriated to some degree. "How bloody dare you run off from Delhi without so much as a by-your-leave?" he roared, eyes bulging with rage. "Leaving me to answer damned awkward questions over your absence at the Viceroy's Ball? Damn it, I won't have this kind of behaviour, d'you hear?"

Minette's face flushed with anger, her earlier anxiety vanishing. "And why do you think I left so suddenly, Patrick? Or are you still too drunk to remember the terrible injuries you inflicted on your little daughter?"

"What I remember is an impertinent besom, who had the nerve to answer me back when told to go to bed! And if I gave her a little smack, she bloody deserved it. I'm sick and tired of these damned brats of yours, forever whining from behind their mother's skirts. Blasted pests every one of 'em, spoiled rotten by you and your gaggle of *ayahs!*"

"It was considerably more than a "little smack" that you delivered, Patrick!" Minette spat. "It was a hard enough blow to cause the poor child to fall back against a burning stove. In any event, I'm not prepared to discuss the issue until you have slept off your alcoholic revels of the past several days."

Seeing Minette standing tall and disdainful before him, the man lunged forward to roughly grasp his wife's arm. "You'll do what I damned well tell you," he snarled close to her face. "And now I intend to teach you a bloody lesson you won't forget in a hurry!"

Seeing his free arm swing back, fist bunched to deliver a blow, Minette did not hesitate. With all her strength, she gave her husband a hefty shove, catching him off-balance and sending him sprawling backwards against the wall. White with fury that violent hands should have been laid on her, Minette stood over the astounded man. She spoke slowly and with cold menace. "Don't you ever, *ever* try to punch me again, Patrick O'Hara! But in the event that it even enters your mind, I shall report you to your commanding officer for domestic brutality. That should do your career as a doctor a world of good."

Stupefied by the enraged virago standing over him, and aware of the ridiculous picture he must present sprawled on the floor, Patrick scrambled to his feet. Glaring at his wife from red-rimmed eyes, he hawked up a gob of phlegm that he spat at Minette before slouching off to the bedroom.

From a distance several pairs of frightened eyes followed his departure.

The man's spittle dribbling down her shoulder, Minette stood frozen, delayed reaction causing her to shake uncontrollably. Drawing an unsteady breath, she forced herself to make her way towards the small group huddling in the nursery doorway. With an attempt to muster a normal tone, Minette instructed the *ayahs* to see to the children's bedtime, and then bent to kiss each child in turn.

It was unthinkable to spend the night with a man who had just threatened her with violence. Minette retired to the spare bedroom and barricaded the door with a heavy chest of drawers. Several hours later, she fell into a restless sleep.

It was still dark when Minette crept out of the house the following morning, desperately needing the comfort of her horses. Frederick might well materialise to accompany her: but if not, she would ride out alone to gather her scattered wits.

Although it had occurred to her that one day, Patrick might turn violent towards her—the reality was nevertheless a hideous shock! Seized by an overwhelming desire to put distance between herself and her husband, the old doctor's warning nevertheless crept insidiously into her mind. It had all seemed simple prior to Patrick's return, but now her courage to carry it through was truly being tested!

How would she cope financially, should Patrick prove mean

with funds? Dare she consider her old home in France as an option? Despite having not heard a word from any member of her family since she ran away with Patrick? Her father was a kind man, and surely he would not allow his grandchildren to go homeless? The thought of remaining trapped in this violent marriage was unbearable.

An hour later, the young woman was no further forward in making a definitive decision. Handing the two horses back to their grooms, she walked briskly home, filled with dread at the thought of further confrontation with her husband. With any luck he would still be in bed, sleeping off his disgusting condition.

Upon entering the house, she could hear Patrick loudly snoring through the closed bedroom door. Good! The boys were having breakfast in the nursery, and acutely aware their father was in the house—they escaped to play on the *maidan*. Clutching pencils and paper, Claire remained with her mother on the veranda. The child had yet to be confronted by the author of her pain and distress.

The remainder of the day passed without incident, in all probability because there was no sign of the man in the bedroom. Let sleeping dogs lie—thought the young woman with relief—the longer the better.

Afternoon faded into evening, and Minette sat alone on the veranda, staring at the open book in her hands. Patrick still had not materialised, so there was every chance he might remain in the bedroom until the following day. Still foremost in her mind was the need to remove herself and her children out of harm's way. But she had yet to resolve the problem of how to manage financially.

It was not beyond the bounds of possibility that Patrick might be glad to see the back of his despised family. Minette already had to subsidise the pitiful amount of housekeeping money Patrick allowed her each month, by tutoring other people's children in the French language. A sticking point would nevertheless be a question of giving his wife any money at all.

Closing her book with a sigh, Minette leaned forward to adjust the flickering flame of the hurricane lantern on the table in front of her. Suddenly aware of a presence, she twisted round to see Patrick standing in the doorway—fully dressed. Advancing towards his wife, he laid a placatory hand on her shoulder.

"Darling, don't let's fight!" Patrick attempted an engaging smile. "You have to admit I was justified in being angry over your unwarranted behaviour in Delhi. But I'm willing to forgive you for that, so let's say it's over and done with."

Incredulous, Minette stared up at her husband. My God, it's a case of *dejà vu*—she thought hysterically. The man's prepared to "forgive" me for abandoning him to take care of my injured child. But no mention of the role *he* played in the atrocious drama!

Shrugging off the hand, Minette rose to her feet and turned to survey her husband, her expression distant. Patrick's face was bloated, his eyes bloodshot and a vein throbbed in his temple. Probably from rage, guessing she was about to reject his so-generous offer to overlook her "behaviour"—Minette thought cynically.

"I don't believe this to be a good time to discuss anything of importance, Patrick," Minette told him evenly. "Since it is clear you are still not yourself. Perhaps we could try again tomorrow morning … provided you refrain from drinking yourself senseless in the meanwhile."

Patrick's mouth fell open at Minette's temerity, and he raised his arm to deliver a back-handed slap to the disdainful face staring at him. Sensing her husband's intention, the young woman gritted her teeth and managed not to step back in fear.

"Don't even *think* of raising your hand to me again, Patrick O'Hara!" Her voice was quiet but menacing. "I advise you to remember what I said about reporting you to the Brigadier—and I mean it."

"Christ, what a double-dyed bitch you are turning out to be!" The man was trembling with suppressed fury. "Your own mother was right about you, and I should have had the sense to listen to her. I curse the day that I came across you, Marguerite de Merencourt! Why, even my mother saw what a … "

Patrick suddenly became aware that he was speaking to fresh air— Minette had gone. My God, that bloody woman needed a damned good lesson in learning to respect her husband, and he intended to see that she got it! For the moment, he was heartily sick of her sour face and intended to pass the evening in more congenial company. But tomorrow, oh yes, tomorrow she would bitterly regret her damned intransigence.

"Madam, you will be more than sorry you took this stand against me, I promise you!" Patrick yelled through the open door. "When I get back, you won't be able to go out in public for a month by the time I have finished with you!"

There was no answer.

Patrick stormed from the veranda and out of the house, slamming the front door so that it reverberated. Standing in the shadows, her breathing ragged with tension, Minette's expression was bleak. If she had required a goad to make up her mind over the future ... Patrick had just given it to her. Everything was now clear as regards what her next step must be.

Tomorrow, she would ask to see the Brigadier and explain her decision to leave India. Fearing further violence, she would request alternative accommodation until a passage back to England could be arranged for herself and her children. She would not continue to live under the same roof as this man.

As for his present destination, Minette shrugged. She had a good idea where Patrick was bound. His favourite haunt was a Country Club up the road from the cantonment, where hardened drinkers could congregate round the bar there, often availing themselves of services from local "ladies of the night." She hoped the unspeakable beast would remain there all night long!

Be that as it may, Minette was certain that Patrick would be blind drunk when he returned. He might also be filled with a burning desire to avenge himself on his recalcitrant wife ... or even the children. It was imperative she took precautions to protect herself and them from possible assault.

Mailie was awake when Minette crept into the children's rooms. She understood at once when her mistress told her to lock the bedroom doors from the inside, and keep the keys under her pillow. Minette told the *ayah* to ignore any attempt from Sahib to access the children. Mailie nodded, and Minette heard the click of the doors being locked behind her.

Satisfied she had done what she could, Minette made her way to the spare room and turned the key in the lock. As an added deterrent, she dragged the heavy chest of drawers up against the door once again. But what of the window? She relaxed, recalling that the bungalow windows were barred against burglars. Suddenly exhausted, Minette undressed and climbed into bed, to eventually drift into a dreamless sleep.

"*Mem!* Wake up *Memsahib!*' Mailie's voice penetrated the fog of Minette's sleep-drugged senses. "Wake up, *Mem*! Old *Doctor-Sahib* here, also Barre-*Sahib* is come with doctor."

Dragging herself up on an elbow, Minette wondered for a moment if she really had heard Mailie calling her … or was it only a dream?

"*Mem* … please wake up now!" The *ayah's* voice held an edge of panic. "Old *Doctor-sahib* here … "

Jolted wide-awake, Minette leaped out of bed and struggled to dislodge the heavy barrier from blocking the door. Pulling the door open, the she saw the *ayah* standing in the doorway, her face anxious in the light of an oil lamp she held.

"Did you say the doctor is here? Why? And what time is it, Mailie?" Minette was hastily shrugging on a robe. "Is one of the children sick?"

"No, no … chil'ren alright! It is four o'clock night-time, *Memsahib*. I hear *jamadar* come to bedroom window, he say two sahibs is come for *Mem*. They now waiting in sitting room."

Her heart hammering, Minette tore down the corridor and burst into the sitting room. Doctor MacElwee and Frederick rose to their feet, their expressions sombre.

"Minette, *chère*, come and sit down a moment," Frederick's voice was gentle as he took the frightened young woman's arm and sat her down on the couch. "I'm afraid we are bearing bad news. Patrick has met with an accident. He was shot—we believe in error—by a fanatic bearing some kind of grudge."

"*Shot?*" Minette lost every vestige of colour. "How … how badly hurt is he?"

"Lassie, ah'm verra sorry to hafta say yer husband was killed outright," broke in the old doctor, sensing Frederick's reluctance to confirm her husband's death to the shocked young woman. "Seems he wuss shot from his hoss sometime during t'wee hours, and t'animal made its own way back to the stabling."

"The groom on duty caught the loose horse, and recognised it as Balthasar, Patrick's charger," Frederick continued. "He alerted a sentry who woke me, and a search party was immediately organised. Doctor MacElwee was included, in case of medical urgency. We discovered Patrick lying by the roadside on the way back from the Country Club. I'm so sorry, *ma petite*, but he was already dead."

"*Dead?*" repeated Minette stupidly. "How can Patrick be dead? He was very much alive only a few hours ago, swearing he was going to—"

A second later, the enormity of the tragedy struck home. With a gasp, Minette held out a hand to Frederick in mute supplication, and then crumpled to the floor. Summoning the ayah, Frederick gathered the limp form in his arms and carried her to a bedroom indicated by the servant. He placed Minette gently on the bed and turned to the *ayah* hovering behind him.

"Your Memsahib has had a bad shock, so Doctor MacElwee will attend to her before we leave. I regret to tell you that Doctor O'Hara has been killed in an accident tonight. Please take care of your memsahib, and we will be back in the morning. Nothing is to be said to the children … they will be told when the moment is right."

Minette remained closeted in her bedroom for two entire days. Dry-eyed and stony-faced, she said little, and ate sparingly. The children were bewildered by their mother's odd behaviour, but Frederick took them over to bring some normality into their lives. Very gently, he told the three older children their father had been in an accident resulting in his death—avoiding any detail.

To Frederick's surprise, all three children remained untouched by grief over their father's demise. Claire declared herself glad not to have to see her father again, a sentiment immediately endorsed by her elder brother, James. Charlie told a shocked Frederick he was glad not to be worried about beatings for being awake at night

In the end, it was old Doctor MacElwee who discovered what was causing Minette's depression. Listening to her description of the destructive scene with her husband, he realised Minette was feeling responsible for Patrick's untimely death—despite his promise of extreme violence towards her the following day.

"Now, now lassie! Understand once and for all, it's no' yer fault the mon died! T'was t'divil drink that saw him off our mortal coil, and ye hafta accept that!" The kindly old man patted Minette's hand.

"Remember what he did to the puir wee gurl ... an' he didn'a show remorse for that, as ah recall! Sooner or later, it was bound t'happen agin ... mebbe even wuss. But now, it's yer bairns that need their ma, so come on, lassie—pull yersel' together fer them!"

Minette roused herself sufficiently to attend her husband's military funeral. An elegant veiled figure, flanked by her two sons, she walked behind the coffin draped with the British flag. The funeral service droning to an end, Minette and her boys returned to the bungalow in silence.

Quite simply, there was nothing left to say.

CHAPTER TWENTY-SEVEN

The days following Patrick O'Hara's funeral were to haunt Minette long afterwards. She was forced to endure tittle-tattle from the usual gossip-mongers who declared themselves shocked that the newly bereaved widow had declined to spend time with her poor husband's body. What dreadful behaviour from that heartless Frenchwoman! She tried to ignore the spite, but it stung, nevertheless.

Minette forced herself to make inroads into her husband's personal affairs, beset by the unreasonable feeling she was somehow intruding into his personal privacy. Those finer feelings, however, vanished into thin air when sheaf after sheaf of unpaid bills began to arrive at the house.

Horrified, Minette conducted a frantic search for existing bank accounts, finally discovering two in different local banks. Her relief was short-lived. Both accounts were heavily over-drawn, and in consequence there were heavy penalty charges in addition to outstanding sums of money. The only funds available to Minette were monies she had earned from private tutoring—kept squirrelled away from her husband's eyes.

A dismal picture began to emerge. Without a substantial sale of her possessions, there would not be sufficient monies to emerge from these debts. The desire to weep and hide from the world was overwhelming, but Minette knew she could not afford the luxury.

Her family was depending on her.

Pulling herself together, Minette sought Frederick's help in disposing of Patrick's five Polo ponies and his two chargers. She desperately hoped the funds they brought in would pay off the overdrawn bank accounts. At once, Frederick purchased Balthasar—despite his great age—for a sum vastly exceeding the old horse's value. Conscious of her friend's subtle kindness, Minette was deeply grateful. In only a week, Frederick had sold the other horses for an excellent price. A solid silver tea set and matching coffee pot—purchased long ago with her own money—were also sold and brought in a substantial sum.

At least the banks were paid off.

As her husband's tangled financial affairs were unravelled and then settled, Minette's spirits lightened. She imagined that Patrick's salary must also soon be due, in addition to whatever settlement the British Army gave to the family of a deceased officer. Able now to plan for the future, Minette wrote to her father, asking for his permission to return to France with her children. She only hoped her funds would last until they left India for good.

A bolt from the blue exploded Minette's tentative plans—in the form of her husband's unsettled gambling debts. A staggering sum of money was outstanding to several people, very much in excess of what the unfortunate young woman had in her possession. Destitution loomed.

Making matters worse for the embattled young woman, a letter from Serena O'Hara arrived—a tirade of abusive recrimination. It included the vicious accusation that her son's French concubine had not been content upon ruining his life, but the despicable creature was also responsible for his early death. Serena hoped the harlot would rot in hell ...

Sickened, Minette ripped the flimsy notepaper into shreds and flung them into the kitchen dustbin. She would consign the O'Haras to the past, for that family had caused her enough grief to last a lifetime.

Staring at the pile of "*iou*" notes on the desk in front of her, a white-hot fury ignited in Minette's breast. Even from the grave, the blasted man was managing to blight her life with further evidence of gross irresponsibility. It was little wonder that money had always been tight, and she was forced to tutor so that the children were clothed and servants paid on time. How little Patrick O'Hara had cared about his family! That was now very clear, since he had made no provision for their welfare in the event of being killed whilst on active duty.

My God, but it beggared belief.

How was she to find the huge amount of money to pay off the clamouring creditors? Minette knew these debts must be paid—one way or another—to preserve her family's honourable name. But how?

With a heavy heart, Minette sold her thoroughbred mare, Fantastique, to a family whose fifteen-year-old daughter had always coveted her. She had intended to take both her horses back to France, but now the mare, although aged, was one of the few things of value she still possessed.

Next went her two Chinese Ming Dynasty vases that she had bought as an investment with her own money, in addition to a solid silver tray. Finally, Minette was reduced to rifling through her jewellery box for saleable items of value.

Finally, the debts were paid, but Minette was left with next to nothing—thanks to that weak irresponsible man she had married without truly knowing him. A heavy price to be paying for youthful folly! Never again would she be answerable to a man—she had been crucified by one or the other of them too often. Her life was her own, and she would personally take charge of it.

Two days later, Minette received a visit from the Cavalry Adjutant. A nice man, burdened with the uncomfortable task of requesting that Mrs O'Hara and her family vacate the bungalow as soon as possible. A new medical man and his family were due to arrive from Madras, and would require the accommodation. Aware the unfortunate woman had suffered recent bereavement, the officer was apologetic, assuring her that temporary accommodation would be made available if necessary.

The future of her two *ayahs* was also on Minette's mind. The other servants had been paid off, so it was only Mailie and Seenta who remained to help with the children and general packing up of the home.

Since she was no longer in a position to pay even them for any length of time, Minette asked if she should intervene with the new doctor when he arrived? She felt a rush of gratitude when both *ayahs* refused the offer, stoutly declaring they would accompany their

"*Mem*" wherever she was bound. They reminded her she would need their help even more when the new *baba* arrived!

God Almighty! Her mind being taken over by the traumatic events of the past weeks, Minette had forgotten she was pregnant. If her calculations were correct, the baby was due to arrive in four months time. It was unlikely that military medical services would still be available to her, so she must think about where to go for the delivery of her child. If only her father would reply to her letter! There was so little time left before it would be too late to embark on a journey by sea.

The days went by, and there was still no letter from the Marquis. Depressed, Minette realised there was now some urgency to find somewhere to go. Then, by a stroke of providence, there came a knock at her door one morning. A smiling nun was ushered into the sitting room where Minette was busy with her papers. It was Sister Ursula of the Loretto Order, whom Minette knew well from her own work with the Charity.

"Sister Ursula, how lovely to see you," Minette came forward with a delighted smile. "You must have thought I had disappeared into thin air these last weeks!"

"We did wonder a little, but then we heard about your husband's dreadful accident! I've come to see if all is well, or maybe you need some help?"

"It's not been … easy, to say the least." Minette looked down at her hands, not wishing to unburden herself on the poor woman. "But I've managed to sort most things out, apart from having to leave the bungalow in only a few days time."

"So, what are your plans? Will you be going back to England?" asked the nun.

Minette shook her head. "Actually, I'm expecting another baby in a few months. I hoped to go back to my childhood home in France for the delivery, but I haven't yet heard from my father. The postal service can be so unreliable, can't it? Now, of course, it's too late for me to make the journey."

"Well, why don't you go to our Convent in Simla?" suggested the nun. "After all you have done for our Charity, I'm sure Mother Clementine would be delighted to welcome you."

"Do you really think so?" Minette exclaimed, brightening a little. "That would be simply perfect, and the climate would be wonderful for the children."

"I'll see about making arrangements right away," Sister Ursula turned to leave. "Don't worry, everything will work out well, you'll see."

The nun was as good as her word, and Minette soon received a letter from Mother Superior of the Loretto Convent in Simla. It contained a warm invitation for Minette and her family to stay as long as she wished. All the nuns loved children—Minette must already know about their orphanage in Simla? And now there was to be a new baby ... how lovely!

Minette replied at once, with a tentative mention of the two *ayahs* who would be accompanying her. And what of Turka, her Arab horse? No problem—came the reply—the Convent already had two donkeys and a mule living in loose boxes in their barn, so Turka would have lots of company. There was also plenty of good grazing available.

Reading Mother Clementine's reply to her letter, Minette burst into tears of relief and gratitude. She had been putting off the problem of Turka's future, knowing the little horse was too mentally scarred to adapt to another owner. Having nowhere to go herself, there could only be one answer: he would have to be put down. But now, thanks to the generosity of the nuns, they all had a home to go to—including Turka.

Her life assuming some semblance of direction at last, Minette was filled with renewed energy. She lost no time in telling Frederick of the nuns' invitation to stay in Simla, and was delighted when he offered to escort her family there.

"And you may be sure I will visit you again, after I return from Home Leave," Frederick added. "I haven't been back to Provence for five years, and my parents can scarcely believe their son will shortly be gracing them with his presence."

Minette's face clouded. "We will miss you, Freddie ... I'd forgotten you were soon to leave for France."

"Well, it's not for a few weeks yet. Plenty of time to see you settled in the Convent, in any event."

"Freddie?" Minette gazed earnestly at her friend. "May I ask a great favour of you? Would you take a letter to my father for me, and personally deliver it into his hands? I've already written to him, asking if I may return with my children to live at the family home, but I've had no reply. He may not have even seen my letter, as my mother and her toady son have probably purloined it."

"Of course! I shall deliver your letter directly to your father, so don't worry on that score," Frederick looked perplexed. "But surely there isn't the possibility that he will *refuse* permission? You told me the two of you were always close ... and he's never seen his grandchildren, has he?"

Minette looked down at her hands. "Until that business of arranging my marriage, Papa and I spent a great deal of time together, especially at the Haras. He and my grandparents tried to protect me from my mother, who always loathed me for reasons I was never able to fathom."

Remembering her mother's icy demeanour towards her, the young woman's mouth tightened. "But then, as you know, I ran off with Patrick ... and I haven't managed to establish a contact since. Whilst I was in the Convent, my Uncle Emile discovered *Maman* was systematically destroying letters from my family to me—and mine to them. It stands to reason that she has never stopped."

"I can assure you that the letter in my charge will reach your father! Now, is there anything I can do for you now?"

"Thank you, but no. I think we are more or less organised, and we'll be ready to leave the day after tomorrow as arranged. Freddie, how can I thank you for all you are doing for me? I don't know how I would have coped with these weeks without your help and support."

"*Chèrie*, it is truly my pleasure," Frederick bent to kiss Minette on each cheek, and then strode away—thinking for the hundredth time how despicable Patrick O'Hara had turned out to be.

The longed-for day of departure dawned, and in the company of Frederick, Minette and her family left the cantonment in Lucknow without regret. Turka was already at the station, making a great fuss about walking up the ramp into his stall on the train. Clutching his lead rope, a Cavalry *syce* stood by helplessly as Turka planted his feet, eyes rolling, nostrils flared.

Having just arrived, Minette took in the scene at a glance, and grinned. Turka was "playing to the gallery" as always! Coming to the *syce's* rescue, Minette took the lead rope. Casting a disdainful glance at the sweating *syce*, Turka meekly allowed his mistress to lead him up the ramp and into a stall filled with deep straw bedding. Moments later, he was tucking into a bulging hay-net.

Several hours later, the journey at an end, the travellers descended from the train in Simla.

Looking about her, Minette spied two Loretto nuns frantically waving to attract her attention. A small cart pulled by a sturdy pony was waiting outside the station. The new arrivals were instructed to climb aboard with only their immediate hand luggage. The Convent handyman would collect the rest of it later in the day.

The nuns' welcome was warm, and the children taken off their mother's hands to be given mugs of hot chocolate and iced buns. Whilst Frederick was in the barn making sure Turka was bedded down in his new home, Minette was shown to the guest wing of the Convent.

The two-story apartment was light and airy. Double glass doors gave out to a balcony, the wrought iron railing festooned with window boxes overflowing with scarlet geraniums. A kitchenette existed at the rear, sufficient for making tea or light cooking. Main meals would be taken in the Great Hall, together with the nuns and their group of orphan children of varying ages.

Satisfied that Minette was in safe hands, Frederick took his leave, explaining that he still had a great deal of office work to do in Lucknow before leaving for France. In his briefcase, was Minette's letter to the Marquis de Merencourt.

Frederick was aware his friend was banking on a favourable reply to her request. On the train, she had talked about seeing her beloved grandparents again, and how proud her father would be to see his grandsons ride. She would take them to see all her favourite childhood haunts.

Knowing that Minette's clandestine marriage to the Irishman was a civil affair—unrecognised by the Catholic Church—Frederick was unable to shake off serious doubts. He recalled only too well the rigidity of social constraints binding families such as Minette's and his own. But maybe attitudes had changed over the years he had been away? For Minette's sake, he hoped so.

As the weeks went by, the O'Hara children settled into their new way of life. Their faces taking on the bloom of health in the cooler climate, the daily routine suited them well. There were lessons in the morning and sports in the afternoons. Sister Gwendolyn, a plump nun of middle years, was in charge of Rounders and cricket games. On occasion, she would even join in, amazing the young team players by hoisting her robes to turn on a spurt of speed belying her size and age!

After the trauma and upheaval of recent weeks, Minette was also grateful for the calm and tranquillity of the Convent and its environs. As her pregnancy advanced, she made a habit of going for a brisk walk each day along the maze of pathways behind the Convent building. Breathing in the freshness of mountain air perfumed by wildflowers growing in the hedgerows, Minette allowed herself to relax at last.

Four months after Minette's arrival in Simla, Sonia Jane O'Hara was born. Delighting in the pretty infant, Minette was inclined to carry her everywhere she went. Claire looked on with jealous eyes, bewildered by her mother's apparent absorption with a new arrival that seemed to scream for nothing. She wished the nasty little bundle could be sent back to wherever it had come from, so she and Christina could have their mother's attention again.

Sensing Claire's increasing hostility, Minette sought to distract her with the suggestion that she and Charlie took charge of Turka's daily requirements. Each morning before lessons began, the two children turned the horse out to pasture. They then mucked out his loose box, and made up a feed for the evening. It was a natural progression of affairs that Turka's stable companions became included in the children's care. Soon Charlie and Claire were habitually making up four feeds each day, and tid-bits were also shared equally between every occupant of the barn.

Far away in southern France, Frederick carried out his promise to undertake personal delivery of Minette's letter to her father. Arriving unannounced at the château, Frederick was shown into the salon. He was dismayed to note the Marquis was wheelchair-bound, apparently the result of a bad fall from his horse.

Behind him stood a woman, whose fair beauty was still striking despite being of a certain age. Minette's mother—Frederick correctly deduced—responsible for perpetuating a continued antipathy towards her only daughter.

Having first introduced himself, Frederick produced Minette's letter from an inside pocket and handed it to the Marquis. He explained that he had been charged with personal delivery of the letter by Marguerite, his daughter.

Frederick's heart sank when the Marquise stepped forward and took the letter from her husband, placing it on a table beyond his reach. So there was not to be an immediate reply. Neither parent asked after Minette or even their grandchildren. It was not a good omen for the eventual outcome of his mission!

Refreshments were offered which Frederick politely refused, explaining he still had a considerable distance to go. Taking his leave of the Marquis and his wife, Frederick resumed the journey to his family home in Provence.

Two months later, Minette had just returned from an early morning ride on Turka, whose nose was now buried in a bucket of feed. As she was putting away the tack, she looked up to see a nun hurrying towards her waving an envelope.

Thanking the breathless nun, Minette spirits soared to see her father's own handwriting at long last! Glancing again at the envelope in her hand, a small frown creased her forehead. Her father had addressed it to Mademoiselle de Merencourt. Evidently an oversight, being unaccustomed to her married name.

Perching on a nearby bale of straw, Minette opened the envelope and drew out a single sheet of the familiar crested notepaper. There were only a few lines.

Mademoiselle,

Your request that you and your offspring come here to live at our family home is denied. Living with a man who is not your husband, and furthermore bearing his children is, of course, inadmissible. It is astonishing to us that you should dare to ask, bearing in mind the great shame you brought down on your family.

A decision has been made to strike the name of Marguerite from family records, since you have ceased to exist for us. Kindly refrain from further communication, for it will go unanswered.

Charles, Duc de Saint Aubrey

Stunned by the cold formality of her father's letter, Minette barely registered the sheet of paper slipping from her fingers and drifting to the ground. He had not even accorded her the dignity of being a married woman. Her eyes filled with tears upon the realisation that her father had signed himself as Duc, which meant her darling Gran'père was dead ... .maybe Grand'mère too.

Suddenly, the terrible import of being no longer recognised by her family crashed down on the devastated young woman. Was it possible? Could they eliminate her from family records as if she had never been born? A surge of nausea rising in her throat, Minette ran outside to retch painfully, her stomach being empty of food so early in the day.

Struggling to regain control of herself, she was unable to prevent bitter tears coursing down her cheeks as the awful reality of her present situation hit home.

Nowhere to go.

Derisory funds on which to live.

Nobody to turn to.

Alone ... with five small people depending on her.

Through the fog of misery engulfing her, a small flame of fury flared that yet *again* a bloody man had blasted her world apart, leaving her scrabbling to survive! So what was the answer? Remarriage? *Never!* Somehow she would manage.

Walking back into the barn, Minette's glance fell on the notepaper lying on the ground where she had let it fall. Picking it up, she savagely crumpled it into a ball and stormed outside to fling it into the manure pit ... where it belonged!

The following week was one of reflection and planning. Sitting up late at night, Minette made up a statement of what monies she possessed, including that in the Edinburgh account. A welcome surprise had been a Statement of Account with Lombards in London, discovered whilst sorting out the chaotic mess of Patrick's desk. Evidently forgotten by him. It held a considerable sum, but not sufficient to keep her family for more than a few frugal years. English school fees for her boys would be out of the question. She must make a credible plan ... and soon!

Minette wrote to Jane Ogilvy, asking her to enquire about the possibility of undertaking nursing training at her hospital on her behalf. Preferably to include midwifery, which had so appealed to her years ago. Might it also be possible to stay with Jane during her training? The children had done so well in Scotland that last time.

A large envelope arrived from Jane by return. A training course for nurses was due to begin in three months, and she had taken the liberty of adding Minette's name on the application list. The relevant forms were enclosed, inclusive of a leaflet outlining the hospital's fee structure. Minette could therefore calculate an exact figure of what she was letting herself in for.

As regards accommodation—Jane wrote—she had leased out her third bedroom to a fellow nurse who took care of her dog as she was often away. Of course, Minette was welcome to stay, but sadly there was no room in her flat for five children. Something bigger would have to be found.

But had Minette thought things through—Jane worried. Renting a large enough flat to house her family would be expensive. In addition, there was a nanny's salary to consider, as well as living costs. Then there were school fees for Minette's two boys. But perhaps Patrick had ensured his family would be financially secure, in the event of his unexpected demise on the battlefield?

Financially secure? What a joke. Folding Jane's letter, Minette slipped it back into its envelope and walked out on to the sitting room balcony. Gazing unseeing at the distant mountain range, her mind was a blank. Just as she thought to have found a solution to her precarious predicament ... disaster had struck again!

Minette shivered—but not from the coolness of the afternoon. She was frankly terrified. How was she to take care of these children of hers, and give them the security they so desperately needed? God alone knew … for she did not.

Without warning, Frederick arrived in Simla a few days later, having cut short his leave. He was worried about the probability of Minette receiving either a refusal of her request … or maybe nothing at all. Either way, he knew it would be devastating for the young woman. He found Minette sunk in despondency.

"My … my father has formally disowned me," she told her friend, trying to control the wobbling of her voice. "And my alternative plan to undertake nursing training has received a major setback, because I could never afford the expenditure necessary to look after and educate my children."

Frederick took the distraught young woman's hand. "Minette, *ma chèrie*, you don't have to do any of this you know. If you would consider marrying me, it would make me the happiest man on earth! I love you to distraction—I always have—and I think the world of your children. It would be a tremendous privilege to count them as my own."

Gazing at her friend's kind face, Minette thought what a very nice man he was. He would probably make a wonderful husband, and the children certainly adored him. Did she love him? Maybe. So what was the problem?

Unbidden, the thought crept into her mind that Patrick O'Hara had once seemed the epitome of everything desirable in a man. And look how *that* had turned out! Turning to answer Frederick, Minette caught sight of a shadow moving on the corridor wall behind him. James, of course. That boy was forever eavesdropping!

"James, I know you are there, so clear off, will you!" she called out sharply. The shadow shifted … and was gone.

Turning back to Frederick, Minette wanted to choose her words carefully, to avoid hurting her very dear friend. She would not slam the door closed in his face, but wanted to explain what was on her mind as things presently stood.

"Freddie, my dearest friend, how sweet of you to want to take on a raggedy old has-been such as myself," she said softly. "Not to mention a gaggle of children. But I'm damaged goods, you know, and you deserve better than to be saddled with that sort of thing."

"But Minette, *chérie*, you must know that means nothing to me. To the contrary, I would be—"

"Freddie, there are a few things I need to prove to myself," Minette gently interrupted. "I want to feel in control of my own destiny—dependent on no-one—and self-sufficient financially. Can you understand that?" Her blue eyes anxiously searched Frederick's face.

"Of course I can," Frederick hid his acute disappointment. "Whatever you decide to do, you know you can count on my support. But don't imagine I shall give up on the marriage issue, my girl! There will never be anyone else for me, so I shall ask you to marry me very single year until you agree … in desperation!"

Minette relaxed with a mischievous grin. "That sounds wonderful, Freddie. On the hard road ahead, I'm sure I shall need to feel desirable from time to time!"

Several days later, Minette was no further forward in her plans. She received several letters from Jane, containing examples of suitable properties for rental within a reasonable distance from the hospital. They were all well beyond her means, and the cost of child-care was also daunting.

Minette was floundering. She simply did not know which way to turn. In desperation, she realised she needed the advice of someone wiser and more experienced in the ways of the world than herself. Mother Superior of the Loretto Order seemed the perfect answer!

A delightful old lady, Mother Clementine's ready smile denoted an approachable personality. Minette was certain she would receive sensible and emotionally detached advice regarding the direction she should take. Yes, Mother Clementine would appreciate the importance of ensuring a decent future for herself and her children.

Acting on impulse, Minette hurried towards the main Convent building, meaning to make an appointment to see Mother Clementine. It was providential that the elderly nun happened to be slowly mounting the steps to the front entrance as Minette breathlessly arrived.

Clementine's kind old eyes took in the young woman's distracted air, and the faint frown of anxiety between the dark eyebrows. Learning of Minette's mission, the nun's lined face broke into a sunny smile.

"Come with me to my study, child … I think a nice cup of tea and a biscuit or two is in order, don't you?"

Holding Minette's arm for support, Clementine led the way into a light room. Looking about her, Minette noticed with pleasure the desk and almost every surface held a vase containing a profusion of flowers.

"Mother, I have a dreadful dilemma to somehow resolve … "

"Before we get down to business, let's have our tea," the old nun said firmly. "The answer to a problem comes far more easily afterwards, I always find."

Her eyes bright with unshed tears, Minette watched Clementine's careful little movements as she went about preparing a tray. Taking two cups and saucers of fine bone china from a cupboard, she piled fingers of buttery shortbread on a matching plate. Noticing her guest's surprise to see the dainty tea things, the old nun smiled in amusement.

"Were you expecting me to serve you your tea in a thick servant's mug?" she enquired, a mischievous twinkle in her eyes. "You know, we nuns don't all wear hair-shirts, and consider everything beautiful or delicious to be sinful! Drinking my tea from exquisite porcelain is a luxury I have always permitted myself … and have no intention of giving it up."

In spite of herself, Minette grinned as she accepted the pretty cup and saucer the old nun held out to her. Helping herself to shortbread, she shut her eyes, relishing the rich buttery flavour, suspecting the delicacy had come from a precious hoard.

"Mmm! Delicious! It's a long time since I have had such a treat." Taking a sip of her tea, Minette sat back in her chair.

Clementine placed her own cup back in its saucer. "Now, tell me what is troubling you so much. We have all the time in the world to talk, so don't concern yourself with bells or people calling. I imagine the children are being taken care of? Good! I believe you recently received a letter from France? Was it bad news, my child?"

To her horror, tears welled in Minette's eyes and trickled down her cheeks. The last thing she wanted was to give the impression of a being a baby—she thought savagely. But the tears continued to fall.

"My father ... he has dis-disowned me, Mother," she whispered. "I was hoping to take the children home to France—but he doesn't want me. My n-name has been scratched from all family records ... as though I have ceased to exist!" Minette covered her face with her hands in a mixture of distress and shame.

Clementine allowed a few minutes to go by, to allow the girl to regain her self-control. "But why, Minette? We know you as a lovely caring person, who has suffered great tragedy in her young life. What happened to offend your family to such a degree?"

Over the next two hours, Minette unburdened herself to the elderly nun. She omitted nothing of her own irresponsible behaviour in running off with a debonair young Irishman. She told of her father being deliberately eluded when he travelled to London in an effort to retrieve his daughter. Her clandestine civil marriage in Gretna Green—never sanctified by the Church—resulting in being branded a harlot, and her children bastards by her husband's family and doubtless her own.

Choking on her tears, Minette whispered of the nightmare years she was forced to endure at her alcoholic husband's hands. Her efforts to protect the children from their father's drunken violence—not always with success. Finally, his violent death, subsequent to roughly manhandling her with a threat of more to come.

Minette went on to describe the shocking discovery of Patrick O'Hara's irresponsibility towards his family—the unpaid bills and overdrawn bank accounts. A mountain of gambling debts he had incurred came as a final crushing blow, all of which she settled from the sale of her remaining possessions.

The British Army had furnished her with monies to cover First Class sailing passages back to England, a sum she had been hoarding for the voyage to France. It was all that remained between her ... and destitution.

Minette felt an odd sense of liberation as she came to the end of her tale. Wiping her nose on her sleeve like a child, she braced herself for condemnation from the nun sitting opposite her. Whilst

Minette was talking, Clementine had listened attentively, but without comment or particular expression.

"Frankly, my dear, I am amazed how well balanced you are in light of the appalling situation you lived through for so many years," Clementine remarked at last. "Well done, Minette! Tell me, how does that nice gentleman, Frederick de Barre, fit into the picture? He seems very attached to you and the children."

"He … he wants to marry me, Mother. Freddie is a wonderful person, and God only knows how I would have coped without his help."

"Do you not think that marriage to your friend would be a positive resolution to your future, Minette? I've observed how fond of him your children are."

Minette hesitated, but then shook her head decisively. "It's tempting to accept the easier option, and I know Freddie would be thrilled if I agreed to marry him. But, I can't bear the thought of a man having control of my life ever again. All my life, I have been buffeted hither and thither on the whim of one man or another, and it has to stop—right here and now!"

"In that case, we must eliminate marriage from the equation," Clementine said equably. "Do you have any ideas as to an alternative?"

Minette told her of the plan to train as a nurse in Scotland, and staying with a friend the children knew well. As a fully trained nurse and midwife, she imagined she would manage to keep her family's heads above water, as well as providing a formal education for the boys. But that plan was in the process of collapsing, as her friend was unable to accommodate herself and the five children. Renting a large enough flat for an extended period, in addition to living and child-care expenses, was beyond Minette's limited resources. How much more could go wrong for her?

Thoughtfully, Clementine regarded the distressed young woman. "It does seem that most of the usual avenues are closed off to you for the present moment," she remarked. "However, I do have a proposal which I shall outline in a few moments. First, may I say that I find your independent spirit in wishing to govern your own destiny quite admirable. It will not be an easy road to take, but I believe you have the strength of character to ultimately gain success and contentment."

The nun paused, to allow her next words to sink in. "But Minette, my dear, there are certain ... *sacrifices* you will need to make in order to achieve that. In essence, I believe your plan to take up nursing is sound, and you should pursue that without delay. However, by your own admission, you do not possess the resources to maintain your family in Scotland during your training. Therefore, I suggest you leave them here, in my care, where they are already settled and happy."

Minette's jaw dropped. "No! I could *never* abandon my children like that! Why, I would never forgive myself for abdicating my role as their mother. And Sonia is still just an infant ... "

"*Think*, Minette! Put emotion aside for a moment, and think about what I am saying," Clementine was unperturbed by the hot denial. "First of all, you would have peace of mind, knowing your sweet children were amongst those who love them, and being cared for exactly as you would wish."

"But, how can I ... "

"Secondly, you would be free to pursue your studies, without the perpetual worry over inadequate funds. Neither would you have the burden of guilt over the inevitable neglect of your children, due to the many and disparate hours you will be obliged to spend at the hospital. Think about it with great care, my dear."

Seeing the agonised expression on Minette's face, Mother Clementine leaned forward to gently pat her hand. "You do have an alternative, you know," She reminded her. "You can marry Frederick de Barre."

"No ... I don't know!" The young woman shook her head as if to clear the confusion she was feeling. "Mother, I don't think I can take the risk."

"Take your time, and we will talk again. Meanwhile, I have a few ideas you may find of interest. Upon your return to India, you will be qualified to open your own Maternity Home, preferably where an extensive European community exists, such as Calcutta. There is little of its kind in existence, so an establishment such as that will be welcome to overworked doctors. Your own business will provide you with an excellent income to cover your needs and the children's education."

"I ... I don't *know* if I have the strength to see the whole thing through, Mother," Minette was almost wringing her hands. "Three years—maybe four without my children? Won't they forget me after such a long time?"

"Of course they won't forget their mother," Clementine reassured the distraught young woman. "It's possible the baby might, but she will adapt when you return."

Minette sat frozen to the chair, tea cooling in the cup in her hand. "I'll try to think about it ... but ... but I don't think I can leave my children."

The elderly nun regarded Minette with sympathetic eyes. "The price of a secure future is going to be high ... perhaps too high? Marriage to your young man might be the better option for you, my dear." Clementine rose to her feet.

"In any event, go and find a quiet spot to think the whole thing through. God be with you, my dear child, and may he help you to find an acceptable perspective on your immediate future."

Minette left the nun's study as if in a trance. Conflicting emotions coursed through her mind as sentiment battled with cold reality. As always in times of crisis, she sought the comfort of a horse.

Twenty minutes later, Turka and his mistress were cantering along a winding pathway leading up to a favourite vantage point behind the Convent. From there, the township of Simla could be seen through swathes of fir trees straggling down the hillside. Only the chirping of birds and an occasional rustle in the undergrowth disturbed an otherwise perfect tranquillity. It was here, in this quiet spot, that Minette hoped to clear the turmoil paralysing her brain.

Reaching her destination, she slid from Turka' back, and threw the reins over his head to allow him to graze. Flopping down in the grass beside him, Minette clasped her knees to her chest, gazing blindly over the panoramic vista.

Slowly, but surely the cold reality of her situation overwhelmed her and she exploded into despairing sobs. Startled, Turka briefly glanced up but resumed cropping grass, nevertheless keeping a wary eye on his mistress who was behaving so strangely.

Exhausted from weeping, Minette finally accepted what was at stake. She had come to a fork in the road of her life. Either she took the easier option and married the thoroughly nice Frederick—or she pursued a nursing career with its attendant emotional drawbacks. Mother Clementine had emphasised the choice must be hers ... and hers alone.

For God's sake, why was she making such a drama? Marriage to Freddie was most definitely the answer, was it not? Think how happy the children would be to have him for their father! Her financial worries would be at an end ... .

And what of those other concerns—asked an insistent inner voice? Was she prepared to subject herself all over again to a man? Obliged to obey directives ... his damned orders? Abdicate her right to choose?

God, the very idea was anathema!

A nursing career would not be an easy path to take, just as the old nun had said. But it would at least allow her to make her own decisions—or mistakes. Would the children understand—and forgive—their mother's absence in their lives? It was a chance Minette decided she must take ...

Gently nudged by Turka, Minette realised the sun had disappeared. There was a definite chill in the air, and the skies were darkening to an early twilight. Time to go. Scrambling to her feet, Minette vaulted on to the horse's back, and together they wended their way towards the Convent lights twinkling far below.

CHAPTER TWENTY-EIGHT

The following weeks were harrowing for Minette. Each day she wanted to change her mind … until common sense came to the rescue. Time and again, she vacillated over marriage to Frederick … and then changed her mind. Torn by the choice she had to make—and soon—the young mother was distraught.

Finally, the sea passage was booked and paid for: Minette would undertake training to be a nurse in Edinburgh. The necessity of conserving funds being acute, she decided to travel Third Class, costing a mere fraction of a First Class ticket. Allowing herself sufficient money to pay her expenses on arrival, Minette left the remainder of her funds with Mother Clementine towards the children's keep.

"I'll send you more when I find a few children to tutor in French," she assured the elderly nun, "but I hope this will keep things going for the time being."

"Nonsense, my dear child, what you have given is more than enough for a very long time," Clementine exclaimed. "I don't want you to worry about such things. Concentrate on your studies and leave the rest to me."

Upon being told of his mother's departure to England, James demanded she accept Frederick's proposal of marriage. In which case—he declared—she would no longer need to go away. Recalling the shadow on the wall when Frederick had proposed to her, Minette realised how her elder son had got wind of it.

"James, one doesn't marry someone out of convenience," Minette attempted to explain, "Frederick is far too nice a person to be made use of like that."

"Are you saying that leaving us is better than marrying Uncle Freddie?" the boy's eyes filled with angry tears. "I really love Uncle Freddie ... and I *hate* you!" Whirling, the boy stormed away. Subsequently, he refused to speak to his mother for the remainder of the time before she left Simla.

Charlie had looked confused, but appeared to accept his mother's decision without much understanding. Claire burst into floods of tears, and threw one tantrum after another in an effort to change her mother's mind. Emotionally drained, Minette constantly had to remind herself why she was leaving her children for the better part of four years ...

The dreaded day of departure finally dawned. The carriage taking Minette to the station arrived, into which the Convent handyman loaded her luggage. Determined to put on a brave face for everyone's benefit—including her own—the young woman turned to the small group waiting to see her off.

Several nuns had come to say goodbye, including Mother Clementine. Beside her stood little Charlie who was trying not to cry, the old lady's hand resting on his thin shoulder by way of comfort. Her face stormy, Claire stood holding Christina's hand. Baby Sonia was comfortably lodged in Mailie's arms, sucking her thumb with a supreme lack of concern over the drama of the moment.

James was nowhere to be seen.

Unable to tolerate the tension any longer, Minette turned and climbed into the carriage, her vision blurred by tears. As the carriage rolled down the drive, Claire broke her sullen silence. Screaming hysterically, she ran after the moving vehicle.

"*Maman...don't go!*" hiccoughed the little girl. "I'll be good ... I'll be nice about Sonia! Please Maman, don't leave meeee!"

Halted by a nun hastily running after her, Claire stood sobbing by the Convent gates. Catching up with her on chubby little legs, Christina stood beside her older sister, howling in sympathy. Together, they watched the carriage bearing their mother away disappear from sight around a bend in the road.

The journey to Bombay was long, hot, and dusty, doing nothing to improve Minette's state of mind. Grim-faced she made her way to the P&O Company Offices to collect her ticket for a Third Class berth. It became obvious the clerk behind the desk thought it to be an error, unable to believe a well-dressed young lady should wish to travel in such mean circumstances. When Minette confirmed her booking was correct, the clerk raised his eyebrows but said no more.

She did not expect the ship's Third Class to resemble accommodation she had experienced on previous sailings—but the young woman was not in the least way prepared for the reality. She stared in horror at the meanness of the cot where she was to sleep, and the pile of coarse sheets and thin blankets, which on closer inspection she suspected were not even clean. Even the washing facilities were distinctly lacking.

But it was too late for second thoughts.

Wedged in an airless cabin with three other women, Minette lay sleepless for many a night—unused to the cacophony of sounds emitted by her companions. Two of them snored horribly throughout the night. The third woman wept noisily for hours, sometimes waking the snorers and incurring their extreme wrath.

"I'll knock yer soddin' block orf in a minnit!" one woman offered the weeping misery, whilst the other advised her robustly to "put a ruddy sock innit, fer Chrissakes!"

Bucking and cork-screwing her way through storms, the ship's sides creaked threateningly despite her great size. Dismayed, Minette noticed the ill-effects the wild weather was having on her cabin-mates, and she hurried to spend as much time as possible outside in the fresh air.

Buffeted by gales, and sometimes soaked to the skin, it was preferable to the all-pervading stench of vomit and stale urine in the cabin. Better than having to listen to the miserable moaning from the afflicted women, their groans alternating with colourful expletives.

Meals provided by the kitchens were definitely not a priority for Minette. The food was far from appetising for the most part, but one dish stood out for the young woman as being particularly horrendous. A kind of greasy stew was too often on offer, unidentifiable lumps of fatty meat floating on the surface. A slice of coarse bread lay beside each plate, presumably to mop up the watery gravy.

Revolted by even the appearance of the stew, on days when it was served up Minette would hastily depart from the dining hall.

Secreted in a bag was a tiny primus stove that Mailie had thrust inside, together with a bag of rice and packets of dried fruit. Making certain she was away from prying eyes, Minette cooked herself a simple meal … mentally thanking the little ayah for her forethought.

Weeks later, it was with infinite relief that the young Frenchwoman staggered down the gangway at Southampton docks, feeling dirty, cold, and very depressed. The journey had been an atrocious ordeal, and towards the end she was tearfully wondering if she had made a colossal mistake in her decision to leave India.

Pulling herself together, Minette made her way to London on the Boat Train, where she bought herself a ticket to Edinburgh. The train was due to leave in under two hours, so to pass the time she repaired to an overheated Waiting Room on the platform.

A canteen had been installed inside, so she bought herself a cup of very strong tea. Gagging a little at the acrid taste, Minette forced herself to gulp it down. Moments later, she felt a welcome warmth permeate her chilled body. Two cups of tea later, and Minette began to feel vaguely human once again.

The journey to Edinburgh proved every bit as tedious and exhausting as Minette remembered. Descending from the train, her spirits lifted upon catching sight of Jane waving from behind the barrier, her round face alight with joy.

The two friends hugged each other, then Jane enlisted the assistance of a passing porter to collect Minette's trunk from the train's luggage van. Arms entwined, the young women left the station and climbed into a waiting hansom cab, their breath misting in the bracing Scottish air.

That evening, Minette and Jane sat up late in front of a dying sitting room fire. Both held mugs of a milky drink containing a generous measure of rum.

"Warms the cockles of one's heart," Jane grinned at Minette, whose eyes were watering from the jolt of alcohol, "from a medicinal point of view, of course."

Both were wearing dressing gowns, feet tucked up under them, their bedroom slippers discarded on the floor. Jane's dog, Jasper, was lying on his back in front of the fire, four paws in the air, now and again emitting a gentle snore.

Minette's cheeks were flushed, the result of a hot bath in her hostess's new roll-top bathtub. She had also washed her hair with considerable vigour, eager to banish remaining vestiges of the ship's odour down the plug hole.

Being the least inquisitive person Minette had ever known, Jane asked no questions about the children except in a general way. She confined her remarks to amusing anecdotes relating to her work at the hospital, or mundane matters to do with Minette's nursing course. For that Minette was grateful, although she intended to fill in the blanks for Jane as soon as she was able.

Two days later, Minette brought herself to recount the series of disasters that had befallen her upon a return to India. Of course, Jane was aware of Patrick's demise, but Minette had not told her about leaving her children with the nuns in Simla. Coming to the end of her tale, she braced herself for Jane's disapproval, recalling her friend's fondness for the children

"Can you understand why I chose to leave the children in India—instead of marriage to Frederick?" Minette asked anxiously. "Throughout these dramas Freddie has been a wonderful friend to me. But I'm petrified of committing myself to a man after my experience at the hands of Patrick O'Hara."

Minette's expression hardened. "I remember only too well how charming *he* was at the outset, until things were no longer to his liking. Lastly, I never, *ever* want to become pregnant again."

"Sweetie, I am the last person to criticise you over not wishing to share your life with a man," Jane dryly told her friend. "As for the children, one must hope they are young enough to adapt to the present situation, and accept your reasoning when you return."

"Right now, it is imperative that you put useless self-recrimination aside, and concentrate on the training you have decided to undertake," Jane continued. "You will have little time to brood, believe me. Remember that once this profession is under your belt, it will ultimately lead to the personal freedom and financial security that you badly need."

"Of course you are right," Minette said with a faint smile. "Dwelling on the rights and wrongs of my decision serves no purpose at this point in time. As you quite rightly say, I came here for a purpose and must just get on with it."

"Exactly! And now we have to go shopping for comfy white shoes for you, and a frightening pile of medical text-books that you are going to need. And whilst we are out, we'll have tea in a nice Tea Shop I know rather well."

Jane's common sense approach to life was precisely what Minette needed to help clear her head of lingering guilt and self-doubt. Whilst Jane was out with Jasper for a short walk, she made out several cards offering private tuition in the French language to put in various shop windows—beginning with the Tea Shop.

It was important to Minette to begin earning as soon as possible. Despite Mother Clementine dismissal of the importance of further financial help, the children's upkeep was a responsibility she did not intend to shirk. Not to mention birthday and Christmas presents the nuns would mostly be buying on her behalf.

Minette's first day as a student nurse was spent acquainting herself with her fellow trainees, after which were introductions to the lecturers who would be teaching them. There were fifteen girls on the course, all of them in their early twenties. Listening to their ingenuous chatter, Minette—not yet in her thirties—felt herself to be positively ancient.

Discovering they had an exotic Frenchwoman in their midst, who already had some nursing experience, Minette came to be regarded by the other girls with something akin to awe. As the course progressed, she earned further accolades through her willingness to spend time explaining to slower learners what they had failed to understand during lectures.

Most early evenings were taken up with private tuition. Then late into the night, Minette sat at Jane's dining-room table, absorbing information from text-books and reams of notes she had taken during lectures, aware of the importance of understanding the complex aspects of drug administration. Unfazed by her daily burden, Minette not only relished the challenge, but she was also relieved there was little time left for futile introspection. Almost unnoticed, two years sped by.

Much to her amazement, the young Frenchwoman discovered she had an admirer! Colin Hartwell, an outrageously good-looking doctor, surreptitiously arranged to be on the wards at the same time as Minette. It wasn't long before he approached her with an invitation to lunch.

"Doctor Hartwell, how kind of you to ask me out," Minette smiled up at the enchanted man. "But perhaps I should explain I am engaged to an Army officer in India. After qualifying, I shall be returning there to be married."

"I should have known you would already be snapped up," Colin grinned. "Lucky fellow! We could still have tea together ... no strings of course?"

"Perhaps one day ... " Minette prevaricated with a smile. "But now I really must get on, before Sister accuses me of fraternising with doctors!"

Hurrying away, Minette grinned to herself, thinking how thrilled Frederick would be to hear himself described as her fiancé! Better not include it as an anecdote in her next letter, or he might think she had changed her mind about marrying him.

Letters from Mother Clementine arrived regularly. The latest included a photograph of the children. The young O'Haras were smiling—except James who glowered away from the camera lens. Nothing there had changed much—Minette thought wryly.

Claire and Christina stood hand in hand, and pretty little Sonia was displaying a set of pearly teeth. Charlie stood on one leg, hair flopping over an eye—as always. With misty eyes, Minette kissed the photograph and put it away in her writing case with her letters.

At the hospital, senior staff members were quick to notice the dedication of the young Frenchwoman to her work, as well as caring for patients on the wards. Her examinations results were near perfect, and a decision was taken to offer her future employment at the hospital.

Aware their best candidate intended to return to India subsequent to qualifying, the hospital authorities nevertheless hoped for a change of mind. Minette was pleased the general opinion of her was so high, but remained charmingly vague about her future plans.

Privately, her intention of returning to India was unchanged. Enough time had gone by for Minette to give consideration to

Mother Clementine's interesting suggestion of setting up her own Nursing Home in Calcutta. It stood to reason that it should do well, in light of a dearth of such establishments. The notion that she would be her own employer was also highly attractive!

Slowly but surely, the nightmare quality of those last years in Lucknow were becoming more distant ...

Late one night, Minette was sitting at her desk on a ward, the gloom relieved only by the glow of a small lamp. It suddenly entered her mind that considerable time had passed since she had last heard from Frederick. Was it just a question of a few weeks? Maybe months? Worried now, Minette tried to approximate the date of Frederick's last letter.

It entered her mind that perhaps her dear friend was offended by her continuing refusal to marry him. Had he decided to cut all ties with her? No, that was not Freddie's way. And in any event, Mother Clementine had mentioned Frederick was a frequent visitor to the Convent. Still, this silence was odd ...

It must be telepathy, a relieved Minette thought upon her return home the following morning. On the hall table was a letter, Frederick's bold handwriting easily recognisable on the envelope. Making herself a cup of tea, she settled down in her bedroom to read.

The reason for Frederick's long silence became clear in the first paragraph. Involved in active service near the Chinese border, he had collected a bullet in his shoulder, and had lost the sight of an eye.

Minette's hand flew to her mouth in shock. The loss of an eye was a permanent injury. Oh, poor, poor Freddie!

Recovered to a greater or lesser degree, Frederick wrote, he had since been honourably discharged from active duty to take up a desk job in Calcutta.

Calcutta?

The city where Minette had decided to establish a Nursing Home—heavens, this was sheer providence! Giddy with happiness not to have lost her dearest friend for whatever reason, she was also guiltily relieved she would not be struggling alone in an unfamiliar city.

Subsequent to her three years of training, Minette was awarded a beautifully illuminated Nursing Diploma declaring her to be fully qualified. Without missing a beat, she embarked on a further three months in Advanced Midwifery. The time flashed by, and at the end of her course Minette gracefully declined the hospital's offer of employment. It was accepted with regret.

Now—at long last—it was time to go back to her children.

Minette was sorry to be leaving Jane. Her sweet friend who had comforted her homesickness, lectured her over occasional bouts of self-recrimination, and had fanned her ambition. Recalling her depression at the outset, it was thanks to Jane that she was returning to India armed with impeccable qualifications. Minette could not help a *frisson* of pride over her achievements.

It was the day of Minette's departure from Edinburgh, and Jane took time off to accompany her friend to the Railway Station. Hailing a passing porter, she wondered when—or if—she would see Minette again. She had enjoyed the company of her French friend, and was proud of the way she had pulled herself together in the face of mighty odds.

Having located the correct train, Jane and Minette stood together in silence, each lost in her own thoughts. An officious Guard emerged from within, and strutted down the platform blowing his whistle, and exhorting passengers to board the train for immediate departure to London.

Turning to Jane, Minette was surprised to see tears in the eyes of her stalwart friend, quickly blinked away. Enfolding Jane in her arms, she whispered her heartfelt thanks, telling her that she had truly saved her sanity.

"Just remember to write," Jane swallowed hard. "And give my love to that brood of yours–especially my God-daughter."

"Of course I will! As a matter of fact, Christina couldn't have been better placed for her religious education than with those lovely nuns."

Minette turned to board the train, but Jane placed a restraining hand on her arm. "Speaking of religion, did you do anything about having your marriage solemnised by the Catholic Church? You did promise, sweetie."

"No. There simply wasn't time before … well, it's too late to worry about now," Minette looked guilty. "Surely it is just a matter of bigotry at the end of the day? After all, we were legally married, I have the Certificate and … "

"I only hope you don't live to regret it, Minette," Jane interrupted sadly. "It's really to do with the status of your children. As adults, they may still have to live within same the rigid codes of today's society."

'Madam!' the irate Guard suddenly barked. "If you intend travelling to London this morning, kindly board the train at once! I will not tolerate a late departure through idle gossiping of you ladies."

Minette hurried to scramble into the carriage, relieved to find there was only one other person inside. With a strident blast of his whistle, the Guard waved his green flag at the engine driver. Amid billowing steam, the train juddered and then moved slowly forward out of the station into bright sunlight. Straining to see through the grimy window, Minette waved until her old friend was lost to sight.

The train journey was lengthy and tedious, but Minette had much to occupy her mind. She stayed overnight in the little hotel where the porter had come to know her from previous visits. The following day, Minette caught the Boat Train to Southampton and boarded the liner that would be taking her back to India.

Minette was very glad she had acquiesced to Jane's robust suggestion that she travel Second Class. Repeating the hideous experience of travelling "steerage" would have been more than she could bear! The cabin she was to share with one other female was small but clean, equipped with spotless towels laid out on the end of each berth. Unpacking her toilet articles and hanging up her clothes for the journey, Minette fervently hoped her cabin-mate would be reasonably presentable.

A knock at the door announced the arrival of a girl barely in her twenties—her cabin companion. Isabel Forsythe turned out to be the very new wife of a tea planter in Assam. She was travelling out to India for the first time to join her husband, and chattered excitedly at the prospect.

Relieved not to be sharing accommodation with some tight-lipped old spinster, Minette enjoyed Isabel's very freshness and enthusiasm. She only hoped the tea planter was a nicer man than some she had come across, many of whom were drunkards to a greater or lesser degree.

God, what a cynical old sour-puss she was becoming—Minette thought with a wry grimace. Let little Isabel enjoy her day-dreams whilst she could ...

The sea journey was one of relaxation and reflection for Minette. No patients to attend to, no books to pore over, and no examinations to worry about! What luxury ... time to herself at last.

Much of her day was spent outside on deck, having a brisk walk, or sometimes standing in the ship's stern and watching the giant propellers churning the sea into a frothing mass. Writing in her journal was a daily occupation she never missed, sitting in a deck chair with a book at her side.

Smiling to herself, Minette envisaged her arrival back to the Convent in Simla. Clementine would have told the children their mother was on her way back from England ... how excited they must be! And they were going to love the presents she was bringing back for them.

Soon, she would have her gorgeous little Sonia back in her arms. Not so little perhaps, since from a recent photograph she had become a pretty four year old, her face framed by a mass of flaxen ringlets.

Forcing her mind back to the present, Minette reminded herself there was one more task ahead before she could think of returning to Simla. A suitable property in Calcutta had to be found. It should be large enough to accommodate her family, as well as the intended Nursing Home. Its situation was of prime importance, so it would be practical to locate it within easy reach of the European community. With any luck, Frederick might be already in Calcutta and would know where to look.

In an amazingly short time compared with Minette's previous sea voyages, the ship steamed into Bombay harbour. Emerging on deck, she encountered the half-forgotten suffocating Indian heat exacerbating the familiar stench of the dark green waters lapping about the ship. The young woman's teeth flashed in an involuntary grin—it was the good old smell of home!

A perspiring Isabel arrived at her side, her nose wrinkling as the stench assailed her nostrils. Minette laughed, and reassured her the whole of India did not reek so dreadfully ... only Bombay Harbour. Isabel's final destination was Darjeeling, where the air was fresh and cool. Despite these reassurances, the girl seemed apprehensive, possibly daunted by the prospect of living with a husband she scarcely knew.

"Minette, *ma chèrie!*" exclaimed a familiar voice from behind. "How marvellous to see you again after such an age!"

Whirling, Minette found herself enveloped in Frederick's arms, and soundly kissed on both cheeks. Leaning away from him, she was struck by Frederick's unusual leanness, a black patch over an eye lending him a decidedly rakish air.

"What a wonderful surprise, Freddie!" Minette gazed affectionately at her old admirer. "What are you doing in Bombay? I thought you to be in Calcutta."

"I am, indeed," Frederick grinned. "Mother Clementine gave me details of your sailing, so did you really think I wouldn't come to meet you?"

"No, I didn't dare to imagine such a thing, but I'm thrilled you came, Freddie."

"So, ma *chèrie* ... have you decided to marry me yet?"

"No. I haven't, you terrible man!" Minette replied with mock severity. "I've had far too much to do over the last few years to indulge in such frivolous thoughts."

"Pity!" Frederick heaved a melodramatic sigh of resignation. "I'll just have to ask you again a bit later on, won't I? Come on, let's identify your luggage, and then we can go and have lunch at the Taj. We do have a train to catch, but not for a few hours yet."

By the time the train huffed into Howrah Station in Calcutta, Minette was certain she had endured more than enough of trains for a long while. Howrah seemed busier—and noisier—than Bombay's Victoria station which she had thought was bad enough. Descending to the platform in the midst of heaving crowds, she was thankful for Frederick's presence.

Coolie porters, balancing improbable loads on their heads and under each arm, wove their deft way through the heaving mass of humanity, and the air was foetid with *beedie* cigarette smoke. Hiring a passing porter, Frederick took Minette's arm and followed in the *coolie's* wake as he elbowed a path through the forest of food-stalls, and hordes of passengers hurrying in different directions.

The transport Frederick had arranged before leaving Calcutta was waiting outside the station. Relieved to be out from the suffocating fug, Minette climbed into the covered carriage. The luggage was loaded, the coolie paid off, and Frederick directed the carriage driver to the Grand Hotel on Chowringhee, the elegant heart of the city.

Feeling grubby and travel-stained, Minette entered the cool of the hotel foyer and sank into a rattan armchair whilst Frederick oversaw the unloading of her baggage. Following the hotel porter back into the foyer, Frederick went to the Reception Desk and spoke to the man behind it. Taking possession of a key, he walked over and handed it to Minette.

"Now then, *jeune fille*, here is the key to your room. Your stay at the hotel is my gift to welcome you back ... and I don't wish to hear any foolish arguments!" Frederick sternly put a finger to his lips to cut short Minette's automatic—and negative—response.

"*Chèrie*, I beg you not to trot out that fearsome mantra of which you are so fond, about needing to retain your independence. That would be very boring indeed. Perhaps, just this once, you can accept a present from me with grace?"

Closing her mouth with a snap, Minette grinned at her friend. "Put so very charmingly, *mon cher ami* ... how could I possibly refuse?"

CHAPTER TWENTY-NINE

Stretching luxuriously in the large brass bed draped with mosquito netting, Minette opened her eyes and then sat up. Instantly aware of noise and bustle in the street below her window, she pushed the netting aside and rang for Room Service. It was unusual for Minette to want to eat early in the day, but to her surprise she was feeling ravenously hungry.

The hotel *bearer* duly arrived to take her order for tea and buttered toast, and salaaming courteously, he withdrew. Padding over to the bathroom to draw a warm bath, she was acutely conscious of sore feet from hours of endless walking the previous day. Even more walking was on the cards for today, this time with perhaps better luck in her quest for a property.

Over the past few days, Minette and Frederick had visited several houses on the market with a view for transformation into a nursing home, as well as a residence for herself and her family. It had been a full week since her arrival in Calcutta, and on her first day, Frederick had taken her on a tour of the great city.

Unlike the relatively rural way of life in Lucknow, Calcutta was vibrantly alive day and night. Businesses flourished apace, and residents enjoyed a sophisticated social scene. During the "cold weather" season, Garden Parties and private soirées were given in abundance, in addition to formal business lunches.

Regular Calcutta Race Meetings were hugely popular with Indian and European race-goers alike. During the last two months of the year, a rash of Dances and Balls were thrown, where the good and the great decked out in their finery would congregate. The end of each year was celebrated with elaborate New Year's Eve parties and a fireworks display.

As the months wore on, the heat and humidity increased, so wives and their families would depart to various hill-stations where the air was fresh and cool. Most businessmen and Government officials remained in town to sweat the summer months away in their offices, maybe joining their families for a few days in late August or September.

Minette was impressed by the city's verdant parks and the manicured flower beds, exclaiming in amazement over the rows of sophisticated shops equal to any she had seen in London. A plethora of restaurants offered cuisine from both east and west. Finally, she and Frederick toured several magnificent Government buildings.

On Minette's second day, it was down to the business of finding a home.

Houses situated in the sought-after districts of Alipore, Burdwan Road, and Ballygunge were precisely what the excited young woman had in mind. She and Frederick viewed immaculately maintained properties, well set back from the road along quiet tree-lined avenues, most of them surrounded by sweeping lawns, trees, and well-tended flower beds. Discovering the exorbitant cost of these elegant houses ... Minette's spirits sank like a stone.

Disgruntled, she was unwilling to listen to Frederick's sensible advice that she should look for something more central ... and affordable. After all, there was one appealing property in Alipore that would suit her purpose perfectly...

Lying in the bath, Minette wriggled her toes, hoping the warm water would help to relieve her tired feet. Frederick had lined up another house for her to see today, this time located in a central residential area. Leaning an arm over the rim of bathtub, she picked up a sheet of paper Frederick had given her with the address—Number 2, Camack Street—near the centre of town.

Town? After those gorgeous properties away from the noise and stink of massed humanity, how could she contemplate setting up home in the smelly centre of Calcutta? Sighing, Minette got out of the bath. In any event, she could not refuse to see this property as Frederick thought it to be a real possibility. But she would make sure the visit was as short as possible.

A knock at the door signalled the arrival of her breakfast tray. Sitting and eating a slice of toast in her robe, she again looked longingly at the description of the favoured Alipore house. Might it still be a possibility if she cut corners on her own living accommodation? She would bring it up with Freddie later in the morning.

Freshly bathed, her dark hair twisted into a shining chignon under a white straw hat adorned with navy and white roses, Minette cast a critical eye over her appearance in the mirror. Elegant in navy and white, nobody would have guessed from her air of breeding that Madame Marguerite de Merencourt O'Hara had every intention of joining the ranks of the despised "trade." With a grin of amusement, she imagined the shock and horror amongst Calcutta matriarchs!

Minette had already discovered the wives of the English community in Calcutta had a fine sense of their own importance and pecking order—horridly reminiscent of the Colonel's wife in Lucknow. Well, they could just lump it. She would do as she pleased, and had no intention of acquiescing to their ridiculous dictates.

Frederick was sitting in the hotel foyer, waiting for Minette to appear. He glanced up from the newspaper he was reading to watch her graceful descent of the staircase. If only she would change her mind about marrying him!

Her reluctance to see any point of view other than her own was often maddening, as was her insistence on independence, but he nevertheless had to admire her courage in the face of personal disaster. Oh, yes, for him the attractive Marguerite de Merencourt was the stuff of dreams.

On the way to their destination, Minette had noticed the carriage driver's reaction when Frederick gave him instructions to go to Camack Street. It was obvious the man was startled, then doubtful, and Frederick had been obliged to repeat the address. Good Lord, the very location of this house must be dubious to elicit such a negative response in the fellow.

The property on Camack Street was the only house on their agenda for the day, and Minette rather wished Frederick had arranged another viewing afterwards. She did not imagine any length of time would be spent on this one.

Ten minutes later, the carriage turned into an almost deserted street. The driver pulled up outside high wooden gates, their faded green paint blistered through neglect and exposure to the sun's fierce glare. They were secured by a rusting chain and a large padlock. Minette hoped uncharitably it would prove impossible to turn the key in it.

On the pavement outside, a portly *Babu* was waiting for them, a capacious leather satchel under his arm. He wore a regulation white dhoti, the ends of which were drawn up between his legs and tucked into his waistband to create an illusion of trousers. A rolled-up black umbrella with a bright yellow handle was hooked into the back of his waistband—despite there being no sign of rain.

Instructing the driver to wait in the shade of nearby trees, Frederick helped a reluctant Minette to descend from the carriage.

"Good-morning, *Babu*, I hope we haven't kept you waiting too long?" Frederick addressed the clerk. "I assume you have the key for that padlock, and also for the house?"

"*Salaam, Sahib*! I am waiting veree shortest time," assured the *Babu* rummaging in his satchel. Pulling out a large key, he unlocked the padlock with some difficulty. Removing the chain, he proceeded to shove the gates open, their hinges squealing hideously in protest.

The gates fully open, Minette stared with dismay at the house looming before her, flaking grey walls doing nothing to enhance its unhappy appearance. An incongruously elegant portico shaded the front entrance, the once-graceful columns chipped and green with slime. Panes of glass were broken in several sash windows on the front *façade* of the house, the gaping holes roughly boarded up with varying lengths of planking.

"Shall we take a look inside, Minette?" Frederick suggested. "It certainly seems big enough for what you want."

Stepping over broken cobblestones, Minette followed the two men into a wide courtyard. In the centre stood the ruined remains of a fountain, its cracked basin almost concealed by a prolific creeper. Even the cobbles were thick with grasses, caked mud, and carpeted with weeds. Minette started to see a basking snake dart away into the undergrowth, alarmed by intruders into its generally peaceful world.

Whilst the *Babu* struggled to open the heavily carved front door, Minette looked disparagingly about her, wondering what other horrors might be in store. A final heave and the door swung open with a squawk, hordes of rodents scattering in fright. As she stepped into the musty entrance hall, Minette recoiled in disgust at the stench of rat urine, droppings littering every surface.

Glancing at the memsahib's stony face, the *Babu* whipped out a cloth from his satchel. With an apologetic smile, he proceeded to wipe off dusty door handles. It wasn't only the door handles that were filthy—thought Minette sourly—the entire place was thick with dust and hung with inhabited cobwebs.

The interior of the house was surprisingly cool and spacious, the ceilings high, and the floors marbled. A rather grand staircase rose up to an enormous covered balcony overlooking a sprawling and very overgrown garden. At the rear of the balcony, eight good-sized bedrooms were located, each one with its own grimy bathroom equipped with an antiquated geyser. Doors hung half off their hinges, and ceilings were crumbling in three of the bedrooms.

Minette was not surprised to learn the house had been unoccupied for many years. It was frankly depressing, and a far cry from the pristine properties she had viewed the previous day. In her opinion, there was nothing to be gained by wasting any more time here than strictly necessary.

Glancing over at Frederick in the hope that he would suggest they leave, she was taken aback to see him deep in conversation with the *Babu* as they progressed from room to room. Surely Freddie could not seriously be considering this ... this mess as a viable proposition? Impossible! Perhaps he was just interested in the history of the place? In any event, she would leave him to his discussion a little longer, after which it should be time for lunch.

Minette decided to pass the next few minutes on the upstairs balcony. Averting her eyes from the disastrous bedrooms at the rear, she leaned her elbows on the balustrade and looked down into the garden below. Through an encroaching thicket of grasses and vines, occasional splashes of vivid colour were visible. Minette guessed them to be flowering plants straining towards the light, an indication that the garden must have been cultivated at one time. All the same, clearing it was too daunting a prospect, being well beyond rescue.

With a dispirited sigh, Minette rejoined Frederick and the *Babu* in the hall. Thanking the clerk for his time, Frederick told him that should the lady be interested in purchasing the property, he would be in contact. With an obsequious bow, the *Babu* set about closing up the house with an air of resignation. He knew he had seen the last of these European buyers ... but he was not surprised. One had to accept this house was quite dreadful!

Half an hour later, Frederick and Minette were sitting in Firpo's Restaurant, sipping cool drinks whilst they waited for *tiffin* to be served. The Italian proprietor lurking behind the bar swore his milk-shakes and ice-creams to be the best this side of Rome. Most of his customers were inclined to agree.

After the bitter disappointment of that last property, Minette's face was glum. She was destined never to find the ideal house for her purpose. Anything remotely decent was well beyond her means. Even that house she had liked so much in Alipore ... Freddie had been emphatic in advising her to forget it. He told her it would be madness to risk ending up heavily in debt.

"Why the dismal air, *ma chérie?*" Frederick asked, his expression quizzical. "Is the heat bothering you after so long in Scotland?"

"Heat? No, of course not, Freddie," Minette answered crossly. "It's depressing not to have found a home yet. Anything that might be suitable turns out to be too damned expensive. Especially when I think of the cost of all the nursing home equipment I will need. We've been searching for ages, and ... "

"*Chérie*, I rather think you have found your house ... yes, the terrible one!" Frederick interrupted mildly. "The asking price is well below your budget, and the *Babu* hinted a reasonable offer would be acceptable to the owner, who is anxious to be rid of it."

Incredulous, Minette stared at her friend. Was this Freddie's idea of a joke? Maybe a touch of the sun? Either way, it was ridiculous! Why, the cost of renovating that monstrosity would be unthinkable, not to mention its jungle of a garden and broken-up front courtyard.

Correctly reading Minette's train of thought, Frederick grinned. "Remember we live in India where labour is readily available and cheap," he continued, ignoring the young woman's expression. "Believe me, putting that house in order would require relatively little money, and be well within your means. Think what a prize you would gain in return for a modest investment."

"And who, might I ask, would deal with all the coolie workmen on a day-to-day basis?" Minette asked grumpily. "I'm not capable of managing that … "

"*Chèrie*, let's not bandy words over trivia! You know perfectly well I'll give you all the help you need. Ah, here comes our lunch. Let's drop the subject for now, but do give Camack Street some serious thought, I beg you."

Back in the hotel room later that afternoon, Minette emerged from the bathroom, much refreshed after a tepid bath. Wrapped in a fluffy white towel, she rummaged in her handbag and retrieved a fat envelope that had awaited her at the hotel Reception Desk.

Stretching out across the bed on her stomach, she smiled, recognising the copperplate handwriting on the envelope. Mother Clementine. And judging by the thickness of the contents, maybe something from the children as well? Slitting open the envelope, letters from Claire and Charlie had indeed been enclosed.

Claire's was short and somewhat stilted, demanding to know why her mother had not returned to Simla at once—as promised? Christina was becoming a dead bore, Claire wrote, forever sucking up to the nuns or reading books. Sonia was ill with a cold and cough as usual. The letter ended abruptly with her signature.

Charlie's letter was affectionate, saying how he looked forward to seeing his mother again. Was there anywhere to ride in Calcutta? He and Turka went out riding every day, so he hoped there would be a nice loose box for him at their new home. Charlie did not mention his brother.

There was no letter from James.

Minette frowned. She hadn't really expected a letter from her surly elder son, but why had neither of his siblings mentioned him? Picking up Clementine's letter, she scanned it for a possible mention of the boy. At the bottom of the final page, the nun had written a telling few lines.

"Unfortunately, James has not accepted your absence as well as one hoped, despite numerous explanations of your reasons. He maintains it was never truly necessary for you to leave your children alone for years. I mention it now, my dearest Minette, because it might be of help to be aware of James' resentment in advance of seeing him."

Putting down Clementine's letter, Minette stared blankly into space. It was daunting to learn her first-born was still burning with hostility towards her after all this time. And Claire's letter hadn't been that friendly either. Long and selective memories were definitely on the cards here.

Minette's mouth firmed. The task of creating a home for her family was of supreme importance at this moment in time. Her older children's tantrums would just have to be dealt with later on. Then, they would be made to understand her actions had been for their long-term benefit.

Her mind returned to Frederick's suggestion that the house on Camack Street was ideal for her purpose. She supposed it was true for the place was big enough to divide into two establishments. If the price was as cheap as Freddie indicated it might be, it was perhaps worth another visit—if one managed to look past the decrepitude.

The following day, Minette and Frederick were once again standing on the balcony of Number Two, Camack Street. Frederick and the *Babu* had resumed their discussion, so Minette passed the time leaning against the balustrade, her eyes roaming over the wilderness below.

With a less jaundiced outlook than on her previous visit, she noticed pink and yellow hibiscus flowers peeping through the undergrowth. Beside two tall trees, flamboyant heads of scarlet cannas lilies were pushing their way through a tangle of vines. The air was redolent of a scent identifiable as frangipani, so reminiscent of Minette's early days in India.

Amazing to see how these plants were determined to live, despite being choked for years beneath a thick blanket of weeds! And those trees over there were really quite beautiful. In the hands of a diligent *mali*, maybe it was possible to do something with this garden after all?

Turning to face the back of the balcony, where doors to the eight bedrooms hung haphazardly on their hinges, Minette tried to envisage how they might transform into liveable accommodation.

Very easily, she realised with surprise. Further more, a seamless division of the house into two separate establishments was possible. Perhaps Freddie had not been so wrong about this property after all. A slow excitement began to build …

"Well, *ma chèrie*, do I tell our friend here that you are a prospective buyer?" Frederick had been watching the changing expressions on Minette's face, and she turned to him, her eyes shining with enthusiasm.

"Indeed you may. Freddie, how right you were about this house—it's perfect! Can I leave the price negotiation to you?"

Frederick nodded. "As a matter of fact, I've suggested a provisional offer for the *Babu* to take to the owner. It's quite a low offer, but he thinks it may be accepted as the owner is moving to Madras next week."

For his part, the *Babu* was beside himself with joy. It was nothing less than incredible to him that this smartly dressed memsahib should wish to live in such an awful house. Thinking of the sizeable commission he would make on the sale, a wide smile spread over his chubby features.

"*Bhot atcha, Memsahib*," the *Babu* wagged his head in approval. "Such a veree good bargain I am making for you with owner-sahib. Yes, yes … I am thanking you from the heart of my bottom!"

For a brief instant, Frederick and Minette stared in disbelief at the little man, uncertain if their ears had deceived them. But from the earnest expression on his face, it was clear the *Babu* was demonstrating his excellent grasp of English.

Keeping a straight face with difficulty, Frederick and Minette took their leave of him and hurried out to scramble into the waiting carriage. Only then did they collapse into helpless laughter—to the consternation of the dozing driver. Gasping, Frederick instructed the stupefied man to go back to the Grand Hotel.

Seated once again in the cool ambience of the hotel foyer, Frederick ordered a bottle of chilled champagne. "To celebrate the end of the property search … and to mark the beginning of your new life in Calcutta, Minette, *ma chèrie!*" He poured the bubbling wine into shallow glasses.

"If the offer for Camack Street is accepted, it's entirely thanks to you, Freddie," Minette looked over the rim of her glass with gratitude. "I was more than ready to overlook that house, as you know."

A deal over the property was swiftly reached, thanks to some energetic haggling with the wealthy owner. Minette was now in possession of a sizeable property that had cost her such a modest sum that she could scarcely credit it. A generous amount of money could now be spent on renovation and clearance of the courtyard and garden.

Broken down stabling at the rear also required attention, and lists of necessary equipment for the Nursing Home had to be purchased. Minette realised with relief that the entire expenditure could be met from funds remaining to her—and without cutting corners!

In the back of the young woman's mind, the ominous comments relating to James in Mother Clementine's letter continued to resonate. Now that she had a home to offer her children, speed was of the essence to complete renovating the residential part of the house. Creation of the nursing home would have to wait!

Recognising the young woman's concerns, Frederick lost no time in enlisting the assistance of Raymond Wilson, an architect friend of his. Unsure if he wished to undertake renovation of the ramshackle building Frederick had shown him round, Raymond had an instant change of mind upon meeting the new owner.

He had heard vague tittle-tattle of a widowed Frenchwoman, recently arrived in Calcutta and set upon running a nursing home. Quite extraordinary that a woman of quality should claim to be a midwife of all things—said the gossips—and choosing to embark on a career unmistakeably in *trade*. Learning he was to meet the widow, Raymond envisaged a burly female of indeterminate age, beefy red hands, and greying hair scraped back in a knot.

To his amazement, Frederick introduced him to a slender attractive woman who greeted him in a softly accented voice, her eyes sparkling with enthusiasm over her project. Bewitched, the architect found himself declaring he was prepared to create whatever Madame Marguerite desired...

As a result, detailed plans for the renovation of both the

Nursing Home and her personal residence were in Minette's hands within ten days. An army of builders and decorators was organised, and Raymond offered the services of his own *mali* to restore the garden, who brought three cousins to assist in the work. Thrilled by the swift progress, Minette went about the purchase of furniture and general equipment for her new home.

Two months later, the new residence was furnished and ready for occupation. Work on the Nursing Home was almost complete, only two bedrooms and their bathrooms still requiring a second coat of paint. The rear garden showed signs of future magnificence, a good-sized lawn having emerged from the tangle of undergrowth, edged by three monkey-puzzle trees. Flowers flourished in swathes of glorious colour, freed from the grip of vines and grasses.

The time had finally come for Minette to travel up-country to retrieve her children. It was something of a blow that Frederick was unable to accompany her to Simla, due to his work schedule. She could not help being apprehensive of what kind of reception she was to expect, and had counted on Frederick's moral support.

"Minette *chèrie*, I have the impression you are a little worried about how the children might react to your reappearance in their lives?" Frederick had perceived the young woman's anxiety.

"No, of course not!" Minette's reply was a trifle too emphatic. "It's just that Mother Clementine warned me James might be something of a problem. But then, that boy has always been difficult. I'm dying to retrieve my family at last, and bring them back to their own home."

Packing her valise on the morning of her departure, Minette was still concerned about what her children's attitude towards her might be. Annoyed, she decided there was enough on her plate without worrying herself to death about things she could do nothing about. She was their mother after all, and they must respect that.

For God's sake, had she not always seen to their welfare, and ensured her children lacked for nothing? She would *not* allow them to perceive her as a weakling, anxious to curry favour. That really was a recipe for disaster. Any trouble making would have to be nipped in the bud at once.

Walking through the front courtyard, Minette turned back to

survey her home with pride. The *façade* was no longer grey but a dazzling white, and not a trace of lichen marred the portico's elegant columns. Even the fountain had been rebuilt, and was now in full working order. Dearest Frederick! Thanks to his invaluable help, an almost impossible project had been achieved in a ridiculously short time.

A nearby *mali* ran to open freshly painted dark blue gates, now silent on oiled hinges. Nodding her thanks, Minette walked through to where Frederick's carriage was waiting to take her to Howrah Station.

It had been arranged that she travel up-country to Simla with three nuns and a priest—insisted upon by Mother Clementine. The elderly nun knew Minette well enough to know she was sufficiently impulsive to attempt the journey by herself. Should the matrons of Calcutta society discover such unconventional behaviour, it would be condemned as beyond the pale. Not the best impression to give in a town where the young Frenchwoman was hoping to make her mark!

For once, Minette acquiesced without argument.

CHAPTER THIRTY

The train journey to Simla proved every bit as long and tedious as Minette recalled. Not improved by the stertorous snoring of the priest slumped on the banquette opposite. A fact, irreverently remarked upon a nun as being reminiscent of a porker with a bad case of influenza. Amused, Minette grinned, and the trio of nuns tittered guiltily.

In the foothills of the Himalayas, the travellers were obliged to change trains, boarding the little mountain train designed to cope with steep inclines and sharp bends. As it wound its way up the mountainside on its narrow tracks, Minette felt an excitement mixed with apprehension build as they neared their destination.

With a final hiss of steam and squealing of brakes, the train juddered to a halt at Simla Station. Sister Gwendolyn—organiser of sports—stood on the platform some distance away, a huge smile on her face.

"Here you are at long last!" exclaimed the portly nun, giving Minette an impulsive hug, then greeted the fellow travellers in a more restrained manner. "Just in time for tea, scones with strawberry jam and lashings of cream. Come on, let me give you a hand with those things."

Hefting Minette's valise as though it weighed next to nothing, the nun led the way out of the station. Two ponies harnessed to a buggy stood in the shade of some trees, and the weary group were herded on board. Ten minutes later, the buggy turned in through the Convent gates. As they passed through, Minette was forcibly reminded of seeing Claire screaming for the mother who was leaving her behind.

Dismissing the unhappy image from her mind, the young woman's eyes searched the premises as they approached the front doors of the Convent. Before the buggy had properly drawn to a halt, a side door opened and a gangly boy flew out, grinning all over his freckled face, red hair flopping over an eye—Charlie!

"Que je suis heureux de vous revoir, chère Maman," the boy murmured with a rather wobbly bow, the formal greeting ruined by an irrepressible giggle. "I've been learning to speak some French ... especially for you."

Hot tears of relief springing to her eyes, Minette fiercely hugged her son. At least this one didn't hate her. "Darling, how terribly I have missed you!"

"Well, we're together now for ever and ever, aren't we?" Charlie's face shone with happiness. "Claire should soon be here with Christina, and Mailie is bringing Sonia to meet you."

Moments later Claire appeared, a tall leggy girl, her dark hair framing a face so like Minette's own ... her expression sullen. A stocky little girl stood at her side, also unsmiling. Christina, and well under the influence of her sister, Minette thought sadly.

Behind the two girls came their *ayah*, Mailie, her face wreathed in smiles to see her beloved mistress again. An ethereal little girl came with Mailie, sucking her thumb, and clutching the *ayah's* sari with her other hand. Flaxen curls cascaded to her shoulders, and she gazed at Minette from wide, pale blue eyes.

Sonia! For God's sake, she's become the image of my mother—Minette thought hysterically. But not in personality one must hope.

No sign of James.

Crouching down on her heels, Minette opened her arms to her daughters. After a brief hesitation, Claire allowed herself to be taken into her mother's embrace, prompting a reluctant Christina to follow her example. In turn, the *ayah* gently pushed a bewildered Sonia towards the mother she did not know. Pale eyes widening, the child burst into tears and hid her face in Mailie's sari.

"Dearest Minette, how lovely to see you," exclaimed a familiar voice. Mother Clementine was smiling at the family scene. Straightening, Minette hurried over to give the elderly nun a heartfelt hug.

After a gargantuan tea, Charlie dragged his mother off to the stables, where a dished little face looked out from a loose box. Turka! Recognition of who was approaching was immediate, for the horse whinnied with joy. Minette ruffled the silky mane and rubbed his forehead, and touchingly, Turka leaned his face against his adored mistress, nostrils fluttering in welcome.

"Maman, I've been riding Turka for ages now. He's such a good boy and hardly ever bucks! We usually go out for a ride after morning lessons."

Minette regarded her son with affection. "Wonderful for both of you. Let's hope he can be persuaded to board the train with better grace than the last time."

Charlie's fair skin flushed with emotion, and he swallowed hard. "Is ... is Turka really coming with us to Calcutta, Maman? James keeps on saying you will order him shot because there is no point in spending money on a useless animal."

Minette's mouth tightened in anger. Obviously, James had not tired of causing grief to his younger brother. Neither had he bothered to put in an appearance to greet his mother. She would attend to that young man later on.

"Charlie, I promise you there has never been any suggestion of having Turka destroyed," Minette laid a hand on the horse's shining neck. "After all, he's a member of our family, and I can see what wonderful care you have taken of him."

"Just a minute, what about *me*?" Claire's tone was sharp from behind her mother. "I looked after Turka as well, you know—or have I become invisible all of a sudden?" Angry tears glittering in her eyes, the girl turned and ran from the stable, Christina scuttling at her heels.

Sighing, Minette went back to the apartment in search of her prickly daughter, but Claire was nowhere to be seen. Instead, the two *ayahs* were waiting to assure Minette they were ready to accompany their memsahib to Calcutta. Regarding the little women with deep affection, Minette thanked them for their unswerving loyalty and care of the children during her absence. It was wonderful that they wished to come to Calcutta, for their familiar presence would help facilitate the children's smooth transition to a new home.

"Mailie, where is James?" Minette voice was blunt. "I've been here for almost five hours, so it's obvious he's not going to bother coming to see me."

"*Mem*, James-*baba* he veree angree wit ev'ryting now," the ayah looked away, uncomfortable under her mistress' gaze. "He hiding many, many hours, no comin' for meals … ony stealing from kitchen. He make Sisters veree worrit, and they getting cross wit him … but James he don' care."

"What you really mean is that James is angry with *me*, Mailie!" retorted Minette dryly. "It's no excuse for downright rudeness, however. Now, tell me where that boy is likely to be?"

Capitulating in the face of her mistress' anger, the *ayah* told her the Sisters had recently discovered some sort of hideaway up the hill behind the Convent. Her face grim, Minette strode away, leaving the two *ayahs* gazing unhappily after her.

Certain she knew exactly where her son was hiding, Minette made her way up the hill towards a particular knoll. It was where she, herself, had gone in the past to reflect on worrying matters. Reaching the spot on silent feet, she came upon a rough sort of hut made up of sticks and grasses. James was crouched inside, munching on a crust of bread.

"Good afternoon, James," Minette confronted the startled boy. "I see you share my pleasure in the magnificent view down the valley. Did you forget I was due to arrive in Simla today?"

James scrambled to his feet his face thunderous. "No question of my having forgotten, mother dear—I've no wish to see you."

"Is that so?" Minette ignored the boy's hostility. "Well, I'm here now, so shall we make our way back before the light goes and the Sisters start to worry?"

"You clear off if you want … but *I'm* staying!" Lunging forward, James shoved his mother aside and attempted to run off. But Minette had not been brought up with brothers for nothing. Her hand flashed out and grasped the collar of the boy's shirt, jerking him to a standstill. Despite James' strenuous efforts to wrench free, Minette maintained her grip.

"Let me *go!*" snarled the boy, infuriated by the humiliation of being held captive by his mother. "You have no bloody right to stop me doing anything I want. Just bugger off back to wherever you crawled out from ... *OW!*"

James ended with an undignified squawk as his mother hand connected with his cheek with a resounding slap.

"Don't you *dare* use gutter language to me!" Minette snapped. "Or I shall treat you as the child you clearly still are, and wash out your mouth with soap."

"Huh! I'd like to see you try!" James sneered, although taken aback his mother should have raised a hand to him. He had expected a syrupy approach, maybe begging his forgiveness? "I want nothing to do with you ... ever."

"What you do, or don't want is not up for discussion at this precise moment," Minette told her son. "Your behaviour is nothing short of a vulgar oaf. Very far from the demeanour of a Marquis's grandson—or the great-grandson of a Duke. Shame on you, James."

Minette watched the changing expressions on her son's troubled face. Recalling James' huge pride in his noble French forebears, she knew she had hit the right note. The boy had frozen at her words, his eyes wide with shock.

"Well, if I'm so awful, maybe it's your fault for not staying around to bring me up," he muttered sulkily. "You could have married Uncle Freddie."

"James, I told you before one does not marry out of convenience. Neither am I about to waste my breath explaining for the hundredth time why I left you here. I know it's been a long time, but now we have a lovely home waiting for us in Calcutta. For God's sake, can't you look forward to the future instead of forever carping about the past?"

The boy remained tight-lipped, glaring at his mother with hard eyes. Suddenly sick to death of arguing with her judgemental son, Minette abruptly released her grip of his collar. Staggering back, James sprawled ignominiously in the grass.

"It is almost dark now, so I am going back to the Convent," Minette's tone was indifferent. "Do as you please, James. I shall be leaving for Calcutta with my family in three days time. Should you wish to join us, you may ... but there will be conditions, I warn you."

Turning, she started down the hill without a backward glance at the boy still sprawled on the ground.

Dusk had fallen by the time Minette arrived back at the apartment. Physically and emotionally drained, she hoped Claire was not about to give her a dose of the same sickening accusation of "abandonment" as her brother. That would be well beyond bearing for her shattered nerves.

Both *ayahs* were waiting outside for Minette, their expressions anxious. One wouldn't mind betting the poor things had regularly come up against James' sharp tongue—she thought acidly. In the event James came to Calcutta, that young man was going to have to mend his ways. No more bullying of poor Charlie, and he could also damned well keep a civil tongue in his head.

Supper was taken at the apartment that evening, Mother Clementine having correctly deduced that Minette needed to spend time alone with her children. It was very important they took the time to get to know each other all over again. The old nun only hoped that neither James nor Claire would spoil things for their mother ...

Sitting at the table, an excited Charlie plied his mother with questions about Turka's stabling in Calcutta, anxious that nothing was overlooked for the little horse's comfort. Claire and Christina chattered together, but neither child addressed their mother directly. Sonia ate little, seemingly reluctant to remove the thumb from her mouth in order to do so.

James was conspicuous by his absence.

Minette's eyes ranged over the four children, their faces rosy with health. Her heart contracted with emotion and immense gratitude to the kindly nuns who had looked after them so well. This was the scene she had dreamed about throughout the years she had spent away, and she would not allow that antagonistic little devil on the hill take away her pleasure.

The remaining days in Simla passed uneventfully, apart from the odd snide remark from Claire. Minette made attempts to draw closer to Christina, but the older girl made sure she was in the way, her attitude defiant, almost as if she was challenging her mother. Irritating though it was to Minette, at this point it seemed better to pretend not to have noticed.

In any event, the three older children were busy sorting out and helping to pack up their possessions ready for departure the next day. Whilst in Scotland, Minette had often parcelled up items of clothing for the children that had caught her eye in shop windows. As a result, the number of dresses the girls possessed—Claire in particular—was astounding. All of which the older girl selfishly insisted she would need in Calcutta. Minette said nothing, but she had different ideas.

After the girls were in bed, Minette removed several of Claire's older dresses and pinafores from her trunk. Adding them to a pile of outgrown boys' clothes, she gave them to the nuns for the orphaned children in their charge. It was the very least she could do.

James still had not put in an appearance. Only the *ayahs* had brief sightings of the boy as he dashed into the kitchen to snatch whatever food happened to be readily available. God alone knew where he spent the night—wondered his despondent mother— probably frozen in that hide of his on the hill.

The following day, Minette realised she must accept her elder son's rejection of her was final. With a heavy heart, she went to make arrangements with Mother Clementine for James to remain at the Convent. Naturally, the apartment would no longer be available to him, so it stood to reason he would join the orphanage. Of course, she would pay for the boy's keep and education.

That same evening, Minette was sitting in an armchair, leafing through an old newspaper and brooding about her elder son. For God's sake, her first-born seemed to prefer being an orphan rather than her son! How could he hate her so much? Why was he always so unpleasant? How horribly like Jérome, her own brother, he was turning out to be…

Suddenly, she was aware of a rather sticky little hand on her arm. Looking up in surprise, she gazed into the pale blue eyes of her youngest daughter. Without a word, Sonia climbed into her mother's lap, nestling against her, thumb in mouth. Overcome by this unexpected show of affection, Minette folded her little girl in her arms, a tremulous smile on her lips.

On the eve of their departure to Calcutta, Minette had been for a final interview with Mother Clementine. She wanted to thank her for all she had done over the years for herself and her children. The elderly nun had smiled, and told her how very proud she was of the young Frenchwoman. Not many would have succeeded as well in the same circumstances, and her future was bright.

Seated round the table that evening, Minette and the children were finishing a light supper, when the door suddenly flew open. A nonchalant James sauntered into the room and walked over to the table. Picking a slice of buttered bread off Charlie's plate without asking, he threw himself down in a chair.

"Cat got everybody's tongue?" the boy mumbled sarcastically, his mouth full. "What time are we leaving tomorrow? And I suppose that stupid horse has to come with us—what a waste of money."

Minette rose to her feet, her eyes glacial. "How *dare* you come bursting in here, grabbing food off other people's plates? Your manners are worse than an animal, James O'Hara! And yes, Turka is most certainly coming with us, and since you are not paying for him, keep your nasty remarks to yourself."

"Oh, here we go again, dearest Maman hot in defence of—"

"Shut up, James!" Charlie's chair scraped as he jumped up to face his brother. "You have no right to say a thing about Maman. Why, when she sent you all those presents and clothes, you were only too happy to grab them."

"One more word and I'll give you a damned good hammering, you miserable little twerp!" snarled the older boy. "And I'll say what I like about the mother who abandoned us like unwanted puppies, to follow—"

"*Enough!*" Minette was white with fury. She would put a stop to this once and for all. "Indeed, we will all be leaving Simla for Calcutta tomorrow morning ... but you, James, will not. In light of your continued absence, I have made arrangements for you to remain at the Convent—at the orphanage, naturally."

"But-but you said I could come if I wanted," James was taken aback.

"Yes, I did. However, since we have seen nothing of you since our conversation on the hill, I assumed you had no interest in coming with us to Calcutta."

"Well, I do, but only because Uncle Freddie will be there."

"Sorry James, that is not good enough. I need an undertaking from you to stop your thoroughly unpleasant behaviour towards us all. No more threats to beat up your brother. A radical change in your attitude to me, your mother. Is that clear enough for you?"

"*You! You!* It's always about you," blustered the boy. "We all know how you didn't care about us ... the others are just too damned feeble to say so."

"Stop right there, you nasty piece of work!" Minette's patience was wearing thin. "I will not listen to any more of your beastly recriminations. Either you keep a civil tongue in your head—or you will stay here and join the orphanage."

Still belligerent, James glared at his mother, his lower lip thrust out. As the minutes ticked by and Minette's expression remained stony and determined, he realised at last there was a real danger of being left behind in Simla.

"I suppose I could try to be more polite," he muttered. "But you can tell little suck-up Charlie to watch his step around me."

"If you imagine this sort of nasty rubbish to be acceptable, you have another think coming," Minette was adamant. "Mend your ways—or else."

"*Alright!*" James stared at the floor. "I'll try to be ... nice."

"Still not good enough, James. Do you actually want to be part of our family?"

"Yes!" James capitulated. "Yes, I do want to be part of the family, and I want to go to Calcutta with you."

"Very well, James, you may join us on the train tomorrow," Minette stood up, heaving a private sigh of relief. "Now, off to bed all of you as we have a long day ahead of us."

Sitting by herself, the children having vanished, Minette found she was shaking with reaction after yet another unpleasant encounter with her elder son. Not for a single moment did she believe there would be a miraculous change in James's general comportment. But it was a step in the right direction. And she would no longer have the constant worry of her son living as an orphan in faraway Simla.

Early next morning, Minette and her five children were ranged on the platform at the station. Turka had already been installed in the train without fuss, and was now enjoying a bulging net filled with hay. Several nuns had come to say good-bye to the family, and Mother Clementine also arrived to join the group.

Without warning, Christina hurled herself at the elderly nun, howling and clinging to her robes with both hands. The child had suddenly realised she was being taken away from the women she adored, and with whom she felt secure.

It was Claire who came to the rescue, extricating her sister's clutching fingers from the nun's habit with a combination of threats and promises. Christina was then bundled without ceremony into the railway carriage, where she cried herself to sleep in Claire's arms an hour later.

This unexpected drama came as a shock to Minette. She hadn't realised what a deep attachment had been forged between her little daughter and the nuns. Sitting in the carriage next to Charlie, Sonia cuddled up on her lap, Minette resolved to make an effort to draw closer to Christina. If Claire persisted in trying to prevent her, she would simply not allow it. For heaven's sake, it was just as though Claire felt Christina needed *protection* from her mother—Minette thought crossly.

Good-byes over, the guard's whistle shrilled, a green flag waved, and the little steam engine moved slowly forward in a cloud of steam and squeal of metallic joints. Huffing and chuffing, the train began its descent to the plains far below.

Her arms about a dozing Sonia, Minette's spirits soared. In the face of unbelievable adversity she had emerged, a trifle battered, but otherwise unscathed. In achieving this, she owed much to many, especially to Mother Clementine for her wisdom, kindliness, and understanding of human nature.

For a brief moment, Minette's mind touched on the family in France who had so brutally rejected her—scored out her very existence. Those people who had caused such terrible grief deserved to be consigned to the past, where she hoped they would forever rot in hell. Henceforth, she would block them from her mind. Cradling the sleeping child on her lap, Minette gazed out of the carriage window. Yes. It was time to turn the page, and allow an exciting new chapter to unfold in all of their lives ...

TRANSLATION OF FRENCH TERMINOLOGY

bonjour .... good morning

bonsoir .... good evening

comme il faut .... as one should

gamine .... tomboy

Maman .... Mummy

Papa .... Daddy

Monsieur .... Mr/Sir

Madame .... Mrs/Madam

Mademoiselle .... Miss

Au revoir! .... good-bye

jeunesse .... youth

faras .... stud farm

auberge .... inn

sièste .... afternoon rest

Mon Dieu! .... My God!

n'est-ce pas? .... is that not so?

Duc .... Duke

Duchesse .... Duchess

Comte .... Count

Comtesse .... Countess

Grandpère .... Grandpa

Grand'mère .... Grandma

enceinte .... pregnant

nou-nou .... nanny

vieillard .... old codger

flambeaux .... garden torches

mon/ma chèri(e).. my darling

penchant .... preference (for)

enchanté de faire votre

connaissance .... delighted to meet you

furore .... row or scene
décolletage .... neckline
tant pis! .... too bad!
de rigeur .... compulsory
c'est incroyable! ... it's incredible!
s'il vous plaît .... please
armoire .... wardrobe
chaise longue .... sofa for one

TRANSLATION OF HINDE TERMINOLOGY

coolie	workman
bazaar	market
namaste!	good morning!
ayah	woman servant
salaam	greetings
wallah	fellow
mali	gardener
chowkidar	guard
kensama	cook
jamadar	sweeper
bearer	manservant/major domo
durzi	tailor
nimbu pani	lemonade
dood	milk
pani	water
lao	bring
baba	child
syce	groom
sepoy	Indian foot soldier
godown	storeroom
mulloch	home village
jaldi	quickly
ider ow!	come here!
beedie	local cigarette
gharri	vehicle
makan	food
bhot atcha!	very good!
quoi hai?	anyone there?
jao	go!
punkah	fan

sala! .... filthy beast!
pugri .... turban
ne mancta!.............. don't want!
Babu .... clerk
rupee .... Indian money
ghora .... horse
badmash .... wicked
kabadarh! .... be careful!
howdah .... seated area on elephant
dhoti .... clerk's trousers
Durbar .... ceremonial meeting place
                       during the British Raj

From Carol Edgerley's provocative new series.
The highly anticipated sequel to
Marguerite

Claire

PROLOGUE

"*Claire!* What did I tell you about bullying Christina?" Minette demanded, taking her eldest daughter's arm in a firm grip. "And you needn't gasp like a landed fish," she went on, "because *bullying* is the right word. It's precisely the sort of thing James does to his younger brother. A behaviour that you claim to hate."

Claire stared, surprised by the unusual forcefulness. Her mother was usually out to please. Realising it was not to her advantage to antagonise her further, the girl hurriedly revised her earlier assessment of her mother's authority.

"I didn't mean it, and Chrissy knows that," she mumbled through stiff lips. "May I go now?"

Giving a resigned sigh, Minette nodded and released her eldest daughter, watching her toss back her mane of dark hair and flounce away. Nobody had won that battle, she knew. But perhaps Claire would be more careful how she treated her younger sister.

Back in her office, the only place in her home where she could be certain of peace and quiet, Minette sat down at her desk to attend to some accounts. After a few minutes, however, she found herself simply unable to concentrate. She leaned back in her chair, gazing out of the window at the garden, where colourful birds usually provided entertainment to anyone who watched them.

Sighing again, she pursed her mouth, her face taking on its now frequently glum expression. These highly unpleasant rows with her two older children had always exhausted her. For heaven's sake, at sixteen and twelve, surely James and Claire should have outgrown these tiresome scenes by now?

Apparently not.

Claire was a blatant liar, using untruths as a social lubricant to ease herself out of a situation. James was avaricious and bent on extracting as much "compensation" as he could, regarding it as recompense for his mother's absence from his life. God in heaven, would those two *ever* stop punishing her? Who did they think paid the bills and ensured they lacked for nothing?

Exasperated, she ran one hand through her dark hair, which was lightly streaked with silver. But at least she had Charlie, thank God! Cheerful and affectionate, he was far from acrimonious towards his mother. He loved horses passionately, and being slightly built, intended to follow a career as a jockey a few years hence.

And of course there was little Sonia. The youngest of her three girls, Sonia was six years old. Elfin in appearance with flaxen hair and pale blue eyes, she was her mother's constant companion. Why, Minette asked herself, why did her older children resent her so bitterly? Ridiculous! Sonia was harmless, a sweet child.

Minette's mouth stretched in a humourless smile. It was incredibly ironic that Sonia should possess the exact colouring of her own mother, the Marquise de Merencourt. An unnatural woman who had rejected her only daughter from the time she was born, who had schemed, with impressive success, to be rid of her unwanted child. Minette had never seen her childhood home again. Strange, how those cold, pale, and disdainful eyes now belonged to a little girl who gazed adoringly up at her.

And what of nine-year-old Christina? A dumpy, rather plain little thing, she was very attached to her older sister. Minette shook her head in frustration. Despite her every effort, Christina had never stopped mourning the loss of the nuns she loved.

Where or how had she gone so terribly wrong with James and Claire? It was now two years since their arrival in Calcutta from Simla. Aside from recriminations over their mother's perceived abandonment of them, both remained loud in belittling the business that fed and clothed them.

The nursing home.

An establishment she had created in the other half of their large house in Camack Street, which had proved a highly successful venture. Herself a fully qualified midwife, Minette also possessed more than a passing knowledge of medication.

Bookings flooded in, not only for the delivery of babies, but also for several days of recuperation in a tranquil environment. The income from the business allowed generous living expenses for the family. In addition, it provided an education for all five children at the most exclusive schools in Calcutta. Minette felt very proud of her achievement.

Remarriage had been a possible alternative to undertaking a nurse's training, but it was one she had always refused to contemplate, not even to her dearest friend, Frederick de Barre, in the knowledge all five of her children adored him.

Reflecting on her recent decision that the older children should learn that money did not grow on trees, Minette folded her arms on the desk. It was largely James's avarice that had prompted this decision, but it was also intended as a simple discipline. The children were expected to help with specific tasks about the house, tasks for which they would be paid. The Nepalese *ayahs* were henceforth forbidden to clean up after them.

Charlie cheerfully went about his allocated jobs. Grumbling under her breath, Claire also complied with the new rule, assisted by her shadow, Christina. At the end of each week, however, all three of them were gratified to discover they had accumulated substantial sums in addition to their usual pocket money.

James, however, was outraged. How *dare* his mother expect him to perform menial tasks? That was servants' work. Waited on hand and foot all his life, he saw no reason why that should change. Plenty of pocket money each week was simply his due.

Minette refused to cave in, and so the older boy was obliged to watch his siblings counting up their "wages" with relish each week, sums considerably in excess of what he received! Burning with resentment, James plotted revenge on his parsimonious mother, even if it took years ... .

CHAPTER ONE

Shoving a lock of dark hair back from her perspiring face, Claire O'Hara adjusted her position on the wide stone steps leading from the veranda into the garden. Christina sat next to her, idly swatting the odd mosquito, aware of her sister's rage.

It was absolutely infuriating, Claire thought resentfully. At her very first grown-up birthday party, *Maman* had found it necessary to charge off to her blasted nursing home. Surely her assistant could have managed on her own? The party had been ruined, her friends embarrassed, and Claire was convinced she would never hold her head up again at school.

Only minutes ago, she had been sitting at the dining room table with her mother, younger sisters, and two girlfriends. Being the birthday girl, she had the honour of presiding over a table laden with festive food. In front of her plate stood a chocolate cake resplendent with seventeen flickering candles. Several presents wrapped in brightly coloured paper were piled on a small table nearby.

Before she had a chance to blow out her candles and make a wish, they heard a flurry from the adjacent hallway. Agnes, her mother's Anglo-Indian nursing assistant, came bursting in, babbling hysterically about a possible breech-birth. Finally drawing breath, she begged for Minette's help, and both women vanished from the dining room.

Minutes later, everybody stiffened, their ears assaulted by the ear-splitting screams coming from next door. A window was banged shut ... too late! The two girlfriends exchanged horrified glances.

Fidgeting for a few moments, they mumbled a feeble excuse to leave. Inwardly wincing to think of the stories that would circulate at school the next day, Claire made no effort to stop them. The entire episode was mortifying in the extreme, and the girl struggled to control her anger and frustration.

"Damn and blast that dratted place!" Claire finally exploded. "None of my friends have to live in a home filled with screeching women."

"Claire!" Fourteen-year-old Christina looked fearfully over her shoulder. "Careful that *Maman* doesn't hear you swearing from over the trellis."

"Heigh-ho, girls!' exclaimed a voice from the door as Charlie O'Hara wandered into the veranda, dumping his riding equipment on a rattan chair as he passed. "Isn't it your birthday, Claire? What is it now? Fourteen? Fifteen?" Grinning, Charlie dodged the cushion hurled at him by his sister. "I'm starving, any chance of some cake?"

"Plenty, since it hasn't even been cut yet," answered Claire grumpily. "I'll tell you all about it later. And do get your smelly stuff off the chairs, Charlie O'Hara! Chrissy and I have to clear everything up tonight...remember it's pay day tomorrow."

Over the last few years, Claire and Charlie had grown close. Both were glad for their own reasons to be rid of their surly older brother, who had left home two years ago to work as their Uncle Frederick's personal assistant.

Claire understood James's bitter resentment towards their mother that flared into life on occasion. Neither she nor James had accepted their mother's reasoning for leaving them with the nuns for four years. Marrying Uncle Freddie would have put paid to that. And the dreadful nursing home need never have existed.

For his part, Charlie was delighted to be free from the person who had made his life miserable for years. The stammer that plagued him had almost disappeared, and his self-confidence grew in leaps and bounds. At the age of nineteen, Charlie had achieved his goal of apprentice jockey and was well thought of by leading trainers.

With his mouth full of chocolate cake, the young man regarded his sister with affection as she fussed over the tack on the chair. Recent comments made by friends sprang to mind, including a request to be introduced to his "gorgeous" sister. With brotherly surprise, he supposed Claire was attractive with that mass of dark hair, vivid blue eyes, and she seemed slender enough.

Nevertheless, she was capable of being something of a ruffian, Charlie ruefully recalled. Two years after Christina's Holy Communion, he had thought to amuse his sisters by dressing himself up in her white chiffon Communion dress and veil. His feet crammed into matching white shoes, Charlie had pranced about on the veranda, striking exaggeratedly girlish poses.

Mortified, Christina had gasped, burst into tears, and rushed from the scene. With a yell of anger, Claire had leaped to her feet and chased Charlie out into the garden. Acutely aware of his infuriated sister close behind, he had hurriedly shinned up a tree to escape retribution. Stretching upwards from a lower branch, Claire managed to grab her brother's ankle and yank. Charlie slipped – the dress ripped, and was transformed into a filthy, green-stained rag in an instant.

Christina had wanted to have a photograph taken in her Communion attire as a gift for the nuns in Simla. That was now no longer possible. The distraught girl had refused to speak to her brother for weeks, despite numerous abject apologies.

Charlie eventually achieved forgiveness by presenting Christina with a small puppy, pitch-black in colour. The wriggling ball of mischief was christened "Lily" by her thrilled mistress, much to the mystification of the family.

"Charlie, have you checked on Turka this evening?" Minette's voice broke into the young man's amused reminiscing. "I thought he was off his feed this morning."

"I was in the stable only a few minutes ago, and he was gobbling happily," Charlie reassured his mother. "It was quite hot this morning, so he probably didn't feel much like eating after being ridden."

Everybody loved the little Arab horse Minette had bought long ago in Darjeeling. Getting on in years, he was still capable of an energetic buck or two on occasion.

Minette turned to her daughters. "Before I forget, Frederick and James are coming round for dinner this evening." Glancing at her elder daughter's sullen face, she pursed her lips. "It's James's last evening in Calcutta, so, Claire, I hope we are not to be subjected to sulking. And please make sure the table is laid with the best silver cutlery and crystal glasses."

Her expression still thunderous, Claire inclined her head and stalked off to the kitchen, Christina in tow. "Why does *Maman* have to make nasty remarks to me?" she hissed through gritted teeth. "Even on my birthday? And what's so special about James coming to dinner, I'd like to know?"

"Well, remember, Uncle Freddie is coming, too," Christina tried to smooth troubled waters. "And he deserves the best of everything, doesn't he?"

"I suppose so." Claire's tone was grudging. "After all, he took our vile elder brother off our hands, praise the Lord."

Later that evening, Minette and her family were sitting in rattan armchairs on the veranda under a slowly whirling fan. Elegantly dressed despite the oppressive heat, they took advantage of the relative cool of open air whilst waiting for Frederick and James to arrive. A small brazier nearby emitted a steady stream of aromatic smoke, which was said to be repellent to mosquitoes and other biting insects.

Earlier in the evening, Claire had observed her mother in the kitchen putting finishing touches to her elder brother's favourite dishes. Let's hope the little beast appreciates it, she thought acidly, knowing what her brother was capable of.

The guests arrived, and contrary to Claire's morose reflections, the evening progressed pleasantly enough. Seated round the oval dining table, the flames from tall candles in silver candelabra reflected in its mahogany gloss, the silver cutlery beside each place setting glittering in the flickering light.

Frederick raised his glass in a toast to James's future as midshipman in the British Navy, and the family joined in to wish him well. The elaborate dinner was deemed perfect, even by Minette's high standards, and rounded off by a rich chocolate dessert.

"Help yourself to some more, darling, I know how you love chocolate mousse," Minette smiled at her elder son. "Oh, James, I can hardly believe you will be leaving tomorrow. I shall miss you dreadfully, you know."

"What? Don't make me laugh!" James's face took on its habitual sneer. "To the contrary, I'm betting you're secretly delighted to see the back of one of us. After all, what have we ever been to you? Shackles? Iron balls and chains weighing you down?" The young man grinned without humour before continuing in a profound silence.

"Of course, with the exception of darling Sonia, whom we know is being groomed to be your old-age companion. Please do spare us further sickening platitudes, I beg you."

"James! What a dreadful thing to say," Minette's face lost every vestige of colour. "Surely you must know by now what my family means to me? How can you—"

"More like a guilty conscience at work, mother dearest," James leaned back in his chair. "It was bad enough that you left us to rot for years, but to abandon your new-born infant for others to bring up? I bet you didn't know that, Sonia, dear."

With an agonised gasp, Minette rose to her feet, battling the sting of her son's accusations. "Stop it! I'm sick and tired of having that abandonment rubbish thrust down my throat, James. How dare you speak—"

"I'll speak as I wish!" James scraped his chair back. "Perhaps you haven't noticed, Mother, but I'm no longer a small boy for you to bully. Thank God for Uncle Freddie here. Who saved my sanity by inviting me to live with him. The relief of getting away from your hectoring voice and miserable penny-pinching ways was indescribable."

"James, I really don't think—" Horrified, Frederick was rising to his feet, but subsided upon seeing Minette shake her head.

"Why, why must you be so vile when you are about to leave?" Minette controlled her anger with an effort. "Heaven knows how hard I've tried to reach you. James, you're my first-born son, but— "

"Well, you've failed. *Dismally!*" James snarled at her. "I imagine most people would agree that you've been pretty useless as a mother. Not to mention making a laughing stock of us in the eyes of Calcutta society, thanks to that frightful place next door. And it's hardly helped our family's credibility that you are seen to be doing the filthy job yourself. Christ, if your family in France could see you now, they would die of shame."

"I'll be off now. Uncle Freddie, see you later at home," the young man laid a hand on the older man's shoulder. Glancing back at his dumbstruck mother, his lips twisted in scorn. "Thank you, mother dear…for a most entertaining evening." With a sarcastic bow, he strode from the dining room and out of the house, slamming the front door behind him.

Without a word, her movements wooden, Minette left the room. Frederick followed, closing the door behind him. The four young people remained at the table, stunned by the appalling scene they had just witnessed. Then Sonia broke the silence by bursting into tears and running after her mother.

Although Claire was appalled that James should have attacked their mother with such venom, a vengeful aspect of her nature secretly rejoiced. Unfortunately for her, Frederick returned to the dining room in time to notice her satisfied expression. He stared at Claire for a long moment in unconcealed disgust.

"Your mother is inordinately upset," Frederick said quietly, "and wishes to remain in her room for the rest of the evening. She asks that you two girls please clear the table for the *ayahs*," he paused to look round the three young faces. "Terrible things were said to your mother this evening, but you can take it from me that she has always, always had your welfare and happiness at heart." He gazed directly at Claire, who seemed to have enjoyed her brother's cruelty. Her face flamed.

Without further comment, Frederick left the house and went home.

Minette emerged from her bedroom the following day, her composure apparently unruffled. She did not refer to the previous evening's events, and neither did anybody else. She did, however, have a few sharp words for Claire about a bright red lipstick, bought in secret from the *bazaar* and discovered in her dressing table drawer.

"I will not have you wandering about Calcutta looking like a lady of the night!" Minette informed her glowering daughter. "You may have a lipstick, but in a tasteful colour of which I approve."

"God, I can't even choose my own makeup," Claire grizzled later to Christina. "I'm surprised she doesn't supervise my bath time into the bargain, loofah in hand!"

"That's just as well," her sister replied, "or she'd see that red ink heart you drew on your bosom. And the one on your right thigh."

"God forbid!" Claire exclaimed. "And don't look disapproving. It was only a bit of fun."

"What's only a bit of fun?" Sonia had appeared on silent feet, startling her sisters.

"Mind your own business!" Claire snapped. "And stop eavesdropping in the hope of hearing a tasty morsel to report to Maman."

"I'm going to tell her what you said," Sonia stuck out her bottom lip. "And she gave me a message for you. So there."

"Well? What is it?" Claire demanded. "Tell me and then buzz off."

"I'll tell her that as well, you horrid thing. Maman wants you in her office straight away."

Claire puffed out her cheeks, mentally sifting through recent misdemeanours that might be the reason for the summons. Unable to pinpoint any particular sin, the girl steeled herself for trouble.

With mounting apprehension, Claire tapped on the door of her mother's office and slipped inside. Minette was standing by the window, speaking to a strange gentleman. To the girl's astonishment, her mother's face wore an expression of unusual happiness that made her look several years younger.

"Come and meet your Great-Uncle Emile." Minette drew the girl forward. "This is Claire, my eldest daughter, who has just turned seventeen."

Demurely casting her eyes down, Claire bobbed a curtsey and extended a hand to the visitor. Raising her eyes, she saw the gentleman was staring at her. She wondered if she had committed some social blunder.

"*C'est incroyable!*" Emile exclaimed, taking Claire's hand and raising it to his lips. "Minette, this child is a replica of yourself at the same age. "*Que je suis enchanté de faire votre connaissance, Mademoiselle Claire,*" he said in French.

"*Et de ma part, je suis ravie d'avoir retrouvé un oncle,*" replied a fascinated Claire.

Smiling in genuine pleasure, Emile turned to his niece. "I see you haven't neglected your daughter's education, Minette. Do all your children speak French so well?"

"No. Only James and Claire have found it easy to become bilingual. Charlie and Christina can't do much more than mutter in an execrable accent. My Sonia has yet to show an interest in learning a second language."

Claire examined the face of this new relative, hoping to see some family resemblance. None was discernible. Emile was a tall elegant man, possessed of smiling pale blue eyes, his fair hair greying at the temples. She felt a frisson of pride that such a distinguished gentlemen should be a relative. Emile stayed for dinner that evening, chatting with the three young O'Haras and enquiring about their interests and ambitions for the future.

"No need to look very far to discover where the love of horses comes from," Emile grinned upon hearing of Charlie's occupation. "Although he is in a wheelchair now, your grandfather is still very much in the business of raising and training thoroughbred horses. As his father was before him."

"Really?" Charlie looked surprised. "*Maman* used to ride, but not since she became too heavy for Turka." Charlie went on to describe the little horse's origins.

Claire's ears pricked up at the snippet of interesting information Emile had let drop. Their mother had always been annoyingly reticent about her family in France. That her father was a marquis had only been divulged a few years ago, when Claire had come home from school, weeping.

Four girls had been taunting Claire about her mother's nursing home. The parents of one had been overheard to remark that the business smacked of trade. Of course, that instantly rendered Claire undesirable as a friend.

Learning the reason for her daughter' distress, Minette was infuriated. "My family can buy and sell most others in Calcutta!" she snapped. "Not many of those pretentious people can legitimately claim a marquis and a duke as close relatives." Minette had then looked squarely at her sniffling daughter. "Ignore the silly creatures, Claire."

Shrugging her mother's advice aside, Claire hugged this new

information to herself. She did not have long to wait before the bullies renewed their attack. Delighted by the misery they had managed to inflict on the previous occasion, Claire's tormentors intercepted her on the way home from school.

"Bloody nerve you've got, trying to pass yourself off as one of us, Claire O'Hara!" one of the girls taunted her. "You and your dreary sister shouldn't be allowed to come to a school like ours."

"God, your common-as-muck mother must have lied through her teeth to get you accepted. Papa says it's a disgrace we are forced to rub shoulders with a creature destined to be someone's maid," declared another.

"Not that attending our school will do Claire much good," sniggered yet another of the coterie. "After all, you can't make a silk purse out of a sow's ear!"

Looking the gang leader up and down, Claire began to laugh. "Why, Cecily, my mother says it's hardly surprising you have such a vulgar tongue in your head, bearing in mind the pretentious family you come from. Before you make yourself even more ridiculous, I think you should know my grandfather is a French marquis of ancient lineage, and my great-grandfather was a duke. Naturally, I speak fluent French, which is more than you do. So keep your ignorant trap shut in future, you brainless ninny."

Giving the gawping foursome a final disdainful glance, Claire turned on her heel and rejoined her friends a short distance away. Satisfactorily vindicated, Claire basked in the warmth of the group's admiration.

Now, with the arrival of Emile, there was the possibility of gleaning even more information about her aristocratic grandparents. Without attracting her mother's attention, of course. But all a disappointed Claire managed to discover was that the grandparents on her mother's side were both very much alive. The young girl ached to know more . . . .

Two days later, Charlie came home, grinning all over his face. "I saw Emile at the racecourse this morning, and he suggested we all go back to France with him for a long holiday. Schools will have broken up, so there shouldn't be a problem for you girls."

"What?" Claire jumped to her feet in delight. "Oh, how terrific that would be! What do you think of that, Chrissy?"

"Well, I-I don't really know." Christina looked stunned as if the idea was too momentous to take in. "Does *Maman* know about it yet?"

Her enthusiasm subsiding, Claire stared at her brother. "*Maman* is bound to find a reason why we can't go," she declared. "Besides, she'll never leave that blasted nursing home for any length of time."

"I suggest we leave it to Emile to approach *Maman*," Charlie said. "Not you, Claire, you have too great a penchant for tactlessness."

"Oh!" Christina exclaimed in sudden ecstasy. "If we go to France, maybe we can visit Lourdes whilst we are there. Wouldn't that be wonderful?"

"Do you ever have thoughts that have no religious significance, Christina?" Claire demanded impatiently. "Not everyone is a pillar of the church, you know."

"Don't be beastly, you know, I ... ." The younger girl's voice trailed to a halt, seeing her sister's attention was already elsewhere. Sighing, Christina swallowed her hurt, knowing Claire didn't mean half of what she said. She adored her sister and would do anything for her...anything except abandon her beloved nuns or the religion that always sustained her.

Over dinner that evening, Claire could barely contain herself in anticipation of a visit from Emile later in the evening. Remembering how happy Minette had been to see her uncle, Claire's spirits rose. If anyone could manage it, Emile would somehow induce her mother to agree.

Why, she thought, she might even be taken to meet her grandfather, the Marquis de Merencourt! How thrilled he would be to see his grandchildren for the first time. Charlie could talk horses with him, and she would tell him—

"Claire!" Minette's sharp voice broke through her daydream. "Why are you grinning in that silly way? Get on with your meal before it's entirely congealed."

After dinner, Charlie set up the green baize card table, and a game of bridge was soon in progress. Claire and Christina excelled at the game, and Charlie also played, if somewhat indifferently. Resentful of her mother's attention being diverted from herself, Sonia sulked behind Minette's chair.

Minette noticed her elder daughter's absent expression. "Claire! For heaven's sake," she snapped, "do concentrate on your hand. Whatever is the matter with you?"

"Sorry! I...I've a bit of a headache as a matter of fact," Claire stuttered, caught out in another pleasurable daydream. "But, I think it's on its way out now."

Claire was saved from further interrogation by a peal of the front doorbell. Moments later, Emile was shown into the veranda. "*Bonsoir à tous*," he said. "Sorry about being rather later than I hoped, but a business meeting went on rather long. Am I too late for coffee?"

"No, of course not." Minette rose with a smile and kissed her uncle. "We were just finishing a game of cards. Charlie, be a dear and ask Mailie to make coffee."

"*Mon Dieu*, Minette, but the hot weather has arrived with a vengeance." Emile mopped his perspiring forehead with a handkerchief. "Even your so-called cold weather feels extremely hot to me! How do you stand it, year after year?"

"Oh, one becomes acclimatised," Minette explained with a laugh. "But at least we have electric fans these days, instead of a fellow pulling the string of a *punka*!"

Claire fidgeted, scarcely able to bear it as her mother continued to reminisce about the bad old days in Lucknow. Was Emile ever going to mention the holiday? Or had the whole thing been a figment of her overwrought imagination?

"Where is your eldest son?" Emile enquired. "He is the only one of your children I have yet to meet."

"James left Calcutta only a day or so ago to join the British Navy. We will miss him tremendously, but he has a wonderful career ahead of him."

"I won't miss James one little bit," Sonia piped up. "He shouted horrid things at *Maman*. And he told lies about her leaving me all alone as a baby!"

"Darling, Uncle Emile isn't interested in silly family arguments," Minette hastened to silence her favourite daughter. "Everyone has them, you know."

"And then James said we—"

"Be quiet, Sonia!" Charlie barked, and his sister lapsed into sulky silence. "You heard what your mother said."

With great diplomacy, Emile changed the subject. "*Alors*, do you still have any of that wonderful cognac you gave me last time I was here?"

Glad of the distraction, Charlie went to the drinks cabinet and poured a quantity of the amber liquor into a balloon glass. "I'd join you, but being a bit of a philistine, I don't care for the stuff, I'm afraid," he explained, handing Emile the glass.

Appreciatively breathing in the aroma of fine brandy, the Frenchman leaned back in his chair. "Minette, *ma chèrie*, I have a suggestion for you to consider. Would it not be an excellent idea for you all to come back with me for a holiday? All expenses paid, of course. It would surely be a relief to get away from this dreadful heat, and wonderful for the young ones to see something of France."

In the sudden silence, four faces turned towards Minette, anxiously awaiting her decision. Flustered, she rose to her feet and wandered over to perch on the veranda wall. It was a bolt from the blue, and one that she was at a loss to handle.

The brutal rejection she had suffered from her father all those years ago had gone deep: in fact, it had never really healed. She still had no wish to see the man who had refused to take in his homeless grandchildren, knowing their father had been killed.

The silence behind her was almost tangible.

"No." Minette's voice was flat. "It's out of the question. I have bookings for the nursing home, and ... ."

"Oh, I don't believe this," Claire interrupted, jumping to her feet, appalled that her beautiful dreams might turn into dust.

"Claire, sit down!" Charlie hissed, seizing his sister's wrist. "Let Emile do the talking."

Mutinous, Claire plumped down again in her chair and stared at the floor. If *Maman* prevented them from accepting this wonderful invitation, she would never forgive her.

Taking a sip of his cognac, Emile wandered over to join Minette by the wall. "*Ma chèrie*, I appreciate that you, personally, have commitments to meet. But why don't I take your family off your hands for a couple of months? Think of all those things you would like to do, but don't have the time? Ah, I thought so. And the young ones should see something of a country to which they partly belong, *n'est-ce pas?*"

"Maybe," Minette's tone was noncommittal. "I'll think about it and let you know. But thank you for your generous offer, Emile."

"It would be my pleasure. I am in Calcutta for another ten days, but remember passages have to be booked if the young ones are to accompany me," Emile concealed a yawn. "I'd better go now, for it's been a very long day. *Bonne nuit et à bientôt!*"

Lightning Source UK Ltd.
Milton Keynes UK
UKOW041853281012

201322UK00001B/25/P